NEWS FROM THE RED DESERT

KEVIN PATTERSON

Random House Canada

PUBLISHED BY RANDOM HOUSE CANADA

Copyright © 2016 Kevin Patterson

www.penguinrandomhouse.ca

Library and Archives Canada Cataloguing in Publication

Patterson, Kevin, 1964– , author
News from the red desert : a novel / Kevin Patterson.

Issued in print and electronic formats.

ISBN 978-0-345-81502-6
eBook ISBN 978-0-345-81504-0

1. Afghan War, 2001– —Fiction. I. Title.
PS8581.A7886N48 2016   C813'.6   C2016-902487-3

Book design by Terri Nimmo

Cover photo: © Ed Darack / Science Faction / Getty Images

Printed and bound in the United States of America

2 4 6 8 9 7 5 3 1

Penguin
Random House
RANDOM HOUSE CANADA

For the dead.

NEWS FROM THE RED DESERT

CHAPTER ONE

Taliban's Last Stand, December 2001

T he automatic and heavy weapons fire gave way eventually to the sound of sporadic pistol shots and isolated hollering. A twenty-eight-year-old sergeant from Boise—Special Forces, thus unnameable—stood and watched as his comrades probed the enemy dead. His bright red beard jutted into the world with the assertiveness of a thorn fence. Beside him stood a twenty-year-old private from Bar Harbor with silky wisps of blond cheek and lip hair but shoulders like articulated melons. As combat frenzy faded from the scene, they could breathe easily again.

They looked around at the holed remains of the building the enemy had defended. Other Government Agency personnel—CIA—stood together tightly in one khaki adventure wear–clad clump; SEALs bunched together in their own tight little sunglassed pod. There was no one left to chase. The enemy who wasn't dead now would be soon.

"This was the last position held in strength," the private said.

The sergeant nodded. "According to the intelligence brief."

"Where'd they all go?" said the private.

"If you'd been paying attention you'd have noticed that we killed a lot of them."

"We didn't kill a whole army."

"Dead, run away—they're gone."

"Gone somewhere."

The sergeant shrugged. "If they're still in formed groups, we'll grease them."

In that moment, the popping of gunfire fell away entirely.

"Kinda blows, huh?" the private said.

"What does?"

"I don't know."

"Yeah."

The CIA men moved to search the bodies of the dead Taliban. The soldiers stood back from this. After other operations, the senior NCOs had immediately rounded up the fighting men and directed them toward the helicopters waiting to take them to the next target. They were given their briefings and more ammunition in the helicopter. High-tempo ops were all about not giving the enemy a chance to regroup, to hide, to think things over. Now there was no one to chase.

The private choked up silently and had to swallow. He got it down, then asked the sergeant, "How many did we lose, all told?"

"Not sure. Not many Americans. More NA."

"How many Talibs did we waste, do you think?"

"Lots. Those things bother you?"

"Not really."

"Okay."

"Think we'll go home now?"

"Not right away. Soon."

"Shortest fucking war I ever heard of."

"There's been plenty of short wars," the sergeant said. "Mostly those are the only ones worth fighting." Tendrils of flame now licked the building and they tracked the smoke as it climbed into the sky. It was long minutes before either spoke. Then the sergeant said, "I spent ten years training for these last three months and now I'll be another fifty, telling stories about them."

"Like one of those brontosauruses at the VFW going on about 'Nam, how they coulda won it if they hadn't had one hand tied behind their backs. Fat and drunk."

"Already got the beard. Just missing the Harleywear vest and the ex-wife."

"Difference being, here, we won."

They both stroked their beards. They were still not used to them. What they used to know about being a soldier, before they ever shot anyone, was: soldiers do not wear beards. Something to do with gas masks not fitting, but mostly because soldiers do not wear beards. Maybe Brits and Frenchmen. If you could call them soldiers. And sailors. Which just proves the point. Then they got to Afghanistan, and in Afghanistan men wore beards. So they were told to throw away their razors. War turns the world upside down.

Overhead they could see fast air—F-18s and A-10s—circling, waiting, silently begging to be called in. In the private's silvered Oakleys the older man, still thinking about his itchy beard, caught a glimpse of himself. "I look like someone's half-Appalachian, half-pedophile uncle, come up from the hollow for prostate surgery. Jesus fuck." He was only twenty-eight years old.

The private continued to look skyward. "You're trying a little hard."

"The prostate surgery?"

"I liked the half-Appalachian, half-pedophile part."

They were quiet for a time while they tried to think up new lines.

The CIA people set to going through the burnt buildings working in two-man teams. One photographed and the other collected. They wore microphones into which they muttered continuously, describing everything they saw. The pair closest to where the sergeant from Boise and the private from Bar Harbor were standing had been in on every operation they had been a part of, though they had exchanged almost no words. CIA disdained soldiers as unsophisticated and rulebound muscle. That was the sergeant's read of them, anyway. As if all of them weren't making it up as they went along, from the moment they had landed two months earlier. How to ride horses, how to speak to angry and terrified village elders, how to know when the interpreter is massaging the story. The soldiers, for their part, considered the CIA to have a scent about them. They'd watched some of the interrogation sessions with Taliban considered important enough to take live. Not pretty. Not anything a soldier would ever do, the sergeant from Boise had told his men. And his platoon commander. And his company commander. Who had nodded and looked hard at him. The sergeant did not look away.

The men in khaki pants emptied the pockets of the dead into plastic bags and they photographed the face of every corpse and then they took cheek swabs. They lined up the bodies and numbered them. As the sergeant and the private watched, they rolled one over and an arm seemed to move. The CIA pair stopped for a moment to look at it. One of them put his hand on his pistol. The soldiers held their breath. Then the CIA resumed their photographing and searching. The soldiers exhaled slowly.

The F-18s and A-10s continued to circle overhead, though they looked more resigned now. Other elements of their force had secured the perimeter and still others were searching the surrounding airfield and roads for traps and unexploded ordnance. In a moment the company commander would be calling the captain for an after-action report. There aren't that many ways of saying what the captain from Salt Lake City would have to say. One: the bad guys are all dead. Two: none of our guys are hurt. Three: it doesn't matter how much ammunition we have remaining because: see One.

❁

It had taken twelve weeks. The whole country had seemed to lift up and tilt their way. The fighters near the Tajikistan border gave way in one long loud night when B-52 bombers out of Diego Garcia, far away in the Indian Ocean, appeared overhead, as faint as satellites. The Northern Alliance fighters were used to night fighting but they had not been prepared for this. Unshaven and muscular *ferenghee* pointed lasers on clumps of men and then watched expressionlessly through starlight scopes as they became unclumped. There wasn't anyone on that battlefield who was as old as the half-century-old bombers flying overhead, turning men into red mist, but that did not matter much. Not to the bombed, and not to the bomb aimers. Two-ton high-explosive Guided Bomb Units dropped into rock cracks four feet wide and the plume of body parts that erupted then was an unholy sight in any religion. Age matters when it brings weakness, but strong old things, like infantry master sergeants and B-52s, are made even more formidable by their age.

Chasing the evaporating enemy, the ferenghee had ridden their shaggy Afghan horses until the beasts fell down beneath them and then they ran on their own feet, mechanically and seemingly without tiring. They called in B-52 and Tomahawk missile strikes on every bit of organized resistance they found. One night a Taliban boy named Atta Door was hiding under a rock that rang with steel splinters. He thought to himself, *The ferenghee cannot be defeated.* With the next concussion, that idea spread from him to the men closest to him, who were frantically trying to operate their radio despite the jamming of the invisible airplanes high in the night sky. From them, that idea rippled out to the riflemen and the leaders and imams of the force. They all sagged, and then the point was no longer debatable. It radiated farther outward, and a few minutes later, it filled the thoughts of villagers in their bedclothes listening to the clear-night thunder filling the valley. Then it swept over the mountains, and headed for Mazar-i-Sharif. And from there it headed for Kabul and Herat.

At the Kandahar Airfield, the thought had just found its full expression. That morning, the smoke from the broken dun-yellow plaster of the shattered airport spiralled upwards alongside smoke from one hundred other fires burning on the field. Twenty years ago, before the wars, this building had been an administrative office. It had once been a version of beautiful. Its graceful dome had a Persian sensuality that looked nothing at all like what the private and the sergeant thought of as airport architecture. If you looked closely, you could still see damage from the fighting that had attended the civil war six years earlier.

But this new assault had been vastly worse. Now the domes were punctured, and rebar straggled free of concrete in half a dozen blasted places.

The sergeant from Boise look at the disarray he and his comrades had created. Maybe it would be repaired this time. But it was a pretty broken country. On their way here in their Chinooks, they had seen the hydro dams to the north, unmaintained since the Soviets left, spilling water purposelessly. And no electricity anywhere, except from chieftains' generators, running on smuggled fuel. A broken place in for more breaking, it turned out.

❀

Three months later the sergeant and the private were lined up on the newly operational Kandahar Airfield, their M-4s slung over their shoulders, and their packs hanging loosely on their backs. Regular army guys ran off the C-130s, turboprops still winding down, scanning 360 degrees for threats, at all times displaying full zeal and outstanding situational awareness. The Special Forces guys, three and a half months in-country now, would have laughed, but that would have made it look like they had noticed the newbies.

Behind them, construction was going strong. Rows of tents being assembled, engineers and signals guys putting up antenna arrays. A stack of crates thirty metres wide and nearly as long as the airstrip sat beside the tarmac. Columns of trucks were coming off cargo planes. Antonovs disgorged bulldozers. A small hospital. Laundry. All military now wore clean and unaltered (no sleeves cut off) combat uniforms. The clerks and cooks proudly carried loaded pistols strapped to their legs. A sign in the dining facility said that if you weren't carrying your personal weapon you would not be fed. After years of peacetime theatre, this was no drill.

The sergeant and the private, along with the rest of the Special Forces lined up on the tarmac, had shaved off their beards. They all looked a decade younger than they had a month earlier. Though they weren't talking now, earlier they had assured one another that they were pleased to be going home, looking forward to getting laid.

The last couple of days they had had Don't Beat Your Wife class, with the shrinks and social workers. Adjustment strategies. Effective and Respectful Communication. Alcohol: THE NUMBER ONE RISK FACTOR. This was when it really hit them that they were leaving the theatre of operations, and they had grown subdued and sarcastic. The uniformed social workers were not unaccustomed to this, though it did piss off the company commanders.

The private from Bar Harbor stepped from one foot to the other and shifted his pack. These had been a dope couple-three months, but he wasn't going to hang around when it was time to go. It wasn't in his nature. And he wasn't interested in doing any more sentry duty. That is not why he had done the jump course and then the Ranger course and then the never-ending SF training. Not to fucking be a fucking sentry for fucking signalmen, that was for fucking sure.

The sergeant from Boise was not ready to go. In his mind, this was just getting interesting. He knew a hundred words of Pashto now and was beginning to like the language. Even among the CIA dudes, the supposed linguists, no one had known much Pashto—at the beginning there had been three fluent Pashto speakers in the whole organization. The Peshawar station chief had had to use an interpreter. Which is why the sergeant was reviewing the personal pronouns in his head as he stood there on the tarmac. He wanted to come back. He had spent years training for this work. Already the tide was taking him out. But he'd be back on the flood.

⚜

As the planes were loading up the Special Forces infantry reluctantly returning home, an emaciated twenty-eight-year-old British man with the startled features of a sock monkey arrived at the airfield. Stewart Robinson claimed to have walked there from the Persian border. He had with him a large Afghan dog he called Fido. The soldiers who had to deal with him assumed, mostly because they had been told to deal with him, that he had some sort of affiliation. Probably as a spook. It was agreed by those who had to deal with him that, if he was a spy, he was not a very good one. You're not supposed to notice spooks—or if you do, only because they never say anything. His handler for the day, an Air Force Reserve lieutenant, watched him from behind his Oakleys as he pretended to watch the SF load up. He was not delighted by this assignment. Robinson patted his dog and studied the lines of soldiers. He'd mentioned that he had been one himself, albeit briefly. That was a more difficult and less interesting life than he could have enjoyed, he had told his handler. You have to admire people who can do it. His Air Force handler had hardly nodded. *Where had he gotten that fucking dog? Had it been vaccinated for anything? Who says "albeit" in conversation?*

"So how come you're walking across Afghanistan?"

Robinson had answered this question many times and did not look away from the airfield. "It started out rather impetuously. Then I just kept going."

"Can you speak Pashto?"

"I read Persian at Oxford. Dari is a dialect of Persian."

"Has it helped you here?"

"More in the north. Kandahar, not so much, and I'm not going to go any farther south. It's handy to be able to talk to people. Especially when you get into trouble."

"So did you get into trouble?"

The skinny man looked at the Air Force subaltern and then back at the airfield. "No," he said.

"How much longer are you going to be with us?"

"Do you mean here on the base, or in the of-the-firmament sense?"

"Here, at KAF."

"I'm leaving tomorrow."

"Are you in a hurry?"

"There are things I want to see before they go away."

"Like what?"

"I won't know until I see them."

"My boss is gonna want to know where you're headed."

"Northeast. Kabul."

His minder wanted to ask him, How? How do you walk through this country of perpetual war, so obviously a foreigner, with a huge dog, unclean to Muslims, and no weapon, no friends and just a little bit of money? How do you not freeze to death every night you sleep outside, and how do you persuade terrified villagers to give you food and how do you just walk into the middle of the busiest new US military base in the world, as a non-American yet, and not get tossed into an interrogation room?

But he did not ask those questions. Instead, he said, "Do you want to go get some lunch?"

Robinson pictured the forced conversation and boiled food pouches. "No thanks, I ate this morning."

He looked up at the outline of Ghar Killay, looming over the airstrip, and narrowed his eyes. He wondered how long it would take to climb it. His dog sensed that thought and groaned. The lieutenant figured the dog was hungry.

❀

A hundred metres behind them, Deirdre O'Malley watched the two men and the dog closely. She had only gotten her press credentials two weeks earlier and had been in KAF for a few days. She had not filed a story yet and was getting heat from her boss, who reminded her daily that this was a once-in-a-lifetime opportunity. She kept asking the press liaison officers about combat ops, about local resistance—their replies were nebulous on those subjects, but they told her they did have a great story about a set of triplet airframe techs who were all posted to the base. Uplifting. Good for morale.

What interested her was this emaciated Brit. She had heard he walked in from Iran. Apparently he had his own book in mind and wasn't inclined to give his story away—half a dozen of the guys in the press tent had already approached him. It was understandable, on one level, if that's what he was—adventurer writer idiot guy—but that didn't mesh with anything else: his access to the base, his fluency in Dari. His survival. The fact that he hadn't been picked up by a patrol and shoved into a sack.

⚜

Master Sergeant Demetrios Anakopoulus had been in Kandahar for two months and the supply point he operated had become the hub of the whole base. He watched his men arrange the crates of materiel as they came off the transports. In here somewhere were pallets of steel framing with which he was to construct a warehouse to keep the rain off the rest of the crates. Warehouses, actually. The field of crates stretched nearly the ten thousand feet of the airstrip. Rifle ammunition. Surgical instruments. Field rations. Bottled water. Uniforms. Boots. Pool tables. Weight machines. Treadmills. Canvas tents. Sunscreen. Computers. Radios. Ten thousand different field manuals. Bread ovens. Telephone poles. Anakopoulus surveyed it all and felt a kind of pride. He liked belonging to an organization capable of bringing the makings of a small city from twelve time zones away in a week. You could preserve civilization with just what he had here. Like logisticians anywhere, he thought of the pallets as his property; he had signed for them, and was responsible for them all. Maybe fifty million dollars' worth of stuff. Maybe more. Until all this was distributed, he had the most important job on the base. Not that anyone would actually say that. But it was the case. You could tell from the number of times his boss and his boss's boss called him every day. His bosses could use a bit of calmness. Anakopoulus was due to retire in a year and he knew what he was doing; he just wanted to be left alone to do his job.

This would probably be his last deployment. By the usual rules, it would have gone to someone more junior than him. But these were not usual times. Still, it was kind of great, seeing what the machine was capable of when it got wound up. When it stopped being just a hypothesis. His satphone rang. No one else he knew of had their own satphone except the commander. It rang again.

"Sergeant Major Anakopoulus!" he barked, expecting it to be the waste-of-rations major who thought he had some sort of charge over him.

"Demetrios?"

"Susie?"

"I'm sorry for calling your satphone."

"That's okay. Is anything wrong?"

"No. I just hadn't heard from you and I was looking at the calendar and wondering—do you think we should still plan on going to Puerto Rico next Christmas?"

"That can wait. We'll do it when I get home."

"Okay. It's just that the fares go up the later you book the tickets."

"I know."

"I'm really missing you already."

"I can't talk too long here, Susie. I'm in the middle of something."

"I know. I just wanted to know what to do about the tickets."

"How's the kid?"

"He's great. I'll let you go now. I know these calls are expensive."

"I'll call you as soon as things settle down here."

"Sure."

"Bye."

"Demetrios?"

"Yeah, Susie?"

"Be safe, okay?"

"You bet."

"Are you drinking?"

"Of course not. Are you?"

"No!"

"Okay."

Anakopoulus hung up and put his satphone back in his pocket and surveyed his maze of pallets. He really needed to get some rain cover built for them.

The skinny Brit with the dog approached and said, "Hello."

"Hello, sir."

"Looks like you have about a thousand balls in the air here."

"It's all under control, sir. A challenge, but challenges are what we do."

"Indeed."

"Anything I can do for you?"

Before Robinson could answer, Deirdre O'Malley joined them. Anakopoulus had been briefed about her, too. "Ma'am, I'm afraid you can't be here. This is a controlled area."

"Oh, I'm so sorry, Warrant Officer—I'm still getting my bearings. Can you point me toward the admin office? I can't get my email to work."

"It's just around back of the hangars over there, ma'am. And it's Master Sergeant."

"I can show you," the Brit said.

"Would you? I'd be grateful."

Anakopoulus watched them walk away. He shook his head. No matter what kind of VIP that man was, he was still a moron.

❁

And then the real killers were on the Herc, strapped in like so much equipment. Soon they were airborne with all of Afghanistan spread below. They flew north for a time and then they flew west to Ramstein AFB in Germany. Most of the men, from long habit, went to sleep. The sergeant from Boise could see out a small scratched window if he craned his neck. Through it, he traced the valleys they had fought through, one after the other. Detail flooded back to him. The audio came in snatches, but the video was uninterrupted and perfectly sharp. Every ridge he had flanked, every man he had shot and had seen fall, illumination flares lighting up startled, sleepy, Taliban sentries, a moment later pierced by tracer fire. He could describe days-long stretches of some of that time down to the minute. There was so little summary in his memory, just all that living, crammed in as tight as it could fit. The valleys below him looked like textured paint. Grey stucco. Like his stepfather's house. Sour cigarette smoke and quiet. As opposed to that RPG hitting the other side of the rock he was lying behind. His friend catching a 12.7-mm round in the chest and exploding in front of them. Seeing the sun coming up over the Arghandab from the back of a Chinook, the morning after they took Spin Boldak. None of this would submit to condensation. It would equally defy categorization and understanding. And so endure. Like a pebble in a shoe.

He had lied to Susie for weeks after he got his notice of deployment, claiming he had heard nothing. There was a reason, more than the simple craven wish to avoid upsetting her. He would be gone soon enough, so why make her unhappy before he had to? He knew she would find this very difficult. They had both gotten their one-year chips just the summer before. She wanted him close to her. For her sake, he thought. But he was wrong about that.

She knew. Twenty thousand soldiers were posted to the base they lived near and every ATM lineup featured military spouses who talked to one another. Anyway, there was the news. After the towers came down, they all expected to be spending time overseas. And mostly, they would be. She knew that every other healthy soldier had been notified when he could expect to go. Why hadn't he? Was there something about his health he hadn't told her?

When he did tell her, it was after she had put her son to bed, and they were sitting in the lawn chairs in her backyard. The sun was almost down and it was quickly growing cool. He said he did not know how long the deployment would be for. And he told her he had found out only today.

He could tell she knew he knew more. She looked away. She looked back at him. She tried to speak but her throat closed up. He tried, too, but he couldn't make sounds. They just sat there, listening to the bugs.

CHAPTER TWO

Kandahar Airfield, April 2007

Of course they did not recognize one another. After five years, they'd hardly have been recognizable to their close friends back home, if they'd still had any. Anyway, even if they had remembered meeting, it probably wouldn't have helped. Deirdre O'Malley would still be the fucking embed who lost her fucking *body armour* somehow and came to Master Sergeant Anakopoulus's warehouse demanding a replacement from him an hour before she was supposed to head outside the wire.

"I didn't lose it. It was with my kit, but none of it arrived from Baghdad." Of course she dropped the "Baghdad" in there just as soon as she could. Her gold-rimmed aviators stayed on her face, even inside. "The fighting was heavy when I left and the airfield was mortared. Maybe that's why." She paused. The supply clerk looked at her for a long moment and chewed on a toothpick, then he called Anakopoulus out of his office to see what he would say.

Anakopoulus had been listening to the exchange between O'Malley and his clerk through his open office door, and had been getting angrier by the second. He was entirely uninterested in the posturings of this woman, who must have been in high school when he first set up the KAF supply depot. By now he had seen everything, or everything that mattered: the quiet two years that followed Taliban's Last Stand, the slow-to-boil insurgency that began after the fall of Baghdad, and the Iraqization of the country underway now. He had seen journalists come through here in a steady stream, incontinent with excitement over being part of the mission. The supply techs saw everyone in their first intoxicating hours on the base and learned to recognize the giddiness of civilians encountering war for the first time. In an environment with limited distractions, one took one's fun where it was found.

The veteran journalists travelled lighter and were usually more careful with the tone they used with clerks and techs. They clung to their sunglasses like Homeland Security agents and they walked faster, looked at less and saw more. They'd picked up some phrases in Pashto and Dari. They were dirtier. Anakopoulus was able to date the embeds like a curator looking at a pot. He figured this one had been among soldiers for a two or three years. But there was an uneasiness folded into her assertiveness that suggested KAF did not quite feel like home to her yet. In a few months, after she had been through the supply warehouses a few times, she would present herself with genial weariness, a much more effective strategy.

"You're responsible for your own kit, ma'am," Anakopoulus said with the obdurate detachment of irritated clerks anywhere.

"I didn't lose my kit. I put it on the runway beside the Herc and it didn't come off."

"Maybe take that up with the Air Force."

"I have to go on patrol in an hour."

That was a mistake and he saw that she knew it as soon as the words came out of her mouth. Journalists loved to affiliate themselves with soldiers, but nothing earned the soldiers' disdain more quickly than that presumption of equivalency. *She* was not going on patrol.

"Maybe ask at the press tent. I could give you directions," he said.

She did not reply. They looked at one another levelly.

She knew these first few encounters would influence the way she was seen for the rest of the time she was on base. She could not lose this, not this badly. Looking Anakopoulus in the eye, she picked up her cell phone. She dialled a number. "Major Horner? Deirdre O'Malley. Yes, I got in this morning. I need some help. My kit didn't arrive with me and that patrol you set up leaves soon. I need some body armour. I'm here at the supply depot, talking to . . ." She looked pointedly at Anakopoulus's name tag. ". . . Master Sergeant Anakopoulus, and he doesn't have anything for me. Sure, one second." She offered the cell to Anakopoulus.

"Master Sergeant Anakopoulus."

"Yessir."

"No, that won't be necessary, sir."

"Yessir."

He handed the phone back to O'Malley. He nodded to the clerk and strode into his office. He slammed the door so loudly everyone in the cavernous warehouse looked up.

The clerk walked into the warehouse to get the journalist her body armour.

Ten minutes later, she emerged into the sun, blinking even behind her sunglasses. So she'd established that she wouldn't be fucked with. That was good, she thought. The master sergeant would pout for a few days and then forget about her. Surely.

❀

Four hours later, 3 platoon, Alpha Company, 1st Battalion, Princess Patricia's Canadian Light Infantry stopped to rest in the shade beside a wadi in the Arghandab Valley. Deirdre leaned against a boulder. She was just getting to know, and to be known by, these men, so she kept her mouth shut.

"All morning long, Taliban on every hill, watching us. But no ROE criteria and so we all just look at each other." This was Sergeant Kyle Wilson, twenty-seven-year-old section commander, pretending to be talking to himself or possibly his section, but speaking loudly enough to easily be heard by his fuckwit platoon commander. The platoon warrant

17

officer, Richard Fortin, forty years old, sinewy and irritated, spun his head and glared at Wilson. That was ill-disciplined and disrespectful. They'd be having a one-way conversation about that later.

"Until we're out of sight, and then the fucking cell phones come out," Private Casey Tilmouth, one of Wilson's section, said.

"Shut the fuck up, Tilmouth," Wilson said, having caught Fortin's searing look.

They chewed on beef jerky and drank water. "Can we smoke, Sergeant?" a twenty-year-old from Lethbridge asked.

"No, you can't. You said you quit." Wilson bit into his jerky, not waiting for or much interested in a reply.

Deirdre listened, but not too obviously. She wondered for the nth time why men didn't become adults until their thirties, when women were full grown by the time they finished college. She used to think the men she knew were made children by sports and gaming and especially by accommodating girlfriends and mothers, but these men were undoted upon and the same delayed final maturation was evident. Compare the twenty-year-old from Lethbridge to Wilson and Fortin. The twenty-year-old had grace and physical power, but in his understanding of the world it was as if he were the son and grandson of the other two.

She was sympathetic to Wilson's frustration about the ROEs. He just said what they were all thinking. In Iraq, before the insurgency came to a rolling boil, the American and British soldiers at all levels constantly used to protest the over-restrictive rules of engagement. Then carnage came and the rules generated less discussion. But as much sympathy as she had for him, her advice would be that he'd want to think twice about challenging Warrant Officer Fortin again. Fortin was formidable. You could tell. She could tell.

It's all so tricky, living in someone else's house, being privy to their drama, when your job is to report on it. You start taking notes on Wilson and Fortin and no one ever talks to you again. But pretending you don't hear stuff would just be bullshitting them. Which would also distance you from them, and when you're sleeping among them, and walking these routes and getting shot at together—well, you don't want distance from these people. You want to immerse yourself. Which is the whole point. To know what this feels like, from the perspective of the soldiers.

She also found it more complicated because these were not Americans, exactly. The spots with American patrols had all been allotted months before she was hurriedly transferred here to replace her predecessor, and this was what had been available. Which was okay with her. She had spent time with UK troops in Iraq and had admired them. She had thought that the Canadians might be a little more like the Brits she'd met but soon realized it was the Americans they self-consciously modelled themselves after. They carried the same rifles, wore the same body armour, and the officers attended the American war colleges and the junior officers even spoke in the same drawled rhythms. But they weren't Americans and she wasn't Canadian. Which was part of why they wanted her to admire them. That made her cautious. The first thing anyone from the US Army's Tenth Mountain Division ever said to a journalist was: "We'd just as soon you weren't here. Don't get in the way."

The interpreter, who'd asked her to call him John Wayne, exchanged a glance with Deirdre. They were both interlopers. They wore different-coloured helmets than the soldiers and they carried no weapons. The body armour that she had been given that morning was military-style camo pattern, rather than the pale blue variety civilians normally wore. It made it look like she was posing as something she wasn't, which called attention to her, and she didn't like that. It gave the soldiers a reason to be suspicious of her. Like they were suspicious of the terp.

The first few embeds she had done in Iraq, she had practised her Arabic with the terps and tried to get a sense of their view of that war. That had offended the soldiers and they had punished the terps in small and important ways thereafter. She learned to be careful. One woman among forty lonely men in their twenties—she could have no favourites. Within a week of meeting her, three of them would think they were in love with her. They would probably be restrained about it, but that did not make it not a problem. She was not sure if it would be easier or harder if she knew who the three were. Probably harder. Still—no special friendships.

❁

The platoon had arrived in Afghanistan two months earlier. After two weeks of acclimatization, they had headed off to their forward operating base. For the last several weeks they had been walking these river valleys and climbing these hills. They were all interested in what Deirdre O'Malley had seen in Iraq. Compared to that, this was still suspected to be a make-believe war. Every few days they heard AK fire, generally too carelessly aimed and too far away to be more than potentially dangerous. Bullets fell short, flew overhead or sometimes among them. It was surprising enough whenever a metal coffee cup suddenly rang out and was sent spinning, or a camelpack geysered, that they found it infuriating. When it was worse than that, when someone's body armour suddenly threw them on the ground, their rage was hyperbolic.

In Iraq there was more threat, and much more injury, and the soldiers were less easily angered. The Brits and the Americans both blew off so much ammunition no one even pretended to keep track. Here, every round was accounted for. After spotting Taliban, the first thing they did was review whether the rules of engagement were satisfied. If everyone in charge agreed after deliberation that they were, they engaged. Most of the time the incident didn't meet the criteria and so they crept away silently. These episodes had given rise to Wilson's— and nearly every other senior NCO's and junior officer's—frustration. But it wasn't as if, when they did open up, they had had the satisfaction of joined battle. The slipperiness of the Taliban was such that all they usually accomplished was make noise and pulverize dirt. Which had its appeal but was not why they had become soldiers.

Deirdre listened to these comments and had to stop herself from laughing. In Iraq everyone had talked like that, too, in the first months of the occupation—especially the guys who hadn't been in on the invasion. Itching for trouble, itching to kill. She knew the desire wasn't quite as monstrous as it sounded. Peacetime soldiers train for years, imagining what it would be like to be in combat. Unbloodied, they all feel like imposters. Then the shit came, and the idea that they had ever longed for anything like it seemed impossible. Listening to these men made her realize just how awful Baghdad had been. Twenty percent PTSD rates. Hollowed faces and empty eyes. Abu Ghraib. Too many non-combatant shootings to even begin to keep track.

Fortin took a swig from his water bottle. "ROEs are about discipline," he said, apparently to the platoon, but really to Wilson. "And without discipline, you can't do anything in a place like this. Chaos is always ready to come roaring in. You let your discipline waver, everything falls apart in a second. We're gonna follow the fucking ROEs." He spat into the dirt and did not look at Wilson at all.

And then he judged that they were done resting and he stood and then so did the section commanders. Water bottles were put away and the platoon rose quickly and without discussion. The men lifted their rifles and tightened their webbing. The platoon commander rose and stood beside the warrant. Those two men nodded to one another and then they started off. Wilson took his section at a trot into the lead until they could just be glimpsed at the next bend. He didn't ask, nor had he been told. It was their turn. And it was a relief to get off by themselves.

❁

Two hours later, the platoon was walking along a dirt road lined by forty-foot eucalyptus trees as thin as a man's thigh. It was a bright and cool afternoon. The scent from the trees was strong. In the distance, a thin farmer steered a wooden plow behind a thinner ox. A rifle shot cracked overhead, so loud it seemed close. The soldiers were all on the ground before their hearts had a chance to beat again. The lower-pitched boom of the rifle discharge rumbled over them. They waited for the next shot.

Which did not come immediately. They listened hard to the abrupt silence. From the sound of it, it had probably been a 12.7-mm PKM Soviet sniper rifle, Deirdre thought. The big rounds alarm even experienced soldiers in a way the AK's seven-six-two doesn't. Against a background hum of ballistic yips and barks, a roar catches everyone's attention.

21

In Baghdad, the 12.7-mm was the snipers' favourite rifle. Body armour wouldn't stop a twelve-seven bullet if it was shot from anywhere within sight. Fired from a few hundred metres, a twelve-seven armour-piercing round could go through three men and their armour. That happened to the Brits once, in Basra. Men had crowded together behind a wall, scanning for a sniper—but another shooter was on the other side. Royal Fusiliers falling as one. Kicking. Shuddering. It was one of the worst things Deirdre ever saw. She knew those men. Had posed for pictures with them an hour earlier. She nearly quit that day—and learned one more reason not to have special friendships.

The second shot is how the shooter tells you where he is. Deirdre and everyone else in the platoon listened hard, waiting for it. The range from which a round was fired can be guessed at by listening to the gap between the crack of the bullet overhead and the subsequent booming discharge from the rifle's muzzle—the longer that gap, the farther away the shooter. It is easier to judge if you're prepared for it. At the sound of the bullet, they had all hit the ground, and somewhere in that excited moment of huffing and swearing, they'd hadn't noticed the gap between it and the rifle report. As they listened for the unforthcoming second shot, the absence of a known direction or distance to the shooter compounded the anxiety the men felt. They looked and listened as intently as they could. The lieutenant radioed his company commander. "Contact. Wait, out."

And then they were all still for as long as they could stand it. Those who had sightlines peered around trees and over the grass alongside the road. Most of them couldn't see anything except the ground in front of them and the knee-high grass growing from it. No one could see anything that looked like a sniper blind.

Deirdre tried as hard to listen for and locate the direction of the second shot as any of the soldiers on the ground. Lying with her face pressed into the dirt, her breath came to her quickly. She tasted fear and she tasted cow-shit-laden soil. She felt a kind of focus and intensity that had been more usual in Baghdad and she realized she was relieved to know it again here. She had thought coming to Afghanistan would be the end of a certain way of feeling the world.

The soldiers glanced at her and they knew what she felt. This amused them and when they grinned at her she felt self-conscious. She made herself stop listening for the second shot. She paid attention instead to the soldiers around her. She took out her pad and made a show of taking notes. She took a sideways photograph of the young man nearest her. She had seen it all before, a hundred times, she was telling them. Telling herself.

At last, Fortin leopard-crawled along the perimeter of their defence and studied the landscape, searching for likely firing positions. There was lots of dead ground—hollows obscured from their view—and there was a stone wall that ran for a hundred metres five hundred metres away. If he were the shooter, that would be where he would fire from. After the shot he could run behind it in whichever direction he wanted.

"Can you see anything, Warrant?" a corporal, Perry Wilton, from Manitoba, with tattoos of freshwater sports fish on every bit of unweathered skin on his body, whispered.

"Shut the fuck up."

They listened. Long minutes passed.

They continued to pass.

Still no more fire.

They kept passing.

The platoon commander decided to request a helicopter surveillance of the area.

"Request Hawkeye reconnaissance of our loc."

"Roger that."

And then a moment later: "Hawkeye en route."

❀

It was the same as it had been in Iraq, Deirdre supposed. In the space between shots being fired, every advantage was with the insurgents.

The Taliban looked like the locals because they were the locals, for the most part. Just like the Anbar Sunni militiamen, they knew every bend in every road and they knew which farmers would hide them and who could feed them. The older men had fought in these same valleys against the Soviets and in the civil war among the warlords after the Soviets left. Experienced guerillas understand the importance of surprise and of terrain and of high ground and they understood the long game.

Ferenghee soldiers could almost not be killed by anything except a head shot. They had armour over their bodies and their vehicles and everything one might want to destroy. They had drones in the air, all day every day, and helicopters and fast air available within a few minutes of the first loud noise. Even when there was fog and rain, missiles found the heat signature breath makes leaving frightened lungs. Artillery boomed out 155-mm shells from the forward operating bases most days, and there was no escaping it: Once you let the Americans—to the Afghans, the ferenghee were all Americans—see you with a rifle in your hands, it was over.

The US Army Apache appeared then, its gas turbine engine roaring and its rotor thumping away as it began to methodically sweep the grid they were in. It paused over a couple of treelines and then continued. It ran the length of the stone wall. Then the pilot drawled to the platoon commander, "We're not seeing evidence of enemy activity here. Can you be more specific about the direction the fire came from?"

"Negative."

"Is it certain that the sound was gunfire?"

"Affirmative." Spitting.

"Have you scouted out your position on foot?"

"Hawkeye: Roger."

The Apache came lower now and the ground pulsed with the wash of the heavy rotor. Deirdre could feel it with her knees and her cheek. She shut her eyes, to keep the dust out. It criss-crossed the fields on both sides of the road and studied the rows of trees with infrared.

Somewhere, a man with a rifle was lying completely motionless underneath something large. Probably far from here, by now, watching the helicopter on the horizon and praying.

"We're not seeing anything that looks like enemy activity," the pilot said.

"Thanks for your help."

"We're returning to base. Best of luck."

The platoon commander radioed Wilson, up ahead. "Send a team around to the north and south sides of this road."

"Roger that."

Half an hour later, Fortin crawled up to where the platoon lay on the sides of the road.

"I think we're clear, sir."

"Nothing, huh?"

"Not that I can find. Probably hightailed it the moment the shot was off."

The platoon commander nodded and the two men stood slowly. The rest of the platoon warily rose as well, Deirdre with them. The warrant nodded and they resumed the patrol. For the next three miles, they moved slowly and carefully and paused to study every copse of trees they came upon. It took two hours. They walked a little more quickly than that for the next hour. And then they were back to normal. Wilson's section stayed way out on point that whole afternoon and he hardly had to speak to Fortin at all.

When the platoon reached the FOB, a helicopter was waiting. Deirdre nodded goodbye to the attentive platoon commander and to the terp and ran under the blades of the twin Huey as it started its engines. Their roar drowned out every other thought and a column of dust rose up like a shroud. A moment later they were headed south, back to KAF. She studied the road they had patrolled that day. Millet and wheat fields thigh-high with grain and the land shimmering under the sun. A man in a loose turban walked along the road carrying a hoe over his shoulder. She lifted her camera, but by the time she had it to her eye they were past him and all she could see was road and setting sun.

❀

While Deirdre was lying in the dirt, Anakopoulus, back at KAF, was still seething at her. Going over his head like that, in front of his men, was as if she had climbed up and squatted on the counter and pissed all over him.

His first response had been a call up his chain of command, to logistics and the base OPS O. Who had considerably more standing than the media liaison major who had ordered him to give O'Malley the body armour. That was the last time the press officer would try something like that, that was for sure. His boss, who understood the resource he had in Anakopoulus, had invited him to listen in on the reaming he gave this Major Horner. You will never speak to Master Sergeant Anakopoulus again, do you understand, Major? You will come directly to me on any supply matters. And if you think you can throw your weight around with me, you just try it. Master Sergeant Anakopoulus is an important part of what makes this place work. You are not. Am I clear?

Anakopoulus did not have a high regard for the officers he reported to. He felt generally that he owed them much less than they owed him. He understood perfectly well why his boss was so enthusiastic about climbing all over Major Horner on his behalf. With him listening, too— that was never done. It was because this was the first time Anakopoulus had asked him for anything. His independence was so complete he had been almost autonomous. And now that he had asked for something, that was less true. He knew that. But he paid the price because nothing like that could ever happen again in front of his guys.

It was gratifying to hear that limp-dicked Major Horner being chewed out, but Anakopoulus's own satisfaction wasn't the point. His men needed to know he wouldn't put up with it. Stand up for your guys, in all circumstances, as best you can—it was his first and almost his only principle of leadership. Avoid being pushed around in front of them. But he had been. And so far as they knew, he could be again, which meant they could be. He replayed his exchange with the embed over in his head and inserted more biting rage and sharp phrases until, in this imagined version, she was left speechless.

She had been about to go out on patrol and he could have lent her some body armour for twenty-four hours. But her superiority—her presumption that she was as much or even more involved in and as important to the mission as he and his soldiers were, and even outranked them in some sense—had made him lose his shit. He had been a soldier since he was eighteen. Thirty years. Then the shooting starts and leeches like her show up to take in the show and act like they're experts.

She would probably say there was a woman thing going on here, too. It was true that his crew were all men and he had been here a long time. Susie was one of only a few women he had talked with at length for years, and now they didn't talk, so he tried not to think about her.

But she snuck in sometimes. Like now. Opening the woman door in his head had let Susie through. He tried to shut it, but all the longing came up out of him even as he refused to acknowledge its existence or even his capacity to feel it.

It was better that his men thought he was raging about someone dis-respecting them. He figured the more alert ones would know that wasn't all it was about. Losing his shit could not become a habit. For a dozen reasons.

At four that afternoon, as the men began to cycle off in shifts to the dining facility, he announced he was going for a long run. It was a good decision, getting out of there. Someone was going to mention her. The embed, he meant. All these rotations later, no one was left who knew that Susie had ever existed.

A fter he had been in Kandahar for a year, he could tell Susie was struggling. She tried to hide it from him. In the beginning she'd told him
everything about her days, wanted to involve him at the distance of twelve
time zones in every decision she made. This annoyed him, made him think
she was not self-sufficient enough to endure a deployment that was looking
to be more and more protracted every day. They spoke often on the telephone but eventually their conversations grew less concrete—she slowly
stopped telling him about the birthday parties her son attended, stopped
asking him how to change faucet washers and how to replace fuses. The
abstract generalities about her days—"busy," "okay," "I'm worried about his
grades"—were dutiful and no revelation at all. He told her he had inquired
about leave to go home many times but had always been discouraged by his
overly dependent bosses. "We're at war, Master Sergeant," he told her they
had replied. He told her he had become sort of indispensable.

"I'm just so tired of being lonely," she said, in response. She went to work,
she made supper for her son and watched television. She told him she went
out with her friends sometimes. She was ten years younger than him and
that made the separation harder for her, she said. Her wants were stronger
than his. Which was a shot at him, for being so far away for so long.

He ordered her presents from stores with websites. The Oprah books she had mentioned wanting to read, a new Gore-Tex raincoat, an opal ring. She appreciated the effort more than his taste, but it helped. They tried having phone sex a few times but he knew the phone lines were sometimes monitored and that inhibited him. He didn't tell her that, though, and she took his attitude as disinterest. She told him her boy missed him a lot, and asked him to write to him. Meaning, to her.

After he had been away for two years, she asked him what he'd think if she went out to dinner with a guy she'd met at a party.

"Like, on a date?" he asked.

"Not really. Kinda," she said.

"That would be fine," he said, taking the dare.

"You must think I'm terrible," she said, her voice teasing and discouraged at once.

He made himself laugh then and after a moment he felt like he meant it. And then he did mean it. He didn't want her to be alone. "You being lonely and sad does not make me love you more," he said. "I love you because you are you. And you are at your core a happy woman. Don't stop being you and I'll keep loving you. Be happy. Just please keep loving me."

She was quiet then and he wondered if he had offended her. Then she said: "No one has ever said anything like that to me. I love you, too, Demetrios. I really do. I just need to get out of the house sometimes."

He laughed, with relief, with tenderness. "I know what you need."

"Well, that too."

"Eventually they'll let me have leave."

CHAPTER THREE

After Anakopoulus got back from his run he showered and ate and walked back to the warehouse. The day shift had ended and there had been no new shipments in or out lately and so most of his soldiers were back at their barracks playing multiplayer Call of Duty. Anakopoulus headed into the back of his cavern, turning on lights as he went. The five thousand discrete objects he kept here were organized by NATO stock number rather than theme and so surprising neighbours were created: latrine disinfectant and chaplains' field sacrament kits stared across an aisle at one another. The smell of oiled canvas was strong. A crate of laundry detergent had been handled roughly and the scent of lavender freshness hung in the air. He could hear a forklift moving slowly and moved away from the sound. He wanted to be alone, and to drink in the feeling of capacity all this equipment lent him.

Though killing defines it, war is mostly not that. It is mostly eating and shitting and driving and washing and watching. For every combat soldier on the ground, there were at least fifteen others, making soup and fixing trucks and reconciling expense projections. A knife that was only edge would be nothing at all. This warehouse was mostly filled with things American men and women need to live anywhere. Toilet paper.

Radios. Towels. Batteries. The quantity of batteries he shipped out every month astounded him. Wet cell, dry cell, nickel metal hydride, lithium, he had them all.

Flammable supplies like fuel and motor oil went to a different depot that he also controlled, and explosives like grenades and ammunition went to one far from the barracks. He had received a memo about airlines' concern with lithium batteries and he had decided to store them separately—a major fire in the warehouse would be a catastrophe that would end his career. It wouldn't be the colonel he reported to who took the blame, that was for sure.

Rifles, pistols and machine guns were sent to him before being distributed to unit armouries; at any moment he had thousands of those here, too. This was a country awash with rifles, and every soldier on the base carried a pistol. Firearms were tools and they were common. You got into considerably more trouble by misplacing a weapon than a shovel, but they were basically the same thing. He had a whole row of .50-calibre machine guns packed in grease. Breech blocks were stored separately, and locked up. Cases of 9-mm Beretta pistols, M-4s, M-16A4s. And a few dozen very expensive handmade M-24 sniper rifles.

Of all the weapons he stocked, the ones he liked looking at the most were the AK-47s. It felt strange, stocking Russian weapons with Cyrillic markings and such a foreign-looking design sensibility. They could not be more obviously the product of a different way of thinking about war. He stocked them because the Special Forces dudes working with local militias carried AKs in order to fit in better.

The AK-47's stock and forestock was of oiled hardwood. The wood was part of what made it a heavy rifle, half again the weight of the plastic-and-steel M-4. The oldest construction material fit well on this weapon. It was chambered for the .30-calibre bullet that had dominated the two world wars and killed forty million. Those big .30-calibre rounds were created to stop charging cavalry.

The rifle had brought death to humans on four continents for half a century because it could be buried in the ground for two months and then dug up, cocked and fired. It was as robust as a sledge and could be built by inept machinists. And in that perfect pragmatism dwelt its loveliness.

In contrast, the M-4/M-16A2 with its black steel in sharp trapezoids and triangles and plastic stock, is menace and precision. You cannot bury it for any length of time and imagine that it will work. It needs to be maintained. The American rifles were more accurate and more expensive to make and lighter to carry and in many ways the superior weapon. They fired a .22-calibre bullet that flew out at half again the speed of the older, heavier bullets, and had a flatter and hence more accurate trajectory over its four-hundred-yard effective range. The bullets killed more by their velocity than their weight. Striking flesh, they blew a cone of kinetic injury that, if it emerged on the other side, could be as large as an orange. If a bullet struck bone, it could be sent tumbling in directions that were almost random. Speed versus weight—the difference between the American and Russian ways of war could not be more concisely demonstrated. The Americans conquered Afghanistan in two months and took a handful of casualties. The Russians killed a million Afghans and lost a hundred thousand of their own over a decade—and still lost: in the modern age, speed beats weight.

And yet. All over the world, the AK was what rebels and dissidents and desperate men who fought in the hills preferred. It was cheap and available and robust. And maybe it couldn't be surpassed. Some things just get as good as they can be and subsequent refinements are not improvements: bicycles, pencils, umbrellas. Killing, at its essence, is stupidly simple: send a piece of steel into someone with sufficient speed and they die. As long as it keeps working, any rifle will do this.

Normally, thinking about the perfectibility of objects would have given Anakopoulus some satisfaction. The perfect flashlight. The perfect folding knife. The perfect desert boot. But the long-ago attainment of the ideal assault rifle made him think about mortality and futility. All those designers' lives subsequently spent trying to improve on it and failing. Whole working lifetimes wasted. These sort of thoughts were more and more on his mind lately, what with the way things were going.

❋

Deirdre showered and made her way straight to bed. She bunked with five other civilian women contractors—cooks and accountants. None of them were around and she was grateful for this. She sat on her cot and rubbed her feet.

That had been the first patrol she had been on in Afghanistan since 2002. After the collapse of the Taliban she'd gone to Kabul, which was where the action had been, in those days: loya jirgas and vision statements and plans to build schools and hospitals. UN agencies were everywhere, and the great miracle of the Taliban's collapse had given confidence to every adventurer who wanted to help. Restaurants opened, serving Lebanese and Italian food, and aid organizations flooded in. She took a room at the Hotel Intercontinental and every night in the bar she drank with the western enthusiasts: reporters—war correspondents, rather, though there was little war in those days—USAID, MSF, UNESCO. Hordes of NGO workers. House and office rents tripled every two months. She put away her body armour. She drove around the ring road with no one but her translator for company. Everywhere she stopped, people crowded around, eager to talk. At least that's how she'd seen it then. Now, it seemed impossible. But then it seemed to her and to everyone she spoke to that a miracle had happened. She remembered the intoxicating joy of those days, the parties and the delight and the self-satisfaction—look what *we* did. Remembering made her shudder. But they knew so little then. Which is why no one really asked any questions when the Iraq drumbeat started.

She'd had supper with Stewart Robinson in Kabul, too, after he'd finished his walk. Most of the journalists presumed he worked for MI6. Those rumours did not keep them from talking to him—rather, the opposite: they lent him an air of substance he would not otherwise have worn. It changed what would have been viewed as a stunt into something more meaningful.

They'd met in La Taverna du Liban, a favourite restaurant of the expats. Walking to her table, she was greeted by three journalists and noticed by another five. It was a poor choice. He had picked it. Next time she would choose the venue. When he arrived he was also greeted by his friends, who comprised everyone she knew plus everyone she didn't. He sat down and smiled at her, then said, "Every ferenghee in the city knows everyone else, don't they?"

"It's one big party. And you're the belle of the ball," she replied.

"It isn't me they're looking at right now."

"The gossip is beginning already," she said, surveying the room.

"Let them gossip."

"I'd rather they didn't."

"They will or they won't. It's trivial."

"For you, it's trivial. For me, trying to work, it isn't."

"I think you'll find that if you just ignore that stuff it goes away. The women here become men quickly enough through their work. No one gossips like that about Alissa Rubin. She walked through the Khyber Pass last month. Did you see her piece on it in the *Times*?"

"Yes. That's her over there, isn't it? Is that Carlotta Gall she's eating with?"

He turned around and waved. "Yes."

"Last time we met you were just about to leave Kandahar on foot."

"Oh, I remember."

She looked at him levelly. So it was like that.

"It was bedlam there, then," he continued.

"I was there two weeks ago. It's settling down."

"The fighting?"

"There's no fighting. The chaos of the place wasn't about fighting, it was about hurried building."

"Well, the hurry is appropriate." He was posturing as an old hand. As if anyone had been here long.

She remembered how she had humoured him. "You think the peace won't last?"

"I think we have a very short period of time to give enough back to the Afghans that we make up for our presence here. And after not much longer than that, no amount of giving will be enough."

"They seem quite friendly on my trips around the ring road."

"There is trouble on the way. Sooner or later. We're occupiers."

She recalled how tempting it was to puncture him, but she'd demurred. She'd figured they would cross paths again and he was bound to be influential. She'd wished she'd known him well enough to mock his sententiousness. He might have enjoyed it. She certainly would have.

"There are a lot of people here, trying to make this place better. They're spending billions," she'd said.

"There are a lot of people here, yes. Most of that money is going to them, though."

"Still. We're not the Taliban."

"The Taliban are Afghans."

"The Taliban are monsters."

"I agree. But we're not Afghans and they are."

"You looked it, in Kandahar, in those clothes and windburn."

"Not to them."

"How is the book going?"

"I'm nearly done."

"Can I read it?"

"I have a draft at my apartment."

And she'd looked up at the waiter as he came to take their orders. Which was a relief. It had given her time to think. But of course she'd gone. He'd turned out to be a much better writer than she'd thought he would be. And she had to concede that what had struck her as arrogant and presumptuous in what he had predicted at that first dinner had turned out to be right. But at that point she hadn't yet been to Iraq.

❀

That was five years ago, already. When she got the call from New York to wrap up her business in Kabul and move to Kuwait City she had not been surprised. Her colleagues were all getting the same calls. It was clear what it meant. The Afghanistan project was looking like the most successful large-scale intervention ever. Another year or two and

Afghanistan would be Nepal. Iraq had even more potential: Dubai, but with oil, elections, and universities with women professors. She left Afghanistan for Iraq eagerly, hoping for the best, and expecting that the best was the most likely outcome. Why wouldn't it be?

The ebullience on the plane to Kuwait City was like nothing she had seen since she had covered a college football game. There were contractors and soldiers and journalists and men and women with the State Department and the Coast Guard, Department of Energy, Justice: America was all there for the party. Fortune favours the bold. Afghanistan had just been the proof-of-concept experiment.

❀

Anakopoulus was glad tonight was one of the few times a month that he got together with his counterparts in the British supply warehouses. As he sat down in the British camp he felt something approaching ease settle over him. Around other Americans, he never relaxed. The request for a favour—that he overlook a lost weapon, that he replace something that could be repaired—was only ever a matter of time. The other senior logistics NCOs of the various ISAF national forces understood one another's problems in a way that their own non-logistician countrymen never could. They were all in the same position: guardians of the cargo, but without officer rank or stature. Warrant Officer David Shipman, his parallel in the Royal Engineers, had brought a keg of ale—forbidden to deployed American soldiers—to one of his less-used tents and Anakopoulus had filled his coffee cup appreciatively.

"How exactly did you wind up here?" Shipman asked.

"I volunteered. You know this."

"The question is, why?"

"When the attacks came I was getting ready to put in my retirement papers. I had never realized how bored I had been my whole life. Suddenly everyone, me included, came alive. It was soldiers that would save our country. Everything stopped being a hypothetical and became real. Everything came into focus."

"Jesus fuck," Shipman said. "You're here because you think it's interesting? You have a weird sense of adventure."

Anakopoulus said, "I'm not here for any adventure."

"I'm here for my pension. Six more years."

"Which will make what, eight years in?" Anakopoulus said. "European fucking pensions."

"Twenty, cocksucker. And you're just jealous of our more civilized society."

If Anakopoulus had a friend, it was him. Not exactly Shipman so much as his position. Anakopoulus had been close to Shipman's predecessor, too, and the man before him and the man before that. He had trusted and felt trusted by each iteration of these men. They were outside one another's chain of command, but they did the same job and often helped one another out. Circumstances brought and kept them here and inevitably, a mutual sympathy developed.

Shipman, who had more of an air of felony about him than any of his predecessors, took a long pull of beer. "Hey, before I forget, I have something for you," he said, and reached into his pocket and handed Anakopoulus a thumb drive. "These are from a mate of mine who was through here last week. Most of the stuff in here was shot in Iraq. We think things are crazy here, but Iraq is a real shit show." Anakopoulus accepted the gift without excitement.

"Have a look through them," Shipman said. "Maybe you haven't seen it all."

"I used to look at all the pictures and the videos everyone passed around. I had the idea that it had something to do with me. But war porn gets dull—all those bodies being propped up, all those intestines—the same way porn-porn gets dull."

This last shocked Shipman. "You, my friend, are getting old. And you have been here too long. I heard about you when I was still in Basra. They called you the fuckin' Highlander. Legendary Immortal within the ISAF logistics community. In KAF continuously since 2002."

"Not continuously." Two years ago, Anakopoulus had a few weeks out, at the insistence of his boss. He spent his time in a hotel room in

Cyprus, reading spy novels. Later, he told everyone he had the best time ever.

"Still. Close enough. Rest of us, we all wish we had that kind of endurance."

"It's not endurance."

"In the UK, the supply techs who had been through here told me about you, too. They made you sound like a cartoon. In reality you are much less hairy."

"Thanks for that."

"There is a story, though, isn't there? A reason you feel so comfortable here and never get sick of it?"

Eventually everyone always probes. "I get fucking sick of it. So what's the rest of *your* story? What made you volunteer to come to Afghanistan?"

"It's my generation's war," Shipman shrugged. And then he poured himself more beer.

"So you were bored and wanted to be a badass."

Shipman: "We're *quartermasters*. None of us are badasses."

Anakopoulus: "I'm a fucking badass quartermaster."

Shipman: "Well, then I am, too. But we were badasses before we came here."

"You can't say you're not a badass and then turn around and say you are. Badasses know their badassishness. Badasses have no doubt."

Shipman, feeling the drink, said, "You are full of doubt, you lying motherfucker. You doubt everything."

"Everything except my badassishness. Which is the lodestar by which I navigate."

"You hear that in a movie?"

"Maybe."

"It probably sounded smarter coming out of the mouth of someone better looking."

Anakopoulus laughed. It was time to go. When he had this much to drink he started thinking about Susie. He stood up and waved.

"Goodbye, Highlander," Shipman said.

❀

When he got back to his warehouse, Anakopoulus sat down at his desk in the dark and listened to the helicopters heading off. Night raids left just after midnight, usually, and came back around five. The uninformed admiration his British colleague had directed at him had left him sour. He really was a cartoon, hairy or not. Living his empty life here in dusty Kandahar. Hanging out with a guy he pretended was, but who wasn't really, his friend—just an occupier of a position comparable to his.

He turned on his laptop and checked his private email. Penis Extenderz, and a barrister from Togo with a dead client. Some friends, dropping lines, wondering why he'd been so quiet. There was no email from her. There never was. She was signed into Facebook, though. One of these days she would defriend him. If she had any idea how much time he spent creeping her, she would have, already. She'd posted that her son was about to graduate from middle school. The boy had been in grade two when he was first deployed here. Which put things in perspective.

He dug into his pocket and pulled out the thumb drive Shipman had given him. He plugged it in and the contents fluttered up as thumbnails over the screen. Even in miniature, they were horrifying—or would have been, had he not become so used to everything.

He started scrolling through them. One of the contributors to this file was actually an ambitious photographer. There was a shot of tailors in a shattered shop making suits that caught his eye. Inevitably, there were the bodies, and the many indignities offered to them. Canadian snipers up in Tora Bora posing with necklaces of little fingers. American Marines pissing on corpses. Danes shooting motionless bodies lying in a ditch. He clicked through the carnage, looking for interesting photos. There weren't many.

And there. Who was that blonde? The fucking embed. Posing with Lancaster Fusiliers in Iraq. Arms around the smiling men on either side of her. Another of her holding an AK-47. Posing like a killer.

"Oh, sweetheart," he whispered. And he thought again of how she had spoken to his clerk. And he remembered the way that media liaison had spoken to him. Reporters posing with weapons. They did it sometimes, especially the young ones and especially in the first few weeks. But those kinds of images? Among other reporters, better a sex tape emerge than a senior journalist be caught posing like that. He thought for a moment about her sneer and then he took a new laptop from a stack of cases in one corner of his crowded office. In a few minutes he had it up and running. Then he signed into the civilian Wi-Fi net and Yahoo using an account that had been dormant for a year—guys who had come through over the years gave him their Wi-Fi and email account names and passwords for lots of reasons. To send things off for them. To say goodbye to someone, if something bad happened. To delete every single JPEG in their account. One of them got killed. A couple of the others killed themselves. He had done his duty by all of them, but he still had a handful of account passwords. He used one of them now. One of the suicides.

He went into a VPN and entered the address for the InformationIsFree dropbox, which he'd heard about it in a routine security briefing months ago. Some joker in Iraq had sent out some documents about prisoner abuse. It was a problem, apparently, because they hadn't been able to trace the leak. So if any of your guys are talking about that site, let us know, okay? Those documents got into the papers just after the Abu Ghraib scandal blew up. Caused all kinds of trouble.

The dropbox was simple to use. Which was good. Because he was still drunk. But not too drunk to find the embed's photo and click send, and shamble off to his cot. Not too drunk to wake up an hour later and wonder why the laptop was still whirring and clicking. He got up, scratching his balls through his military issue green boxers, and peered at the screen. And then he was abruptly sober.

Select all.

He pulled the thumb drive and frantically signed off the internet and out of the Wi-Fi. He flushed so deeply his hair hurt. And then he puked into his wastebasket. He had sent every file on that thumb drive to the dropbox. Every fucking cuntsucking file.

He stuck the drive in again and scrolled more methodically through the images. There were photos of uniformed Americans and Poles and

Brits and Australians looking sunburnt and euphoric. There were pictures of children in the street and of women in the market. Some of these were beautiful. But most of the photos were of bodies. Sometimes they were powerful enough to possess a sort of anti-beauty. There was a short video of a Bradley Armoured Fighting Vehicle running over a ditch with enemy in it. Parts flying back. All you could hear was the racket of the armoured fighting vehicle. There was a helmet cam video of one of Saddam's palaces being looted. Another helmet cam video of a firefight in Tikrit. And a series of videos taken off the gunsights of Apache helicopters and A-10s. This stuff was never intended to get out to the public. Not by the people who made these images, nor by the soldiers who traded them. He fell back on his cot, nauseous and dizzy. He laid an arm over his eyes. He could not believe he had just done that.

❀

The next morning, Anakopoulus sat on the edge of his cot in his office and pushed his hands into his face like it was putty. The base was stirring. His posting to the dropbox hung in his thoughts with ill-shaped and shadowed self-contempt.

There was a knock.

"Yeah?"

"You okay in there, Master Sergeant?"

"Yeah."

Robertson stuck his head in the door. "Base Supp O called a minute ago. On his way over."

"'Kay."

"Be here in fifteen."

"'Kay." He stood and dressed. It was six-thirty. The current base supply officer was the twelfth he had worked with since 2002. By now, the person everyone was terrified of was usually Anakopoulus. Today he was the one who was scared. He stood up and started to shave. He cut himself twice.

*I*n March 2005, the former private from Bar Harbor was told by his platoon commander that soon he would be a sergeant. He had been in Baghdad continuously for two years and no one had more combat experi- ence than he did, between Iraq and Afghanistan. Anyway, they needed more NCOs with field experience. Promotions come fast in war. All you had to do was not get in obvious trouble. Not get caught letting your guys do crazy shit, not shoot your mouth off to some reporter or another.

Which is why the sergeant from Boise learned on the same day as the same platoon commander that he would be commissioned and that his transfer to intelligence had been approved. It meant leaving the Special Forces, which bothered him. He would be promoted to captain, in recog- nition of his experience as an NCO. The platoon commander, a captain himself, told him this as if it was the biggest gift imaginable. But leaving the Special Forces pained the sergeant from Boise so deeply that he hardly knew whether to be happy or not. He had decided to apply for the com- mission because he wanted more thoughtful work and because he was tired of killing. That distaste had not yet been discerned by his comrades and so there was still time to act. Another six months or a year, though, and it would be too late. He would be rotated home and given a dead-end desk job. Recruiter, maybe. So it was time to make a move.

The captain from Utah who had been with them at Taliban's Last Stand was now a major. He was sitting in an office not far from them, and had just learned that he would become a lieutenant colonel. He had been surprised by the news, and spun his pencil around his finger, thinking.

In peacetime, a promotion was a life-changing event. You called your wife immediately and you could expect to buy many rounds of drinks at the mess. Promotions came twice a decade, at best, and often they did not come at all. Perfectly competent and ambitious officers retired as majors at fifty-five. But demonstrated ability in battle propelled anyone to the top of all the lists. Lieutenant colonel. He would get his own battalion. More time over here. His wife would pretend to be pleased, for him. He would call her. In a minute.

CHAPTER FOUR

Green Beans café, KAF

Rashid Siddiqui

I met the manager, Rami Issay, when I arrived here after a four-day bus ride from Islamabad. He was excited about just having bought a chess set for his establishment. He said that it was so that he could improve the atmosphere. "What is wanted here on Kandahar Airfield is a proper café—not some industrial-scale coffee-dispensing *depot*," he declared.

"In a proper café, people linger. They do not buy their cappuccino hurriedly, and run away back to work, before anyone sees them idling. *Idling* is what a café is all about. Or else coffee would just come as a pill of some sort. And anyway, idlers," his voice dropped conspiratorially, "need the cover of other idlers."

Rami Issay was a jowly jolly little man from Karachi. He told me, his new employee, that he'd lived in Leeds for a dozen years before having to return to Pakistan. There he built and then spectacularly exploded a computer sales mini-empire in the middle of the longest economic expansion Southeastern Pakistan had ever known. If perhaps he were one ten-thousandth as perceptive as he clearly imagines himself to be, he would not now be a migrant worker and bankrupt employed by the Kellogg Brown and Root corporation to run one of their Starbucks-in-camo Green Beans coffee shops on bloody Kandahar Airfield in what

44

amounts to a large shed. Indeed I soon found out his own expertise was in idling, and in this matter, he knew of what he spoke.

When I signed up I was not told where precisely I would be working, only that it was a distant but faithful place. The commitment was for one year, and I was also told it would be difficult and expensive to return early. Everyone knew what was meant by these phrases, though when I signed the document, I briefly entertained the notion that I would be going to one of the Gulf States. I also received an advance, representing a substantial fraction of the total remuneration.

For my fellow passengers on the bus out of the country, the advance and the distance was life-changing. This much was apparent from their demeanour and our silence as we wheezed our way through the mountains. Our minder had our ID; our direct interaction with the police at the checkpoints was limited. Hardly a meaningful sentence was uttered until we were ushered out of the bus into the bright sunlight of Kandahar. And there in front of us were our employers, bellowing our names and waving ID tags and passes. Rami Issay had brought a placard, I guess to spare himself the indignity of raising his voice. It had just one name on it, mine: "Mr. Rashid Siddiqui." If he had tried such a tactic in my place of origin, he would have been trampled to death by like-named respondents.

But I should not be so unkind. If the events of my life had proceeded differently, I would be an engineer by now, and treating men such as him badly. We all have our circumstances and my task is to accommodate myself to my own.

When I approached him, he grinned widely and bowed. Peace was upon us both, and he took me through the process of getting through the camp gate. His combination of imperiousness and ebullience seemed to work well with the soldiers and soon enough, within a few hours, and after a body search of unprecedented thoroughness, we were through. From my first view of the ferenghee soldiers up close, my impression was that they were quite uncomfortably warm. They were English, that day—their uniforms said Royal Air Force regiment—and as pink in the face as pomegranates. They carried their odd, short English assault rifles slung over their shoulders. It was the first time I had seen those strange little weapons; in this part of the world, the AK-47 is the way people kill one another. How anyone shoots accurately with those British rifles is beyond me. One hears them called them "bullpups" and the word sounded appropriately silly to me. I couldn't help smiling at them as these thoughts ran through my mind. But Rami Issay shot me a look and I sobered and glanced down. I thought then about a thousand Pashtun shredded by these toys and the tiny vicious bullets they spit out. I sobered further.

The base at Kandahar Air Field looked like the disaster relief camps they set up after earthquakes. Apart from a few shattered Soviet-era shacks, everything was prefabricated aluminum or canvas. Hardly a structure was more than a couple of years old. Whole building complexes were put together out of shipping containers. Every object not mounted upon an axle was surrounded by blast barriers: ten-foot high fences of sandbags, wire mesh and concrete. The colour was monochromatically dun: dun uniforms, dun dirt, dun sandbags. It was early spring and, presumably, about as verdant as things got. By mid-July even the greens of the few eucalyptus trees lost whatever undertones of colour they had possessed and everything was as desiccated as glassblowers' sand. They call this part of the world the Red Desert and perhaps it is, for a few weeks before and after the vernal equinox. But otherwise it is the colour of fly ash.

Colourlessness in other contexts connotes lifelessness, but so far as humans went, there was nothing lifeless about the airfield. Twelve thousand people worked here—soldiers, mercenaries, maintenance men, cooks, launderers, construction workers. The hurly-burly never stopped. Trucks and combat vehicles were always rumbling around, Chinook helicopters lifting off, Antonov heavy-lift air freighters roaring up, up, up and away, and small packs of tired men, walking together and talking: off-duty soldiers from Jordan, Romania, Holland, England, Estonia, France, Canada and twenty other places—including the Great Satan—together with the local and Pakistani and Bangladeshi workers. Always there were some of us kicking at the dust and whinging about women and money. There were two things to do in KAF—work and complain.

Once I was admitted into the camp, my new boss conducted me to his café. It was truly a small place, only fifteen tables and eighty square metres, including the public area and the back, which is where I was to sleep at night, along with the rest of the staff, among bags of coffee beans and crates of non-dairy creamers. Dividing the space was a narrow counter of espresso machines, overtaxed refrigerators and questionable pastries. The punctured building they call Taliban's Last Stand was on one side of us and the hospital on the other. Behind was the flight line; we could almost always hear the steady whine of jet engines.

Rami Issay showed me the hook where I could hang my bedding during the day and then gave me a quick lesson on the operation of the espresso machine. He forgot to tell me about steaming clear the nozzle. My co-workers watched him with skeptical sparkles in their eyes as he clumsily tightened and untightened the knobs of the gleaming stainless steel product of Puglia-by-way-of-Taiwan. He would have introduced me to them if he could have remembered all their names, but he spared us all that embarrassment by announcing that he would just let everyone get to know one another, he said, "without undue formality." Then he wandered off vaguely in the direction of the boardwalk.

None of the others would speak Pashto or even Urdu with me at first; every time I tried they shifted into English. I was puzzled by this but, later, as I understood the psychology of KAF better, I learned to share their caution. They had heard that I had studied in America from Rami Issay, I think. He felt a kinship with me, he said, because we both know the size of the world. And after the planes had hit the towers, the world had tossed us both back on our cancelled-visa asses to a country we had never wanted to see again.

Fazil was the head baristo, as he termed himself; he had a wife and two sons in Peshawar. He had been here nearly continuously since the shop was opened in 2003. Then, he'd handled the place by himself most of the time. The preparation for the invasion of Iraq had seen the numbers of soldiers in Kandahar drawn down, and for months he had expected his position to be eliminated. Within six months of Baghdad falling, the idea of IEDs was evangelized and bombs started exploding everywhere around Kandahar. Since then he and his wife have slept easily every night, he said, knowing his job is secure. Both his boys are in a good school and they will become engineers, he thinks. His wife has paid off all the debts that drove him to Kandahar in the first place and soon they will purchase a modest home with an electric washing machine.

The next man to introduce himself was Fazil's friend, the one-eyed Amr Chalabi. Men in groups instinctively establish a hierarchy of who could, if it came to it, beat whom to death and Amr, tall and powerfully muscled, occupied the apex of our list. He had worked at the café nearly as long as Fazil, but he maintained an entirely different posture. Where Fazil was solicitous and engaging, Amr preferred rarely to speak, and then only to Fazil or the boy, Mohammed. Amr did his work quickly and helpfully—he was the first up every morning, washed, shaved and sweeping away the previous night's insect accumulations while the rest of us were still blinking at the bare bulb overtop us. When he worked the counter he usually operated the espresso machine, nodding as the orders were called to him and handing the paper cups of milk foam and coffee out with precision. He was the oldest, too, perhaps forty years, maybe forty-five. I have never learned whether or not he has a family or children. I did know that he had terrible insomnia, and that when he lifted his patch, his left eye looked like it was filled with cotton. Sometimes, in the sleeping area at night, one caught sight of him lifting the patch as he lay on his back, staring at the ceiling and waiting for morning.

Mohammed was scarcely eighteen, and by scarcely, I mean thirteen at the outside. He must have claimed to be older in order to be hired, and while he attempted to sustain the fiction, he shaved once a week and then only for the ritual of it. If he possessed any hair but the shock of blackness rising straight up from his scalp, none of us had ever seen it. Fazil would not allow him off the coffee shop premises after dark. I dismissed the boy as an ignorant villager. Everything about him suggested dullness: his accent, his relentless piety, his inability to look anyone in the eye or say the first thing about politics, or anything else.

My first night there, they told me they had been waiting for me for months, as if it were somehow my fault I had not been hired earlier or had my papers processed more quickly. They gave me to understand that I would be starting with a debt owed to them, which would require paying off. My detested predecessor, a Bangladeshi named Hamid, had developed tuberculosis four months earlier, and was immediately loaded into a truck headed for the border. Since then, the population of the camp and the workload had increased steadily. Rami Issay had told them I was supposed to have arrived every day for the last three months. And now there were the Gurkhas and the Australians and the American Marines landing here and the English Marines too. Some days the queue wound out around the coffee shop all the way to the massage parlour. I was pleased to be here, I said. I would change my mind soon enough, Fazil said, though without much conviction. We all laughed harshly.

Fazil was the one who taught me how to use the espresso machine. Mohammed swept out the place, as he would twenty more times that day. Amr carried more bags of coffee beans from the back. Rami Issay returned to the café and sat in a chair and read a copy of the *Harvard Business Review* he had found somewhere. The pilots began coming in about then, looking for their cappuccinos. Rami watched to see if any of them would notice what he was reading. None of them did. He did not betray any disappointment. The pilots, headshorn and enormous in their green flight suits, stood around the entrance together and laughed like great braying camels and enjoyed being themselves, so muscular and so erect. Rami Issay just sat there, out of the pilots' way, and looked out a window toward Ghar Killay, the mountains silver peaked and jagged in the distance. The air above them shimmered in the midafternoon heat. Then someone else walked in and he rose, grinning, to greet them.

Master Sergeant Demetrios Anakopoulus

Five years on this base and the one place I'm still not used to is this coffee shop. First year here, we were on hard rations most of the time—foil bags of ravioli and omelets and beef stew, and coffee that came out of green metal urns and no one would even have admitted knowing how to spell cappuccino, let alone drink one three times a day. Now my guys run over here after every meal and bring back trays of foamy cups. At first I never came here. It seemed too fancy for an operational base in a combat zone. Then I did and it turned out that it's the one place on the base where people give one another a bit of space. So I spend quite a bit of time here. The only place I can be alone. Which is sort of the point to my being here, as far as I can tell.

I do find it a treat. Today, more than a treat. *Select all.* How could I have been so stupid?

First thing, I guess, is to act normal. Hope the site doesn't post anything. Resist the temptation to write and ask them not to. Just disappear. No more contact. They'll probably want to confirm things. If they can't, they probably won't use the photos.

The thing is to not lose my shit.

That Asian woman—the masseuse—has been staring at me too long for months now. Settle down. She doesn't know anything. She stares because she wants you to know she isn't afraid of you. Which is worth knowing. So thank you, Asian woman. Who gave me a great massage last year when I hurt my back. But likely doesn't remember. Which is fine by me.

Mohammed Hashto

The Americans don't look normal. No one else is as big as them. The Dutch are tall, too. All these foreigners are tall. Not the Gurkhas, not the Jordanians, so much. But the Americans' arms are the size of normal people's legs and their chests like sacks of grain. They talk big, they stand big. Who would ever want to fight them?

I was afraid of them at first. I thought they would yell at me. Then I realized that that wasn't going to happen. The soldiers in the Tribal Areas, they notice you. They think about whether you have some money they can get out of you, or whether you're going to shoot them in the back after they walk by you. They look you in the eyes and watch for fear, and if they don't see it, they pay attention. The big men here don't care whether you're afraid of them, and don't look at you long enough to tell whether or not you are. They just want their coffee. Which is how Fazil prefers it. But someone like Amr is used to being noticed. Me, I don't care whether I'm noticed or not.

The giant bald man comes in three or four times a day. He drinks triple-shot cappuccinos and is polite. He watches the Thai woman pretty closely. He never lets her notice him. Or she never lets him notice her noticing him. Many of the other soldiers seem to be afraid of him. They get out of his way when they see him coming. Maybe they work for him. They all come out of that long yellow warehouse near the airstrip and return to it when they're done here. You can see them working, when an airplane or a truck convoy comes in. The bald man walks among those men and watches. But not like he watches the Asian woman.

I did not like Rashid at first. I did not like how he spoke with so many strange words. And that he kept using them after he knew the rest of us could hardly understand him. Maybe even more, then. I understand English. I listen to the radio and read the newspaper. Maybe he spent time in India. They talk like that there, like English is their own language, and that the more of it you know the smarter you are. In Pakistan it is different. We use English too, but Urdu is what we live in and think in. When he tried to talk to us in Urdu and then Pashto I was surprised that Fazil kept changing back into English. But then I understood. It was too soon to show him what we thought.

Rami Issay bought the first chess set when Rashid arrived. It was a strange thing. Rami Issay is normally so bored by his coffee shop. I think meeting Rashid made him more interested. Rashid is smart and suddenly Rami Issay wants the Kandahar Green Beans to be smart too, like cafés in ferenghee cities.

I asked Amr about chess. He told me that chess was invented by Muslims. That it is still a game, but less sinful than the card games the Americans and English are always playing, or dancing, or the music videos you see them watching in their compounds. "But is it a sin?" I asked him.

"I don't know. I am not an educated man."

"But there are no holy men here to ask."

"I think that we should remember to pray, and fast on the holy days, and be pure ourselves. We think the ferenghee are sinful and most of them probably are. But the Taliban would think we are sinners, too."

"But there is only one God."

"Yes. And he made the world and the people in it."

"So the others are not blasphemers?"

"No. They are blasphemers. And you are not them."

"I don't know what to think."

"Be pure in your own heart and actions," he told me.

When the bald American stands in the line for his coffee, he usually looks a little angry. But he isn't any more or less impatient whether the line is long or short. I don't think it would make any difference if he walked in and a free coffee was waiting for him, made already. Or if Rashid had to make it over again three times, like he did on his first day. He would always be the same amount of impatient. He doesn't usually sit down. Usually he stands on the deck and drinks his coffee. Fazil says he's been here since before he opened the shop. He's like that dried-up tree outside his warehouse. He has become part of his place. No wonder he's so angry.

Just Amachai

The boy, Mohammed, is just a baby. He should be living with his family but in this part of the world, who knows how that story goes? Probably nothing you would actually want to hear. In Thailand he'd have become a monk. So pious and eager to please and so pretty. Shave his head and put him in a robe and he'd fit right in.

This place is swarming with French and British and every other sort of western soldier, and every day is busier than the one before it. It's just a matter of time before they kick us out of our shack to make room for more barracks. It's just a matter of time before that Special Forces general, that warrior monk, Lattice, decides that we are an unnecessary luxury anyway, along with the Burger King and the Pizza Hut. Which isn't to say that I was sad to see those go—my little belly was getting so big! This is not something anyone wants in a masseuse. Back to rice and healthy food. Which is probably what the general was thinking, too. No one wants to be soft here. Not even me. Especially me. After they closed, I lost five kilos and my tips doubled.

You never see the generals here. Drinking coffee at a coffee shop would be too leisurely for the likes of them. The generals should be more like the pilots. The pilots come in here when they're not flying and they make no apology and do not act embarrassed. They have less anxiety, I think, because they know what they do. They fly their helicopters and if they get where they're going safely and pick up and drop off whatever they're supposed to, then they did things right. It's nice to have certainty like that. I have it. I know when I'm doing my job right or not. I didn't used to. Which is funny because in those days I was younger and more beautiful and that was my job, to be young and beautiful. If only I could have known that then, I'd have saved myself from the shame and the embarrassment. But this is what it is to get older, isn't it? Finally we are understanding that we were so stupid to have been so anxious about everything back then. Later is when the real trouble comes. Like now. Things generally do get worse. We Buddhists see this more clearly than the puritans. Life is suffering. The more life, the more suffering.

This is what I think about when I watch the boy moving among the men, never smiling, working so hard and not looking at anyone at all, hauling racks of coffee mugs into the back to wash, and so worried that he might do the wrong thing. But we all do the wrong thing, honey. The tricky bit is that it isn't usually the thing we think is the wrong thing. It's the problem with the stern religions. We have Muslims in Thailand, too, but they are not as severe as this. Maybe because the rain comes more often. And we have our monks, too, to be holy for all the rest of us.

Amr Chalabi

The Japanese woman should stop staring at the boy. She knows it makes him uncomfortable, knows it makes him feel like he is sinning, and she keeps doing it, over her cup of green tea. Half-dressed and fresh from the brothel, still reeking of the ferenghee she has been with. I asked Rami Issay two times if he would forbid those women from coming here, but he laughed and said I didn't know anything about café culture. But the boy has no choice about being here, would prefer to be at a madrassa someplace, and ought to be, inshallah. I would die to protect him, but I don't know how to protect him from this torment. If ever the prostitute lifted her eyes from little Mohammed, she would see me and know she is seen. But she never does.

CHAPTER FIVE

G eneral Thomas Lattice sat in his office within the Special Forces compound, a hundred yards from the Green Beans café, and sipped from his cup of hot water. He had left his door wide open. It was after midnight, and apart from the duty officer and NCO, who were being conspicuously attentive to the security of the compound, it was generally quiet. He could hear locks being checked. One of the sentries coughed, once.

He was reading summaries of the media coverage of the war over the last month. Both he and General Jeremy Jackson, commander of the whole Afghan operation, had been posted here from Iraq four months ago—and not because things were going well. Still, one of them seemed to be doing just fine in the court of public opinion no matter the facts on the ground. Lattice had been briefed by his staff about how skilfully General Jackson was managing his media profile. Every mention of him included his Princeton PhD and his ability to run a mile in less than seven minutes. Lattice's response to this was disdain. The two had once been friends. Lattice had been Jackson's best man when he married, the summer they graduated from West Point. But even when they were friends, Lattice had understood how interested Jackson was in everyone's opinion of him. He had silently predicted that such a weakness would limit his Jackson's career success. But he had been wrong. Jackson's attention to how he was seen—image management, it was called now—also included a finely attuned sense of whether he was seen as too concerned with his image. An essential component of field craft is how to observe without being observed.

Lattice's aide had made the point: Jackson was a celebrity. And that status accorded him certain capabilities here and in the future. The same aide had prepared a summary of the reporters Lattice himself needed to cultivate if he wanted to have similar influence. Deirdre O'Malley's coverage of the war had historically been very useful: 88 percent of it positive or message enhancing. (The aide actually hadn't needed to point O'Malley's effectiveness out to him; he'd read her profile of Jackson in *Time* early on in the Iraq war, and understood the role it had played in making his old friend a star, not only in the media but at the Pentagon.) But lately her stories were slightly muted. The success of the surge in Iraq had not been duplicated here, Lattice thought, and she was responding to that. Then there was the matter of how she was seen to cover Jackson long-term. She could not have sustained the admiration she'd revealed in the profile and retained credibility with her editors. Still, 88 percent.

Stewart Robinson was about to visit the base. Robinson had fashioned himself a public intellectual—an unusual step for someone so junior and from the intelligence community. Not that Lattice knew anything explicit about Robinson's covert roles. But he could smell spook. Anyway, in Robinson's op-eds and lectures he supported the war or furthered the message 64 percent of the time, but was judged to have a higher impact than O'Malley because of the walk that had made him a celebrity and because he had been publicly critical of the military in several instances. "The Fox News guys don't change anyone's minds, sir," the aide had said. "People who could go either way listen to other people who could go either way. We need him on our side."

Then the aide added: "Jackson's lustre is bound to fade here. You'll want to position yourself for that." Lattice looked hard at that young man with his master's in communications. Ten years ago he would have fired him on the spot. Not now.

❁

Stewart Robinson walked off the RAF Herc and hoisted his bag over his shoulder and looked around. He put his Oakleys on and silently took in the familiar hills south of the airstrip, even as a Major Horner—with dual appointments in public affairs and the base adjutant's office, the man quickly explained—fell in beside him. The major said he was really quite pleased that Robinson could come. He imagined that the book tour for *Country of Stone* had been pretty exciting. As he had discussed with Robinson's publicist, he had arranged a reading for the soldiers that night. There were ten media requests for interviews, seven of them television. Was there any way Robinson could extend his stay? Had he followed the reviews in the American and British press and did he ever expect a response like this?

By this point, they had reached the holed and patched-over building they all called Taliban's Last Stand. Its rooms were being used as offices now. Horner and Stewart paused for a moment and looked at the pockmarks of machine-gun fire on its walls.

"You have powerful memories of this place, I'm sure," Horner said.

"I do. It's where it all started, you know."

"Your writing career?"

"No. The Taliban."

"Oh, of course."

"So what's next?"

"I'll bring you to your room and let you get cleaned up. Then we're having lunch with the ISAF battalion commanders on base."

"Who wants to interview me?"

"Peter Morgan from CBS, Tom Parry of CBC, Caroline Rudolph from NBC, Jim Ackers from Fox, Clark Smith from ABC."

"Is Deirdre O'Malley here?"

"Yes. She's been back for a few weeks."

"Has she put in a request to interview me?"

"No. But I'm not sure she knew you were coming. She's been out on patrol a lot."

"Does she go by the press tent?"

"Only when she needs something from someone."

Robinson grinned. "Have you ever worked in the media?"

"I was a reporter for the *Times Picayune* for a couple of years before enlisting. That's in New Orleans."

"Six years ago?" Robinson asked, glancing at his rank insignia and calculating.

"Yes."

"Was it a good decision?"

"Are you kidding? Best decision ever. I was going nowhere as journalist. Hardly anyone was. And it's even worse now for the print media, I think."

"Think we're getting much done over here?"

Horner paused. Brits—even ones immersed in the intelligence world—are not Americans. "It's a really tough job we've taken on. We might not succeed." He prayed he would never be quoted saying that. "But that would be a strange kind of effort—only trying when you know you'll win."

Robinson conceded, "It's got a better chance of working out than Iraq does."

"Iraq will work out, too."

"Will it?"

"Already has, partly. We've gotten rid of a genocidal tyrant."

"That's not the story the Iraqis are telling one another these days."

"If we're going to win, we have to change that story," Horner said, smiling.

"Or the facts that drive it?" Robinson asked.

"I heard you wrote a book," Horner replied, his smile growing ever wider, and his eyes narrowing almost imperceptibly.

Okay, he was smarter than Robinson had thought. Maybe no more interesting. "I did. I told a story about people I met and what they told me."

"Why?"

Robinson let that hang and they walked a while more, until Horner stopped them in front of a barracks. "Is this where I'm staying?" Robinson asked.

"It is. Room 104. Here's the key. I'll meet you here in an hour. Don't drink the tap water."

❀

Horner returned to his office while Robinson was cleaning up. He found a stack of messages on his desk. The one on top was a high-profile memo, addressed to public affairs personnel in theatre. Signals intelligence had recorded large volumes of data being exchanged through InformationIsFree.com. Some of it, the memo speculated, may have compromised operational security and may have pertained to military operations involving Operation Enduring Freedom and Operation Iraqi Freedom. Any contact with media personnel who ask about or refer to that website shall be reported to the sender of this briefing, the memo concluded.

He set aside the memo and shuffled through his inbox. There were last-minute confirmations of attendance at Stewart Robinson's discussion. *Foreign Affairs* had loved his book, as did *Foreign Policy* and the *Times* and the *Post*. Reading those reviews, Horner thought he could detect the envy of every foreign policy wonk in the country—intellectuals all, longing to be adventurers. And Robinson worked it well. He was charismatic and, when it served his narrative purposes, funny. Equally, the soldiers who followed the lay discussion about the war—and all the ambitious senior officers did—were struck by the meteoric rise of Robinson's media profile. Speed trumps weight, pithy paragraphs trump credentials, and individuals' stories are more gripping than collective ones: the sort of thing that made soldiers hate the press. Jessica Lynch becoming more famous than Tommy Franks. "Welcome to my world," thought Horner as he adjusted the attendance figures for the talk.

Robinson would be done his shower by now. Horner stood. He told himself he was still a journalist. It was just that now he worked on one big story. What a book he himself could write. He should start keeping notes. Then he felt ridiculous for even thinking that. But he should be keeping notes reflexively. A journal, maybe. He'd come here for a reason, after all. He had wanted to have a larger life.

❀

Horner parked his truck in the lot a few hundred yards from the barracks. When Robinson emerged, Horner was waiting near the door. "Better than a tent, isn't it?"

"When did these go up?"

"Three years ago, I think. There were here when I got here."

"When I was last here, everyone was under canvas."

"But you were used to it."

Nodding. "On my walk I slept under the sky, most of the time." The two men headed for Horner's truck.

"Does it still seem real to you that you did it—walked across this country?"

"It often doesn't."

"What do you remember the best?"

"How shockingly cold it gets on a clear night in winter."

"I can't imagine."

"You could, though. Go out on patrol with the guys."

"I was just thinking I should, actually. Anything you want to know about this reception we're going to?"

"Who's coming?"

"Mostly senior field officers. Majors to full colonels. The generals usually keep out of these things. Undefined terrain and all that. There will be a couple of CIA guys there."

"No doubt they'll stick out."

"They usually do. Though they rarely say much."

"Will there be Special Forces or Joint Special Operations Command there?"

"I don't know. Depends on how busy they are. They don't RSVP."

As they neared the truck, the sirens sounded and they exchanged a look, Horner inexplicably grinning and Robinson puzzled by Horner's reaction. The major ran then, waving Robinson to follow him. They got to the blast shelter just as the first rocket struck. A hundred and three millimetres in diameter: you wouldn't think it would pack so much explosive. But the report left their ears ringing and they both felt the concussion deep in their chests.

Horner was not used to the rockets yet. Every few days there was an attack. Every few weeks someone was hurt, though no one had been killed by one since he had arrived. He was telling this to Robinson when he noticed how amused the Brit was by it all. By him. He realized he was talking too fast. He sounded scared and—worse—delighted. He stopped talking. The all clear siren rang. They stepped out from under the blast shelter and headed back to Horner's truck. When they got to it they noticed that the tires were all flat, and then they saw the crater in the ground beside the driver's door. They both shrugged, then turned to walk to the meeting room. Each of them waited for the other to mention how close they had come. But neither did.

❁

The session with the battalion commanders went well. Robinson knew how to work a room. As funny looking as he was, the camera loved him. The military photographers were all over him. The way he handled the colonels was masterful. He announced that his hope for the meeting was to hear from them, what they, the local experts, were experiencing on the ground.

A French colonel, first regiment, Foreign Legion, raised a hand, then asked, "Your walking journey was magnificent but foolish, in the best sense of both these words. Surely it is our foolishness that yields the

most insight, no?" They all chewed on that for a moment, trying to figure out how drunk the colonel was. And then Robinson asked him if he
thought the farmers he patrolled among considered him the problem or
the solution.

The legionnaire shrugged. "He considers me another man with a gun.
If I'm not looking at him he doesn't even see me." The journalists in the
room wrote that down.

Recorded Nov 13 2004; Transcribed August 12 2007 by request of JAG for investigation Ref# 2007-7-21-56789345DAnakopoulus

SUBJECT A: Hey, I was hoping you'd call.

SUBJECT B: How are things?

SUBJECT A: Great, thanks. Jose just got back from science camp. That was a good idea, thanks. He loved it.

SUBJECT B: What was the best part for him?

SUBJECT A: I think he liked the rocketry a lot. He keeps asking me if you have anything to do with drones over there.

SUBJECT B: I probably shouldn't talk about that. I heard if you use certain words on these lines they alert computers to record the conversation. But the answer is, not really.

SUBJECT A: It's great watching him really get into something. He's talking now about studying engineering. After all my endless math homework lectures last winter.

SUBJECT B: It's like with my guys. Truth is, you can't really make anyone do anything. All you can do is make it easy to do the things that they also want to do.

SUBJECT A: That doesn't sound very soldier-like, Mr. Military Man.

SUBJECT B: There's a lot of theatre in soldiering. It serves a purpose. Then there's the non-theatre part of it.

SUBJECT A: Like in banking.

SUBJECT B: And how are the interest rates?

SUBJECT A: Variable. [laughing]

SUBJECT B: At some point we'll get tired of that joke.

SUBJECT A: Jose used it at science camp, he says.

SUBJECT B: Has he been listening in on our phone calls?

SUBJECT A: No. He heard us make that joke a hundred times.

SUBJECT B: Good, because that would be alarming.

SUBJECT A: Oh my God, could you imagine?

SUBJECT B: I would be mortified.

SUBJECT A: There's no chance this is being listened to, is there?

SUBJECT B: I don't think they have the manpower to listen in on all the calls from the base to America that are going on right now.

SUBJECT A: Course, I did use the word "drone."

SUBJECT B: And you just did it, again.

SUBJECT A: Drone, drone, drone.

SUBJECT B: Asking for trouble, missy.

SUBJECT A: Are you . . . flirting with me?

SUBJECT B: Maybe. So what did you do while Jose was away at science camp?

SUBJECT A: Well . . . if you must know, I had a date.

SUBJECT B: With the bookstore guy?

SUBJECT A: Leonard. Yes.

SUBJECT B: What did you do?

SUBJECT A: Went for dinner. At that Greek place on Third Avenue.

SUBJECT B: Was it good?

SUBJECT A: It was. I had swordfish. It was amazing, actually.

SUBJECT B: Did you drink retsina?

SUBJECT A: It did not seem necessary to remind myself how foul that stuff is.

SUBJECT B: And what else?

SUBJECT A: What else, as in, what else did I eat?

SUBJECT B: Or whatever.

SUBJECT A: [laughing] I had fun, he was interesting to talk to. I have my reading list now for the next three years. Then he drove me home.

SUBJECT B: And that was it?

SUBJECT A: Well, he came in for a glass of wine. Then he went home after about a half-hour. We were both tired. We had worked that day.

SUBJECT B: Ah.

SUBJECT A: If you must know, there was some kissing.

SUBJECT B: Is he a good kisser?

SUBJECT A: Pretty good. Not as good as you. You're also more interesting to talk to by a wide margin.

SUBJECT B: Why?

SUBJECT A: Well, you do go out into the world and do things. He, well— he reads about things.

SUBJECT B: I meant about the kissing.

SUBJECT A: [laughing] Oh, of course. Well, he's altogether too tentative, for one thing.

SUBJECT B: I'm taking notes. "Don't be tentative."

SUBJECT A: Take this note: "Be *here*."

SUBJECT B: [laughing] Hey, I gotta go.

SUBJECT A: Okay. Hey, I love you.

SUBJECT B: I love you, too, sweetie.

[SUBJECT B HANGS UP.]

SUBJECT A: Come home soon, okay?

CHAPTER SIX

Green Beans Café

Deirdre O'Malley

A paper letter from Peter, forwarded from Baghdad to the press officer here in Kandahar. It was a surprise it got to me and it was a surprise to hear from him.

It's been six years since the start of all this. I came home that day and told Peter that I had been approved to go to Afghanistan. He hardly looked up from the magazine he was reading. He told me I was too excited about it, for the wrong reasons. That pissed me off and I hit back. He'd pretended he was just worried about my safety, but that was not what he had meant and I called him on it. He ended up walking out of our apartment and by the time he got back that night I was packed and gone.

I slept at the airport and flew to Washington the next morning. Shitty way to end things, though—he was a sweet man. From his letter, it sounds like he still is. He said he saw one of the last pieces I filed from Baghdad before coming back here and said he wanted to write to me to congratulate me. It isn't the whole truth. He doesn't say it in so many words, I know he wishes he wasn't still stuck covering the metro beat for the *Plain Dealer*. Which anyone can understand. But it wasn't me that rejected his application for a pool position.

Imagine being a journalist these last five years and not being able to get over here. How could you go to work every morning, knowing you'd be writing about zoning bylaw debates when the colleague who had been in the cubicle beside yours was now a war correspondent?

I dated a succession of soft men in college and after. I thought I loved some of them. I thought I loved Peter. When we were both working for the *Plain Dealer* he was helping edit the comment page. I'd envied him the wider importance of his stories. Then the press pools were being formed and I had a shot and I took it. I don't miss that old life. I don't even miss him. That sounds severe, but the world was always harsher than we were pretending. You face it, you get into the middle of it and you understand what you are capable of. It's pretty exhilarating. Which is why the young guys all around me who put down their bongs and put on uniforms have done so well. Hard things reveal your strength. Peter's strength is buried under all that equivocation and reasonableness. I wish he had gotten a spot, too. It would have been interesting to see him lose twenty pounds, get some lines on his sweet face.

The sirens sound, but before anyone can move I hear the boom. Where was that? I look around the coffee shop and people have stood up—in Baghdad, that rocket wouldn't have been noticed. You want to know the difference between this place and that? There it is: here there are 103-mm rockets, one at a time, whereas there it's mortars, twenty at a time and with way more precision. Two hundred people a day killed, twenty of them our guys. The numbers here are a hundredth of that. Baghdad was hell. This is Minneapolis.

Though I heard about another green-on-blue shooting today, an Afghan national taking out Americans in Bagram. That's a difference between Afghanistan and Iraq that makes you worry about Afghanistan. This is the third this month. Afghan soldier, police officer, interpreter, loses it and picks up a rifle and runs amok. Shoots up a mess tent or something. Some of them look planned and maybe are the work of Taliban plants. The others just look like someone going postal. Someone's pride is offended. Someone's PTSD gets clicked to "high." The central story of Afghanistan, supposedly, is that the Afghan people

67

want us here. It's hard to know how true that is, but every time one of the best employed and privileged Afghans decides to commit suicide-by-massacre, it looks a little more false. I need to do a story on that. Maybe not right away—I'd rather not alienate the Public Relations officers just yet. But in a couple of months.

So what do I write back to Peter? That I miss him and still think fondly of him and hope that we can always be friends? Or that he needs to quit his job right now, ditch his wine collection and get scared for a change? Poor guy. He could be me. Was me, until all this horror. And the most horrible part of all is that I wouldn't change a thing. How do I say that to a smart and gentle man who thinks the life change he needs is to start watching his carbs?

I slept beside him for two years. Slept, day and night. At my desk, at the gym, and underneath him. Then woke up.

It's the evil truth about wars: they're not all bad for everyone.

Fazil Palwasha

I think that most of the non-Americans don't know what exactly they are doing here. This place is American, the money is American. And it is American contractors who serve the food in the dining halls and fix the electricity and give haircuts and all that. Screaming Eagle Way intersects with Freedom Boulevard and everyone drives on the right.

It's maybe why the non-Americans come to the coffee shop so much. Which is not to say that there are not many very large and loud Americans here all the time, nor is it to say there is any doubt about who runs this place. But on the base, this is the place where it is not all the time always America.

We can live in Dar al-Islam even though Dar al-harb is everywhere around us. A house of peace can stand even within a larger house of war. We can keep the faith. Say our prayers. Fast when we must. Be as pure as we can be.

Major Dan Horner

I'm surprised no one has done a story about the baristas here. I might suggest it. I read all the stories written back home about how our mission here is hopeless, that this culture is too alien to western sensibilities to ever really be understood and will always remain hostile to our values and aid. I know that those pieces could not have been written here at Green Beans by people drinking macchiatos prepared by men who two years ago had never met a westerner. Jobs are the best anti-extremist measure ever invented. Better than a Hellfire. And cheaper. Plus you get a steaming cup of espresso rather than a smoking hole. That would be a good line. I should suggest it. Like, in a roundabout way.

I could put them on to this man. I don't know his name but he has a reliable efficiency about him that I admire. And his English is excellent. I've seen him reprimanding his co-workers at times for dogging it. In contrast, his boss, that Issay fellow, seems only reluctantly in charge. That's often the way things go, though. Battalion and ship XOs are reliably ferocious, because they want a command. Their bosses get to be beloved because someone else is being ferocious. Oh, the more I think about it, the more I like the idea. Could even be a *New Yorker* piece, or a *NYT Magazine* profile. Get all psychological. Is C.J. Chivers on the base these days? I should get hold of him, and suggest it.

Rami Issay

I am not a stupid man. I understand what Fazil and Amr think of me. I can discern contempt. There is the crew boss, who everyone admires, and there is the man the crew boss reports to. It is this way with construction workers, too. Everyone makes fun of the architect. Crazy ideas about what will look good and what won't and what is feasible to build. But imagine a city built with no architects. All would be functional tedium.

69

Our world is saved from tedium by whimsy, but the whimsical are usually punished. Look around this place: what do you see? Gunships lifting up in great cylinders of dust, conscripted Jordanian boys so lonely they cannot bear it, hardly a shred of greenery anywhere, and rockets coming in like shooting stars. Dying boys being pulled off the flight line and taken to the hospital, not a glass of beer to be found anywhere, and hardly any women, no music, no babies. This, we are constantly told, is an operational base. By operational, they mean industrial efficiencies. No pleasure, no ornament, and no resting, except to prepare for more fighting. You will see corporations behave like this when they are under the direction of especially severe accountants. But accountants are motivated by net profit/loss figures and austerity is a means, not an end.

These people here are uninterested in genuine economies—they fly their *fuel* out to the FOBs by helicopter at the cost of three hundred dollars a litre—I read it in the *New York Times* on the personal computer. Austerity for them is merely a posture they adopt to shore up their own anxieties about their level of ferociousness. The Pashtun, genuinely ferocious, are austere, and they are the ones who are winning this war.

The Americans decided to take down, therefore, the fast food trailers on the boardwalk, and permit no one any beer. If they become more Pashtun, they hope, they will be more likely to win. In Pakistan, we understand the Pashtun better than that. They are barbarians, and will fight barbarically to keep ferenghee—anyone but them—out of their valleys. They fear the larger world, which is what makes them fight so hard for their highlands, but that is also why they have no interest in the lowlands. To them, the lowland people are unholy and strange. The Pashtun have no envy. That's the key to understanding them—it's what limits them and what makes them unconquerable. The rest of us are slaves to our needs. Take me. Without restless ambition I would never be here. Would never have built and lost my business, would not be trying to start over by running this café. Would have remained on my father's farm and hurried to plant my winter wheat every autumn, before the rains came. And then sat back and watched as it and my children grew. It would have been a very different life, but not a worse one, maybe. Fifty years old and managing a coffee shop for the Americans in Kandahar for two hundred US dollars a week. It would not have been a worse life than this one.

Look at that sky. It's going to rain any second. If it is heavy the helicopters will not fly and then the flight crews will come to the café to wait out the weather window. We will need more pastries.

FIVE THINGS TO UNDERSTAND ABOUT WARTIME EMBEDS
Deirdre O'Malley
(BuzzFeed Listicle, July 3, 2007)

1. Journalists do not stop being journalists just because we travel and eat with soldiers. The press travels with President Bush, too, and eats the Air Force One food, such as it is. Clearly, that does not stop them from criticizing him.

2. The alternative to having journalists report these wars as embeds would be minimal reporting at all. No foreigner can travel long in Southern or Eastern Afghanistan now, or in Anbar, without being kidnapped or murdered. This would leave all the reporting in the hands of uniformed military-affiliated war correspondents, as it was in previous conflicts.

3. Understanding the war from the perspective of our soldiers does not distort journalists' depiction of it, it makes available the most important point of view. These are our soldiers, after all, and they die and suffer in our name.

4. The soldiers are quite direct about their attitudes to embeds. They wish we weren't with them. They don't see us as their advocates. They see us as snitches and snoops. Oddly, it's only the critics, completely removed from the battlefield, who view us as cheerleaders for the war and for the military.

5. Bodies dominate any field of view that contains them. Reporting a battle after the fact inevitably lends a certain sombre, grief-stricken tone. There is another truth available to the embed at the instant of combat: the fear and the excitement and the courage and camaraderie of the moment, which is at least as important to understand. Battlefields are not crime scenes. Covering them as if they were is misleading. And a betrayal of the young people who just fought on them. Battlefields are sites of contest, more like football fields than held-up banks: places where victory and heroism are acted out—and defeat and injury suffered—all as a function of the luck and effort and courage at work on them.

CHAPTER SEVEN

W hen Stewart Robinson got to the airfield it turned out that his flight was delayed—bad weather and unspecified operational issues. He waited around for two hours and then noticed that everyone else who was to have left on the same flight had gone. He was the only one still there, sitting on his suitcase, reading a copy of the *Economist*. He approached an air traffic officer and was told that it was almost certain that he wouldn't get out that day. He was told to come back the next morning by six.

Robinson was two parts frustrated to one part relieved. He took the opportunity to wander around KAF unescorted. He recognized almost nothing from his first visit here. There was construction underway everywhere. The population on base had doubled every eight months for the last four years, someone told him.

Robinson did not remember a cappuccino bar on the Kandahar Airfield, that was for sure. He ducked as he entered the Green Beans and smiled as he took in the sight of doctors and nurses and pilots drinking their coffees and eating biscotti. He ordered an espresso and made his way to the one free table he could see. He sat down and as he lifted his cup to his lips he noticed Deirdre at the table to next to his, staring into her laptop screen. He had to double check that it was her. She looked different.

Not older, exactly. More contained, perhaps. Every bit as attractive but more formidable. He watched her drink her own coffee and type away. It looked like she was writing one of those BuzzFeed listicles. Slumming, he supposed. Oh, that would be fun to tease her about.

Or perhaps she was no longer teasable. The set of her mouth was different than he recalled, more serious, probably angrier. In a moment she would notice him staring. She had always been stared at a lot and she had her techniques for dealing with it. He wondered which she would use on him.

"Hello, Stewart," she said, without making eye contact. Then, looking at him over her coffee cup, and clearly with intent to injure, "I had heard you were on base."

"Nice to see you, Deirdre."

"Are you here peddling your book?"

"I finished touring it last year, but someone here in public affairs asked me here to talk about the Pashtun to them."

"One more thing you are an expert in, now."

"Well, no. But I gave a talk about what I understand of them."

"I'm sure they loved you."

"I'm sure they thought I was an idiot."

"Little did they know . . ."

". . . how right they were."

"Are you still in Kabul?"

"Most of the time. I travel a lot. I was supposed to fly there today."

"The plane isn't coming. Thunderstorm."

"I heard."

"What are your plans?"

He looked around and opened his arms. "My day is wide open." The second he said it, he knew he sounded overeager.

"I saw your piece about Michael Hastings," she said.

"I saw yours."

"Oh?" They said in unison. They paused, and smiled at each other.

"I didn't like it," they continued together.

They both grinned.

74

"How come?" he asked.

"I thought what he did was cheap. Hang out with that general and his aides for weeks straight and then report back on every indiscreet thing he overheard them say. If I or any of the other embeds did that, there would be no embedding programs. And there you were, saying he was re-establishing journalistic norms."

"And there you were, saying he had no right to criticize the general that way, that he had never served his country the way the general had. Who do you think journalists are responsible to? Who is your constituency?"

The café was quiet now. He had raised his voice. He looked at his coffee. That was not what he had intended.

She nodded. "I'm afraid I'm on deadline. I have to get back to work."

"Of course."

And then she stood up and closed her laptop and collected her things. She walked out of the café. He watched her leave. She didn't look back. He was surprised. He had been half playing. She used to be able to tell.

❦

After filing her story, Deirdre dropped her gear on her bed and showered. Then she walked to the press tent. There was no one there she wanted to talk to. She wasn't sure what she was hoping for. She lingered beside the coffee pot, and looked at an article in the *New York Times* about the drone.

> WASHINGTON—On May 6, a Central Intelligence Agency drone fired a volley of missiles at a pickup truck carrying nine militants and bomb materials through a desolate stretch of Pakistan near the Afghan border. It killed all the militants—a clean strike with no civilian casualties, extending what is now a yearlong perfect record of avoiding collateral deaths.

That sounded like Peter Sullivan, at the agency. He'd become their favourite unnamed source lately.

She wandered over to the bulletin board, where another piece, this one from the *Washington Post*, was tacked up. It discussed the leadership at the CIA and their resolve to prosecute the drone strikes ethically:

Brennan's bedrock belief in a "just war," they said, is tempered by his deep knowledge of the Middle East, Islam and the CIA, and the critical thinking forged during a classic Jesuit education.

Some White House aides describe him as a nearly priest-like presence in their midst, with a moral depth leavened by a dry Irish wit.

One CIA colleague, former general counsel John Rizzo, recalled his rectitude surfacing in unexpected ways. Brennan once questioned Rizzo's use of the "BCC" function in the agency's e-mail system to send a blind copy of a message to a third party without the primary recipient's knowledge.

Right, she thought. And then Deirdre checked her mailbox, where she found a letter. She almost never got mail there. She opened it.

Dear Deirdre:
I've asked Major Horner to get this to you. Isn't he quite a specimen of military press liaison? I think he will go far. You should have seen him steering me around the room after the talk I gave to the senior combat arms officers this afternoon. I was a prized piece of flesh, let me tell you. (One hopes he is not reading this. If you are, Major, shame on you.)

I had hoped I would run into you but I am told you are out on a patrol with some Canadians. I hope they know what they're in for. I am back to Kabul in the morning, and it appears that I am unlikely to see you. In the event that our missing one another was entirely accidental and you'd like to have a drink, drop me a line. I'll tell you my Iraq stories if you tell me yours.

Either way, it's very nice to have you back in Afghanistan. You were always my favourite memory of Kandahar.
Stewart

*T*he Special Forces sergeant from Boise, soon to be a captain in military intelligence, was stateside, with more days of leave available to him than he knew what to do with. He drove his truck into the badlands and camped in the dust. He had had an idea about doing some antelope hunting, but as it turned out, he'd had no appetite for shooting. He watched the pronghorns through his binoculars as they drank at sloughs, eyeing the horizon and trying to decide if they smelled danger or not. He was struck once again by their skittish intensity. Three weeks in hunting season, their heads jerked in all directions and they sniffed the air compulsively. They appeared incapable of ease. This, he thought, is what hypervigilance looks like.

He slept in motels when it rained and on a mat unrolled in his truck box when it was clear. He drove through western Washington, Idaho and Montana, circling through the arid high country with its failing farms. He ate in diners when it was convenient, and other times he cooked for himself on the tailgate of his truck. He did not go into bars. He could count on being left alone over a meal, but not over a drink, and he had no interest in answering anyone's questions. Or in being thanked for his service. Eventually he found himself parked in the driveway of his stepfather's stuccoed house. He had not seen the old man since he was twenty. Ten years now. His mother had left him and then she'd died. He had no idea where his biological father was. So this old man was it, his only tenuous remnant of family.

The screen door opened and the old man looked out. The sergeant got out of his truck.

"Jesus Christ, look at you."

"Hi, Dick."

"Could you fit another tattoo on your arms?"

"It's been a long time."

"It has. Care for a beer?"

"Yes."

"Inside or out here?"

"I'd as soon sit inside."

"It's about what you might expect. C'mon. I'll clear some space at the kitchen table."

They talked about the Mariners and about his mother. They agreed that with that bullpen there would be no excuse for not doing well and that she was a good woman. The thing about good pitching is that it normally makes for better hitting and base running, too. People feel supported. It took a long time for the war to come up. The old man's own forearms were tattooed, if less exuberantly than his onetime stepson's. On his right arm were the letters "U.S.M.C."

"So how come you're not in the city, partying?"

"I seem to have lost my taste for that."

"Growing up?"

"Too much time in the field, I think. I don't enjoy company the way I used to."

"Ah. So what's left that you enjoy?"

"Being in the field."

"You know the war is going to end."

"It's a problem."

"One you'll want to fix. You have lots of years in front of you. You don't want to spend them alone."

"I've been commissioned. Into intelligence. That has dialled back the field time."

"So you're a lifer, then."

The sergeant nodded. "Probably was a few years ago."

"Big difference—between visiting that place and living there."

"Yes."

"When do you go back?"

"Next week."

"You looking forward to it?"

"Yes."

The old man poured him another bottle of Coors.

The younger man nodded. He wasn't going to argue. On the old man's arm, under "U.S.M.C," was "Da Nang."

CHAPTER EIGHT

Within days of its purchase, already the Green Beans chess set had been used a number of times. Rami Issay's capacity for self-congratulation was such that he could perceive vindication in the colour of his own waste water. And so he immediately bought more chess sets in the market, and soon there was one available for each of the little tables in the café. With successive purchases, he had grown less particular, buying wooden sets and then ones made of injection moulded plastic.

He and Rashid sat down in the lull after lunch. There were only three games going now. The younger man set up the pieces while his employer congratulated himself: "We will be selling more coffee, too. Customers draw other customers. The chess players occupy their tables for half an hour or more, but many people come in to watch some moves and have a latte."

Rashid pushed his king's pawn forward two. "The staff enjoys the game, too." He nodded at Amr and little Mohammed Hashto, who were playing behind the counter.

Rami Issay put his own king's pawn up. "I'm more interested in the response of the military and para-military personnel of the

International Assistance Force. Many are, for the moment, wary of being seen as too thoughtful."

"Why would that be?" Rashid said, his king's pawn taking Rami Issay's queen's pawn.

"Everywhere in the world, these qualities are cast in opposition to one another," Issay said. "Action versus reflection and understanding. A man may possess one set of these qualities but not the other. Men of action disdain things as impotent-looking as chess playing and book reading. And the book-readers, it must be admitted, scarcely participate in things like this Global War on Terror. Why do you think this is?" Queen's knight advancing.

"Well . . ." Rashid said, studying the board. Advancing his own knight.

"Because they've reflected on the matter, and see the folly of it? Not so, my young friend. Look online: read on the personal computer the organs of London and New York—the thinkers advocate for this business," he waved his arm lazily overhead, "as blood-thirstily as any warrior. Precisely because they don't participate."

He switched to Pashto and whispered, "It's because the scholars— there, and here—do not fight, would not permit a situation where anyone might yell at them, or hurt them, that they don't know the nature of war. They advocate it, imagining it to be a tool, something that can be controlled: smart weapons and surgical strikes. Limited inputs producing predictable outputs. No one faces up to the madness at the essence of war."

At the sound of the Pashto, the contractors had looked up. They had thought this to be their place.

Queen's bishop to the third rank.

King's knight up.

In Pashto, whispering back, Rashid said, "Boss, you really have to think about what you say out loud here. Who knows who's listening?" Advancing a knight.

Still in Pashto: "I want to say, who cares?"

"But that would be crazy," said Rashid, in English.

"You are not without a point, my young friend."

❈

He wasn't always able to look on the bright side. When his visa difficulties emerged in the UK, Rami Issay had had to leave for Pakistan within a few days. Saying goodbye to his wife and daughters was agony then and agony every time he thought about it. His daughters were three, five, six and nine years old at the time. His wife, Sula, was angry with him. She did not understand any better than he what had happened to prompt the revocation of his UK permanent resident card, but she was correct in her view that he could have gotten his citizenship long ago. She suspected strongly that he knew more than he was letting on. He didn't. There had been some minor scrapes with the police in Pakistan that he had not told her about when they'd met. But he had nothing to do with Islamic radicals, as everyone had concluded when he was made to leave the country in the first crazy days after the towers came down.

In the subsequent years he had sent her money and when the computer sales company he started up was doing well, he sent her a lot. Then it failed and the money stopped. Now she was living with her uncle in Leeds. The girls had all been born in the UK and were citizens. He'd last got a letter from his youngest daughter a year earlier. Since he had come to Kandahar he had not heard from any of them, though he'd been able to send money again. He should write to them himself. He should write to Sula.

Rasia, the oldest, would be fifteen now. She had a Facebook page. She had friended him. He looked at it nearly every day. It appears she was a fan of the Arctic Monkeys. He had listened to their music in order to understand something of what her tastes had become. The exercise was not very productive. She was so beautiful, as beautiful as Sula had been. In pictures of the two of them that Rasia had posted, Sula looked tired and old. Her life there must be hard. He knew her uncle was a controlling man who drank. She did not like him and it must have been very painful for her to ask him for help.

There were pictures of Rasia's sisters in her photo album, too. He scarcely recognized them. It was painful to contemplate that. Goddamned internet. He made an effort to turn his attention back to his surroundings.

❀

Just Amachai walked in then, followed a minute later by Deirdre O'Malley. The two women did not acknowledge one another and found tables at opposite corners of the café. Mohammed hopped off his stool while Amr continued to study the chess board between them. Mohammed approached the American journalist first because he knew her less well.

Deirdre had been out all day on a helicopter with the regional commander, a Canadian brigadier, visiting FOBs. She was exhausted and dirty. She asked for an iced latte and Mohammed nodded.

He approached Just Amachai less cautiously. She reached to tousle his hair and he grinned. "How are you today, Madam?" he asked. Amr was already making the latte he had heard Deirdre O'Malley order.

"My arms and fingers and back are tired."

"Was the day very busy, madam?"

"It was. A battalion of French engineers and one of English infantry came in from their FOBs today." She leaned forward. "Such tired men. So many muscle knots."

Mohammed blushed deeply, which had been Just Amachai's intention. "Perhaps some tea would help you feel better, madam."

"Yes, please."

He knew how she liked it. He couldn't wait to show her.

❀

Deirdre eavesdropped on the boy's interaction with the masseuse with the vague idea that she might write about the massage parlour. It was surprising that such a thing existed here at all. It predated the media's

83

time in Kandahar; no one seemed to know exactly how it had come here or when. The perverse purpose of the parlour: reassuring everyone that the suspension of their sexuality was possible. If they could not do that for a few months, how could they possibly win the Global War on Terror?

Formally, the suspension of sexuality was a cardinal principle of the camp: no fraternization of any sort, between any of the five hundred women and eleven thousand men on the base, even among those who happened to be married to one another. The barracks were segregated and visiting was forbidden. It was like summer camp. Campers were sent home for transgressing the rules all the time. They were often greeted with divorce petitions, given that the army made sure the circumstances of their return were known. And laid charges when adultery could be proven.

Everyone who came for a massage understood that physical release would not be tolerated, even if it was inadvertent. The gender and attractiveness of the attendants were apparently simply a happy, or perhaps cruel, accident. Deirdre had had a massage there, when she was very sore from riding in a Stryker, and she had found her masseuse skilled. She had been Czech, she thought, and so beautiful that Deirdre wondered how the men could find the interaction more therapeutic than agonizing.

Her BlackBerry buzzed and she saw an all caps message from her boss in New York: CALL ME. She did.

"Kenwood, what's up? Why are you even awake?"

"ABC and NBC and the *Guardian* and *Le Monde* have all received huge leaks about the fighting there. Do you know anything about this?"

"No. What are the leaks about, exactly?"

"From what we hear, footage of helicopters gunning down civilians, footage of drone collaterals, incredible stuff. No one's published anything yet, but the talk is deafening. Have you pissed someone off? Why are we excluded?"

"I've pissed a million people off, Kenwood. But it doesn't sound like this could be a sanctioned leak. No one I deal with would have done this."

"But someone still did it. Find out who."

"There will be a lot of people trying to do just that, I think. Most of them with sidearms."

And then one of their phones cut out. She'd blame it on his later, if she had to.

✿

Rami Issay said, "I have a good idea."

Rashid rolled his eyes, but only after he put his hand over them. "What's that?"

"I think we should have a chess tournament. Excellent move. An imaginatively used knight is truly one of the game's great pleasures."

"Of course you do."

"What?"

"Nothing."

"Sometimes you mystify me, my young friend."

"That is a well-supported bishop, isn't it?"

"What would we have as a prize?"

"For what?"

"The chess tournament."

"Boss, this is Kandahar."

"All the more reason to introduce a bit of civilization."

"Boss, this place has had civilization scrubbed from it. Look around you. No one will thank you for your efforts."

Rami Issay did not reply to that. "That was a truly good move."

"Thank you."

✿

Deirdre watched the videos on the InformationIsFree site as her thoughts raced about the leaker. Who would do something like that? Who has even the vaguest sympathy for al-Qaeda and the Taliban? No one. And no non-American would be given access to those sorts of files. Some pissed-off American, then. A missed promotion, a felt-to-be unjust reprimand of some sort. The signals intelligence people would be all over the original files, looking for signs of where they came from. God help whoever sent these out. She felt a kind of moral injury herself; she could not fathom why someone might have released these files. She had to get some of the other journalists to talk to her about this. She hated the press tent. Wankers. Whiners. Leches. Who among them would talk to her straight about what they knew? No one. Who would even pretend to? A couple, anyway.

Just then the terp she had patrolled with walked into the café. She stared at him for a moment before she caught herself and then she nodded. She wondered what he was doing in the Green Beans. Terps never came in here. The only locals in here normally were the baristas—though, hundreds of kilometres and a country away from their own homes, the baristas would be surprised to learn they were considered locals. Everyone in the café looked up at the terp, especially the baristas. He caught Deirdre's eye.

She waved the terp over. He came to her gratefully. "Hello, ma'am," he said, as he sat. Mohammed walked over and he ordered a tea.

"Deirdre."

"Pardon me?"

"My name is Deirdre."

"My name is John Wayne."

"I remember. Is it really?"

"Well, no, of course not. We use pseudonyms for the sake of our families."

"Why John Wayne? Why not an Afghan name?"

"It feels less deceitful."

"Where do you come from?"

"I would prefer not to say, ma'am."

"You speak Pashto well enough that you must be from the south."

"I thank you for the compliment." He began to rise.

"No, please stay. I won't pry anymore."

He sat again.

"Do you enjoy the work?" Deirdre asked.

"Yes. I am learning one hell of a lot."

"What have you learned?"

"American vernacular. I learned English from textbooks the British left behind half a century ago. The Americans have always been mysterious to me. When I watched their movies, I always thought that they were speaking another language entirely. And, not understanding their language, I have not understood them."

"Do you, now?"

"A little more than I did. I understand that they are as mystified by this place and the people who live here as we are by them."

"Maybe don't tell your employers that."

"I have been indiscreet. I apologize."

"Not at all. I think you are right. We do not understand this place well. But perhaps you are part of the effort to teach us."

"This is the hope. People who understand one another have less reason to fight."

"Do you think if the Taliban were understood better it would be less necessary to fight them?"

"The Taliban are, as you suggest, extremists. They did many evil things when they were in power, and it is not wrong to see them like that. But if Americans knew Afghanistan better it would seem less useful to make war with the Taliban."

"That might be another thing you should not say to the soldiers."

He smiled. "The men I work with did not make the decisions that brought them here." He noticed then how quiet the room had become. He had hoped it would be comfortable to come here and drink a cup of chai or play some chess. He leaned forward. "I should go, ma'am. It was a pleasure talking with you." And he stood and walked quickly out of the café.

The tension in the room dissipated. Everyone returned to their own chessboard or magazine or conversation.

Deirdre's BlackBerry buzzed. CALL NY.

❦

Just Amachai watched Deirdre pack up her notes and laptop and stride out of the coffee shop. Just Amachai was not as tired as she had pretended to be with the boy. That had been to entertain him. But it had been a busy day. Busy days were fine by her. Since she had arrived, six months earlier, she had saved fifteen thousand dollars, mostly in tips. She wasn't a prostitute, and never had to explain that here. Just not having to have those conversations was worth putting up with the dust and the dreadful food and the absence of a temple to pray in.

That writer-lady annoyed her. She never acknowledged other women in the room, and hardly acknowledged non-westerners, except when they came to take her order. She was here to write about the war in Afghanistan but, from reading her online, it seemed that the journalist considered it to be only a story about westerners. Except for how grateful, or not, the Afghans were for the labours of westerners on their behalf.

Mohammed came over to ask if he could bring her another tea. She smiled and said, "No, thank you." She could see his disappointment—he had wanted a reason to linger. "Tell me about your day, Mohammed," she said. He glanced over his shoulder. Rami Issay was staring at the chess board, tapping his fingers on the edge of the table.

"It was a little busy, ma'am," he said, perching on the chair opposite her.

"Your English is coming along, Mohammed."

"Thank you, ma'am. The new boy, Rashid, helps me."

"Where is he from?"

"Pardon?"

"Where did he live, before living here?"

"Islamabad, ma'am. But he has travelled many places in the world. He was a student of engineering."

"Stop calling me ma'am, please."

Grinning. "Okay."

"Where did he study engineering?"

"In the United Kingdom, I think. Near Massachusetts."

"Not in Pakistan?"

"Maybe in Kabul."

"Does he know Pashto?"

"Oh yes, he speaks it well."

"He is Pashtun?"

"I don't know who his family are but he knows many things. The entire periodic table of the elements, for instance."

"Well, he did study engineering."

"Yes, he did, m—"

As he caught himself, Just Amachai felt a surge of maternal affection so strong she had to restrain herself from hugging him.

"Perhaps you could ask him to teach you about the periodic table of the elements. A knowledge of science is a useful thing."

"In Taiwan, does everyone go to school until they are married?"

"Not Taiwan," she said gently. "Thailand. No, not always. The rich do, though. Which is part of how they stay rich."

"What is the religion in Thailand?"

"Buddhism, mostly. There are Muslims in the south."

"Are they persecuted?"

"They would say they are."

"Is Buddhism an old religion?"

"One of the oldest."

"Why does it mistreat Muslims?"

"It isn't the religion that mistreats them, my dear. It's the army."

"Which is not Muslim."

"Yes."

"Muslims are mistreated wherever they are not the majority," the boy said.

"Is that true?"

"Yes. My teacher told me that."

"Who is your teacher?"

"I must not say."

"Oh, so mysterious. Well, my dear, you may have your secrets. I certainly have mine."

"If you really want, I would tell you."

"You should not betray a confidence, Mohammed."

"Okay."

"Where does your family live?"

"I have no family now, ma'am. But my father lived in a village in North Waziristan. It is where he is buried."

"Oh, I am very sorry."

"It is okay. I am reconciled to it. My mother had to remarry and her new husband was not interested in me living with them. He already had many children."

"Do you have contact with your mother at all?"

"I have not spoken to her since she told me I must leave."

"Do you understand the position she was in?"

"Of course. It was her wish."

"That you not contact her again?"

"No. What came before." And with that his voice broke and he stood and wiped her table with his cloth repeatedly until he could talk again. "I must return to work now, ma'am."

"Mohammed, you are a beautiful boy, and I know your mother loves you."

He nodded.

"Go back to work before you get into trouble."

Mohammed scurried back to the counter, where Amr had been watching his exchange with the masseuse. Business was very quiet that afternoon. Fazil had been doing books in the back. He had poked his head into the kitchen looked out at the café, surveying the room. He looked at Mohammed cleaning the coffee machine and then he went back to his books. Once he was gone, Amr pointed to the chess sets and raised his eyebrows at Mohammed. Mohammed looked toward the back, where Fazil had just retreated, and nodded.

❀

A soldier walked through the door and took off his hat. For a moment no one realized who he was. And then the contractors did and they abandoned their chess game and stood. Rami Issay glanced over to see who had checkmated who. Seeing that no resolution had been achieved, he looked up at the men and then followed their eyes to the door. Another younger officer had come in behind the soldier, following him closely. The contractors slid past them and out the door.

The soldier was Lieutenant General Jeremy Jackson, United States Army, the ISAF commander in Afghanistan. His companion was his chief of staff, Colonel Fred Shaw from Fayetteville. "Would you like a game?" the younger man asked the older.

"I would."

Shaw collected one of the onyx and alabaster sets from the shelf beside the till. He carried it back to a table and began setting it up. Fazil approached and Jackson ordered two cappuccinos. Fazil nodded and retreated. Shaw held out his closed fists to Jackson. Jackson picked the left. Shaw opened his hand. White. He nodded.

Shaw replaced the two pawns and considered his opening. His objective here was complex. He could not, would not, try any less than his hardest against the general. But there were other considerations. In baseball, Jackson was fascinated by knuckleballers. Shaw decided the Reti flank opening would be better, here. King's knight to f3. This was the hypermodern style, where the goal is to control, rather than occupy, the centre of the board. It would strike the general as creative. Shaw moved his king's knight.

Lately General Jackson was spending more time in Kandahar than in Kabul. The war was going poorly here. He had been in meetings all day with the regional district commanders, reviewing the progress of the war in the south. The Brits and the Canadians were taking casualties and holding the most contested territory, as they pointed out, endlessly; the Dutch, the least of either. All were doing about as well as far as quantifiable metrics went: girls in school, electricity availability. Lots was being done, but not much was being achieved. Iraq had been like that when Jackson took command of his division there, too. If it was a simple problem to solve it would have been solved already.

Shaw had heard about the chess sets at the coffee shop and thought that after the long morning of bad news meetings, Jackson would like to play. As he thought about his own answering move, Jackson wondered how Tom Lattice, the Special Forces—outside Jackson's control—commander felt about it. No doubt it would strike him as a distraction. With the recently escalating tempo of operations, Lattice was in KAF frequently these days, too. A lot of the time he was the ranking general on the base. To Lattice, pretty much everything was a distraction—even eating. Right now, he was probably resentfully chewing on some uncooked rice in the Special Forces compound, a hundred metres from the coffee shop, with its own walls and wire and gate and sentries and prison even within the base: the whole SF mind-set rendered physical.

"I'm surprised this exists, a hundred metres from the SF compound," Jackson said to Shaw.

"A bit frivolous for the likes of them, isn't it?"

Shaw wondered why Jackson had never transferred to SF. In the months after 9/11 it had been clear that it would be the growth industry in the military. Jackson would have been a lieutenant colonel then. A little senior to make the move, maybe. Shaw had been a captain, and had known Jackson only by reputation. He was famous for taking his battalion's second lieutenants—twenty-four-year-olds—running every Friday afternoon. And not stopping until they asked if they could. When they learned later, over beer and Tylenol in the officers' mess, about his Princeton PhD and fluency in Arabic, it wasn't from him. And so they would be impressed by it twice over. From those stories, Shaw hadn't liked him.

Jackson was still staring at the board. It had been a long time since he had had to respond to the Reti opening. The general's estimation of Shaw, already high, rose incrementally. Meticulous, but sometimes unorthodox—a useful pairing of traits. It was how he viewed himself, of course. Queen's pawn, up two. Predictable, but still the strongest response. The interesting part of that opening would unfold in the next half-dozen moves.

"Here's the thing," Jackson said, scanning the room. "Places like this should be less strange. The only way to win this war is over years and years. We should build these bases with the presumption that we'll be here for years and years. Because we will be. The alternative is just losing. We should be building with brick, not plywood and canvas."

Shaw moved his king's bishop to king's knight two. Immediately he was taking control of the centre of the board. Jackson stopped talking for a moment.

He moved his knight to cover the pawn. Reacting, not initiating. He had to brief the Joint Chiefs of Staff the following week and he had been thinking about how he would describe the situation here. He had been brought here to do the same magic he had done in Anbar. It's dangerous to be considered a magician.

"Of course, the country is sick of war. More tired of it than anyone even realizes. No one wants to talk about being here for decades to come," Jackson said. The country he was referring to wasn't Afghanistan.

Shaw brought out his own queen's knight.

"I like this place. I like that no one here even knows who I am," the general said.

"The contractors who left when we walked in knew who you are."

"Oh." That disappointed Jackson. He had flattered himself to think he could be anonymous if he wanted and he had flattered himself that he could tell if he wasn't.

Jackson decided that if Lattice moved to shut the coffee shop down, the way he had the Burger King, he would veto him. He also decided that if a surge was coming, he had to figure out how or even if he could steer it to any purpose. Otherwise, he should get as far away from here as possible. While he waited for Shaw to move, he took out and wrote on his field message pad: Ret'ment Date? Across the room from him, two South Asian men, possibly Bangladeshis, played chess. A father and son, from the similarity of their noses. Likely from Dacca, given the chess playing. Their positions were carefully constructed, but both players betrayed an excess of caution: they had each castled within the first five moves. Reasonably well thought out aggression would shatter either of them. Get a rook onto the father's seventh rank and his position falls apart. The son's queen's rook was vulnerable in half a dozen ways.

Clearly he was still learning the game. What kind of man would make his son work in a café in a war zone when he should be in school?

This place was unexpected, like Shaw's Reti opening. The soldiering part of these wars was all anyone at home talked about. But wars are way more than the shooting. Even within the same side, they're about competing ideas about how to live, about what is disposable and what is essential. A place like this stands for something. Which is why Lattice would be so suspicious of it. And why Jackson thought he should defend it.

❀

In the back, Fazil paused in his bookkeeping to twirl his pencil around his finger and stare at the little jets of light that spurted through gaps in the café walls. It was so hot his hands ran with sweat, but that was not what distracted him. He had seen Mohammed talking to Just Amachai and was surprised by how much his acquaintance with her was starting to bother him. He did not know what the Thai woman wanted with the boy. If Mohammed were another year older, he would have told him not to talk to her, but he was still such a child, and he had to sympathize with Mohammed's desire to talk to someone the same age as his mother. Even if she was a whore.

But everyone was a whore here. Himself included. Taking money from the Franks to make them coffee. Dishing up their little pastries. Doing these accounts.

It was much too hot to do this work. He got up and walked back out to the counter. He watched General Jackson finish his cappuccino and stand. The general nodded at Fazil and Fazil smiled back. The general's servant stood, too. The general walked out the door. His servant followed him.

❀

Ten minutes later Deirdre came back into the café and sat down. She did not want any more coffee. She wanted a moment to think. Fazil began to approach her and then, reading her correctly, turned around and went back to the till.

This was going to be the biggest story of the year and her service had been completely left out of it. You could tell it was important by how quickly the lies had started coming when she'd asked her colleagues about the leak. "Sorry, I haven't been kept in the loop on this. Sounds like a huge story, though. Let me know what you hear?" Not that lying wasn't normal, but normally journalists lie in the other direction: they say they know all about everything. The *Guardian*'s Mick Sheppard had been marginally less deceptive: "If the London and New York reporters can do this story, sharing credit with and involving the people in the field isn't going to be top of mind for them, is it? They resent us like ass itch, Deirdre, you know it." Which was all true, but did not answer her question. The CBS reporter, David Mitchell, was more frank: "Honestly, it sounds like it could mean my job. All anyone back home can talk about is how we haven't been included and how that must be my fault somehow. Who have I pissed off? As if pissing people off isn't supposed to kinda be our jobs—there and over here. What are you hearing, Deirdre?"

"Not much." Already she was scanning the media tent for other people to talk to. In a moment he would be telling her how much he admired her Iraq work, and suggesting they go for coffee sometime.

"So listen . . ."

"Talk to you later, David." She spun away. That had been close.

❀

Master Sergeant Anakopoulus walked into Green Beans having just seen the stories about the helicopter video. They had seared his eyes. So much for this blowing over.

He ordered his usual coffee and cherry pie. He did not end up even picking up his fork, but he sipped his coffee and held that down, at least. It had surprised him how quickly the first of the snipers-with-trophies pictures had been disseminated. He'd have thought there would have been more fact checking, more verification. Nobody had yet mentioned the embed-in-arms pic, the one he had intended to send.

The trick with the laptop and the inactive email account wouldn't keep him safe for long. He had taken that computer and burned it at the dump, but the signal traffic from his location to the dropbox could still give him away. Did the NSA monitor all the dropbox's incoming traffic? They would if they could. If they had thought of it. Certainly he couldn't access the dead man's account ever again. The only way forward was to act perfectly normal and pretend nothing had happened. Probably five thousand wireless accounts on the base. Just don't give them any way to narrow it down. Every one of their suspects would be under surveillance today. He looked around the café. There were no unfamiliar faces. So either he wasn't being watched, or he wasn't being watched by amateurs.

Normal. Act normal. Do what he usually did. Come for his coffee and then go back to work. Look after his guys. Snarl from time to time. Don't drink anymore. Write emails to Susie and don't send them. He stood up and made his way back to his warehouse. His coffee cup was almost full and the pie untouched.

❀

There were no televisions in the café—this had been one of Rami Issay's non-negotiables—and so those who spent much of the day there remained unaware of the collective frenzy over the leaks. A few hours after the journalists had begun to hover anxiously at the press tent to whisper about how little they knew, and a couple of hours before Anakopoulus had come over to not eat a slice of pie and not drink a cup of coffee, the websites of the *Times* and the *Guardian* and *Le Monde* and *Der Spiegel* all put up preliminary stories about the magnitude of the leaks that had been shared with them—though they were all assiduous about not saying anything precise about their content. That discipline had not lasted long. Pretty quickly, the *Guardian* decided that *Der Spiegel* had broken their agreed-upon rules of disclosure, and responded by releasing the helicopter video, with the justification that there were no secrets in it, merely embarrassments. The *Times'* editors wrote to each of the German and British editors reprimanding them and, receiving no immediate response, went retaliatory and released three snipers-with-trophies videos and two more guided bomb-sight clips.

In the café, all anyone noticed was that the journalists were absent that afternoon. If it was something going on with war, the flight line would have been active, but it wasn't. Maybe a party of some sort, then.

❁

In the early evening Rashid slipped into the back of the shop and went to stand in the open doorway facing the airstrip. He could see uniformed men working on the rows of Chinooks and Blackhawks and Apaches; khaki-grey clothed men stood on ladders and looked at rotor gearboxes.

When the pilots came into the coffee shop they described the war as almost entirely an air-to-ground effort. Regular force infantry maintained the perimeter around the airfields at KAF and Bagram and patrolled some of the roads radiating out from them. From the airstrips, and from the carriers in the Indian Ocean, and from Diego Garcia, and from the smaller airstrips across the country, the Air Force flew thousands of missions a day—during large ops, tens of thousands—air strikes, medevacs, reconnaissance, resupply and personnel rotation: everything by air. The SF teams dropped off in the villages by helicopter at night were just another payload—for which there were other, equally lethal, alternatives, which never had to be subsequently extracted under fire.

Rashid sat behind the café on a trash can and listened intently to the evening sky, but all he could hear was conversation from the coffee shop and steam hissing from the espresso maker. He stared south, concentrating on the line where the mountains abraded the sky. He saw nothing. It grew darker. Then he heard them.

The drones sounded like faraway chainsaws; high-pitched and buzzing, fading and resurging as stray air currents brought the sound forward or arrested it. They were audible long before they could be seen. A few seconds later, he spotted them descending abruptly out of the sky, their stick-insect landing gear unfolding and flaps hung low. Rashid thought they were beautiful, otherworldly and chilling. He loved that they could fly for days, and, apparently, tell the time showing on your watch from twenty thousand feet. He presumed that he could be seen even now, as he watched them line up and plunge toward the airstrip. The first of them taxied toward its handlers, its missile rack empty. Imagine sitting and drinking tea with your comrades or your family, no idea there were Americans anywhere near. And then, boom. You could see why, when they got it wrong, the survivors were so upset. Why everyone in the Tribal Areas seethed about them. Which didn't change how beautiful they were.

The last of the drones landed just before the night's blackness came and taxied to its handler before shutting off the engine, and for the first time since Rashid sat down to watch, it was quiet. Then the Apache and Blackhawk helicopters began winding up and the night raid soldiers lined up beside them.

As the sun set, the shadows from the mountains to the southwest raced out across the plain. When they reached the airfield, darkness swept over it as if sprayed from a hose. The sun slid below the mountains and in a moment the stars emerged. Lights all over the base flicked on and the helicopters began taking off. The Apaches left first, and then the long stream of Blackhawks and then finally the twin-rotor Chinooks, with their heavier thumping beat. A few minutes of noise and then they were all gone. Great plumes of dust settled back on the base. The lights of the helicopters winked out one by one in the distance. Tonight, like most nights, they flew south, into the Red Desert, where the trouble came from. Rashid waited until the last of those lights were gone and then he walked back into the café.

Deirdre stood and put her laptop back in its case. She looked right at Rashid as he came in but did not acknowledge his nod. She flung her bag over her shoulder and left. The place was empty except for a pair of chess players. Rashid filled the mop pail.

*J*oint Special Operations Command insisted on autonomy and so General Lattice, the commander of American Special Forces in Afghanistan did not report to General Jackson, the commander of the rest of the American forces in the country. This would have been less of an affront to Jackson if Special Forces had remained the niche asset they were considered to be when that division of responsibility was negotiated. But the war had now become largely a Special Forces undertaking, and General Lattice would hardly return General Jackson's calls, which made Jackson seethe. Lattice had the latitude he needed to do anything he wanted, operationally, and all the political blowback, the outraged calls from Afghan leaders, even from the Afghan and American presidents, would be directed to Jackson. Accountability without control or even much influence: Jackson felt like the electrocuted dog in the box in a 1950s behavioural experiment.

His protests about this state of affairs achieved nothing. He had been in Afghanistan four months now, and the magic he had wrought in Iraq was impossible here. So his star was fractionally less bright than it had been, and Special Forces—as an idea, as a community—just rose higher and higher in the estimation of the Congress and the media. SF were the *only ones who ever seemed to get anything done. And they never took casualties. Or photographs of themselves defiling bodies.*

The first rule of war is: don't fight wars you won't win.

Lately, Jackson had been waking up at three, his thoughts roiling with the complexity of the situation. Tonight on the Kandahar base, with thoughts of the leak on his mind, and somewhere, circling, if he had to be honest, the notion that he might run into Deirdre O'Malley, he rose and put on his running gear rather than lie there the prisoner of his own problems.

Lattice was famous for his own early morning runs. The nonsense the media wrote about him—abstemious of alcohol and caffeine, sleeps three hours a night, sips only cups of hot water—always mentioned his four a.m. runs. As if one million middle managers at home who were try-ing to lose weight didn't jog in the morning, too.

As Jackson slipped out of his room and into the pitch-black night, he was aware that Lattice was likely doing the same thing.

❀

Thomas Lattice asked Jeremy Jackson to be the best man at his wedding after they graduated from West Point because he had never in his life met anyone with the vigour and presence of his classmate; their friendship had expanded Lattice's understanding of the possible. Knowing Jeremy had inspired Thomas for the first time to aim for the very highest results, and aspire to the best and most demanding appointments. Thomas had stopped thinking of himself as well above average and started thing of himself as singular. That's what Jeremy did.

When they'd emerged into the spotlight as superstar generals, it felt to Jackson like his due, and to Lattice, like unending enhanced interroga-tion. But Lattice had come to believe fervently in his vision: for the SF, for the war, for Afghanistan. And when he was persuaded that his celebrity could be used to further those ends, he used it as he would any other useful weapon. He hated that Jeremy was so much more comfortable and skilled with this stuff than he was. He hated that it mattered. Professionally, though, they had never been rivals until Iraq went so bad.

As the two men headed out into the night to run around the airfield, there was almost no sound. The flight line was quiet for the moment. Jackson saw Lattice halfway down the airstrip, a thousand yards away. It looked like it could be him, anyway. Lean almost to the point of skeletal and remorselessly fast. He could not try to catch him, Jackson realized.

Of course Lattice had spotted Jackson, long before he even reached the airfield. He got a thousand yards up in just a few minutes and when Jackson reached the running path around the airstrip, Lattice was far enough away that he did not even have to acknowledge seeing his former best man. Lattice would not look back.

They ran like this for an hour. At the end of the hour, they had covered fifteen kilometres and Jackson was on the verge of vomiting. Lattice had the kept the distance between them constant, and even now remained a distant dot, his posture and his pace nearly exactly what it had been.

Jackson was going to be late for his first meeting. He took an exit and ran, but not as fast as he had been running, back to his barracks to shower. Lattice saw him leave. He waited another five minutes to make sure Jackson wasn't coming back and then he slowed to a walk and then he hunched over, his hands on his knees. He vomited once and then stood straight. He started running again, but more slowly, toward the Special Forces compound.

CHAPTER NINE

It was the first time the sergeant—now captain—from Boise had been back to Kandahar. The remustering into intelligence had not been as complicated as he expected; he had been commissioned and promoted and right away sent to Baghdad. He had been surprised by how much he missed the Special Forces. He found the regular army uninspired. NCOs did not know their soldiers the way they did in the SF, and the difference in level of physical fitness was shocking. For the first few months he was in Baghdad it had been all he could do to bite his tongue. To his new colleagues, he knew he seemed standard issue SF: arrogant and contemptuous. When he saw himself in their eyes his first response was to stand even straighter—but then he remembered whose patches he wore on his shoulders now.

Since he was out of Special Forces, he could go by his real name: Rob Waller.

When the order came through for him to return to Afghanistan he had been surprised. He asked his company commander if he had put his name forward. His company commander assured him he would have discussed it with him before doing something like that. "I would have asked you not to," Captain Waller said.

"Really?"

"Yes. I need to establish myself here. I can't always be the ex-SF guy."

"The order came through to me as a done deal."

"Okay."

"They remember you well there, I'm told. I hope you've kept in shape."

Waller nodded. His superior held out his hand and they shook.

"Stay safe," he told him. Waller nodded again.

❈

He had not forgotten that he'd liked Afghanistan so much better than Iraq, but the particulars of that affection started to come back to him even as he walked off the airplane. He remembered the smell of the Arghandab River and the scent of trees that grow at altitude—resinous and sharp. No palms here. Which was fine by him. Cold winters and summer nights and real trees, real country, real people. Real reason to be here in the first place.

The private-now-sergeant from Bar Harbor met him at the airstrip. "Good to see you again, uh, sir."

"Yeah, get used to it."

"Figured you were an SF lifer for sure."

"Like you?"

"Well, who knows? Till something better comes along. Just hard to imagine what that could be."

"Wars end, buddy."

"I know. Not for a while though, it looks like. You here for long?"

"Probably not. Just looking into a few things."

"That leak come from here, then?"

Waller met his eyes.

"OPSEC, huh?"

"I didn't say anything," Waller said.

"Yessir."

"Why do you think I'm looking into that?"

"It's all anyone is talking about. INT dudes and FBI and CIA have been pouring in for the last three days, from Iraq and the States, both. Guys in the field are furious, apparently. Everyone says we're gonna see way more action out on the FOBs now, way more suicide bombers around KAF. In town you can tell everyone has watched those videos just by the way they look at us."

"They always looked at us like that. One Afghan in a hundred, maybe, has access to a computer."

"Well, they hate us now."

"They started hating us the day after we arrived. And have hated us a little more every day since."

"If you say so. Sir."

Waller let it drop. "It's strange being back."

"It's not Falluja, anyway."

"It's not just the not-Falluja part that I like about this place. There's going to be plenty of fighting here, too."

"So what is it?"

"The smell, maybe."

"Doesn't Jet-A smell the same everywhere?"

"It's clean."

"It's always clean. Pilots are fussy like that."

"Iraq is an unholy mess."

"So is this, Rob."

They walked on.

"I mean sir."

❀

They saw the hole in the road from a thousand metres away. Deirdre and the soldiers knew what had happened long before they reached the remains of a burnt-out British Scorpion lying on its side in the ditch. At last, the Taliban had learned that they, like everyone else, would always lose firefights with ISAF soldiers. But in any country with fertilizer, kerosene and pressure cookers, there were other, one-sided, ways to fight an occupier.

The scene was days old. It had rained enough since that you could no longer smell blood, except when you got too close to the shattered vehicle. There were no bodies.

It pissed Warrant Officer Fortin off that the Brits had not removed the Scorpion yet. "People see something like this and they reach conclusions," he grumbled. He turned to his soldiers. "Move on. Don't touch anything." The platoon took a last look at the death site and resumed walking. Deirdre took a quick photograph and followed them. They were relieved when the road finally turned and they could no longer see the shattered British vehicle.

It was overcast for once and the heat had given way to a still coolness that had the soldiers wearing jackets. The rain had greened the country appreciably, washed the dust from the tree leaves. For once the landscape seemed to contain something other than desiccated menace. But intention does not live within landscape. Mountains are indifferent to humans. What they are is gorgeous. And large. Way bigger than you.

The soldiers lifted their eyes beyond the closest treelines, to the mountains in the east and the ridgelines and valley bottom before them. The sense of foreboding that the shattered British Scorpion had brought to the day lifted a little. A bit of breeze played among them. They stopped scanning every hollow for evidence of a sniper blind and started looking at the country itself. They were not used to its austere beauty yet.

Deirdre remembered the place as it had been when she first arrived, when optimism hung over it like a weather system. She remembered it as greener and less hot then, but war distorts every lens. It was true that the drought that had come with the war's resurgence was not caused by the war. But without the revived war, the irrigation canals would be working. When there's a war going on, most of the bad things that happen can be blamed on it.

Optimism. Once it's gone, how do you get it back? Vanished hope is worse than original skepticism, because of the hole it leaves behind. So long as they'd felt invincible, they had done amazing things. Build three thousand clinics and schools in fourteen months. Walk across the country with nothing but a dog and daring. Rout the only fighting force that ever defeated the Red Army with air strikes and a handful of bearded soldiers. The world really was tipped in their favour those days, like the first flush of love, summer sunshine, and he likes you back.

Most of these guys here now knew nothing about what the place felt like back then. Some of them would have been in middle school. She watched them looking around, their eyes lifted a degree or two higher than usual, and she felt what they felt—a pause in the sense of jeopardy that allowed the loveliness of the place to sneak into them. Like when you're in the process of moving your stuff out of a boyfriend's apartment and you stop and notice how kind a man he is, really, however flawed. A hole in the cloud wall. Just to make it all maximally painful, later, when you find yourself yelling again.

❀

Four in the afternoon, and the day had brought to them no other sign of war. Fortin realized his men were relaxing. That worried him, and he scanned constantly for a reason to start shouting. But there was none. And the harder he looked at the edges of the fields and down the road stretching before him, the more this looked like the land outside Pincher Creek, Alberta. Without the oil or order. Or Seagram's Five Star Canadian Rye Whisky. Or hockey. Or Ford F-150 pickups.

But the size of the sky felt the exactly same. And the blue mountains on the horizon. And the arid foothills that seemed barely to hold grass between rainstorms and erupted in green every time the sky darkened. And the ferocious love the people who lived on it had for the land.

They were climbing a long grade now, and Deirdre was sucking wind. "Too many years at sea level in Baghdad," she said, aloud. They knew what that was the second she said it. So did she, once the words were out of her mouth. She winced and didn't say anything else, opting to use her breath to breathe.

Her consolation was that everyone else was puffing too. Most of the infanteers were carrying sixty-pound loads, including body armour and weapons. Then there was the man with the 7.62-mm machine gun, another forty pounds. Fortin increased the pace a little. In another circumstance, the men would have been irritated. But now they felt like they had been let out for a run. Beneath them they could see the oxbows of the Arghandab as it wound sinuously across its valley. In the distance, the woodsmoke haze of Kandahar, where the markets sold fist-sized blocks of polished lapis lazuli that could have been formed out of this perfectly blue sky, compressed to the point of substance. Deirdre had bought some, as had each of the soldiers, the first time they saw it in the bazaar, though heaven knows what any of them would do with it.

❀

As the afternoon rapidly slipped into evening, the café was still hot in a way it usually was not so late in the day and when the room was nearly empty. Fazil was behind the till. The heat made him think of summer—soon his children would be let out of school. His wife had made arrangements for them to continue religious instruction at a local madrassa, but nevertheless, they would have more free time and little Hamid and Aisha would be excited. He had not seen them in a year and when he skyped or spoke to them on the telephone they were shy and anxious with him. He wished he could travel home more easily, or at all safely. But he couldn't. Another convoy of buses and fuel tankers had been attacked the night before. The Taliban had run them close together and then lit them on fire and let the occupants—workers bound for American bases like KAF—burn. War had brought him here and war kept him here, so far from his children. Who would be all he would value as an old man, memories of whom would be all that remained to him as he breathed his last breath. And here he was, making less of his fatherhood, the only thing that would endure. Would war even be possible if all the parents of the planet just stayed with their children?

❀

That thought leapt from Fazil, brooding silently behind the counter, into the mind of Just Amachai, who normally exerted herself greatly not to pine for her own son, being raised by her parents in Thailand. From whom she had heard almost nothing in six months. They lived in a village near the Malay border with neither telephone nor electricity. They went to the post office to use the telephone when they could. When they managed to call they always told her everything was fine, and that her son was doing well at school. Absence had diminished her place in his life. She slept on a cot on a dusty Central Asian air base surrounded by coarse people just so she could send money home, and in return she was forgotten. Of course she was. Every absent parent in the world is forgotten. Still, she told herself, one does what one must to provide.

To provide what, if not herself? Money. Tuition. School uniforms. Food. A new roof. Electricity. A scooter. And did her son want any of those things as much as he wanted her on the day she left? She had come here and remained here also because it was easier, for her. She went to work and mailed the money home and her parents did the loving of her son and she did not have to live in the back of her parents' house and listen to all the other children in the neighbourhood go to school in the morning, but not her son. She told herself that her parents loved her son, too, and that he knew it. And that soon she would be home.

❀

Anakopoulus sat at the table beside Just Amachai. He had glanced at her when she walked in but now he looked out the window at the dusty land beyond, and the blast barriers and the sandbags that partly enveloped every standing structure. He looked at all this, but he did not dwell on any of it. He thought about how many weeks had gone by since his error and how he had not been contacted by anyone from the various security branches. Maybe he had gotten away with it after all. Maybe it was all going to be okay.

Of course it wouldn't be. Like they were ever going to stop looking until they caught him? Like they weren't burrowing into the internet right now, looking for the traces that would lead to him? The internet was big, was all. There was a lot of code to examine. Any moment there would be a knock on the door. "Please stand up, Master Sergeant." At times he thought that everything after that point would be easier. The fear was what was so painful. As an adult, he had not been afraid much. How do frightened people bear this? He felt anxious dread sweep up from his prostate and spread throughout his body like a rigor, making it quiver and making him feel short of breath. He forced himself to clear his thoughts for a moment. Just breathe. Think of nothing at all but your breath. And that created a blank space that allowed Just Amachai's ruminations about her child to spread from her thoughts into his.

He experienced a pastiche of images of tender women, introducing their daughters and sons to him. Anakopoulus had been with women with children since his late twenties. At the end of each relationship he felt nearly as much grief for the lost children as for the lost woman. He found mothers more appealing than childless women. He liked that there was always something in their lives more important to them than him.

Susie's son was fifteen now and, he knew from his Facebook lurking, still basketball-mad. This was not Anakopoulus's sport—he followed football and baseball—but for the sake of the boy, he'd acquainted himself. He had bought season tickets to the Mavericks and he'd taught himself to admire the fluidity of the game. When they played together, whatever advantage he had due to his size—the boy had been nine, then—was offset by his unfamiliarity with the game. They returned to his house after long afternoons at the park, spent wordlessly bouncing that ball, and leaping and throwing. Sometimes they had gone hours without speaking. With his technique it was only a matter of time before he tore his rotator cuff, he figured. Which would be fine by him. In the meantime he would bounce that damn ball as many times as he needed to.

The boy had to be thinking about college. Soon, he'd be studying for his SATs, looking at the different scholarships. As this thought occurred to Anakopoulus, the clamp tightened again on his chest. The child was on his way out of childhood, and the one tendril of adult manhood in his young life—Anakopoulus—had been pulled from his fingers with no regard at all for what the boy had to say about that.

If he got caught and prosecuted for treason, that would be bad. The kid would see his face in the paper. Though maybe he had written Anakopoulus off by now.

❀

That night, Facebook and YouTube leapt to life after InformationIsFree posted another treasure: 9 minutes and 42 seconds of a helmet cam–recorded assault on a compound near Gardez crowded with senior Taliban leaders meeting to discuss the upcoming fighting season. An AC-130 led it off with a two-minute-long 30-mm cannon burst—eight thousand rounds—through the walls and the ceiling of the compound, immediately followed by tracer fire from three platoons of Marine infantry. It was like watching an explosion in reverse, sucking in all that light and heat and ferocity.

And then the fire team advanced through the objective and secured the target. Shattered men lay behind the compound's gate, groaning and expiring. It was the women who caught the eye, though. Among them, bedecked in wedding silks, growing dull with congealing blood, was the bride.

The company commander could be heard giving a rapid series of unintelligible orders. Then came the last one, loud and clear. "Cut out the bullets. This was the Taliban that did this." A soldier looked at him for a moment afterwards, not moving. "You know they'd do it to us," the commander said.

The camera was turned off then.

Anakopoulus had not seen this clip before. Surely that had been faked.

CHAPTER TEN

A sunny late-spring afternoon, warm enough that all the windows of the café had been flung open and the door jammed wide, but not yet hot-hot, in the ferocious way it would be in a few weeks.

More, better: Rami Issay had not been in the café since dawn. The mood of the place reflected these two gifts. Even Amr smiled as he instructed Mohammed at chess. The coffee shop glowed with reflected golden light and the usual squalor retreated. The warmth of the sun brought out the odours of damp soil and desert flowers; even the tired eucalyptus tree beside Taliban's Last Stand was obvious to the senses, a hundred metres away, mingling with the scent of the coffee and the baking pastries. Fazil swept the floor and Deirdre O'Malley paused for a moment in her texting and laptopping and looked out the window at a platoon of Jordanian soldiers lined up outside the PX waiting to buy personal hygiene articles and then she looked at Fazil, and then her gaze wandered over to Rashid, who sat behind the counter reading a copy of the *Stars and Stripes*. Mohammed moved his king's knight to king's bishop three. Amr let slip a low whistle.

Just Amachai walked past outside, carrying a parcel. She glanced toward the café but did not wave. Anakopoulus, on one of his increasingly extended coffee breaks, drank his latte and watched her until she disappeared behind the hospital. The young colonels had been through the café earlier in the morning, oddly energetic. Something going on in the OPS world, Anakopoulus supposed.

He was not interested in what it was exactly, because in a way, he already knew: a brigade-scale sweep through the Panjwai was coming. Or a new movement of Taliban elements through the mountain passes. Or semi-credible reports of hand-held surface-to-air missiles being deployed by Taliban elements in the east.

Anakopoulus wondered why Rami Issay was not around. He'd eavesdropped on Fazil explaining to Rashid that, at dawn, General Jeremy Jackson had stopped in alone for a cup of hot water after his twenty-klick run. He had surveyed the night-shift chess players and the small lending library, then had picked up a copy of *The Things They Carried*. An hour later, someone from Kellogg Brown and Root, the company that managed the civilian-provided services on the base, had called and left a message requesting the manager come to the headquarters building to see him.

The collective suspicion was that Rami Issay was now riding a bus to the Khyber Pass. More hostile imaginings chose different geographies: Bagram's black prison; ISI compounds and hoods. He had turned out to be a spy, an AQ operative, a brother-in-law of Mullah Omar. He had been caught embezzling or diverting hundred-kilo bags of coffee beans to friends of his in exchange for opium. He was behind the much-whispered-about canola oil incident last month. None of the worst suspicions were said aloud.

Deirdre noticed Anakopoulus sitting alone, as usual, resolutely not noticing her. She was used to men who adopted that posture, just to show how indifferent they are, and she understood what it meant. There is a kind of war that is intensely sexual, where the soldiers, women and men, all want only to fuck and tell stories and exult and drink. Gulf War One had been like that, apparently. The first two weeks of Iraq, maybe. But not this, and not what Iraq became. Sour misogyny ran through it now, with weariness and cynicism flowing alongside—different results from a common origin.

She had heard of General Jackson's visit here and she wondered what he had thought of the café. He would have liked its scale, she guessed. Just a few tables and a staff so small you knew all their faces by the third visit. If there really was an OPSEC issue with Rami Issay or the coffee shop, the general wouldn't have come near this place; it would all have been dismantled by OGA or the contractors by now. Indeed, he had probably just been curious about the place. Jeremy (she still allowed herself to think of him as Jeremy) was one of the most curious men she had ever known. He had to know about everything he saw, especially anything not in keeping with the pattern. A chess club/café in the middle of his war would catch his eye. It crossed her mind to ask him to pose for a photo here, but she knew that he would never allow that. But still it would make a good picture. For later, maybe. When they'd figured out how to deal with each other again.

She felt the quiet pleasure of the café evaporate abruptly before she knew why it had. And then she saw Rami Issay, beaming his way through the door with the ebullient self-satisfaction of a man who, long derided, believes himself on the verge of vindication. He replied to people who had not greeted him, every word heard throughout the café. In an instant the suffused happiness of the afternoon was replaced by wary irritation. He annoyed, by level of annoyance:

1. Fazil, who felt an incandescent and homicidal rage, though this manifested itself outwardly only in the increased frequency of his sweeping. To proud Fazil, who had run a textile factory and who was used to being acknowledged for his competence, the presence of this buffoon, Issay, was a constant torment. The man's loose talk and profound indolence were surely in a footrace to see which would end his time here. If a gallbladder attack or gout or some other fat man's disease didn't first, inshallah. But here he was, back and happy and, it would seem, with some new scheme, meaning more work for them all. Allah be merciful.

2. Rashid, more obviously, but less deeply felt. He merely rolled his eyes and set aside his newspaper. A morning without Issay constantly hanging over him, desperate to impress him with his taste and worldliness, had been a great pleasure. Too good to last, it appeared. Put your face back on, now. "Hi, boss. Did they leave marks?"

3. Deirdre O'Malley, looking up from a piece she had just spotted on the *WashPo* site that scooped the story she was one day from filing, about the results of the poll ISAF had conducted on the support they enjoyed among civilians in the western provinces. Someone had leaked this, and not to her. She would speak to Major Horner. Why had the press liaison officer given it to her, if he had given it to someone else even earlier? And now, all this commotion around the fat man. Can't they see she was trying to work?

4. Anakopoulus, who just wanted the café to stay as it was. He had been on the verge of losing it for days now and it would really be his preference for that idiot to keep it down.

5. Mohammed, just about to fork Amr's bishop and rook when the fuss began. First Amr turned to see what was going on, and then he rose to stride pointedly out of the room. Game over.

Frowning at Rashid's odd question and ignoring the barbed glances, Rami Issay announced in a whisper easily audible in every corner of the café, "I need to meet with the staff immediately." Mohammed and Rashid and Fazil all shuffled behind the counter to join Amr.

Puffed up like some giant mushroom burst forth from the forest floor, Issay followed them. His voice breaking, he declared that, in view of his success with the café, he had had the honour of being asked by his employers in the Kellogg Brown and Root corporation, private contractors administering the base's civilian-operated aspects—including the Green Beans—to establish a cinema club for the base.

"I will bring some brief bit of colour to this godforsaken place yet, I tell you," Rami Issay declared. "And even if that small bloom is buried five minutes later under a great pile of fresh donkey dung, then it will still have been an accomplishment of which I may be proud."

Fazil and Amr stepped away and resumed cleaning.

"Anyway," Issay added, after a moment, "I have been a cinephile since I was old enough to sit upon my father's knee on Saturday afternoons and watch Sultan Rahi kill brigands. This will be enjoyable."

Rashid said, "Boss, listen to me. Nobody—not one person here—wants to watch the legends of the Pakistani silver screen twirl their mustache ends and swing their swords about."

"Oh, I know that. And I know well who our audience will be and what is the most vital and sophisticated film canon. American movies are what we will show."

Rashid gestured to the café's patrons. "Can you name a film made in the last decade that these people will be interested in watching?"

"I'm not going to give you the satisfaction of saying *Lawrence of Arabia.*"

"Can you even tell me who is Megan Fox?"

"We will most assuredly not be showing those sorts of films, my young friend."

"Boss, right now, she's the highest-paid young actress in the feature film industry."

"Well, then, perhaps I shall be making her acquaintance, one night when the best way I can think of to spend my evening is to watch a film inspired by a plastic car toy."

That gave Rashid pause. "And where will we be getting our films?" he asked at last.

"I have found a distributor."

"Do they know they'll have to fly their films into Kandahar?"

"Don't you worry about anything."

"What is this outfit's name?"

"BitTorrent."

Rashid rubbed his face with both hands. "This is going to be an almighty disaster."

"I'm only joking. Must you be so unrelentingly pessimistic, Rashid Siddiqui? The military will try to bring in what we ask for—so long as it is not sexually licentious, they tell me. They've given me a list of films they have immediately on hand. I will show it to you and perhaps you can suggest some titles that will resonate with the yoot here."

"The yoot?"

"Have you not watched *My Cousin Vinny*?"

"I have seen it," Rashid said, into his hands.

❀

Later that afternoon, Rami Issay wandered out and left the nearly empty café to Amr and Mohammed. Amr told the boy to sit down and have something to eat. Mohammed turned on the computer in the back that they were allowed to use. He entered "Taliban" into the YouTube search field and the first result showed the bodies of four schoolteachers who had taught at a school built within sight of Bagram. Mohammed thought they looked like kind men and wondered why anyone would shoot them. What had they been teaching? He would have to ask about that. Then he entered "Americans in Afghanistan" and the first link that came up was the just-released video of the helicopter machine gunning people in the street. And the clip after that was the colonel telling his men to cut the bullets out of the bodies of the women. Then his break was over and so he signed off the computer and walked back into the front of the café to help with the lunch rush. He was so nauseous he was no longer hungry.

❀

At the same moment, Deirdre got twenty emails simultaneously, all with links to the *Guardian*, which had just posted the helicopter video. Soon it was also on *Le Monde* and *El País*. It had been taken through the target acquisition camera of the 30-mm cannon on the nose of an Apache helicopter based out of Bagram. While it hovered a kilometre away from a clot of men standing at the intersection of two alleys in a village purported to be on the outskirts of Jalalabad, its camera recorded the view through the gunsight. The audio recorded the discussion between the pilot and the weapons systems officer. She put in her earbuds and turned up the sound on her laptop.

Blurry footage and on the audio, the thump of a helicopter. It was hard to tell for sure where they were, but it was a city: a jumbled sprawl of one-storey houses, flat roofs and chaotic streets. The helicopter was descending, and through the gunsight camera the weapons officer was studying a particular intersection.

The conversation between the pilot and the weapons officer was casual and focused. She had listened to hours of such discussion in her time in Iraq and she knew how normal and efficient a mode of communication it was for the soldiers— and how callow it would sound to a domestic audience.

Those words in their casual tone would be played and replayed on a million earnest weeping people's blogs, she knew. She felt badly for the men. They would know those voices were theirs. Maybe their girlfriends and parents would, too.

And that footage of the people stopping to help and being shot in turn would be inflammatory, too. As would the reporters being shot— the foreign-national reporters. She didn't know what to say about that.

She closed her eyes for a long moment. She removed the earbuds and set them down on the table. She opened her eyes. She began to feel a rising sense of indignation about the fact that this was being viewed by people who had no context in which to judge. Who would leak something like this? What could the motive have possibly been? Surely they would have known what effect this would have on the mission. Abu Ghraib all over again. Every internet café from Baghdad to Jalalabad would be playing this over and over again. Deirdre replayed the clip, starting with the exchange between the helicopter pilot and the gunner referring to the parents of the children who had just been shot:

PILOT: Well, it's their fault, for bringing their kids to a battle.
GUNNER: That's right.

She could just hear that line being quoted over and over again. Someone would probably release it as a ringtone.

She had seen worse up close, a hundred times. War is shitty. People know that. Or they ought to when they send their soldiers off to fight. Even if they never get to know the details, they can depend on that. If you haven't seen war, the details will just confuse you.

Then she thought again about the guys on that recording. Jesus. Everyone who recognized their voices will look at them a little different for the rest of their lives. This stuff is not supposed to be public. This was a horrific violation. She hoped the leaker got caught fast. She made a fist.

❀

Rashid studied the list that Rami Issay had passed to him. He was to pick five films for the next month, which was to be a trial period for what the boss proposed to call the Kandahar Kinema Klub. "Sometimes, the young people will deliberately misspell words. It is the fashion today."

Oh, for God's sake. "I know, boss. But that mostly has to do with music. This is not music and we are not in Los Angeles and we are not cool. And we cannot call it anything that can be abbreviated to three Ks."

"Why ever not?"

"Trust me." Because it is only me that keeps you from being summarily fired for ideas like that one.

"But still, can we not try to have fun with this?"

"Boss, trying is the least cool thing of all."

"If having fun must conflict with being cool, I think you know what I would pick."

"Whatever you say, boss."

The films would come from Germany, on any of the resupply or repatriation flights out of Air Force Base Ramstein. An anonymous but helpful and clearly informed clerk had provided plot summaries.

True Lies: *Schwarzenegger and Jamie Lee Curtis struggle with their marriage, his secret career as a special operative and a woman's need for affirmation as they are attacked by terrorists.* NOT RECOMMENDED FOR MUSLIM AUDIENCES.

The Matrix: *Keanu Reeves, Laurence Fishburne. The machines have taken over. Nothing is real. Sunglasses and black leather trench coats have never been more cool. You can do anything, create anything, with code. But even if you're the One, no one touches anyone. Except, possibly, as code. But if you are equating that with the real thing, soldier, then you have been deployed far too long. Recommended.*

Gone in Sixty Seconds: *Nicolas Cage and Angelina Jolie, when she still did movies like this. There are some very cool cars, the theft of which is the core of the plot. Spectacular chase sequences fill most of the screen time. Cage becomes extremely agitated. Highly recommended.*

Mr. and Mrs. Smith: *Like* True Lies, *but less Schwarzeneggerish. Brad Pitt and Angelina Jolie are hired assassins, each unknown to the other. Like all spouses, whether they acknowledge it or not. Recommended.*

Wrote the presumably married clerk. There were pages of this.

❀

Deirdre almost bumped into General Jackson outside the dining facility. He was leaving, she was entering. He said it first because someone had to; there was no ducking her gaze and anyway. "Hello."

"Jeremy." As level as voiced-over Japanese movie dialogue.

"The press liaison officer told me you were here."

"He said the same thing to me about you." A riposte to what had not been intended as a jab.

Jeremy Jackson's eyes crinkled. Long pause. Then he said, less distantly, "What do you think about it all?"

"That's a pretty broad question. And anyway, what I think doesn't matter. What do you think?"

He looked around. "It isn't Iraq."

"It is not."

"But it is complicated."

"The best stories usually are."

"Which story are we talking about?"

"I think you said, 'it all.' Which story is that?"

"Western hegemony?"

"Will you do an interview with me on the subject of western hegemony?"

"No."

"Then that's not the story I want to talk to you about."

"I'm almost reluctant to ask what is."

"Whatever you *will* talk to me about. You hold the cards here."

"I really don't."

"You still have my cell number?"

"It works here?"

"It has worked wherever I've been for the last two years. The wonders of modern technology: SIM cards and roaming plans. Ask Fred about it."

"I'll tell him hello for you."

"Give him my best."

"I will."

"Don't shut me out, okay? I have to do my job here, like everyone else."

"Why would I avoid you?"

"Why, indeed."

"Nice seeing you again, Deirdre."

And they paused, maintaining eye contact, while they both decided not to shake hands, and then they walked on. Neither of them could take a full breath for at least a minute. They both hated that.

※

Anakopoulus locked his office door and then sat down and poured himself a glass of whiskey. His guys knew better than to disturb him once that door was locked. He opened his email. His military inbox was one long list of *where is*. Where is that refrigeration unit you were holding for me? Has that container of oil filters arrived yet? He forwarded these to his clerks to chase down. Which is where they should have gone in the first place. It's always the same story, people have two conversations with you and they think they have an in with supply. *Write the big man directly, he'll take care of it.*

In his personal account were notes from his brother, and from guys who had rotated through sometime in the last seven years and couldn't stop thinking or talking about it since. Like unwrapping bales of uniforms here is an entirely different experience than it would ever be stateside. The guys who had been or subsequently went to Iraq didn't obsess over this place as much. Though with three rocket attacks this week, it was getting so that the difference wasn't as big as it had been.

One of the guys had sent him a link to the helicopter video that had just been posted. He clicked on it. As the images flickered on his screen he felt a hand around his throat. By the end of the video, his shirt was visibly damp and, once again, he was nauseous.

❀

Deirdre had seventy more emails waiting for her when she opened her eyes the next morning to the sounds of Harriers taking off. She scrolled through her phone, scanning subject lines. Most of them were about the leak investigation. What did she know? Were there MPs on the ground, asking about it? How offended were the soldiers? Had there been any local outrage expressed? How much violence had it provoked?

She was eating her eggs in the DFAC when David Mitchell sat down without asking.

"Hey!" he said, "I've been meaning to grab a coffee with you."

"Hi, David," she said.

"So, the story of the year keeps getting more heated, huh? Did you see the *LA Times* editorial this morning?"

"Yep."

"Everyone is *furious*."

"I see the point. Inflaming anti-American sentiment is going to cost lives here and in Iraq. Real lives, real people."

"Isn't every Afghan who is disposed to killing Americans pretty much doing it already? Would the idea that a helicopter crew might machine-gun innocents and laugh as they watched through a gunsight surprise any already aggrieved Pashtuns?"

"It's fuel added to the fire."

"Do you think the *Times* considered not running the story?"

"The *Guardian* had the story, too. Whoever organized the leak knew what they were doing. Everyone's hand was forced."

"What do you know about who did the organizing?"

"I know what you know: InformationIsFree.com. They run a dropbox out of Liechtenstein. I heard about them when they released a bunch of Greek government accounting statements showing corruption. Otherwise, there isn't much out there about them. They say they don't want to become the story. All that will change, though."

"Their name says what you need to know about their motives, I guess," he said.

"The Afghans who support the coalition operations here only do so because they believe the Taliban to be even worse than having unbelievers driving in their streets. That 'even worse' part is the only thing that gives the mission and this country a chance. And the truth is that the Taliban *are* much worse. But they have to be seen as that for there to be any chance."

"Is that our job? To make the mission successful?"

She felt her temper rise. She had twenty times as much time in the field as he did. "Nobody in NATO stones women in soccer stadiums. The Taliban are shitty. That is just true. It's part of the story."

"How much popular support do you think the Taliban have?"

"I was in Iraq until five minutes ago, David. I don't know any better than you do. Don't try to trap me. Of course we're not brown and not Muslim and we kill Afghans. So, no, we are not universally loved, and the Taliban do have some support. It doesn't make them not horrible. Which, again, has to be part of the story."

"We?"

She sighed and looked away. "Americans."

"'Cause I'm not killing any Afghans. How about you?"

"Point taken. Aren't you clever."

"How do you see this all playing out back home?"

"I think the response has been really mature. Normally, all leaks are embraced because everyone wants to know a secret. But the press is being pretty critical about this. I think InformationsIsFree deserves the shit-kicking they're getting."

"Because of the fuel-fire problem?"

"Yeah. Soldiers are going to die as result of that leak."

"Yeah."

"And when they do, the public will need to understand that part of the story, too."

"Fox News will make sure of that."

"Soldiers are real people. And they really can get killed by reporters."

"Those kids with 30-mm holes in them were real people too."

"Of course," she said, and stood up with her tray. "Have a good day, David." She dropped her tray at the bay and walked to the exit. *Asshole.*

❀

Anakopoulus was sitting at his desk reviewing air manifests when one of his men poked his head inside. He looked up. "Hey boss, just got a crate in from AFB Ramstein marked for your attention personally."

"What is it?"

"Looks like movie equipment. Some films. A popcorn popper."

"Right. I got a call from the base commander's ADC about this. I think he's doing some kind of entertainment night or something. I'm supposed to get this to the Green Beans. Do you wanna call them for me?"

"Sure."

"Thanks."

"Hey boss?"

"Yeah?"

"Everything okay?"

"Get back to work."

"Gotcha."

❀

Rashid's first thought on seeing the film crates in the big sergeant's warehouse was *of course*. The posters had already gone up in the café and around the base, advertising *Red Dawn*, the first screening of the KAF film society, but according to the packing slips that was not what had been shipped to them. Of course.

Fight Club. It could have been worse. Could have been some dismal Hugh Grant romantic comedy. Any of the Sandra Bullock vehicles that the boss had wanted to order would all have been disasters. This, they could deal with. Rashid tried to recall what he could of the movie. He remembered fetishized violence, though he could not recall the use of any weapons, which would have been better. The homoerotic Brad Pitt–Ed Norton tension-but-not-really-cuz-they're-the-same-guy would simply have to be overlooked, as it had been by most of the world already. The title would bring the audience in. If they didn't like what they saw, they could just look away.

The sergeant said one of his guys would bring the projector over to the café on a loader. Rashid carried the film reels back on his shoulder. They were surprisingly heavy. Perhaps they should have just used something off BitTorrent, after all. They would have known what they were getting, and there would have been no need to worry about shipping mistakes. As he lumbered down Screaming Eagle Way, a platoon of Poles marched by, a short bullet-headed NCO striding alongside with fierce attention. Land Rovers from the RAF regiment bumped their way over potholes behind them. Rashid heard a circular saw screeching as it bit into a two-by-four. He smelled the wood. He smelled the DFAC's bread ovens. He adjusted the film canisters on his shoulders and he realized with surprise that he was at that moment almost happy. The smell of cut spruce and bread. There was even the prospect of talking about a complicated movie—whose reels he was carrying to a strange café so that it might be shown to soldiers. He permitted himself a small smile.

Rami Issay was not dismayed by the shipping mistake. "I only acquiesced to that *Red Dawn* in deference to the recommendation of the officer commanding, Ramstein Cinema. This is much better."

"Maybe, boss. I worry a little that it will seem . . . degenerate to them."

"Do you mean the Pitt-Norton interaction? They are simply two men shirtlessly fighting with each other. Is boxing degenerate? Are the mixed martial arts?"

"There's all that anti-materialism. It will seem socialist."

"My young friend, have some sympathy for what the soldiers endure. They have few comforts and poor pay and danger everywhere. They think their compatriots at home are cosseted and narcotized. That part will resonate with them."

"I think they will dislike it. Look what they read when they come here. Not Chuck Pahalniuk novels. Tom Clancy, *Soldier of Fortune Magazine*, things like that . . ."

"I do look. And I see that anti-materialism and reverence for the community is as much a military thing as a left-wing thing. What our customers here recoil against is compulsion. This is actually the sentiment of *Fight Cub*. It's almost libertarian."

"Boss, keep your voice down." Switching into Urdu: "You can't be seen to be political in any way."

"It'll be fine. If anyone objects, it was Ramstein's doing. Let us have a cup of chai."

And they walked from the storeroom into the front of the café. It was busy. Little Mohammed and Amr were working hard. It was consistently busier than it had been. The chess sets were part of it. But there were more non-players coming in, too. Rashid thought that the presence of the chess players had altered the feeling of the place, made it seem less bleakly functional, and that drew soldiers.

Rami asked Amr to make two cups of chai. As Amr nodded and went to prepare them his irritation was as obvious to Rashid as it was invisible to their boss. Amr's cheeks had flushed subtly beneath his beard and his eyes had tightened with restrained violence. Amr had been operating the espresso machine just as fast as he could, pulling double shots and steaming cups of milk one after the other in a steady blur and shriek. Mohammed scurried from table to table, his devotion to his position at all times evident. He made no mistakes with orders. Amr's point was: Rami Issay and Rashid Siddiqui could make their own chais—and would have, if they'd bothered to think about the people they were supposed to be working with rather than this blasphemy of a cinema show they were planning.

Mohammed put their chais up on the counter. They picked them up and surveyed the café. They sipped their chais. Eventually Rami Issay said, "It must be time, my young friend."

Rashid rose without answering and walked outside the café with a crowbar. He opened the crate the projector had been shipped in. Taped to the projector was its operator's manual. Relieved, Rashid sat down on the crate and opened it.

Rami Issay watched through the window as Rashid consulted the manual and then set up the projector such that it would illuminate an outside wall of the café. They had borrowed enough chairs and benches from the big sergeant to seat two hundred people.

The screening was to begin a half-hour after sundown—an hour away. There were some rules. The projector was never to face the airstrip, lest it cost a pilot night vision. In the event of a rocket attack, the screening was to be halted immediately. No smoking would be permitted in the audience. Fazil had been working in the back kitchen since dawn. He had baked three hundred apple carrot muffins and made one hundred roast beef sandwiches. Whenever he lifted his eyes from arrays of sliced bread in front of him, he glowered at whomever he saw. Rami Issay had stayed out of his way since ten that morning.

He turned away from the window to survey the café, which was buzzing away happily enough under the attentions of Amr and Mohammed. There were four chess games going of unremarkable quality. Just Amachai sat alone and drank her tea and watched everyone. Deirdre O'Malley walked in, sat down, and immediately descended into her laptop.

❀

Deirdre looked up as a UPI reporter whose name she couldn't remember, uninvited, sat down at her table. "Hey O'Malley, I was hoping I'd run into you."

She couldn't recall meeting him. Then, after a moment, she remembered. "Oh, hi." He had been in Baghdad doing vacation relief for someone for a few weeks three years ago.

"So, have you seen—?"

She cut him off. "Listen . . ."

"Don."

"Dude, I'm on deadline here."

"Okay, okay. I didn't see you writing."

She watched him get up and walk out of the café. She looked back at her computer: every journalist who had ever been in Iraq and then run home, overwhelmed, had attached themselves to this story. An ex-boyfriend had just published the transcript of the helicopter crew's conversation, salted in a few mostly inaccurate explanations of the technical terms, and got the front page over the fold of the *Independent*. Another ex-less-than-a-boyfriend got a quarter-page op-ed decrying the media co-operation with the leaker: THIS IS DAMAGING, his headline protested, before he launched a rant upon the leaker. "The soldiers I embedded with did not endure all manner of threat so that their most difficult moments would be served up on the internet . . ." Three weeks in Iraq and one IED and one firefight and he had been finished. Pale and anxious and unable to work.

The real question—the story—was still: where had the leak come from? InformationIsFree wasn't saying. No one in the media tent seemed to know anything. Maybe someone in Bagram had leaked it. Or even Langley. But it was only a mission like ten thousand others, so why would anyone on the inside bother? She wondered then if it hadn't been exchanged informally. War porn.

Just then Mohammed approached her and asked if she wanted another cappuccino. She did not say anything for a moment, just looked at him, as he looked back at her, nervous and quizzical. "Sure, Mohammed." It was the first time she had used, or let him know that she knew, his name.

What she thought was, the spooks would find the leaker. And then there would be an arrest followed by a helicopter ride to an aircraft carrier. And the story would be released in a choreographed sequence of Bob Woodward whisperings and then news conferences with slides and evidence displays. She and every other field journalist would be left on the outside while the Sunday morning shows would clean up. It would be the year's biggest story. You could already tell that audiences were getting bored with the combat camera pieces. Urgent-sounding correspondent speaking excitedly into a mic. Helmet askew. In the background, dust and mud-brick huts. All that no longer captured people's eye the way it had. People already had their Call of Duty. They wanted something with narrative, now. A spy novel. Secrecy and treason.

❀

As the café filled to capacity, Fazil appeared from the back and put on an apron and began taking orders. Rashid began helping behind the counter, too. They were none of them happy except Rami Issay. He leaned back in his chair beside the back door and closed his eyes, smiling. Amr muttered to Fazil that it looked like the boss was having a shit. Fazil scowled at the indecorous language but did not rebuke him.

Jeremy Jackson and Fred Shaw came in then, bending low and removing their Oakleys in the dimness. They both scanned for and saw Deirdre, who was staring at the wall three feet over Anakopoulus's head. They looked away. Shaw thought she was probably ignoring them; Jackson thought he would have been able to tell if it was purposeful. They sat down, Jackson with his back to her. Mohammed brought over a chess board, unbidden. They thanked him, and asked for drip coffees, black.

As the sun slipped behind the mountain, Rashid, operation manual in hand, walked outside to turn the projector on to prewarm the bulb. After confirming that the cooling fan was turning and that the vents were unobstructed, he said to Rami Issay that it looked like everything was working fine.

The twilight sky was still a little too bright, but along Screaming Eagle Way soldiers were walking toward them. Most of these were unfamiliar faces—dressed in varieties of Under Armour and North Face fleeces. As they coalesced into a crowd outside the café, it became clear there were far too few chairs. Rami Issay grinned at his agitated young friend. Some of the audience sat down on the ground beside the chairs and others stood behind them. The popcorn maker was soon going full blast and notwithstanding the enormous sack of kernels that had accompanied it, Rashid worried that they would run out.

The sun dipped farther behind the mountain and Rashid watched the shadow racing across the airfield toward them. And then the moonless night descended, black and silky and punctured only by stars. He hit the button, the film flickered to life and conversation stopped. But the opening sequence contained no fighting at all and those in the audience who had been led to believe they would be watching a mixed martial arts flick shifted in their chairs. Rashid thought, this was the minute the success or failure of the Kandahar film club would turn upon. And then the title sequence lit up the screen. And the people almost all stayed, for the same reason almost all of them had come. Spectacle captures the brain by wrapping a fist around each eye.

⚜

John Wayne's roommate, who also an interpreter, told him once, in elegant classical Pashto, "We are not bound together by a capacity to kill. It's the shared threat of death that welds men to each other." He was older than John Wayne and presumed from time to time to instruct his younger acquaintance. It was easier to listen to him than it would have been to tell him to be quiet.

This night John Wayne had gotten off his helicopter after a long day's patrol and walked to the interpreters' barracks past a flickering cone of horizontal light sprayed against the coffee shop wall. He considered stopping in to watch the movie for about one second but he had been up since five and had walked twenty-eight kilometres that day in body armour and boots. He had to be awake at four the next morning and already it was dark.

When he got to his room he saw light seeping out from under their door: his roommate was still up. He hoped to God that he was not feeling poetic.

When he opened the door the first thing he saw was the Baluchistani glowering at him from a steel chair. Then he saw three American men in khaki adventure wear standing around his bed. They had their pistols out. One of them held his laptop and another his cellphone.

❁

After the movie ended, Rashid watched the crowd slowly disperse. He did not see General Jackson leave, though he'd been there earlier, standing at the back. So he had slipped away before the end of the film.

"What did you think?" Rami Issay asked him.

"Ed Norton is a brilliant actor."

"And Brad Pitt?"

"He is very beautiful in this film."

"Did you find the politics in the film distracting?"

Rashid began picking up and collapsing the folding chairs. "I was surprised that such a liberal movie would resonate with all these soldiers. Maybe after all these months I still misunderstood them rather badly. All these people came here. Presumably to make the world better. That is not a conservative impulse."

Rami Issay watched Rashid folding chairs. "Some people may make war for noble reasons, I suppose."

❁

Captain Waller sat in the corner of a cell made out of shipping containers inside the Special Forces compound. He was making notes in a binder with numbered pages. John Wayne sat on a metal chair in front of him, with the CIA interrogator hovering over him. Waller had anticipated not having to use an interpreter, but as John Wayne grew more upset he claimed to lose his English, and eventually one of the SF's interpreters was brought in.

The SF interpreter grew ferocious when he realized that John Wayne was also an interpreter: one of them, on the inside. CIA told him he had been caught sending large files to an ISP address in Pakistan. When the contents of the file were examined, they found hundreds of pictures of casualty trophies, including some of those that had been posted on the internet. John Wayne claimed they had been given to him by his friends, the soldiers, and he had sent some to his brother, because he wanted his brother to know how difficult this work is. He wanted to impress him.

The SF terp would have none of it. Every phrase was prefaced with "He claims . . ."

The CIA officer slapped John Wayne until his mouth was bloody. Then the SF terp joined in, with a closed fist. Captain Waller looked up at that, but the CIA officer shook his head, and so he let the beating proceed.

John Wayne began weeping, leaking bloody foam and tears with each gasp. No, he couldn't name his friends; no, he didn't remember who had given him the pictures. A tooth was knocked out. He vomited, spraying the walls of the little room with bloody bile. CIA put on a smock. He had brought extras. He handed one to each of the other men in the room. When Captain Waller put his on, his face was so wooden he looked as if he was dead.

*D*eirdre *felt a sense of foreboding from the moment she got off the plane in Jerusalem. She had always loved the city, but this time, all she could think of was what had to happen. He knew it, too. Their lovemaking was perfunctory, and their conversation clipped. The long, meandering conversation that had filled their days together was gone. He had been profiled in the* New Yorker *that week. There was talk about a run for the presidency. All eyes would soon be upon him, or were, already. And those eyes would then be upon everyone near to him. Which is why that could no longer include her.*

"I'm saying this because we have no choice," she said.

"I know. Thank you," he said. He was sitting on the bed, still naked, watching her dress.

"Then you agree?"

"I understand your point."

"And you agree with me?"

"Yes."

"Good. I'll take a cab to the airport. Can you wait a little while before you go, too?"

"Of course."

And then she bent to kiss him goodbye. She wanted him to see how much this hurt her. As she stepped back she looked at him, to show him. All she saw was relief.

CHAPTER ELEVEN

After the KAF film club's successful debut, Rashid started doing more night shifts at the café so that his days were free to organize future screenings. He did not mind this so much, and wouldn't have at all, were it easier to sleep during the day. Most of the time, after it got hot, he got up and helped out anyway. It occurred to him that this may have been what his boss had anticipated.

Of course, Rami Issay wanted to show another film right away. Rashid supposed that if a thing was worth doing, it was worth overdoing. Issay had heard from his supervisor that his effort was appreciated—a phone call had been placed from General Jackson's office to the Kellogg Brown and Root managers and they were thankful for the goodwill he had earned them.

As he took the chairs off the tables and returned them to the floor after he'd finished mopping the place, journalists, up to do interviews with American evening news programs, lined up outside the door. The sky began to lighten faintly in the east. The air temperature reached its nadir and the fleece-shrouded writers and broadcasters huddled together and complained about the time difference, the cold and the café's habit of being especially busy just when they had to start work. Deirdre O'Malley stood in that line and listened to the groaning and did not participate in it. Pointedly.

When Jeremy Jackson joined the queue a few people behind her, Deirdre did not turn around, though everyone else did. They all wanted to interview the general, but understood that no impromptu questions would be answered and it would be much better to win a nod from the general than to pointlessly irritate him.

Jackson wished it was less busy. Deirdre acted as if she hadn't noticed him. He was grateful. He would reciprocate.

Deirdre had just been told by a source that the leaker had been found, and wasn't American. She was skeptical. It seemed too neat, too exculpatory. And there were no details about who it was they had. She decided that after her coffee she would go by the Special Forces' compound and say hi to the long-suffering ("We never comment on operations. No, you can't print anyone's name or rank.") public affairs officer there. She would ask to see General Lattice. She had asked before and been rebuffed, but she'd try again. She knew him from Iraq. He had even thanked her for some of her better pieces, but that was back when that made her uncomfortable and she hadn't responded with any particular warmth. He'd continued to grant her interviews when it suited his agenda, but the thank-yous stopped. He was a proud man and an egoist, like anyone who ever gets anything done.

She wondered if he knew about her and Jeremy then gave her head a shake. Old news.

Jackson was thinking about how his reputation had been made in Iraq, pacifying Anbar. As he waited in line and watched the sky begin to lighten, he thought about how much easier a problem that had turned out to be than this was. In Iraq there had been an established civil society, until right before the invasion. Kids went to school, hospitals admitted sick people, engineers ran water plants, and the army had uniforms and paid wages. There were sectarian and tribal divisions that could be put to use, too. Here the situation was more

different than similar. And there were mountains. And an open border to Pakistan. And the ISI. And every month the security situation
was worse, not better, notwithstanding the declarations of the PA guys.
Notwithstanding his own assertions in the media.

Not for the first time, he thought that accepting this command may
have been a mistake. The next cycle of primaries would start in three
years. He had worried the War on Terror would be fading from memory by then. Now he wondered if he should worry that it might not.

She had spent enough time pretending not to and wishing that she
didn't, the realization was painful: she missed him. He was standing
just a few feet behind her now, and in that undefended proximity—he
couldn't see her face—the tenderness she still felt for him revealed itself.
Even if she'd have liked to hit it with a stick.

She'd first seen General Jackson in the Green Zone a few weeks after
the fall of Baghdad, walking to a press conference. She saw why the
reporters liked him. He didn't swagger. He was the only skeptic about
the Iraq war who still had senior responsibility. All the rest, Shinseki
on down, had been marginalized or retired. But Jackson was insulated
because everyone conceded that his technical skills were needed, and he
was pretty careful with his media profile. He did not get involved with
controversies. When the insurgency began truly to announce itself, he
became indispensable. By that point, his technical skills were in daily,
even hourly, demand.

Falluja felt like it was fifteen minutes ago. Car bombs going off every
twenty minutes and snipers on every rooftop. Whispered conversations,
urgent and potent, about all the players in that complex stew of actors:
Zarqawi, Moqtada al-Sadr, the wary Sunni tribal elders and all those
boisterous and disappointed young men with no jobs, no women, no
houses and nothing to lose.

One night they'd talked for four hours in a basement about the aes-
thetics of battle, about how manned fighters, paratroopers and first-light
stand-tos continued to stir people long after these things were practically
useful and so they were retained, like glinting swords on the parade
ground. In war, the warriors must be given reasons to think themselves

ferocious. Look at the Republican Guard and they how they folded once they realized they weren't. Or not as much as the First Marine Division, anyway.

Two days after that conversation, she got a call to do a long, in-depth interview with him, no conditions, no no-go zones. The results of that interview got her the cover of *Time* magazine and a Pulitzer nomination. It made her career—and contributed to his own ascent as a celebrity general.

Afterwards, they did not want the other reporters to view them as too close to one another. So they began meeting in places where they would not be seen and recognized. There was a hotel in Jerusalem—the Inbal. Journalists and soldiers did not often stay there and that suited Deirdre's and Jackson's purposes. Jackson supposed that Mossad probably watched him when he was in the country wherever he stayed, and so he had to be careful about what they talked about—it wasn't just her discretion that was at issue. Deirdre thought he was joking the first couple of times he said that.

When he was scheduled to go to London or Berlin, he found reasons to mention it and she found reasons to be there, too—though in those cities they were careful not to stay at the same hotel. The surprising thing was how long the fiction that they were creating for the outside world endured for them, too. They did not so much as touch one another on the first five trips to western European capitals. They met for suppers in his room. They walked in Luxembourg Gardens late at night and in Kew Gardens and along Wilhelmstrasse and on Leidseplein. They discussed the nature of war, and the way it suspended normal discourse.

They both knew it was a mistake from the start. But the war made it inevitable. At the end of their walks along the Seine, they got back on separate airplanes to Baghdad. Every week they lost colleagues to IEDs and snipers. They both learned Arabic and they both stopped going back to the States. Jackson's kids were all grown and his wife was self-sufficient, in the way of military spouses. They felt more alive than they had, ever. Three years earlier she had been reporting city council meetings and he had been supervising a training centre in Georgia and running a hundred kilometres a week. On five different occasions she had held a bleeding cameraman in her arms. In all this mayhem, they felt there was just one other out there who understood and who was not a rival.

The amount of time they spent thinking about one another vastly outweighed the amount of time they managed to spend together. They went weeks between email contact, and everything written was composed with an eye to a third party reading it. As far she could tell, Jackson worked a hundred hours a week, and she was at a loss to account for how he sustained the pace. She read and wrote long into the night most days, too, but everyone worked hard. What Jackson managed was something else entirely. She remembered how her boyfriend in Cincinnati would sleep in on Sundays until one in the afternoon and refuse to shave unless they went out for supper someplace nice.

It was not just that he was a powerful man. With her, he seemed unconscious of that power, and that drew her even more. He did not boast and rarely even talked about the current famous version of himself. When he spoke personally, it was about growing up in Michigan, going ice fishing and trying to find interesting books in his local library. She could picture him then, wiry and shy, asking the librarian for history books and sucking them up like a grain auger. Late seventies rust-belt economy and he would not be dragged under. Every man she met told her over and over again what a good job he was doing, how smart he was, and how strong. Jeremy's version of this was just that he had a great staff, that Fred had taught him lots. She broke all her rules for him, and the breaking of those rules greased the skid on her better judgment. Reservations were tossed out like articles of a lapsed faith.

She wondered what he was thinking about now. She'd heard he had been to the café to play chess. It would be inconvenient if this turned into his favourite place, too. She guessed she could spend her time at the press tent, if she had to.

❀

He missed her, too. He stared at the spot between her shoulder blades and remembered watching her laughing hard and the way her whole body had rocked. He remembered that first long interview he did with her, with public affairs handlers hovering, and the way she looked right past all of them and pushed away his talking points with pointed ease. He was surprised to find her so aggressive and subsequently warned the PA guys and his boss that the interview hadn't gone well, that whoever had recommended that he sit down with her should be warned about her—and reprimanded. Seymour Hersh's piece about Abu Ghraib had just come out; she had asked many questions about accountability and the legitimacy of the American example. He was worried about it right up till the piece came out. Every one of those points made it into the article—but in her account of their interview, he'd responded with an air of worldly calm that he did not recall possessing. The PA guys told him he had conducted the model interview. Acknowledged the hard questions and faced them squarely, and tried to contextualize them. They suggested he sit down with the *New York Times* editorial board the next week, and he did. While he was in the city he did the Sunday talk shows, and then that became a regular thing. People were so desperate to see some evidence of calm competence. That became his label.

But in that first interview she had not been patient with his contextualizing. When she'd asked about enhanced interrogation, her cheeks had flushed. She'd looked angry when he'd equivocated about the difference between modes of interrogation and her next question, about the courts martial of Japanese war criminals who had employed the same techniques, had him backpedalling like a sophomore debater.

He could not account for the piece that came out of it. Every time he was congratulated, he became more puzzled. He thought he had hurt his career deeply and had phoned his wife afterward to fret. She soothed him, as she had countless times, irrespective of the details; she always grasped perfectly the essence. He invited Deirdre to his office in Baghdad a week after the article appeared. He did not refer to it and neither did she. He asked her what she was hearing in the street from the Sunnis. Who did they hate more, the Americans or the Shia? It was the first time she had been asked a question by a senior officer. Months later, over breakfast in the airy hotel room in Jerusalem, she'd said as much. That had become another one of his labels: the general who asks more questions than he answers. Every journalist mentioned the habit and assumed it to be an old one.

She'd told him that for the Sunnis, it depended on who was in front of them. You want to be less hated, you have to put your face in front of them as little as possible. He said that could be mistaken for a lack of resolve. She said, "By them? Or by your colleagues?"

"Precisely," he'd said.

He was too disciplined to let the conversation meander too far and anyway he knew how that would be seen. He concluded the discussion and invited her to return to talk any time she thought he might be helpful.

She began getting invitations from his aides to go out on patrols he was accompanying—always in a vehicle other than his. Most of the time they didn't even speak. He was congratulated by his media relations advisers for his press savvy. He got a call from the theatre commander telling him he wished some of his asshat colleagues in the other sectors handled themselves as well.

It was all her. He had given the exact same interview to a dozen other journalists. She was the one who made him sound the way he did. And once that calm competence narrative got started, she propelled it. She changed everything.

❀

Anakopoulus was in line behind Jackson. The general looked distracted and that was fine by Anakopoulus. When he spotted him, his instinct was to go back to his office, but he suppressed it. He was afraid that leaving would call attention to himself.

Another story had come out, up on all the papers' web pages overnight: 101st Airborne troops shooting up a wedding party. Some other joker wearing a body cam. Jesus Christ. Did no one have control of their men?

A body cam? The audio was the worst part. The screams. The shots. The screams ending. Three million YouTube hits in six hours. He'd watched it. Someone will go to jail for that camera, he thought. They'll identify the night and the unit involved and then it will just be a matter of time. Get a list of the names and cross off everyone you see in the shot—then start recording voices and find a match. The moment the guy who made the video saw that it had been released, he would have begun sweating everywhere. Whole days would go by feeling like he was about to pass out. The sound of doors slamming would be terrifying. Every siren would be for him.

❦

And because Deirdre had decided to try to see him right after she had her coffee, while she waited her thoughts turned to Jeremy's rival, Thomas Lattice, whose impact on her life had been just as forceful as Jeremy's. Life-saving, in fact. After she got back from that last night in the hotel in Israel, she had a chance to go on patrol in Sadr City with a Marine rifle company. They had turned a corner onto a narrow street when the ambush erupted. The three men in front of her were shot immediately. The platoon commander called on everyone to withdraw but she was paralyzed by fear and remained huddled beside the body of the man closest to her. She felt his body shaking as more rounds hit him. Then she heard her soldiers returning fire fiercely and her ears rang like a struck steel beam. Something gripped her ankle and she was dragged to the side of the street. She assumed it was someone trying to help her and she wiggled toward them. There were stairs she was dragged down and then a door opened. A basement of some sort.

Inside were tense men speaking Arabic. She was quickly tied with coarse rope that hurt her and she was blindfolded. For the following hour she listened to helicopters and armoured personnel carriers thumping outside. She heard American voices yelling. She tried once to yell back but she was kicked so hard she retched and then a rag was stuffed in her mouth.

There was a lull then. It seemed to her that her soldiers had stopped looking for her. That would be the worst possible development. If the men who held her were able to move her to another place, they would be able to keep her just as long, or as briefly, as they wished. Her Arabic had reached the point that she could understand calmly uttered phrases, but no one in this room was calm. They were much more concerned about the soldiers outside than they were about her, but she agitated them, too. And they wanted no more cause for agitation.

She elected not to reveal that she understood any Arabic. She cried out in English a few times, and she was kicked hard each time she did. "Humanize yourself," she had been taught, in the class. "Speak to them, weep, show emotion." She began sobbing. It was not difficult. Then she was dragged into another room and a door closed behind her.

When the soldiers burst through the street door she fell to the floor as fast as she could. Bullets whistled past her, just over her head, through the space she had just occupied. Then the door to her room was kicked open and she was grabbed and a blast blanket was wrapped around her and she was hustled out into the street. There was a Humvee idling and she was propelled into its back seat and they leapt away.

Beside her was an SF intelligence guy who wanted to know right now, as fast she could tell him, everything she had seen or heard or smelled— everything. And she told him everything. Every couple of moments he stopped to bark things into his cell phone. "It's secure," he said, in reply to her look.

The man in the front passenger seat just stared straight ahead. Did not acknowledge her. Did not look at her. Did not pull his eyes even for one second off the windscreen. Jumped out the passenger door when they slowed for moment, back in the Green Zone. Didn't look back, just walked away fast. Thomas Lattice.

❀

"Could you tell General Lattice that Deirdre O'Malley is here?"

"Hi ma'am," the private-now-sergeant from Bar Harbor said, abandoning the position that he did not know her. "Nice to see you got out of the Suck." It was 0700 and the sky was lightening quickly now.

"Good to see you, too, Sergeant. That's two promotions in three years. Things are going okay for you, aren't they?"

"Well enough, ma'am."

"So is he even around?"

"I can neither confirm nor deny that, ma'am. But I will get him a message."

"You told me you were in KAF at the beginning." He had told her that in Iraq. He had been, like a thousand other men before and since, trying to impress her.

"Yes, ma'am."

"Here at KAF?"

"Taliban's Last Stand, yes, ma'am."

"Strange being back?"

He paused for a long beat. "You get used to the strange, after a while."

"I know. There are problems with that, though."

"If you say so, ma'am."

She looked for the smirk she remembered. It didn't come. She wasn't one of them.

❧

A hundred feet from them, John Wayne was sobbing noiselessly, his head on the table in front of him. His voice was shattered; it was all he could do to whisper. The terp who had been hitting him was spent but still enraged. He had beaten the man so hard for so long that both of them were covered in perspiration and blood, and it wasn't until John Wayne's head was pulled up once again by his hair that you could tell who had been beaten and who had been doing the beating. CIA did the lifting by the hair. Captain Waller leaned into the corner of the sea can and listened for intelligible words. Nothing had been intelligible to him since about ten minutes into the session, the sobbing being pretty much a one-note song.

Every time a fragment of a word was said in Pashto or English, CIA directed the SF terp to ask him to expand. Then it was the SF terp hitting him some more and the CIA officer asking questions. The terp relayed them, but the effort of the beating took nearly everything he had. And anyway, the sobbing required no particular interpretation. It was the first the time the SF terp had been so involved in an interrogation. The CIA guy had been in many of these and sobbing was nothing new to him. It irritated him, because it functioned as a kind of screen to hide behind. The weeping, the despair, the no words at all. The CIA guy stood now, and directed to the terp to stand aside. He adjusted his smock.

The point now wasn't to get him to say anything. The point was to seal the impression they had made. To make the contrast between this and the reasonable man he would meet tomorrow as striking as possible. He wiped and then put away his notepad. He told the terp to go get a shower. He suggested the captain do the same. Captain Waller replied that he would remain. The CIA officer shrugged. He put on a pair of disposable latex gloves and lifted a paddle from his case.

※

Deirdre could hear none of this. She waited for one of the soldiers to either ask her to leave or to invite her in. They remained seated in the same position they'd been in when she arrived. They were experts at making regular army feel unwelcome—a civilian was hardly worth their effort. Had she not known some of these guys in Iraq, she would have already been escorted to the gate. She tried to think of something she could engage them with—but remembered watching them laugh in Iraq at every rookie journalist who tried that. Still.

The door behind the desk opened then and Thomas Lattice walked through it. He seemed unsurprised to see Deirdre there, though no one had phoned anyone since she'd arrived and no one had left. She looked around for CC cameras.

"You harassing my guys, Deirdre?"

"They're like a brick wall, general. You picked them well."

He nodded curtly. "Come this way."

"How long have you been in KAF, now?" Lattice asked when they were settled in his office.

"Couple months."

"Who have you interviewed?"

"A few NCOs, for perspective—the PA guys approved it. A couple of battalion commanders, who said nothing meaningful at all. Some Canadians. Why? Wanna talk?"

He dismissed the suggestion as a joke, waving his fingers. "You filed a good piece about that patrol in the Panjwai the other day. Got a sense of how limited conventional army tactics are here, without saying it in so many words."

He was talking despite himself, she realized. "Those guys I was with wouldn't put it that way."

"Course not. They're still waiting for the Soviets to break out of the Fulda Gap. They think artillery and armour are the keys to dominating a piece of territory."

"Can we get into this a bit more?" she asked, pulling out her notepad.

"No."

"How about the leak?"

"That is a serious business. No war porn in SF. My guys are the real thing. None of them needs photographs to remind them what they're capable of."

"Every division and nearly every brigade in Afghanistan or Iraq seems to be in those files. But so far no SF, you're right."

"We take OPSEC a little more seriously."

"To say the very least."

He almost smiled. "But you know all this."

"I don't know much about the leaker. Are you involved in the search for him?"

"I'm an operational commander. I'm too busy trying to find bad guys to worry about some whiny twenty-one-year-old sharing his war porn with the world. I know it matters. It's serious. But it's not my mission to solve."

"Whose is it?"

"SIGINT. NSA. Your friend's."

Ah. Jeremy. So he knew. Knows. "Will it affect your tactical decisions?"

"You know I'm not going to answer that."

"Okay. Have you seen a change in the population's attitude toward your forces since these videos were made public?"

"I haven't seen evidence of that yet."

"Really? You're more plugged in to local attitudes than any of the regular army guys, aren't you? How could it not have?"

"You heard my answer. But the local liaison officers don't report to me. Maybe ask them, if you need to get the answer you want. Maybe ask the guy who wrote the manual on counter-insurgency."

She set her notepad on her knee and eyed him. "Is there something you're trying to say here, general?" He had not been spoken to like that by anyone in ten years, not since he made colonel, and never by a journalist.

He liked her courage, a little. Not enough to listen to much more of that tone. But he liked it.

"My men and I, we spend less time theorizing."

"I see." She picked up her pad again. "Last time we spoke, you said you thought that industrial armies were obsolete, that mechanized divisions were the battleships of this century. Is that as true here?"

"More."

"Why?"

"It costs a million dollars per soldier per year to put them either here or in Iraq. Twenty billion dollars for an infantry division, with all its bottle washers and mechanics and clerks. Per year. And when regular army gets here it puts up wire and stays behind it mostly, except to go out from time to time and try to find the IEDs the locals planted the night before—by driving over them. No one speaks the local languages. What they know really well is how to fight World War II over again. And if there were a Wehrmacht or a Red Army out there wanting to fight us, that would be fine. But our problems aren't like that anymore. There isn't a front line. Or if there is, it's the wire around the FOBs."

"So the whole army should be SF?"

"Should be multilingual and exceptionally fit and mobile and smart. And organized in much smaller independent units. Able to move and sustain itself anywhere."

"Doesn't someone have to wash the bottles?"

"Here, KBR does it. Have you gone to that coffee shop?"

He knew she had. "Yes."

"Those aren't soldiers making you your coffee."

"They're Pakistanis."

"Exactly."

"Do you approve?"

"Of the Pakistanis or the coffee shop?"

"Either."

"I approve of Pakistanis. They're ferocious. Coffee shops are part of what industrial armies bring with them. They make it easier to stay here, when soldiers should want to get it done, get out and go home."

"SF: men of peace."

"SF: men who get the job done."

"They call you the warrior monk here."

"I don't care what they call me."

"Do you really only drink hot water? Sleep three hours a night?"

"How does any of that matter?"

"What do you think of the president's strategy in Afghanistan?"

"Well, it's gotten worse here. I was here in 2001, as a colonel. We had it settled down."

"Was it Iraq that got in the way?"

"It was incompetence."

"Really?" Meaning: are you sure you want to say that? I'm writing it down. You can see my notepad.

"Of course."

"At what level?"

"At the level where the decisions were made that let the Taliban leadership escape through Tora Bora, let them regroup in Pakistan, to not control the border, to not learn the local languages and customs and become a part of these communities, to stay in our convoys and drive sixty miles an hour through the villages. To run over their kids and buy the silence of aggrieved parents and the co-operation of corrupt tribal chiefs with dollars instead of deeds."

"What should be done differently?"

"Watch this space."

"How is Mary, if I may ask? You've been deployed for what, seven straight years now?"

"Mrs. Lattice," he said, correcting her, "knows what it is to be a soldier's wife. She does a lot of volunteer work with one of the veterans' support organizations—Fallen Fighters."

"Runs it, actually, doesn't she?"

"She's the CEO, yes."

"And founder?"

"Along with Sherry Jackson," he said, deadpan. *Fucker.* She had forgotten about that. And she'd walked right into it. Jeremy's wife was not a subject she wanted to discuss. "But she's not so involved anymore," he added.

It was a famous story, about how the two women, intimate friends at the start of the decade, became antagonists as their husbands were promoted. By the time the husbands each had their own divisions, their wives refused to speak to one another. Deirdre had met Jeremy's wife once, when she'd visited Baghdad at Christmas. Deirdre felt an ache in her gut when she thought of Sherry. Guilt. Jealousy. Anger.

Lattice was playing with her and was so accustomed to having people submit to him that he was surprised for the second time when she asked him if she could go out on patrol with him.

"Our patrols are very, very difficult."

"I'm up to it, General."

"Are you?"

"You know I am." Meaning, she had covered Lattice's execution of her own rescue at length. She did the first interview about it as she was being driven back to the Green Zone. It had helped Lattice. Tit for tat.

"My men will be in touch," he said, smiling. And then he stood and walked out one of the room's two doors. She finished the note she was making and then tried the knob of the door he had just walked through. It was locked. She tried the other one. It led back to the office she'd been waiting in. The sergeant from Bar Harbor nodded at her. "Lawson here will show you to the gate, ma'am."

"Thank you."

And then she was back on Screaming Eagle Way and making her way to the Green Beans, still wondering what the hell had just happened and whether Lattice meant it when he said she could accompany him on a patrol. His offer was unprecedented and would make his PA staff, who spent their time refusing to elaborate and declining interview requests, howl. But she knew that he would not allow himself to be seen to be overruled. She would be available the moment he offered.

❈

Rashid stepped away from the espresso machine when Amr emerged from the back of the shop. He had been working for fourteen hours and was glad to be relieved. Already it was hot, though, too hot to sleep, and so he did not immediately make his way to his bed. He sat on a stool at the back of the service area, winning an annoyed glance from Amr as the older man set about making the coffee orders he had taken. Mohammed emerged, too, and began clearing the tables and carrying orders to those waiting.

Between them, Amr and Mohammed served the customers quickly, and as the morning rush settled into a more manageable rhythm, Mohammed came into the back to wash cups. He looked at Rashid, still sitting and yawning, and said, in English, "How did you like your film the other night?"

Rashid did not immediately register that he had been spoken to—Mohammed hardly ever said a word to him. Then he looked up at the boy and smiled. "*Fight Club*? It was a bit of a surprise."

"Had you seen it before?"

"Yes."

"So you knew what was in it."

"Yes."

"Do you find that interesting? Helena Bonham Carter and her shame?"

Rashid laughed. "Who are you quoting?"

When Mohammed did not reply, Rashid continued, "Helena Bonham Carter is always interesting. At the very least."

Amr shot him a searing look then and Rashid got up and went to his bed.

The coarse woollen blanket was itchy in the heat and he could not sleep. He nevertheless closed his eyes and pretended to, if only to avoid being given a task. These moments when he first got off shift, when Rami Issay was still sleeping, were the only empty minutes in his schedule. He found them distressing. They allowed him to remember.

This morning he replayed the moment when he was told that his student visa had been revoked. He had foreseen most of what would happen, at least in outline. Ms Johnson, the woman who called him at the rooming house, was efficient and crisp. She told him when he had to be out of the country. No, she was not privy to the reasons behind the revocation, she said, in a tone that asked at the same time, "Are you kidding?" The holes in Lower Manhattan were still smoking.

He tried to ask whether the decision was final, but his voice broke and she told him good day. He slipped down the wall where the telephone was mounted, the handset still against his ear. He did not weep. But he bit on his lower lip so hard he tasted blood. He knew precisely how his father would respond. His mother's dismay. He would not be able to live in his parents' house again. He would be on his own in Islamabad, a city he had so scorned on leaving that it would be certain to punish him.

This is what he thought about when there was nothing else to occupy him, which was why he tried so hard to remain occupied. He was to have started his master's in electrical engineering at MIT that autumn. And now, for no reason known to him, he was on the American no-fly list and apparently the subject of ISI interest in Pakistan. There was no engineering career ahead of him. That future was gone. He had tried to conduct himself as if it wasn't. When he got back to Pakistan he went to his father's house and he was told that he would have to pay back the money he had been given to live in America, that whatever he'd done to bring this upon himself was his responsibility and that he had shamed his whole family in squandering such an opportunity. No, he could not stay there. They wanted no visits from the police and, anyway, there was a new baby brother in their already crowded home.

Rashid had wept then, as he left that house, thick globular tears running down his cheeks like the New England summer rainstorms he remembered from his time in Boston. It was the first time he had cried since he was twelve. That night he slept in an alleyway among street children. One of them showed him a knife. He resolved to approach his situation like a difficult chess problem. The disadvantage was the essence of the problem. He needed to find the best possible response, and in finding it, win. He didn't completely convince himself. But as he wrapped his arms around his knees and shivered, it was how he decided to behave, going forward.

The chance to come to KAF solved several problems at once. It represented a place to live; after a few nights of improvised sleeping situations, that seemed more important than he could have anticipated. The pay was modest, but there was an advance, which he gave to his father, prompting no words of thanks or acknowledgement. His anger at his son was undiminished. One more reason to get away.

There was a rudimentary security check, but Rashid bought the papers of one of the poor boys he'd met in the street for a few American dollars and the boy's background was desperate enough to have been largely unverifiable.

But, as in chess, bold solutions to difficult problems only rarely pan out. This life here in Kandahar was as empty as anything he could imagine. Even making fun of Rami Issay was no longer very interesting. Rashid let out a long sigh and rolled over in his hot and lumpy bed. It was like sleeping on a burlap-covered corpse. Where was this going to end?

❀

Lattice drew back the curtain on the one-way mirror and watched the interrogation of John Wayne. Protocol was that interrogators were to be made aware when they were being observed but this was Lattice's turf and CIA is not SF. Waller, the intelligence officer, remained sitting in the corner. He had been up all night. Speckles of blood were on his cheeks. The terp had stopped speaking long ago. The CIA officer refused to let him collapse. He had tied the man to the chair and pulled his head back by his hair.

"Just tell me who you got the files from. Then you can sleep. We'll clean you up and you can go back to work and forget this ever happened."

He did not answer.

"Wake up!" the CIA guy yelled, and slapped him across the face.

John Wayne was not asleep and he was not unconscious. It was clear that he would not be going back to work. He had decided he was going to be killed. When the Americans were done with him they would give him to the NDS, the Afghan security service. And then he would die, either immediately or in a cell, in Sarpoza in a few months or years. Everyone knew about the NDS. Everyone knew about Sarpoza.

Lattice knew something about Captain Waller. Ex-SF sergeant. In Waller's impassive face, Lattice correctly read disgust at what was happening in front of him. He recognized the response. He decided to keep a careful eye on Waller.

❀

Rami Issay walked into the base adjutant's office and waited for his clerk to acknowledge him. The clerk was on the telephone and several minutes passed. Finally, he looked up. "Yes?"

"I would like to speak to the base adjutant, please."

"Do you have an appointment?"

"No, but he told me to drop by and talk to him the next time I wanted to have an event."

"Who are you?"

"Rami Issay. I run the Green Beans coffee shop."

"What sort of event do you want to have?"

"Forgive me, but are you the adjutant?"

"No, but I can take your name and see if the adjutant will grant you an appointment."

"General Jackson told me to work things out with the adjutant."

Long stare. "I'll see if he is in."

"I think you know very well whether he is in."

"Just a minute, please. Sir."

The clerk got up and opened a panelled door and closed it behind him. A few minutes later he re-emerged. "This way, please."

Rami Issay followed him into the office where Major Horner sat behind a large desk. Rami Issay put his heels together and stood at attention. "Good morning, sir."

Horner looked up from his computer. "Are you mocking me?"

"Goodness no, sir."

"Then stop that, please."

"Yessir."

Horner rolled his eyes. "General Jackson's chief of staff asked me to keep an eye out for you. Now what is this about?"

"I would like to undertake a morale-improvement initiative, sir."

"Please stop sirring me. What kind of initiative?"

"A chess tournament, sir."

"Will there be gambling?"

"Goodness gracious no, sir."

"Well, I don't see why you would even need to ask permission to hold a chess tournament. Do you?"

"Yessir, I mean nosir."

"Good heavens, man, calm yourself. Please sit down."

"Thank you, sir." Sitting.

Horner fell silent for a long minute. Then he asked, "Do you know what reality television is?"

"Nature documentaries?"

"No. Shows where there is a contest of some sort. *The Amazing Race. Survivor.*"

"I'm afraid I am not familiar with such shows."

"It doesn't matter. There's going to be one shot here at KAF. It strikes me that you and your café should be a part of it, lend some local colour."

"What is this show?"

"They're calling it *Stars Earn Stripes.* Good title, huh? Celebrities and ex-SF dudes, attempting heroic and difficult feats."

"Which celebrities?

"Nick Lachey. Todd Palin."

"I am not familiar with these people, sir."

"The American public is."

"What will they be doing?"

"Demonstrating their skill at arms and their courage."

"Are any of them soldiers?"

"Some are ex-soldiers. Still."

"This is to boost morale in America about the war?"

"You'd think the facts about the Taliban would suffice, but they don't. So, yes. I'll tell you what. I'll help you with your chess tournament if you help me with the TV shoot."

"But I, sir, am no ex-soldier or American action TV star."

"Don't worry, the producers will find your café interesting. And there might be a contest of some sort you could play a part in. A Know Your Enemy quiz, or something like that."

"I am not America's enemy, sir."

"I know. Just thinking aloud."

"Have you been to my café?"

"Your café?"

"The Green Beans beside the flight line."

"I didn't realize it was yours."

"Well, I run it. We have chess sets now. We've started a film series."

"Why?"

"To make life better here for all the lonely people."

"Why does that matter to you?"

"I'm just trying to do my part."

"For the mission?"

Rami Issay looked around the spartan office. Flag. Portrait of General Jackson on the wall. Metal bookcase in one corner. Field manuals and boxes of preprinted forms. He felt an enormous sense of fatigue. He felt it rise and then with all his strength, he fought it down. "No sir."

Horner's eyebrows rose.

"For America."

"What do you mean?"

"You aren't really trying to win a fight here. You're trying to sell something, right? An idea about how to live. I'm trying to show that idea. As are, perhaps, your television colleagues."

"Thank you, Mr. Issay. You may go. I'll be in touch."

CHAPTER TWELVE

The platoon walked slowly and carefully. The intel had been unusually specific that day, about the level of threat and its nature. They had seen drone footage of men planting IEDs and of them being summarily dispatched by Hellfire missiles, their colleagues emerging from the ditches moments later to pull the wounded to cover. In the meantime, new digging happened up and down the same road. Surely the insurgents all understood that those new bombs had been seen, too? The order had come down to shut off movement on that road until the engineers cleared it with counter-blasts. It had been closed for two days, but now the road was considered safe.

The question the soldiers had asked themselves as they listened to the intel briefing was why? What made it worth it to the Taliban to lose men to close the road for a couple of days? The intel officer didn't answer immediately. Then he said, "We can't see evidence of large enemy formations moving through the area. As far as we can tell, these were all local actors."

It hadn't been a wholly satisfactory response. Trying a little harder, he offered, "They are not us. And more to the point, we are not them. We do not feel about this land the way they do. What makes it worth fighting at all, and taking the wrong end of a 100:1 kill ratio? We're here building schools." He was twenty-six years old and had a degree in Middle Eastern studies. He had learned Pashto at his fancy college with the intention of coming here. He was an object of mockery among the troops, considered at once too thoughtful and completely out of touch. The sentence he had just uttered did not help him on that score and he was smart enough to know it. "They take their directions from their leaders. And every local commander needs to be seen to be fighting us, as much as they do actually fight us. Not just for their superiors, but for every farmer in the valley who hears the IED go off."

Fortin indicated that the briefing was over then. And the men stood up. The intel officer gathered his notes up and left. The men lifted their weapons and made their way to the departure point. It was late afternoon.

That was four hours earlier, Deirdre calculated. After her meeting with Lattice, she had had run to catch her helicopter out to the FOB where she met the platoon. She had been looking forward to talking to John Wayne and when she realized a different terp, calling himself Joe, had taken his place, she wondered where he had gone. Normally they kept a terp with one unit, to build trust and cohesion. The new terp would not utter a single word about John Wayne. He had gotten drunk, then, or got in a fight. Or something more serious. When she asked Joe if he'd be back, he told her she'd have to ask someone other than him. Maybe a soldier. That alarmed Deirdre and interested her. Terps love to gossip about each other's petty crimes as much as soldiers do. If it had been a fistfight or drinking, he would tell her.

By now they had covered twelve klicks. They'd walked past one huge crater that the engineers had left. Apparently there were plans to pave the road, with a view to making the business of concealing IEDs more difficult.

"It would cost ten million dollars a mile here," a master corporal from Manitoba said. "More, if you have to fly in the asphalt."

"Why would you do that?" a corporal from BC asked.

"'Cause the roads are so dangerous."

"Apparently we don't understand the big picture."

"Shut the fuck up back there and watch your arc," Fortin said.

Walking on more quietly now. The eucalyptus trees shone silver in the heat. The soldiers could smell them even more strongly than they could smell themselves.

Fortin watched his men sweating and worried. This was a short day patrol but no one was carrying much less than thirty kilos of gear and ammunition. None of them would complain about the discomfort, but even as the sweat darkened their uniform pants, the backs of their heads moved less and he knew that if he could see their eyes they would be less alert than they had been. He could not make it less hot. Heat is hard.

Up in the mountains, the problem had mostly been keeping everyone warm, which meant keeping them dry, which meant not letting everyone's combats get this soaked with sweat. No one would have to sleep in their clothes this night. They should be back to the base by midnight. It was an unusual luxury to be based so close to KAF, with hot showers and fresh eggs whenever you could get in. An unusual luxury that had only been prompted by the proximity of the enemy to the main base. Which was itself concerning. But still—fresh eggs. Showers.

He rechecked their weapon discipline for the hundredth time. They were good soldiers and they had trained hard. Even the men who had multiple tours in knew better than to think they had it all figured out. And so he needed to bark at no one. They all faced where they were supposed to be facing and held their weapons carefully and did the drill perfectly. Problem was, this wasn't a drill. He would have preferred less precision and just a bit of loose nervous tension. But nervous tension is exhausting. And heat like this anaesthetizes.

His young lieutenant did not understand these nuances. The men were following the SOPs and he was reassured by that order and precision. Until you've seen men shattered in front of you, you find the drills reassuring. Fear submits to familiarity. Death doesn't. Death revels in routine. Every successful ambush depends on it.

As they walked, Deirdre kept at the new terp. He would not say anything more about John Wayne but she found out that he was from a village to the east. Yes, he spoke Pashto, of course. Yes, he had been a terp for a while. He wasn't sure how long. Time kind of ran together here, had she noticed that?

❀

The first shot threw Sergeant Kyle Wilson on his back. Too loud, too powerful to be anything but a 12.7-mm round. When it roared out at them, the report and the sound of bullet hitting body armour came right on top of one another. There was the briefest instant when the platoon looked at Wilson uncomprehendingly, before going to ground themselves. In that beat, automatic weapons fire lit up from the tree lines along the road on either side: AKs and at least a couple of belt-fed weapons. It wasn't obvious until they hit the ground who had been thrown there and who had thrown themselves. Rivulets of blood ran from arms and legs and heads. Wilson did not move. The lieutenant, ten yards ahead of Fortin, was on the ground, leaking brains from his ear. Fortin began barking. "Robinson! Get that Minimi on that treeline. Bring up the GPMG! Who has an M-50? Vadaboncour, put a rocket over there. Who else has one?!" And then, more clearly but just as urgently, and into the radio: "Niner, this is Red Team Alpha. Contact, wait, out."

Gunfire erupted from their hastily formed perimeter in an almost continuous roar of automatic rifles and machine guns and rockets. The light machine guns ran their fire expertly, a foot above the dirt at the tree-line. Lopez put his M-50 rocket into a likely looking hollow. The saplings on the treeline opposite fell as if scythed. Within a few moments a cloud of fine dust had been thrown up so dense that nothing could be seen beyond the patch of dirt they lay upon. Fortin gestured to stop firing. The cacophony petered out over the following ten seconds. Everyone's ears rang. The air was so still the dust just hung there. When the echoes of the last shots finally faded, all that could be heard was nothing.

Deirdre was on her side, gasping. A bullet had hit her backpack as she had thrown herself down and pierced her water bottle. At first she thought she was bleeding but then she realized the liquid all over her was too cool to be blood. The dead lieutenant's brains had sprayed out in a plume behind him and she had bloody grey goo on her neck. She lifted herself a little and looked around.

The deep breaths of the wounded men rose up in the stillness. The medA leopard-crawled over to the platoon commander first, and established that he had been head shot and was pulseless. Wordlessly, he made his way up to Wilson, who was coughing red foam and moaning. The medA pulled off his body armour and found the entrance hole under his left armpit. The exit hole took up most of his right armpit. A sucking chest wound, but with not enough chest left to seal. It was amazing he was still breathing. He wouldn't be for long. The medA cut open his sleeve and injected twenty milligrams of morphine into his shoulder. Then he moved on to the next bleeding man, a corporal from Regina, who took an AK round in his lower belly. Feces leaking through a quarter-sized exit wound in his side. Breathing easily. Pulse strong. Not in shock, but pissed off. More morphine. He'd need a laparotomy and a colostomy in KAF, but he looked like he'd be okay. One other man had been shot through the forearm. He cradled it on his chest as he lay on his back. His arm was a mess, dangling from where his elbow had been. Might need an amputation at the elbow—it was hard to say. The surgeons hated amputating anything, and hardly did it anymore, so long as there was something to graft and fixate. There was a bright arterial bleeder in the shattered limb and so the medA put a tourniquet on his upper arm. More morphine. He bent a splint into shape and tied it above and below the wound. He crawled over to the sergeant major. "The lieutenant is dead and Wilson will be soon. The other two will live, I think."

Fortin nodded. "I'll get a medevac in as soon as it's safe."

The medA crawled back to the wounded men. Deirdre fished her notebook out of her pocket and began scribbling.

Fortin crept to the position perimeter and lifted his binoculars, looking through the grass. Along the treeline he saw broken saplings and rocket craters but no signs of men. He got on the radio and raised the company commander. The news of the casualties, and especially the loss of the platoon commander introduced a particular focus to the exchange. Nothing like emotion was betrayed. When Fortin requested air assets, he was told fast air was already en route. They had drone imagery up already, but could not discern whether there were combatants in the treeline. Fast air would settle the matter in a moment.

The pair of A-10s came into view a moment later. He rang off from his company commander. The lead pilot of the A-10s raised him a moment later and he described where the firing positions had been. The A-10s circled around twice and then they approached low and slow, along the treeline. When they were five hundred yards away their 30-mm cannons lit up the road with the shriek.

A 30-mm round is the size of a thick dill pickle, packed with explosive. Individually, their concussions have would have been a little less powerful than that of a grenade. But these cannons fire at a rate of four thousand rounds a minute. The roar stretched into one long, basso profundo note. Four thousand beats a minute. Faster than a hummingbird's heart.

The platoon's fusillade had shredded the saplings at the start of the firefight. Now thigh-sized trees fell stupidly, in all directions, shedding leaves and tendrils of their shattered trunks as they pitched into the dirt. The road was impassable within seconds. The roar of the cannons competed with that of the jet engines; the summation of the two represented more noise than humans could actually hear. The men covered their ears with their hands and felt the dirt under their chests rippling. Deirdre thought that, as painful it was to be in the vicinity of this attack, to have been the object of it must be unthinkable. The combat she had seen in Iraq had been mostly urban where air power was less useful.

It was the least of the differences between the Afghanistan and Iraq wars, she would have conceded, already writing the lede to her piece. Urban, rural. Nationalist, Tribal. Secular, religion-addled. Rocky, sandy. No oil, oil. *And here, we're losing*, she added to herself, really realizing it for the first time. She lifted her hands from her ears as the aircraft finished their run and rose high into the air, the roar of their engines fading as they climbed.

She listened, then, for the sounds of dying men in the broken trees, but all she could hear was her own ears ringing. And the two wounded men near her moaning, and the A-10s, climbing and circling and getting ready to come back again. She hunched down into the dirt and pulled her helmet tightly down, as she covered her ears.

This time the A-10s came in even lower. The earth shook so hard that dust rose from the ground immediately under them and most of the men were coughing even before the cannons opened up. And they did open up and the whole earth erupted in man-high dirt geysers, shrapnel flying like sideways hail. She felt steel splinters bounce off the Kevlar of her helmet so hard and so many times she tried to crawl up inside it.

And then they were gone.

Fortin designated some of the men—all new guys or reservists—to remain with the dead and wounded; he formed everyone else into an assault party, and prepared to advance to the treeline. The belt-fed weapons—the 5.56-mm Minimis and the 7.62-mm GPMG—opened up, splintering the splinters further, atomizing wood into a pale haze of dust and cellulose. After a minute he halted them, then sent the platoon across in sections, the soldiers diving into the trees and searching for evidence of the enemy. After a moment they found a man, a boy, really, lying on his back and coughing up bloody froth. His smock was a mat of congealing blood. Beside him was an RPG. He had had no rifle, or it had been taken. He looked at the soldier who found him with wide eyes, and mumbled something between coughs. The terp was brought up. He knelt beside the boy and asked him something in Pashto. The boy replied in a couple of short phrases. The terp said something else. The boy looked away. Fortin asked the terp what the boy had said.

"He said, 'Please don't leave me here.'"

The platoon had by now stretched out along the ambush site, crawling through downed trees and branches. There were no other bodies alive or dead. When the terp asked the boy how many men he been with, he just looked away. Deirdre had by now caught up with them. She asked Fortin, "Can I take his picture?"

"No, ma'am."

"Okay." She put her camera away.

Fortin got on the radio and spoke in crisp, controlled words to the OPS O at KAF. A drone was in the vicinity now and they could see the platoon alongside the road, and the men guarding the wounded. "Can you see any enemy?" Fortin asked. There was a long pause.

"Affirmative. Wait out." Then, a long minute later, "We have twelve personnel in traditional garb headed north and away from your position." A moment later, "They appear to be armed."

"Can you deal with them, or shall I pursue?"

"Wait." Then, "We can target them."

"Roger."

Fortin looked up and down the narrow road. He saw nothing. Deirdre had positioned herself behind him, keeping out of his field of vision, but close enough to hear everything. He did not pay her any attention. "McLeod! Get your men under cover! Everyone away from the road!" The men began crawling into the trees. Then they heard an explosion about a kilometre north of them. A black cylindrical cloud rose slowly into the sky. The radio squawked: "The enemy appear to have been destroyed."

"What is their location?"

"Grid reference: two three niner eight four eight."

"Roger. Will investigate." Eight hundred metres north-northwest of where they were.

"Understood."

"We need a medevac for my wounded."

"Roger that."

Fortin crawled through the treeline until he came to the field on the other side. He could see a smoke and dust plume at the northern extremity of the field. The platoon advanced along the edge cautiously, pausing frequently to listen. It was very quiet. When they reached the far corner, they could see the crater the Hellfire missile had made.

He set up flanking positions on either side of the explosion site. Then he sent in alpha squad. McLeod radioed back a few minutes later. "Objective secured. Not much moving here."

When Fortin got there, Deirdre trailing close behind, he saw McLeod facing away from the impact site, scanning for threats. Excellent. A less experienced squad leader would have been preoccupied with what was before him.

Which was twelve shattered men, who had bunched up as they had been preparing to cross open land, making a perfect target. Their weapons were strewn around a hundred foot radius. Shining bloody bone jutted out of trousers and brains out of skulls. An older man carrying a radio, possibly the commander, had been eviscerated. Deirdre began taking photographs. She forgot to ask permission. No one said anything to her.

Two men were still breathing. Adults, at least, this time. Beards as thick as brown brambles. One man's femur made a seventy-degree angle in his mid-thigh. The soldiers removed the AK-47s and the RPGs the dead and wounded had been carrying and piled them a few paces from the impact crater.

⚛

Deirdre photographed the shattered Taliban one after the other. The wounded men looked up at her, embarrassed at being seen in such a state by a woman. They covered their eyes with their arms. She moved on. The dead were mostly quite young. Farmers' sons, presumably sent to fight in lieu of the parent. The oldest were two men who could have been in their thirties, and she photographed these with particular care. They were hardly marked—the explosion had tossed them twenty feet from the impact area—and looks of nearly comic surprise were etched on their immobile faces. Deirdre had seen men dead of blast injuries before. IED dead were often unmarked and were unnerving to look at. She wondered what that felt like, to have a shock wave passing through you, scrambling your insides until all was hemorrhaging mush. Did that kind of death take long?

If she were to be killed, she would prefer being shot. Bullets were honest in their bloody piercing. No mysterious startled looks with intact skin containing a pulped interior. She would want the means of her own death to be apparent. These perfectly intact but lifeless bodies had an obscene absurdity about them that repelled her.

The platoon divided the enemy's weapons into twenty-kilogram bundles and distributed them among themselves. The intelligence guys had asked that any recovered weapons be brought to them. There was some question of recently manufactured Chinese weaponry entering the country and they wanted to establish how significant an issue this was. Then the soldiers turned and made their way quickly and carefully back to the men they had left at the ambush site. As they headed out, Deirdre looked back to the wounded Taliban. One of them waved. She waved back. Sergeant Major Fortin gave her a glance that required no verbal elaboration.

When they got back, the wounded were still alive, though the gut-shot man was pallid and losing consciousness. The medic told Fortin he needed to get to a surgeon immediately. Deirdre took her place in the centre of the defensive perimeter. She could see a farm in the distance that she hadn't noticed before. There was no movement visible in or around it. The family would have retreated inside the moment they heard the first shot. Some of the young men she had just watched die might have grown up there.

In the distance, the sound of helicopters. Then they were visible. Two Chinooks and two Apache escorts. The Apaches circled around the position, hovering and inspecting, before drawing back and allowing the Chinooks in. When the Chinooks landed, the rear doors gaped open and medAs ran from them.

Deirdre was pushed into the helicopter as soon as all the wounded were aboard. The platoon collapsed its perimeter as if it had been inhaled by the great noisy beast, and then they were all aloft and on their way back to KAF.

The Chinook settled down on the tarmac a hundred metres from the Green Beans. An ambulance drove up the moment the helicopter was stationary. The back doors opened and the medics carried the stretchers down the ramp and into the ambulances. Deirdre thought about the Taliban fighters they had left to bleed to death in the dirt. Then she thought about the schoolteachers who had been lined up and shot outside their school in the Panjwai the week before. She hoped the men lying out in that field now were the men who had shot the teachers.

There were medical officers with the ambulances, and they immediately set to inserting more IVs and running in saline. They had blood waiting for the wounded. They moved in an urgent and precise way that reminded the soldiers not at all of their chaotic crises. No one was shooting at the doctors. Within seconds the ambulances were headed off to the hospital, whose ambulance bay opened up to the flight line. The soldiers watched the ambulances back into the bay and then the whole hospital seemed to vibrate, lines of men and women moving to surround each ambulance.

The soldiers lined up on the flight line and walked off together to their after-action debriefing, with the young intel officer from the fancy university. Deirdre turned left when the rest of them turned right and walked to the gate leading to the base. She needed a shower and then she had a piece to write. She noticed bit of flesh on her arm—someone's skin and fat. She brushed it off. She took two more steps toward her room. Then she stopped and leaned over, her hands on her knees. And tears welled up and ran down her face noiselessly. Soldiers walked past her on both sides. They looked at her with concern and embarrassment but did not approach her.

After a long minute she straightened up and carried on.

CHAPTER THIRTEEN

Green Beans café, KAF

Rashid Siddiqui

Once again, it was impossible to sleep. The heat made every bit of my body that touched the wool blankets sting. The smell of the man who had slept in my bunk before me was pure ammonia—I think he slept about as much as I did. And then the Apaches and A-10s started taking off all at once. Something had happened out in the desert, presumably.

Never mind, there are things that needed doing anyway. Rami Issay is intent on recapitulating the *Fight Club* fiasco and wants me to pick the film for next week.

I wonder if Captain Tom Allan, officer commanding, Ramstein Base Cinema, as he titles himself in his correspondence, has any more intention of sending us what we ask for this time than he did last time. Oh, one mustn't get paranoid. Mistakes happen, and after all, it might not be the most fastidious souls who, in the middle of two wars, are attached to the base cinema.

So *Magnolia*. Umm, no. Not the right film for an outside show. *Pan's Labyrinth*? Okay, he's having us on. At least we're clear about that. *Borat*? Well, he has a sense of humour. *The Departed*? No. Too much dialogue. *Rambo: First Blood*? Could the same person have recommended this as the earlier movies? *Kill Bill: Vol. 2*. Possibly. *Pulp Fiction*.

Pulp Fiction! Dialogue heavy, to say the least, but lots of action, too. And Uma Thurman. This could work.

Rami Issay would have to agree, of course. He probably would, though. He has hardly been in the café for the last few days, so busy with getting the approvals for the chess tournament. And he claims some sort of television crew is coming to interview him about his attempts to lighten the lives of the brave soldiers here. No doubt, I shall be organizing that too.

Was he ever so happy running his curry shop in Leeds? Or his computer sales network, whatever that was, in Islamabad? I doubt it. Those were situations grounded in reality, and men like Rami Issay do not prosper faced with taxes that must actually be paid and competitors who work harder than they fantasize. War is unreal in a way that resonates with fabulists like him. So long as the general continues to find this café amusing, there will be no other opening across the street from it. It's the perfect arena for a man of his talents. Talent.

I have to spend more time thinking about what I am doing. My contract will be up in a year and the question is, were I to leave, where would I go? I am three-quarters of an engineer, persona non grata in America and a subject of interest to the secret police in my homeland. A return to Pakistan is not attractive to me and I may board no western aircraft, receive no western visas—all for reasons that cannot be discussed with me. Never mind, it is what I must face. The question is, what next? I must not get trapped by entropy here in this coffee shop. Next thing you know you're thirty and your life's trajectory is set. Next thing you know, you're Rami Issay.

Mohammed Hashto

Rashid is an impure boy. He helped Rami Issay, who is also impure, show that movie with the shameful women, Helena Bonham Carter. Rashid and Rami Issay are supposed to be faithful Muslims and they are not. They spend too much time with the ferenghee and care for nothing but their approval. Rashid lived among them too long, I think, in America. And Rami Issay lived for a long time in Britain. The ferenghee bring only death. Before the Americans came, there was no war here. It was like in Pakistan. People grew their crops, fed their children, went to weddings and studied the Holy Book. Why can't it be like that again? I want to go home so badly I can't think about anything else. These people are not my friends. They are impure. The only faithful men here are Fazil and maybe Amr. Though Amr struggles, too.

As I do. I like Just Amachai, for one. But she is an unbeliever and she works in that shop of hers and I am told that what goes on there is wicked. Prostitution is an abomination to Allah. It is adultery and involves things that must only happen between men and their wives. Why would she do this?

As I learn more about my faith, I understand that the righteous life is a strict one. And that the devil wears a pretty face sometimes. She seems so kind. But you must look at the whole of someone's actions. If they cannot honour God then how can they honour your friendship? "Do not mix with the ungodly," the religious men say, "and understand that they may not announce their ungodliness to you, for that is Satan's way."

I was shown a hadith about this yesterday and I thought of Just Amachai and then I wept. To me she does not seem wicked. Is everyone who does not appear wicked, wicked? Is my teacher wicked? Maybe Rashid is in truth holy, because he does not pretend to be? There would be a long list of holy people around here, if that is the way it works. It cannot be. We must use our eyes and our ears, even if they may be deceived. For what else are we to use to look upon Allah's wonders? To listen to them? To think about them?

Just Amachai

That boy has such light in his eyes. Short and quick and with a shock of black hair as thick and upright as a shoe brush. He moves like he thinks every critical eye is upon him. He is so quick to smile when he discerns tenderness. Constantly I have to stop myself from touching him.

These days he is trying to figure out his religion and is full of powerful feelings. His adult person is bursting out like a lily. He thinks for himself and this is where the turbulence comes from. Most people just accept what they're told and pray for prosperity. His adolescent sincerity is what reminds me so much of my own boy. They would enjoy one another, I think.

Any day now he will start falling in love with girls and women. He should get back to his home village—this is an unnatural place for him to be at this age, with no girls and only a few women around. Me and the other masseuses. The nurses from the hospital, the women soldiers. No other children.

This is a childless place. Except in the hospital, I suppose, where the wounded children are brought. But there are no children walking these roads, playing, laughing. Maybe I have stayed long enough. I have made some money and it is time to go back to my son. My parents are kind but they belong to another century and my son must learn about this one. With the money I have made here, he can go to secondary school and university, if he gets in. It is tempting to stay a few more months and put a bit more away. But every day I stay is another I will not spend with my boy. I must make some decisions, I think. No doubt my supervisor, the Russian woman, will make it difficult to leave. But the Americans oblige the employers to get us home when we are finished working. I must time it so no pay is owing to me when I tell her I am done working here.

If only I could take the boy back home. I could send him to school, I could find him a mosque to attend. It is a daydream, I know. But he is trying to make his way in this world without a family and it seems so unfair. He just wants to be loved and to be safe. I would love him and I would keep him safe.

I have been away from my own family far too long. This will have to be my last month here. I don't care if they do keep some of my pay. I will tell my employers today.

Deirdre O'Malley

That ambush messed me up. More than it should have. Ever since getting off the Chinook that brought us home I've felt like I'm swimming in clear jelly. It was the first time that the war here felt dangerous to me, in the way that Iraq was, continuously and unpredictably. Was I like this there? Anxious and rattled and unable to sleep? At the end I was, I guess. After the abduction. Was that why Kenwood sent me here? For a fucking break?

It's not like I even got scratched. I do need a new pack. But that's happened before. What I can't stop wondering is what it would take to break the will of the Taliban. They took twelve dead, against two dead and two wounded. And they had all the advantages. We walked into an *ambush*.

No matter how resolved they are, though, the Taliban can't sustain a loss ratio like that any more than the Iraqi insurgents could. I heard from Lattice's aide-de-camp this morning. They're going out on a long patrol in three days and I can come along. He was cryptic about where we'd be going or even how I should pack. "I suggest you prepare for all eventualities, ma'am. We'll go through your pack before we leave, and prune what needs pruning."

I wonder what Jeremy will think about this. He's bound to see whatever I write. I'd let him know, but we have hardly spoken. A handful of nods across rooms at press conferences and a couple of crossed paths around the base. He'll have an opinion. He'll think I'm being manipulated—or set up. He'll think it's an effort to get at him, narcissist that he is. But the senior generals are all that way. They're easy to love, these people with the light inside them. The rest of us deep-sea creatures move toward it by reflex. Which serves their purposes.

I could use some of the Thai woman's equanimity. I could use a massage. She must be tired of being here. The only person she talks to here is the boy. She puts up walls for the same reason I do, I think. The difference is that I need to be able to open those walls from time to time in order to do my job, and she really doesn't.

Still, look at her. Such perfect posture as she sits in the corner with her tea and looks out the window. She looks completely at peace with herself and the world. I want that. When she notices me, what does she see? Frenetic journalist-bitch, typing fast or reading her email, glowering at people who sit down with her uninvited. No one is ever invited. When she wonders what I am doing here, what I want to achieve, what does she guess? That I am ambitious and aggressive. That I keep colleagues away, for reasons she, as a woman, understands. That I submerge my loneliness in work.

How is she not lonely, too?

Fazil Palwasha

The Thai woman should just leave the boy alone. She is not his mother and even if she were, he is too old to be treated the way she treats him. He should respect her and be kind to her but not familiar with her. He has not made the progress he needs to. I will speak to him about it.

I myself am sounding like his father. I am not his father, he has no father. He has become his own father. And Amr, evidently, his uncle. They play chess constantly. Three or four games a day. I would say that time should be spent more productively, but how exactly would that be? Those two work harder than any of the rest of us.

It is such a strange bubble we all find ourselves in. Cappuccino and streusel muffins and mocha frappes. This will only go on so long. I will work here while I am able. It is humiliating but I am making more money for my family here than I would be selling magazines on the street in Islamabad. I am being excessive. I would not sell magazines in the street—they prefer boys for that, anyway. But my prospects are limited at home. The problem is my children. I must not allow them to go astray in the manner of the boy here. My wife has them going to a good school and they go to the mosque often; I spoke to the Imam before I came here. He will watch over them and their instruction. My brothers will also help. But they need their father, too. They don't matter as much to anyone else as they do to me.

What I wish my co-workers to understand is that they should not be envied, these ferenghee among us. They are not happy. They are far from home and they miss their children, too. They are rich—there is no denying this. But listen closely to their explanations for why they have come here and you can hear their self-disdain. They know their lives are degenerate, that their wealth is stolen from poorer people, poorer countries. They come here, as individuals, to escape that wealth, when the reason their countries are here is to expand it. They feel that contradiction and it makes them unhappy. Look at the reporter. She could break into tears any moment. What she needs is faith. They all do. A single person is too small a thing to be worth caring about. Which is what draws them into armies. They seek the community we have in the House of Peace by going to war. I will look for a hadith that addresses this.

Amr Chalabi

Fazil is a difficult man but it is good that he is taking an interest in the boy. He needs to have educated men in his life, to show him the importance of learning. I cannot do that but Fazil can. And if the boy is saving his money the way he says he is, then perhaps when he goes home he can attend school. Though I wonder how long he will hold onto his money when he has no family to live with. If Fazil could take him with him that would be the best thing of all. But Fazil has his own family and his own sons to look after. What will probably happen is the boy will end up back home, spend all his savings and be back where he was before he came here. I would take him back to my village if I was sure my brothers would give him work and be kind to him. I have no land myself. Being poor is one thing when you're just looking after yourself.

It is much worse when someone needs your help. If he were a few years older he could join the army. But he isn't. He needs to go to school. He needs to be a boy. And have a father.

We must get him home. I will speak to Fazil about this.

Rami Issay

I thought having to take this job was the low point of my life, but now I wonder if it won't prove to be the biggest opportunity I have ever had. The more I hear about this reality television show idea, the more I think that this could be my redemption. Sula may yet forgive me.

It's a brilliant idea, really. If you're going to make a reality television show, what could be more real than war? I told Major Horner I thought that was profound and said of course I would be interested in helping. Rashid thought I was joking, though. He'll see. Nick Lachey himself is coming! He has his own page on IMDB. And Picabo Street! She competed in the Olympics!

They are interested in my attempts to bring culture to the war zone, the major tells me. They are planning a segment called "Stolen Information." They want to have a mock interrogation, maybe have me play an interpreter. Or portray the man being interrogated. I have not done any acting before. I asked them if there would be lines to memorize. Major Horner thought they would probably prefer a more organic approach. Perhaps I will bring them some suggestions. I wonder if I should attempt to lose some weight.

Announcing *Stars Earn Stripes*

Hosted by General Wesley Clark (ret'd) and Samantha Harris, *Stars Earn Stripes* is an action-packed competition show that pays homage to the men and women who serve in the US Armed Forces and our first-responder services. The star-studded cast includes four-time undefeated world boxing champion Laila Ali, actor Dean Cain (*Out of Time, Five Days of War*), actor and former National Football League player Terry Crews (*The Expendables 2, The Newsroom*), multi-platinum recording artist, actor, producer and television personality Nick Lachey (NBC's *The Sing-Off*), Alaska businessman and four-time Iron Dog snowmobile race champion Todd Palin, NBC's *The Biggest Loser* trainer Dolvett Quince, Olympic gold medalist Picabo Street, and WWE diva, Eve Torres.

In this fast-paced competition, the eight celebrities will gather at a remote training facility where they will be challenged to execute complicated missions inspired by real military exercises. From helicopter drops into water to long-range weapons fire, the contestants will be tested physically, mentally and emotionally. Each will be paired with a special operative from a military branch or one of our first-responder forces, including former US Army Delta Force and Green Berets, US Navy SEALS, US Marines and police officers, who train alongside their partners and compete in the missions with them. Each of the teams is competing for a cash prize on behalf of a military, veterans' or first-responder charity.

Committed to hiring recent vets on the crew, *Stars Earn Stripes* hopes to inspire other employers throughout the country to make similar commitments to our returning heroes to show audiences just how incredible these heroes' missions really are. Dick Wolf (NBC's *Law & Order, Law & Order: SVU*), Mark Burnett (*Survivor*, NBC's *The Voice*) and David A. Hurwitz (*Fear Factor*) serve as executive producers. The series is a production of Universal Television, One Three Media, Wolf Reality, LLC and Bill's Market & Television Productions.

CHAPTER FOURTEEN

Rami Issay sat up in his cot. The sky was still black and the morning birdsong was building. He sat and listened to it for a few minutes while he tried to decide if it would be possible to go back to sleep. Since he had to consciously stop his thoughts from racing, he concluded there would be no more sleeping. He did not remember the birds being so loud so early before. He would have to be sharper than this to carry off his responsibilities with the chess tournament.

When he finally dressed and walked into the café it was five and the sky was lightening in the east. Rashid was alone, mopping the floor. No one was outside. It had been quiet on the tarmac, too, the post-mission traffic light. It was a blessing to have had a quiet night.

It was the day of the chess tournament. All the slots had been filled within twenty-four hours of the posters going up. Even better, the secretaries of generals Jackson and Lattice had called, asking if their bosses could still enter. Of course they could.

And if that weren't enough, Major Horner had telephoned Rami Issay to tell him that Mark Burnett of *Survivor* would be arriving the same day. He had been told about the chess tournament and thought it might be a useful thing to depict on this television show of his.

At six Major Horner telephoned Rami Issay to ask if everything was ready for him when and if he arrived.

"Of course it is. But, pardon me, sir: if?"

"Mr. Burnett is an extremely busy man. He is the producer or executive producer of no fewer than twelve currently active productions around the globe."

"Will he need something to eat when he arrives? Does he eat dairy? Gluten?"

"We've taken care of that. Please, on no account should you feed him anything from your kitchen."

"What's wrong with my kitchen?"

"Just let us feed him. Okay?"

❀

"Who was that, boss?" Rashid asked.

"A very excitable Major Horner."

"He's taking quite an interest in your chess tournament."

"He says Mark Barnett may be coming to see our chess tournament."

"Mark Burnett?"

"That might be it."

"The guy who made *Survivor*?"

"Yes. Is it good?"

"It's huge."

"Rashid, is the food we serve here in any way suspect?"

"No, boss. The food safety officer comes by every month. We always pass easily. I sign the form for you. Why are you asking?"

"No reason."

❀

Rashid and Rami Issay began laying out the chess boards as the sun came up. Customers wandered into the café to buy coffees, but faced with sets and RESERVED signs on the tables they took their coffees to go

177

and the café remained quiet with anticipation. Rashid set out the game clocks his boss had procured and hung blackboards from every wall—one for the tournament round-robin schedule, and four to depict the progress of games for those spectators unable to see the boards.

The tournament was scheduled to begin at eleven a.m. At eight a woman knocked on the door of the café before trying the handle and realizing she could walk in. She looked as if she were nineteen, if that; she wore a black hoodie and carried a messenger bag adorned with band stickers. "Hello," she said. "Is this the Green Beans?"

"Yes it is, child. How may I help you?"

"I'm Chayse Simpson. I work for One Three Media. Are you Rami Issay?"

"I am. You must work for Mr. Mark Barnett."

"Burnett. Well, sort of, yes. I'm here to scout your location and learn about the job you do here at KAF. The network people are curious about you."

"When will Mr. Barnett be arriving, if I may ask?"

Simpson didn't correct him again, just smiled. "He does not spend a lot of time talking to me. I really can't say."

"Today, though?"

"Who told you that?"

"Major Horner suggested it."

"Who is he?"

"The base adjutant. He is most looking forward to meeting Mr. Barnett."

"Burnett," she tried again. "Okay. Well, I'll just start by shooting some video of your café. Is that okay?"

"Of course it is."

She pulled out a measuring tape.

❀

By 10:30 the café was crowded. Those scheduled to play later in the day had come early to watch the first round of games. There was a contingent of Romanians, a few Germans, half a dozen Poles, and a dozen Americans. Ten minutes before eleven, General Lattice walked in. One minute after that, General Jackson arrived.

General Jackson was to play a Romanian NCO who spoke no English. He did not appear to understand his opponent's rank or role, and that struck Jackson as fortunate, as least at first. Lattice played a Polish captain who was very aware of whom he was playing against.

Both generals had looked around for media when they arrived, and together their eyes fell on Chayse Simpson and her small video camera. She shot them close up as they shook Rami Issay's hand in turn but not one another's. Her camera swung from one general to the other for long minutes as they each sat down in front of the boards.

Rami Issay stentoriously read out the key rules of the tournament. One hour of playing time would be permitted to each player. The second round would begin immediately following the conclusion of the first. Anyone not ready to play when called would be disqualified. No cell phones could be used during play. He urged spectators to remain as quiet as possible.

And then he said, "Players, you may begin."

There was a clicking sound as pieces were advanced. Of the sixteen tables, twelve players had opted for the king's pawn opening. There were two queen's pawn openings, a knight's pawn and a Reti. Jackson had played the Reti. He had evidently been thinking about Fred Shaw's insouciance.

The clocks were tapped nearly as one. But after the third move the number of possible responses began to grow and the clock striking was no longer synchronous. The pace of the poorer players slowed first and then all of them slowed down, except the Romanians. The Romanians played like demons, their hand movements precise and sharp. The sophistication of the play was quickly beyond what Rashid could follow. He watched Simpson instead. She filmed all the players but was most drawn to the generals.

Jackson began struggling early. He glanced up at the camera on him and, dispelling his irritation, smiled good-naturedly. Lattice refused to look up from the board for the camera; by the twelfth move, he was beating the young Pole by two pawns. Clearly the younger man had been cowed and had made several elemental errors. The general did look up at the Pole after each of his moves, and smiled. The camera caught these. Lattice knew how that would seem and that darkened his mood. Jackson knew equally that he looked both more gracious and less clever than Lattice; this infuriated him and lent his good cheer an insincere quality. He began hoping for a rocket attack.

Lattice, for his part, regretted coming here at all. One of his communications staff had learned that Jackson had signed up and had argued that so must he. It was the most idiotic thing he had ever heard of and the only thing that made it remotely tolerable was the realization than Jackson was losing his first game. Lattice captured a knight in the next move and with the one after that he forked the Pole's rooks with his own knight. The Pole leaned back in his chair, smiled, and then reached over the board to shake the general's hand. He stood and walked to the counter to get a coffee. The captain's happiness at being done with the game was evident.

Simpson walked among the tables, filming the event without much concern for her effect on it. The contestants tried to ignore her as she took close angle shots of the most interesting faces. In addition to the generals, she paid particular attention to Rami Issay as he acted his role of host and adjudicator. Rashid was surprised by this.

The Romanian playing against Jackson had traded pieces for position with a confidence that puzzled his opponent. By the twentieth move the Romanian was behind three pawns, though he dominated the centre with presciently positioned bishops. By the twenty-fifth move, Jackson no longer questioned his opponent's wisdom. With the bishops' support, the Romanian's knights came slicing down the middle and within three more moves, Jackson had to trade a rook for a bishop. Six moves after that it was all over. Jackson hadn't even seen the checkmate coming. His ego was sufficiently robust that this didn't shatter him, though he was irritated that his schooling had been caught on film. Deirdre would have told him it only made him look more confident, playing chess against people better than him. "How many generals anywhere would do that?"

she would have said. "Describe it as an education you sought." He wished, again, that they could still speak with that sort of ease.

Lattice, on the other hand, played steadily better through the day. The next two opponents did not give him anything like the difficulty the Polish captain had. He checked the time often; he had not expected the tournament to take as long as it did. As he progressed, he relearned some long-ago lessons about flashy attacks and pawn development and patience. And then he was up against the other undefeated player—the Romanian who had dispatched General Jackson.

The Romanian felt the game with a depth that Lattice did not. They were both clever enough players but there was a nuance to the Romanian's game that was not in the general's, and the victory eventually was his.

Lattice posed uncomfortably as he was presented with the small, second-place trophy Rami Issay had had built by one of the carpenters. When the general said he would not allow photographs, Simpson stepped forward. "General, what would make a photo acceptable to you? Are you concerned about the trophy?"

Lattice turned to her as if only noticing her now. "No. No more photographs. Please put down your camera." Simpson found herself, for the first time in her professional life, acceding to such a request and lowering her camera.

❀

Deirdre was supposed to meet the general at the café with her gear. She had come ten minutes before the appointed time, and now stood at the door watching Lattice dismiss the photographer. When he saw her there, he caught her eye and nodded. He strode to the door and held it open for her. "Is that going in your piece?" he asked.

"Of course."

"Just for the record, I had no idea there would be a camera there. Did you bring rain gear?"

"Impermeable and semi-permeable both. Like your man said."

"Good. There's a low-pressure system coming in off the Indian Ocean."

He walked so fast she had to run to keep pace with him. She was carrying ten kilos: besides the rain gear, a thin sleeping bag, a single change of clothes, camera and film. It was about as light as you could go for a long trip and too light if they were going into altitude, but she didn't want the general's man going through her stuff and tossing things out.

"Throw your gear in the back of the truck and get in with it," he said, nodding to the deuce-and-a-half parked near the SF compound. It had just started its engine. He climbed into the cab. She did as she was told, and with a heave, pulled herself up the five feet to the top of the tailgate. When she rolled into the truck's covered box she found herself among unsmiling bearded men in Afghan garb. "Hello," she said.

"Hey," the man nearest her replied, with a deep Alabaman accent that was the only American thing evident about him. He moved to make room on the bench. There was no rank insignia on his clothes, but she thought he was probably the squad leader. She sat down beside him. Someone slid her pack toward her. The truck was put into gear and they lurched off to the flight line.

On the tarmac, five Chinooks were waiting for them. The two-and-a-half-ton trucks began disgorging men in a steady stream from their boxes and straight into the backs of the helicopters. Deirdre was directed into the back of the fourth bird in line. She watched as Lattice spoke with the meteorology officer at the edge of the tarmac for a most recent weather update and then turned and ran into the back of the first helicopter. She wedged in between two silent young riflemen. SF was not used to embeds—everything they did was by definition secret.

Lattice had proposed at a senior OPS meeting earlier that month, that if they allowed more discussion of things that weren't really secret, they could draw a sharper circle around the stuff that was. That started a debate. One battalion commander said that the mystique their secret status lent them was valuable. Another said, "Look, the media can become the enemy, like it was in Vietnam, or it can remain our ally the way it has been so far. But you have to give your allies reasons to be your ally. Find a particularly loyal one, and give him a glimpse. Flatter him."

There had been no riflemen at that meeting and so the men in the truck were not aware of the debate. What they did think they knew was that the journalist was here because the general was. And, to the extent that the patrol did anything different for her sake or his, they would be paying for it. She read this thought in the half-dozen exchanged glances she caught in the first minute after she sat down. She kept her mouth shut. Then the ramps went up and the engines started.

❁

With the generals gone, Simpson put down her camera. Amr and Mohammed began moving the tables back to their original places, and she reviewed some of the footage she had shot. As she made notes in a large black binder, Rami Issay brought her a cup of tea and a piece of poppy seed cake. He sat down with her. "Did you get what you need?"

She looked at him. Then she pulled her toque lower on her head and put a large pair of earphones on so that she might assess the audio. Ms Simpson lifted the cup of tea and mouthed, "Is this decaf?"

"No, but I could bring you some chamomile if you prefer."

"Thank you."

He took her tea back to the counter and filled a pot with steaming water and put a bag of chamomile in it. He brought it back.

"Do you have Sweet'n Low?"

He did not know what that meant. But he was pretty sure he did not have it. "I do not, I am sorry to say."

"It's okay," she said, and resumed watching the video on her Alienware laptop, which was the size of a large atlas. She did not touch her tea or her cake.

"Is there anything else you need?"

She looked up from the screen. "No, thank you. I think I'm good."

He sat there for a few more minutes and then he got up and went back behind the counter. Mohammed was sitting there. The café was quiet, for the first time in hours.

"Anything you need, Mohammed?"

"Like what?"

Rami Issay shrugged.

Mohammed got up to clear off the tables.

CHAPTER FIFTEEN

A s the Chinook lifted off, a great cloud of dust rose up around them and for a moment nothing could be seen through it. Deirdre always found helicopter takeoffs in dirt claustrophobic and imagined that it must be worse for the pilots. They needed the helicopters to rise faster than the clouds they created, lest the dust destroy the turbines—and so they rose quickly. Within a few seconds they were through to blue sky and KAF itself fell away under them like a big olive-drab tarp. Dust billowed beneath them, obscuring the airstrip but otherwise all was sharp. The ordered lines and ranks of barracks and tents covered an area even more vast than she would ever have supposed walking around it. The sewage treatment plant—universally called "the Romanian swimming pool"—shone pungently green in the afternoon light, and the rows and rows of new construction ran around the perimeter of existing buildings like a thick, pallet-crowded shell.

The birds skirted Kandahar City for safety reasons—one of these days a shoulder-launched SAM was going to appear—but the prominent buildings were nevertheless visible: the governor's palace, the central market, the football stadium, Mir Weis hospital, Sarpoza prison. She had patrolled through these areas as an embed half a dozen times since she had returned from Iraq. In 2002, she went anywhere she wanted, with only her translator for company. She had known those places before; now she knew them again, in their altered version—more moneyed and more scared. There were things in the shops. There were cars on the streets. And in some of the cars were bombs.

It's not like there hadn't always been violence in Kandahar—the whole of the senior Taliban leadership came from here, and the civil war that had erupted after the departure of the Soviets scarred this city almost as much as it did Kabul. Asceticism and fury seemed to grow out of the parched soil itself. And now the land was in full blossom.

Sarpoza prison. As they passed over it, Deirdre wondered if this was where John Wayne had wound up. The first rumours that he was the leaker of the collateral-murder video had died away and from number of FBI and MPs running in and out of the command headquarters, she could only conclude that no one thought the problem had been solved. So what had they accused the terp of now?

She pictured the terp in a cell below her, his alert features blunted by beating and weeping and no sun. She wondered if he had in fact done anything wrong. She hoped not. The innocent stand up better, she had found. Though no one stands up well after having their kneecaps shattered—a favourite introductory gift of the NDS, when they've decided they're not likely to let you go. She thought for a moment about the ferocity of the Iraqi interrogators in Baghdad and how the Americans had looked away as their allies did exactly what was expected of them. She had had friends—local journalists, sources—who had wound up in the vortex and miraculously emerged alive. They had no interest in discussing what had been done to them but neither was it necessary. There was more information about it on their faces than she could bear thinking about.

She forced herself to study the fields. She had memorized the important landmarks around Kandahar, the crossings of the Arghandab, the principal and secondary roads, the feeder towns, the FOBs. She thought for a moment that she had found the road on which the British Scorpion had been destroyed. She looked for the wreck but either it had been removed or she was wrong about the location. To take her mind off the terp, she began mentally naming the villages she recognized.

❀

Sarpoza *was* where the terp had ended up. He'd heard the rotors of the helicopters overhead and he lifted his head to listen carefully. He had long fantasized about the soldiers he had worked with learning of his mistreatment and coming to rectify things. He knew it would never happen. He guessed that they knew where he was. But he was not one of them, and was no longer useful to them. He clung to the rescue fantasy anyway, because there was nothing else in reach except concrete and straw. Lately, the fantasy had taken shape around the embed learning of his circumstances and doing a story on the way the NATO armies used NDS as their torturers. He knew enough of how reporters thought to know that they would be shocked. For that matter, even the soldiers who sent him here would be shocked. Even the ones who had beaten him first, who thought they were the dangerous men.

His thought, about Deirdre writing an exposé of the treatment of prisoners handed over by ISAF to the NDS, leapt through the air from him to her as she passed overhead. She received it and considered it, thinking it had arisen out of her own anxieties. That sort of story was part of what she had expected to be doing here when she first came. She had been in Iraq when Sy Hersh had written the first Abu Ghraib story. He had been able to write it because he was at the end of a great career and could neither be punished nor lose any future opportunities. And, most of all, because he was eighty and did not travel out on combat patrols as one of the platoon. He did not love soldiers the way she and the other embeds ended up doing. At one level or another, ever since he broke the story of the My Lai massacre in Vietnam, he'd probably hated soldiers. And you couldn't blame him. That was his experience of them. Neither could Deirdre and her colleagues be blamed: their experience was of wise-cracking, brave and terrified young men, with more love and loyalty in them in those circumstances than anyone could know in any other.

When Hersh's *New Yorker* story appeared, the hurt and frustration of the soldiers still in Iraq was impossible to convey to unembedded journalists or editors back home. The sense of betrayal among the soldiers was deep and sincere and pre-rational. Because she loved these goofy, earnest young men, Deirdre felt it as well.

She thought about asking Jeremy if she could tour Sarpoza, him saying yes, and her writing about the broken terp, chained to a wall. She had given up everything for this life here—Peter, her friends back home, even maybe her ability to live back home again. She imagined the soldiers talking about her the way they'd talked about Hersh. For a moment she felt paralyzed. Like when that hand had grabbed her ankle in the Baghdad bazaar. Then she went back to naming the villages.

❖

The helicopters flew south, toward the mountains. No conversation was possible over the noise of the rotors. The loadmaster eventually handed Deirdre a pair of earplugs and she nodded thank you and put them in. The man beside her, who looked to be twenty years old at the outside, was sleeping, his hairy chin on his chest. Underneath the Afghan garb was a kind of body armour she hadn't seen before, so thin you could barely tell it was there. Like Frodo Baggins and his mithril. What the regular army guys would give for that, she thought. And then, "Really? *Lord of the Rings*? I have spent too much time around twenty-year-old men."

Four Apaches met up with them as they approached the mountains. Sleeker and more lethal looking in flight even than they were on the ground, they flew beneath the Chinooks and scanned the valley for radar or thermal traces of the enemy. Helicopters settling into a hot LZ being the nightmare scenario they wished most to avoid.

The Chinooks held back as the Apaches scouted the primary and alternate insertion sites. Drones would already have been monitoring movement in the area for the last several days, she supposed, but a hovering helicopter is vulnerable to RPG or machine-gun fire: the rotors and turbines cannot be armoured and still function, and the two-hundred-gallon tanks of Jet-A are bombs awaiting sparks. They could search the area just as much as they wanted, she thought to herself, and maybe a bit more than that, just to be safe.

When the Chinooks approached the insertion site, they dropped into it quickly and threw open the ramp the moment the bird was down. The engines remained at a roar and the men sprinted off, as eager to get back into the comfortable terrain of sharp grass and spiny succulents as the pilots were to get some altitude. Deirdre followed the man beside her off the ramp and ran as fast as she could to the perimeter they formed. Their Chinook roared up off into the sky toward KAF. The Apaches were still circling around the insertion site. The arrival of the helicopters had alerted local forces to their presence, and their thermal imaging now detected activity on two ridgelines. Probably Taliban, but you couldn't know they weren't just shepherds. There was no knowing anything until an RPG was fired at them.

The soldiers plunged into the grass, one after the other, as the other helicopters disgorged their passengers. It felt strange to Deirdre, watching the familiar drills being run by men who looked hardly at all like soldiers—so sun- and wind-burnt they were the same colour as the red earth they trod upon. Gowned in coarse woollen shawls, and carrying AK-47s, they looked more like the men they were trying to find than American infanteers.

The last man off the last helicopter had just thrown himself into the grass when the group got up as one and began moving to the closest treeline. Deirdre could hear no commands being barked, nor did she see any hand signals being exchanged. The long familiarity with one another allowed them to rely on subtler cues. For the platoon commander, it was like driving a car that knows where you want to go. The sergeant walking in front of Deirdre had been a private in 2001, and had ridden a shaggy Afghan horse through these same hills for the few weeks they were in this area. He thought about that now. It was surprising how much he remembered of this terrain, considering how much he had been through since—Iraq and the Korengal and Waziristan. But it had been his first taste of sustained lethal operations and those memories were bound to linger. He thought about all the crazy shit he had seen and done since and still he recalled the ridgeline to the west perfectly: Ghar Mabar it was called on the map. He could remember his younger self marvelling at its knife-edged profile.

Deirdre would have been interested to know this, but not a word was said to her as she walk-ran in the file of silent men. It was just as well, since she would not have been able to converse and move at that speed. And she knew that all eyes were upon her, waiting to find something that would allow them to call in a helicopter and extract her.

The five Chinooks had carried 150 men. This was too large a group to manoeuvre quietly as one. She had not been told any of this, but the plan was for the company to divide into five 30-man teams and radiate out from a common point. The men had been briefed in detail and they all knew their assignments. Each of the teams had a junior officer and a senior NCO leading it. The lieutenant colonel commanding the operation had his own team and additional signalmen, but the assumption and expectation was that the manoeuvre teams would remain substantially autonomous. Local initiative and improvisation were the essence of SF OPS, as every public affairs officer told every journalist every chance they had. They reached a rendezvous that looked no different to Deirdre than any other part of this parched terrain, and the five teams headed off on five different compass bearings. No words were exchanged. Every man in each of the five teams felt more comfortable in the smaller groups. Company-sized formations of SF were training and administrative structures only. Putting 150 SF on the ground in one spot was unprecedented in these men's experience.

Deirdre was waved forward with the team that included the lieutenant colonel and Lattice. She did not approach either of them. She stayed in the middle of the column and did her best not to puff as she walked. They were following a trail that was so narrow it could be imaginary. The soldiers around her —she had to remind herself that that was what they were, in their shawls and caps—seemed to relax a little, now that they were in a smaller group. They walked faster, too. Open air, un-uniformed, bearded and unquestioned: this life offered those things as recompense for what it asked.

The trail headed uphill. Because it had presumably been made by normal people, she expected that the slope would ease off; normal people do not walk up fifty-degree inclines. It did not, and this made her wonder whether the path had been made by the lead man in the column. She decided not to think any more about where they were walking. She lifted her eyes from the ground and looked up the column. She could see the general at the head, and the colonel behind him. The general was making a point here, she realized. He was breaking trail, and going so fast the kids in the rear could barely keep up. The sweat stains running down the shawls in front of her were deep and black and the odour of men formidably sharp. They did move quietly; the constant barking she had heard from every other infantry NCO out on patrol was absent here.

They reached the top of the ridgeline and finally took a knee. The men dispersed into a defensible circle and Deirdre remained in the centre. The general looked over his shoulder at her. She nodded at him. He did not appear to notice. He turned back to the colonel and the two of them looked at a map. Then they set off again.

❀

As the sky had darkened, Deirdre had expected the platoon sergeant to lead the patrol toward a bivouac, probably prepared by an advance party, with a defensive perimeter and possibly some hot food. They just kept walking. They had been walking for seven hours and now they followed a trail lit by the moon. They made almost no noise. The men in the lead wore night vision goggles. When they turned to look behind them, she caught their distorted faces in the moonlight and shuddered. What the Afghans must think when they see these men, moving through the night so fast and then disappearing without noise. As she thought these words she realized that that would probably be the lede of the piece she would write about this patrol. Kenwood would like it. Then she tripped on a tree root that everyone else had stepped deftly over and she told herself to concentrate on the matter at hand.

As they climbed the side of a steep river valley, they did not slow their pace. She had not exchanged a word with anyone since the general told her to throw her gear in the truck. She'd worried that she had packed too lightly, but now she wished she'd brought half as much as she had. It was all she could do to keep up. The men around her carried thirty-kilo packs, plus weapons, ammunition and radios. Even the general.

Just when she was starting to conclude that they were going to walk all night, the column halted. Without a word, the men dispersed around a small clearing on the ridge. Some of them unrolled sleeping bags, others crept farther uphill and downhill—sentries. Someone tapped her shoulder and pointed to the base of a tree. He said, "No lights." She nodded. She unrolled her ground mat and placed her thin sleeping bag upon it. She crawled into it, her clothes still on. She looked around the moonless dark. She could not see anyone else. She listened for any sound of the bearded men all around her, but all she heard were night insects.

❀

It was 0400 when a booted toe nudged her and all the men around her were rising and folding their sleeping bags into their packs in one easy movement. The faintest light showed on the eastern ridgeline. She did as they did and within a few minutes of opening her eyes she was also ready to move out. Every eye in the platoon, as well as the general's, was upon her.

Someone handed her an energy bar. She took it gratefully and began eating it as they set out. She was cold at first, but with the movement she warmed quickly. General Lattice fell in beside her, letting the lieutenant colonel lead today. Or more accurately, feeling comfortable leading the patrol from back here.

"Good morning, General," she said.

"Good morning, Ms O'Malley. Did you sleep well?"

"Excellently, thank you. Yourself?"

"As well as I needed to."

"Ah. Warrior monk. Three hours a night. Boiled rice and hot water."

"Less sleep than that, in the field. And more protein and calories than that, too."

"Do you prefer it out here?"

"To desk work? Of course."

"How much time do you spend in the field now?"

"Since the last promotion? Hardly any. It was easier in Iraq, for some reason."

"Where are we going?"

"We're making high-density patrols through the Panjwai. The whole group."

"Your men look as ferocious as the Pashtun."

"That's the idea."

"You think the regular army guys aren't considered ferocious, in their body armour and shaved faces and sunglasses?"

"I'm not interested in how they are seen. However it is, it doesn't seem to be helping them."

"I heard your men speaking Pashto to one another last night. Was that for me?"

"They weren't trying to impress you. They probably just didn't want to be eavesdropped on."

"They resent having a journalist along."

"They resent having a general along."

"Which of us is the bigger issue, do you think?"

"Oh, me, by far."

"Why do they resent having you along?"

"Because they know I'm not here to help them with their work."

"Why are you here?"

"No reason good enough to justify making them suspect my motives."

"Is it because I am here?"

"You wouldn't be here if I hadn't decided to come along."

"Why?"

"That wouldn't be fair to anyone, least of all, you."

"You don't think it'd be safe?"

He laughed harshly. "For whom?"

"So why the beards and the Afghan clothes?"

"It sets them apart."

"From regular army?"

"Yes."

"Don't the Taliban know perfectly well who is American and who isn't?"

"Of course."

"So why the Pashto speaking and the shameez wearing?"

"It's symbolism. Soldiers love symbols."

"What does it symbolize?"

"That we're aware this place is not America, that we're interested in how people think here. That we have our eye on the long game, too."

"Is that how the villagers around here receive it when they see you coming through their doors in the night?"

"The night raids are different. They're done by dedicated teams from Bagram and KAF. We're not those guys."

"These guys here aren't. But surely you are. The night raid teams work for you."

"Yes, they do. But they won't win the war. These guys will."

"You think you're going to beat the Taliban?"

"It would be impossible to ask anyone to risk their life to that end if that wasn't going to happen."

And then he nodded to her and ran forward. The team was approaching another ridgeline. The lieutenant colonel was looking at a map and clearly had something to say.

❀

"Chayse, can you hear me?"

"Of course I can hear you, Sara."

"I'm amazed cell phones work there!"

"Well, they do."

"Listen, we've been going over the footage you shot."

"Yes?"

"We think it's *fabulous*."

"Good."

"You are doing excellent work."

"Can I come home now?"

"Not yet. I'm going to come over there. We've pretty much decided to shoot an episode on the base."

"Which one?"

"Well, according to the episode map, the third. 'Stolen Information.'"

"What does the café have to do with that?"

"The writers are still hashing that out. Your friend the café owner, though. We definitely want to involve him. Would that be okay with the military, do you think?"

"Manager. Not owner. The only military I've dealt with has been falling all over themselves to make this happen."

"If you get any static from them at your end, let me know. The PA officers I've been talking to at the Pentagon would be only too happy to clear up any difficulties."

"Sure. When will you arrive?"

"I'm flying out in a few hours. They're putting on a special transport for me!"

"You don't have to go through Dubai and Bagram?"

"Direct from California!"

"Wow, the brass really are enthusiastic. What do you want me to do in the meantime?"

"Local colour, Chayse, local colour. Get to know as many people as you can. Become Mr. Issay's friend."

❀

Rami Issay and Rashid both held their breath when they prepared to open the crate marked FILM—HANDLE WITH CARE. It had been dropped off at the café sometime the night before. Rashid Siddiqui inserted his screwdriver and pried. Packing foam spilled out and he reached inside for the heavy grey disks. He withdrew the first one he touched. It said REEL THREE, SIN CITY. They both sighed.

Rashid said, "Boss, I know this film. I watched a bootleg copy I found in the bazaar a few months ago. Frank Miller cannot be successfully shown in a military environment. They will call this pornography. It will be the end of the film series."

Rami Issay held his head in his hands. "I saw the review on Rotten Tomatoes. I was told the *Stars Earn Stripes* producers might come tonight, though."

"Well, you have a decision to make."

❀

Deirdre and the soldiers were lying in the shade of a stand of poplar trees that overlooked a poppy field. The colonel had put spotters and snipers at each end of the ridge. He was watching a video feed from a drone high above them on his laptop. Deirdre could see him whispering into his headset, but she couldn't make out what he said. He looked up and caught her watching and covered his mouth with his hand. He watched too much NFL and read too many spy books. No, she couldn't read lips.

Lattice was aware that he had not successfully resisted his temptation to take control of all things, always, and so he had forced himself to come sit with her. He would have much preferred to be watching the drone feed and positioning the spotters himself.

"Can you tell me what we're waiting for here?" Deirdre asked him.

"No."

"Because you don't know or because you can't tell me?"

"Do you have a more general question?"

She sighed. "How is the poppy crop doing this year? That field looks healthy."

"The conditions for growing poppies are nearly ideal. Which means there will likely be a record crop. Which is not good news. Largest crop since 2001, anyway."

"In 2001 there were no poppies grown, though, were there?"

His voice tightened. This was well-trod ground. "The Taliban had one of their spasms of ideology and, yes, banned the poppies. But they'd financed their civil war with poppies, and the war against the Soviets before that. They are quite okay with infidels becoming addicts. When it suits their purposes. Like now."

"So are we waiting for opium smugglers to show up here?"

"I'm not advocating poppy interdiction as a strategy against the Taliban. It just pisses off the farmers."

"Is this an ambush?"

"Myself, I wonder why we don't just buy the entire opium crop. The world needs morphine. And prosperity takes the spring out of extremism everywhere."

"Have you advocated that?"

"I'm not going to say that at a press conference. It's not my field. But it does make sense to me."

She thought about what he had just said. Did he think this was all off the record? He knew better. Was it her job to clarify the point? She wondered for a moment and then she decided to see where it went.

"Can you shoot likely opium smugglers on sight?"

"Everything that enrages these farmers has to do with the industrial army. Poppy eradication, which is stupid, the high-speed vehicle patrols through their villages, which are lethal to the villagers' kids and livestock, and most of all, the sheer, obvious presence of Americans everywhere in their country, years after we invaded. Every man up there," he nodded, indicating the soldiers on the ridge, "wants to know when we're going home. And so do they."

"Which will be?"

"Depends on how much latitude I am given."

"What do you need?"

He looked away from the ridgeline and at her. "It would be a fairly short list."

"God, you're opaque," she replied.

He looked back at the ridgeline and frowned. He liked hearing that. She knew it immediately.

❀

Chayse Simpson walked into the café. She wore a Black Flag hoodie with the band's name scrawled in white across the front. Her headphones were around her neck. She wore sunglasses. She sat down at the table beside the door. She opened her messenger bag and pulled out her laptop.

Rashid was at the counter, placing a tray of cinnamon buns on wax paper. He looked up when he saw the sullen American woman come in, but he did not interrupt his bun placement. Then he saw Rami Issay come in from the back and he closed his eyes, for the boss's sake.

"My young American friend!" Rami Issay called out, approaching her table. "What can I get for you? Would you like a cinnamon bun?"

"No thank you, Mr. Issay," Simpson said.

"How about a mug of chai?"

"Mr. Issay, I sent the footage from the chess tournament back to our producers in America."

"What did they think?"

"They thought it was interesting. They would like to meet you. One of them is on her way here now."

"Would they like me to arrange another chess tournament?"

"No, Mr. Issay. Their interest is in the reality show. But they are trying to figure out what sort of role you might have in it, if you want to be a part of it, that is."

"What are they considering?"

"I'm not sure what all they are considering. They did say they found you quite charismatic."

"Well, that's wonderful. Are your quarters adequate for a longer stay?"

"Is there an alternative to the barracks? It would be great to have my own room and shower."

"I don't really know. Myself, I sleep with the rest of my staff in the back of the café."

"I see. So there's nothing you can do, is there?"

"I can ask."

"Thank you for that."

"How long do you think you might be here?"

"It might be weeks. Maybe more."

"Well, you can have all the coffee you want, while you are here. On me."

"That—" She caught herself. "That's very generous of you, Mr. Issay."

❀

Walking now, along a well-established footpath. The soldiers seemed more relaxed. Lattice was just ahead of her. "Is this a denial-of-terrain patrol?" she asked.

"No. We don't really do that. The regular army does that fly-the-flag thing. We generally have more concrete objectives."

"Can you say what that is, today?"

"You know I can't."

"Can you tell me after you've achieved it?"

"No. But you might draw your own conclusions if you pay attention."

They were being listened to by the men in front of and behind them. He could no more be seen to be toadying to her than she could, to him. Though everyone in earshot understood that each of these was more interested in the other than anyone on the patrol actually carrying ammunition.

"What you're seeing here is pretty important, even if there isn't a lot of noise right now."

"Oh?"

"It's like when the tanks were first used at Cambrai in 1918, and suddenly barbed wire could be overcome. Or the sinking of *Prince of Wales* and *Repulse* by Japanese torpedo bombers in 1941. In an afternoon battleships became obsolete after sucking up wealth from nations aspiring to greatness for half a century."

"So what are the current battleships?"

"Armies."

"Guys like you?"

"Armies aren't guys like me."

"Every time we invade Iraq we seem to need them, though."

"We really have to stop doing that."

"Were we just going to leave the Republican Guard in Kuwait?"

"For a little while, yeah. And blockade them completely. And work from the inside to paralyze the administration. Support the Marsh people uprising, like we said we would. They would have left Kuwait. "

"It worked out, though, that first time. One-hundred-hour ground war. We kicked butt, and got the Japanese to pay for it."

"The 'kicking butt' is exactly the problem. All that rah-rah media attention and war-as-infotainment. The worst thing you can do is win a war so handily."

"The worst thing you can do is win?"

"A war like that, yes. CNN all the time, hardly any casualties, no pain at all at home."

"Why?"

"'Cause then you're just going to go back for more."

"Winning Gulf War One caused Gulf War Two? Caused 9/11?"

"In about a hundred ways."

"What's the alternative?"

"SF. No media. No rah-rah. Quiet and shameful things done away from the light. Things that reasonable people understand to be necessary but no one is proud of."

"Is this off the record, General?"

"No. If something can't be printed, I won't say it."

"People back home are pretty proud of you guys," she puffed, as they began to climb a slope.

"They have no idea what they're proud of. Industrial-scale armies need that pride, that rah-rah, because they're so expensive and obvious and visible. So they work it all up, have parades, surround themselves with cameras. And that makes more war inevitable."

"From your point of view, that's a bad thing?"

"We haven't won a big war since 1945. We should stop fighting them. We do pretty well with the little ones, though."

Deirdre caught her breath enough to say, "This isn't all just off the top of your head, is it?"

❀

They obtained a goat from a shepherd. A sergeant from Wisconsin, an avid deer hunter, cut its throat and dressed it. It took them a long time to get a fire lit and a bed of coals established, but now they had it on the spit and were roasting it. An hour until sunset. The fire was smoky.

"I thought you guys were on hard rations all the time."

"MREs are heavy. We try to be self-sufficient."

"I doubt you've let them roast a goat before, though. The smoke, the conversation with the shepherd—this is for my sake, isn't it?"

"For the sake of your article."

"Which is the whole reason I've come along."

"Of course."

"I mean, you have an agenda."

He looked at her. "Everyone has an agenda. Ask me what mine is."

"What's your agenda?"

"To save this shit show from descending completely into chaos."

"How are you going to do that?"

"By changing the conversation about another surge of mechanized infantry and armour divisions to a different, smarter strategy altogether."

"By spending half your afternoon on Roasting-Goat Theatre?"

He laughed. "No. Now go get your plate and line up with the men." He sharpened his KA-BAR on a whetstone. He would be doing the carving.

"Sir, yessir."

He looked up at her sternly. His mouth was tight. His eyes were not, however, and she nodded at him and stopped herself from smirking. He did-not-smirk back at her. She walked over to her pack to pick up her plate. And her camera. That crackling goat was an arresting image, however staged. Pity they weren't still patrolling on horseback.

❀

When the C-17 finally came to a halt and throttled back, Chayse Simpson, Rami Issay and Major Horner had been waiting for Sara Miller's arrival for three hours. As the roar of the turbo fans settled, the people on the tarmac took their fingers from their ears. Those really were preposterously large transports. Three times the size of the C-130 Hercules. The ramp went down and the battalion of engineers began filing out. There seemed to be no one plausibly associated with a TV network on board, but then a tall woman, dressed in black combat boots, black jeans and a black leather jacket, emerged onto the tarmac with the pilots and the battalion commander. She lowered her sunglasses and looked around. Simpson waved and Sara Miller walked toward them. Major Horner thought she was walking toward him with anticipation. Simpson had dealt with her enough to wish that she really was.

As she drew nearer, Rami Issay worried out loud that he was not sufficiently well dressed. Simpson snapped: "For the love of God. This is Kandahar. She doesn't want to see you in a business suit." Then: "I'm sorry. I didn't mean to speak sharply."

"My child, think nothing of it. I understand the stress you are under."

And for a moment she thought, maybe he really did. And she felt both grateful for his kindness and guilty for her part in what was about to be done to him.

❀

"So, just to be clear. This was never about me learning about SF in the field at all, is it? It's about you launching your broadside. Strategy debate in the media age. You're going to be a YouTube video."

"If you wish to post this online, I have no objections."

She balanced the video camera on a rock so that his face remained in frame. "Don't you have to run this sort of thing through your people?"

"They suggested I write a book."

"What's wrong with writing books?"

He snorted. "There's been a lot of books written. They change nothing."

"What does?"

"A *Rolling Stone* cover."

"Jann Wenner would be horrified to hear that generals want him to help them shape policy."

"No, he wouldn't."

She paused for a second and considered the point. "You're right. He probably wouldn't."

"Everyone wants to control the narrative."

"Clearly."

"Except the amateurs, maybe."

"Like who?"

He didn't smile. "So you wanted to ask me about what we've learned from Operation Enduring Freedom?"

"All right, General. Ready? Okay: 'General Lattice, what would you say have been the important lessons of this war?'"

※

That night at their barracks, Simpson sat on Sara Miller's bed, taking notes. They'd spent an hour or two at the café, watching how it all worked while Rami Issay did his best to impress them.

"The thing is, we need a narrative entry point, to bring Rami Issay into the arc of the show," Miller said. "I'm not sure what that will be, but we have to find it and find it fast."

"Which episode do you see using them for?"

"We are still thinking 'Stolen Information.' We'd use Rami Issay as an entertaining stand-in for some local man who has somehow gotten hold of some information—like the InformationIsFree leak or something. We could have the celebrities 'interrogate' him. Afterward, he could award them points based on how intimidating they were. What d'ya think?"

Simpson could not think of anything to say.

"I know, lame. But obviously he's a talent. Charming and odd. Big presence."

"Plus there's the Rashid relationship mixed in."

"Are they an item?"

"I don't think so."

"They might be though, right?"

"I don't know."

"That could help with our demographics."

"Your audience will have tuned in to watch Todd Palin shooting targets."

"Don't stereotype. We have to find some way of injecting narrative tension into this. It can't just be Nick Lachey racing Picabo Street and Todd Palin over an obstacle course. What does Todd Palin represent? The father of a soldier in peril. Why does he care about stolen information? Because of his son, who is in combat. He hates the leaker. The leaker represents everything wrong with our society. Selfishness, indifference to community, cowardice. What about Nick?"

"You can't smoke in here."

"Relax, it's an e-cigarette."

"Ah."

"Nick is a patriot."

"Aren't we all patriots?"

Sara Miller looked over her glasses at Simpson. "I would not say that for a second, Chayse. Are you? Am I? How can you know?"

❁

"Taliban move at night, so if you want to catch them on the march, this is when you have to do it."

"Makes sense to me. Where are they during the day?"

The general looked at her. She was smarter than that. "Where do you think? Sleeping."

"Where?"

"Under trees. In grape-drying huts. In the grass."

There was no moon, and if it weren't for the ambient light amplification devices, it would not have been possible to see one's own hand in front of one's face. The general had provided Deirdre with a set. She had worn night goggles before, in Iraq, but these were better and sharper and lighter. The whole valley beneath them was lit up by the stars themselves. In the distance, a farmhouse had a candle lit within and the entire building glowed with a pale green light.

"See them?"

"No. Where?"

"In that millet field, one o'clock. A thousand metres."

"I have the field. But there's no 'they' there."

"Look harder. The far edge. Moving east."

"I'm looking."

"Now they're coming up to the corner of the field."

"Wait. Yes. I see something."

"There are nine men."

"There are not."

"Yes, there are."

"Jesus. I must be blind."

"No. You have to learn to see."

"Yes, sensei."

"See them?"

"Yes. Not nine. But I see a moving dot. Dots. Not nine."

"Want to know who they are?"

"Yes."

"They're part of the outfit that ambushed your Canadians."

"Really?"

"Want to get them?"

"Yes."

"The mistake amateurs make in ambushes is scripting the whole thing in their heads. You imagine the enemy will come in from this direction and then respond to your attack in that way, but often they don't do what they're supposed to. You have to be flexible. And have a range of responses prepared for different situations. Still, when you have tech, and you do them well, ambushes are highly satisfying."

"Sir."

The general looked up at the sergeant who had just whispered to him. He nodded. He thought he had been speaking quietly enough that no one could hear him, whispering directly into Deirdre's ear, breathing the words as much as he had been enunciating them. It was exactly the same way he spoke to his men when he wanted to be maximally quiet. But yes. He had wanted to continue talking to her. Which was the next best reason to have stopped. He glanced over at the sergeant in gratitude and closed his eyes tightly for a moment and then opened them.

CHAPTER SIXTEEN

They were four hundred yards back from the trail behind a low ridge of dirt that afforded them just enough cover to be able to glimpse the path without exposing themselves. Deirdre, the general, the medic and a radioman hung back. The Taliban were coming.

Deirdre thought about the Canadian boys who had been killed when they had been the ambushed, and of the gurgling sound that young man had made as he had bled into the dirt.

Lattice had said that these men approaching them were under the command of the same man who had directed the ambush on the Canadians. The fighters who did that had all been killed, but they would have been known to these ones. Would have eaten together, trained together, prayed together. They could as easily have been the men that crouched behind that treeline and trained their weapons on those beautiful boys. They would have been pleased to learn of those deaths. Would have prayed for the souls of the martyred. She thought, *Kill them. Kill them.*

The trail doglegged sharply to the left thirty metres past where the soldiers lay, perhaps eighty metres now from the lead man in the column of Taliban. In the dark, the insurgents had bunched up tightly, so as to not lose track of one another. More experienced men would not have done that, would have just moved more slowly, carefully maintaining long spaces between them. Several valleys to the east, a shepherd boy had told them about being compelled to give a team of white Taliban one of his favourite goats. So they knew that there were ferenghee, probably SF, about. They knew that the drones watched these trails every minute. And so they walked close to one another and, were they not carrying weapons, would very much have preferred to hold hands. A night ambush, which is what they feared now, turns into chaos more quickly than any other type of combat. In the dark, the roar of machine guns and rockets sound twice as loud and close and there is no reassurance to be found in the faces of ones unseen comrades. Night ambushes were a specialty of the white Taliban, whose night vision aids gave them the advantage in such scenarios. It felt to these men like they were young goats themselves, being led toward a tree.

Lattice had had to force himself not to direct the ambush personally. Lieutenant Colonel Matheson was a strong man, too, was the problem, which was, after all, why he had come to command a battalion of SF infantry deep in the wilds of Kandahar. He had been the captain in charge of the final assault on Taliban's Last Stand, and had enjoyed a reputation ever since of being a man who would bring tasks to their conclusion. Once the general had made the men cook that goat, the colonel had become so brittle and terse, Lattice worried that Matheson's head might just pop right off his shoulders. Lattice wished he could have explained the goat to the colonel, but that the war was going to be won or lost on the cover of *Rolling Stone* and on the set of the *Daily Show* was not a thing he was able to say to men who had been in the field continuously for most of a decade.

He would have dispersed the belt-fed weapons a little more, though he liked how the claymore mines were positioned. And the choice of the doglegged part of the trail was good. The eight automatic weapons that would imminently open up along the length of the enemy column would be devastating. Night combat always gives an extra fifteen seconds to the initiator. It takes that long for the men being shot to realize just what is happening, what direction the threat is coming from, and where they should hide.

What happened in those first fifteen seconds was that men started dying, fast, and their first response—the leaping to the side—did nothing to stop the dying.

And what happened next is that the ambushed realized that they were not safer, lying flat beside the trail, that the fire was coming from above and in front of them and that the men lying with them were being quickly killed. And so they stood up together and made to break away to the forest and the dark, as far from this shrieking inferno and one another as they could get.

Which was just the moment the ambushers set off the claymores, spraying ball bearings through the chest of every man standing in front of them. The stragglers—the few remaining paralyzed and too-frightened men—went down too. Even if they were not hit by the claymores, they were no more able to move and stand and escape than their mortally wounded compatriots. And so ensured their own death.

Beside the trail huddled one last undamaged man who, looking around himself, could see only muzzle flashes in the dark, like two dozen fluttering torches. He aimed his rifle at one of them and fired three-shot bursts at it, over and over again, until one of the machine gunners spotted his muzzle flash and trained his own weapon on where the last flash had come from. The machine gunner waited. And when three quick pulses appeared again, the man fired one hundred rounds at the spot. Seven of those rounds entered the body of his target, the only man who had been firing back at the ferenghee. His name was Mahmoud Daoust and he was twenty-two years old and had begun fighting with the Taliban for one excruciating year, since his father's house had been night raided, his younger brother taken away in a helicopter and not returned. His enraged grief lead to him to approach a man who lived in his valley. A week later he was walking in the night with a rifle and convinced of his own righteousness. In the subsequent year he had mostly slaughtered Afghans, people like him. He shot a farmer who had taken money from the Americans to compensate for damage they had done to his build-ings. He shot a schoolteacher who might have been his own teacher for the three years he attended. He had killed and killed. And every time the ferenghee's airplanes and tanks appeared, his experienced and respected commander had made them hide. He had killed no Americans, had not even shot at one. Mahmoud Daoust died with those seven bullets in his chest, his lungs welling up with blood. What he felt mostly was relief.

But one of his rounds had headed toward the side of the trail where Deirdre and the general were watching. They saw great gorgeous swaths of white tracer fire stretching out in front of them like lethal artwork and then the blue, blindingly bright explosions of the claymores. And then there was a pause in the firing as the men operating the Minimis paused to place new belts of ammunition in their weapons, and the ser-geant in charge of them all yelled for them to hold their fire. He listened to his radio, waiting for the colonel to adjust his fire or redirect it, but no direction came. Another of the sergeants, closer to that side of the trail, radioed that he could detect no movement among the enemy.

They all waited for Matheson to reply.

It was the sergeant who had shushed General Lattice who found him. Mahmoud Daoust's AK-47 bullet had caught Matheson in his armpit as he had shifted to see the firefight better. It entered his right chest. The ribs under his armpit were broken and the pleura surrounding the lung was opened. Every time he inhaled he sucked as much air into his chest through his armpit as he did through his mouth. His lung was collapsing. In the abruptly silent night, the whole combat team could hear their colonel's gasping and, as one, they seemed to holler for the medical assistant, who arrived one moment later, with a chest tube and one-way valve in hand.

General Lattice flung himself into action. He directed the men to secure the perimeter, to examine the dead and establish that there was no residual threat. Simultaneously, he called in a medevac and identi-fied a level spot nearby where a helicopter could land.

There was no residual threat. The Taliban were all dead or dying. The medical assistant started IVs on the colonel and began running concentrated salt solution into him as fast as he could. Within minutes, a medevac helicopter was on site. A medical officer leapt out and helped load him into the bird. The colonel was losing consciousness now, and the doctor put a tube in his trachea to help force air in and out of his undamaged lung. Then he nodded to the pilots and the Blackhawk rose up and away and a moment later, all that could be heard of it was the rapidly fading thump of its rotors.

❦

With the chest tube inserted, and the valve allowing the air around his lungs to exit but not return, his left lung began to re-expand and Matheson did not feel as desperately short of breath as he had. He still coughed up blood and, with each paroxysm of coughing, he felt a stabbing pain in his chest where the chest tube rubbed against his lung. But he felt now that he could survive, whereas back on the ridgeline before the medic put the chest tube in it seemed quite clear he was dying.

He knew if he opened his eyes and revealed that he was awake he would be sedated. He wanted to remain awake and so he kept his eyes closed and listened to the din all around him.

He had seven children stateside. It occurred to him that it would be wildly irresponsible of him to die. He and his wife, Lisa, had gone to church their whole lives and loved one another in a wholehearted way since they were fifteen years old. His oldest daughter was eighteen and a freshman at Brigham Young. His youngest was three, and if he died now, she would not even remember him. Lisa, so bright and lively, would wilt overnight. Everyone would tell her how strong she was, and how lucky she was to have her faith and her community, but the truth was that she would crumble inside though she would confess that to no one.

He knew that she ached during these deployments and that she had spent six years now praying for the wars to end. And now, maybe, they were at an end for him. Even though each breath hurt, it was so much easier to breathe now. Through narrowed eyelids, he watched the valve as it flapped open with each expiration and closed with each inhalation.

He would live, he thought. And now he would go home. With all his limbs, too. Could be worse.

❀

They were scheduled to be out for another three days. Lattice had asked Deirdre if she wanted to go back to KAF on the medevac with Matheson.

"I think this is still where the story is, General. But thanks."

Lattice shrugged. He would have preferred that she head back behind the wire now, but he would lose more by ordering her to do so than would be worth it.

She got it. She had a point to make, too.

Every mammal with ears now knew the SF unit was in the area. And so the team gathered their equipment up and prepared to march, notwithstanding it being 0300 and dark. These soldiers were always quiet when they moved, but the usual outward-focused silence was now joined by an inward one. They had worked with the colonel for five years, as he was promoted again and again. These men were proud to be in his battalion and doubly proud to be in the fire team he accompanied in the field.

Letting the general direct the field ops of the team was like letting your boss's boss move into your house and decide how the roast should be cooked. It felt strange and intrusive to everyone except the general. This was Colonel Matheson's house. They were all grateful that the general had taken charge. But they wanted Colonel Matheson back. In the meantime it was night and the path needed to be studied. And the forest listened to. And fuck only knows who else was out there—drawn by the gunfire and then the medevac. They needed to get away, and they needed to remember that they would be looked for.

When the sun rose the next morning, they were still on the move. The sky had lightened in the east slowly, and then the sun burst out all at once as it topped a ridgeline. It was cool still, but the soldiers and Deirdre were warm from the effort of walking. Every one of them was still thinking about the colonel. SF formations took few casualties—the

IED strategy did not affect them much, as they avoided roads and used helicopters to take them anywhere they couldn't walk. But most of all, because they were careful and well led. Every casualty they did take made a lasting impression and Colonel Matheson was particularly well known. Everyone knew about his faith and his seven kids. No one had ever heard him swear or seen him drink alcohol or even coffee. They had ridiculed him for his rectitude but now what they remembered was that he had never once reprimanded any of them for their language or their intoxicant use or for anything that wasn't soldiering. And that when it came to soldiering he was obsessive. He knew the state of every bit of equipment his men carried, he knew the state of their feet and of their marriages. He insisted that every plan and the fallback and fall-back-back plans to every undertaking be defined and understood by all concerned. He'd kept them safe.

❀

When the sun came up over KAF, Lieutenant Colonel Matheson was in the base hospital being examined by a Danish trauma surgeon. A Dutch anaesthetist stood by. The American OR nurses had been woken when the helicopter radioed in. They were setting up the operating room. Everyone was anxious. When Matheson had arrived he was cold from the IV fluid run into him and from the altitude the helicopter flew to avoid ground fire on the way home. Cold because he had spilled so much of his blood out of his chest and into the soil.

Problem being, cold blood does not clot. And when he arrived his blood pressure was faint and if he were less fit than he was, he would have been more distressed with such a low blood pressure, but as it was, he indicated he felt fine, even though he was far from stable. And when the nurses transfused him with four units of packed red blood cells, he indicated he felt even better. And he meant it. But his hemoglobin on arrival was fifty grams per litre, and after the packed cells, it was still fifty grams per litre. Which meant that he was bleeding fast. The tube in his throat precluded him asking questions, but he heard enough of the conversation between the surgeon and the anaesthetist to understand.

The doctors transfused clotting proteins, more blood and platelets, and tranexamic acid but he was still bleeding fast. As he was brought to the operating room, the anaesthetist whispered, "You're going to sleep now, Colonel." Matheson nodded. The milky white propofol slid into his arm and his eyelids sagged. The anaesthetist watched the blood pressure carefully and ran in more fluids. When he judged the colonel to be unconscious, he nodded to the surgeon.

The surgeon opened his chest on the left side, excising a rib to get better access to his wound and cranking a set of rib spreaders. He found a hole in Matheson's subclavian artery. With his low blood pressure, the pulse of blood from it welled rhythmically, rather than spurted. The surgeon clamped it and sewed it carefully. The anaesthetist continued pumping in packed cells and plasma. In a desperate effort to warm the colonel enough that he might clot, the anaesthetist put a heated-air blanket on top of him ran all the blood and fluids he was giving him through a fluid warmer.

Finally the clamps came off the subclavian artery and the surgeon studied the repair. The suturing held. The hole was mended. He was still bleeding, however, in a diffuse and generalized way from a thousand places—his stomach lining, every suture in his chest, his lungs.

The surgeon closed up the incision as best he could, dabbing constantly at his suture lines in order to see where he was placing his needle. He looked up at the anaesthetist. "This is getting worse," he said.

"He needs whole blood," the anaesthetist said.

"Yes."

The military used walking blood banks—cadres of soldiers on base who volunteered to donate blood for mass casualties. They were all screened regularly for infections and unusual antibodies and in the sexless and drug-free environment of KAF this was a strategy that could be workable where in other contexts it would not be. When they were needed, the donors were called in and a half-litre of blood was taken from them and run right into the wounded.

With fresh warm blood, the battle wounded revived with unprecedented speed. Their disordered clotting normalized and their colour improved fast. Fresh warm blood contained things that the distilled and chilled product did not, and it turned out that those things were more important than anyone could have guessed.

The anaesthetist asked the lab to activate the walking blood bank. The tech hesitated, as the walking blood bank was supposed to be used in mass casualty situations. But the anaesthetist insisted: "This is Colonel Matheson." The debate stopped and the donors were contacted.

But by the time they had come in and were giving blood, Matheson was in worse trouble than ever, the urine in his catheter bag was claret, the secretions coming from his endotracheal tube were pink and frothy, his oxygen requirements were climbing and still, and again, the acidosis was severe. The anaesthetist had heard he had seven kids.

❧

In the café Rashid had noticed the agitation of the senior officers when they came in after the morning briefing, but there was no saying what was up with that. There never was. Agitated officers were not uncommon in the days and weeks before operations were to unfold.

Mohammed was in the back at the computer, reading the news. He had been told to google "Bagram Black Prison" and he had. But as he read the pieces that popped up, he resented having been told to do this. He shut his eyes in angry confusion. He opened them up again. He looked out at the soldiers in the café. Could any of them have been a part of such things? Hooks in the mouth? Electric shocks? How could this ever have happened?

❧

The Danish surgeon and the Dutch anaesthetist stood at the foot of the colonel's bed and watched the ventilator wheeze and sigh. The surgeon said, "The whole blood isn't helping. Could he have an ongoing bleeder we didn't see?"

The Dutch anaesthetist: "It's not impossible."

"Maybe his only chance is that there is, and we could fix it."

"He's not going to survive the trip to Landstuhl, that is for sure."

"We're just watching him spiral, now. And we're almost out of B-pos donors."

"He might not survive another thoracotomy."

"He won't survive another six hours like this. His kidneys are shutting down. His acidosis is worse. Every time we draw blood everything is more deranged. Multi-organ system failure. We can't just do nothing."

❀

That night was another movie night at Green Beans. At seven thirty it was growing dark and the crowd was restless. The turnout was even larger than for *Fight Club*. Rami Issay had grown anxious that Sara Miller was not coming, and had been deliberating how much longer to give her when the door opened and she walked in.

"Sorry I'm late," Miller said.

"You aren't at all," Rami Issay replied. "We have plenty of time." Then he stepped outside and gave a thumbs-up to Rashid, at the projector. Sara Miller and Major Horner followed him. Chayse Simpson was already there, and had videotaped the arrival of the crowd.

"Is that Rashid, running the projector? Oh, this is perfect," Miller enthused.

They sat down in the chairs that had been reserved for them. Amr brought Miller a cup of coffee—with almond milk, just as she liked it. Rami Issay tapped his foot nervously. He was aware that *Sin City* was not the sort of film normally shown on military bases. Several of the more pious soldiers would probably leave partway through the screening. Rami Issay wondered what they could possibly have made of the title when they opted to come. That there was a retribution theme? Well, there was, actually, but not in an Old Testament sense. It didn't matter.

In a few minutes the crowd would be rapt. This was a movie, not a DVD watched alone in a bunk with headphones plugged in and the rest of the world plugged out. They had gathered as a crowd to eat popcorn together. The object of their shared attention was less important than the fact of it. Rami Issay, cinephile since he was six years old, understood this.

He looked at Simpson, who was pointing her camera at him, and smiled. "It is lovely, is it not?" he whispered. "So many lonely people, just wishing to sit among friends and watch a show. I know exactly what they seek."

And then the sinning began: comic-book gore and bilious greens flowed into sulphurous yellows and Bruce Willis, full of taciturn rage, would endure anything to spare his daughter the suffering his enemies would subject her to if they could. Old Town was run by machine-gun-packing hookers full of lethal carnality. Crime kingpins and crooked cops were cartoonish in the darkest overinked sense, and the corrupt politician protected his monstrous son.

Most of the soldiers took it all in blank-facedly. There was some stirring in the back when the violence was interspersed with lurid graphic-novel sexuality. Some stood and left, but only a few. Rashid paid particular attention at the non-Americans in the audience: there were a couple of Jordanians, a few dozen Romanians, lots of Brits and Canadians, a smattering of Gurkhas—and the interpreter pool. As the film proceeded, the lurid comic-book carnality caught their attention. An animated, even a quasi-animated, film is allowed to be vastly filthier than live action movies, without drawing the attention of the censors, Rashid thought. Though this was certainly drawing the attention of everyone here. Poor little Mohammed's eyes were the size of chicken eggs.

Rami Issay was in his element: happy and validated. The host of a successful party, three hundred new close friends, sitting in metal chairs and eating popcorn with butter flavouring and too much salt and laying down a carpet of empty plastic water bottles. Every one of them, man and woman, rapt at the sight of Jessica Alba in chaps, twirling her lariat. Simpson zoomed in on him again, as he merrily, obliviously, chewed on his own popcorn.

Ninety minutes later, when the evildoers had been mostly punished and the muted and qualified victory of the righteous was obtained, Rashid finally looked up and around and was surprised to realize how engrossed he had become in this odd cartoon. It had felt so purifying to loathe a despicable scumbag villain and cheer his comeuppance. He looked over at Mohammed and saw an expression on the boy's face he had not seen before: a heavy-lidded blankness that could have been sleepiness, except that in his limbs was an agitated restlessness that he could not suppress. Rashid glanced next at Fazil and Amr. They looked as they always did. He looked back at Mohammed. Someone should have told him not to watch this. Too confusing for him. He did not need to see that scene with Brittany Murphy. Even in Boston they would have called that nasty.

※

"Mr. Issay, that was fantastic. I loved every second of it. Chayse, did you get some good footage?"

She nodded.

"Great. Clearly we can do something more interesting here than episode four of *Stars Earn Stripes*. I want to shoot the whole event the next time you put on a film. Can you do another one soon?"

Issay nodded. "Of course."

Miller put an arm around his shoulder and led him inside, where they sat down at a table. "I've already spoken to my contacts at NBC and Sony. They need to see some HD footage in order to commit, but your movie night will fit in nicely with the chess tournament footage. We might have most of a pilot right there."

"A pilot? You mean for the *Stars Earn Stripes*?"

"Well, I'm just thinking aloud here. But like I said, I'm seriously considering doing something altogether more interesting. A docu-dramedy about you and your café."

"Good heavens."

"You will have to get yourself an agent, Mr. Issay."

"Really? But I would be willing to work for free. I require no additional compensation."

"You'll want to think about that, I think. You'd need to come to Los Angeles. There will be test shoots and the writers would need to meet you."

"I'll need a visa."

"We'll take care of everything. What I am trying to work out now is how to tell your story in a way that the American public will connect to you."

"Am I so opaque?"

"We are all opaque to one another, Mr. Issay. The only redeeming feature of television is that it can break that down sometimes."

"Muslims from this part of the world are not well understood in America."

"I think you mean two things by that," she said.

"Yes?"

"I think you mean that they are not liked and I think you mean that they are not understood. For our purposes, these are very different problems. The dislike can be used to our advantage. The not understanding part is trickier. Americans don't like feeling stupid. The more they realize how little they understand about this place, this situation, the less engaged they will be as an audience. So our job is to familiarize them without them realizing it. We can't puncture the confidence of our viewer. On no account should we force on them an insight they do not feel they have come to mostly on their own."

"This is human nature. My staff, they are the same."

"Precisely. We want the viewer to come to understand the perspective of someone like you because they figured it out on their own, they're so smart. They know what you or someone like you thinks."

"Madam, I am at your disposal. I do not really understand how or what you are going to do. But I will help anyway I can."

Chayse Simpson and Sara Miller and Rami Issay sat at the café until long after everyone else had left. Simpson made notes. What this would be, they proposed, was a marriage of drama and reality television. Issay's character would be unveiled one episode at a time, with successive revelations alternately alarming and reassuring the audience. The thing would be to keep the audience fond of him, even as they feared him.

"Maybe make him torn himself, about his feelings about the unfaithful," Miller said.

"Ladies, if our purpose is to educate our audience I feel I should point out that the dominant tradition in Islam is one of tolerance," Rami Issay said. "Look around you, after all—you are surrounded by Muslims who are not angered by you."

Miller paused, then said, "We have to be conscious of the audience's expectations about you, though. And there has to be tension to sustain their interest. A whole lot of tolerant kumbaya will not be interesting to watch."

"I do not understand the kumbaya."

"Neither do I, Mr. Issay, except when I've been drinking."

❀

Climbing a hill fast now, the men kept the distance between them constant nevertheless. Deirdre followed Lattice closely and tried to pay attention to what he was saying. Clearly he was not minding being in command. He sounded as if he was not in the slightest tired. He was thirty years older than her. Where do they find these guys? And he kept talking.

"The movies get war wrong so constantly yet that version of combat is what prevails as normal, even among soldiers, even among ones who have seen a lot of fighting. You should see them coming back from particularly intense patrols. They have so much cognitive dissonance the first thing they do is run for their game consoles and immerse themselves in Call of Duty. The first few times I saw that I just stared. These guys are the original first-person shooters—why do they need the games?

"Because the games present violence as ordered and controlled and understandable, the same way movies do. The narrative arc is completed, there is a kind of choreography and beauty to a firefight shot by Michael Bay, or a bar fight even, in any sort of film. And we love that narrative. We apply it to situations where it doesn't apply in the least. Which is always.

"We've all seen bar fights. Stupid, fat, drunk men blowing saliva and blood and roaring at each other. No narrative about it. Nothing beautiful. Movie bar fights bear the same relationship to real bar fights that movie war does to real war.

"In movies and Greek poems, violence is a corrective, a settling of scores, a meting out of justice. It is necessary and useful." He paused and glanced behind him. Deirdre was right there. "Did I just hear your tape run out?"

Deirdre caught her breath. "No, I have . . . twenty more minutes," she said, checking her recorder. "We could do this when we stop, if you like."

"No, I think this is good, the sound of gear rattling, and you puffing for wind, puts it all in context."

"Okay."

"In the real world, chaos lies at the heart of violence. The men who shout and punch walls back home do it because they feel more comfortable, more powerful in a chaotic environment. Same thing here. This is the central reason war doesn't proceed logically and predictably. Phobos and Deimos, fear and dread, are the moons of Mars. But Chaos is her core."

"Is that the first time you've used that line?"

"No. But it's the first time for publication, if that's what you're worried about."

"Just wondering. So you keep track?"

"Of what I've been quoted saying?"

"Yes."

"Of course I do."

❁

The intelligence on the Taliban they had ambushed in the night was that they had been followed by drone for three days, right until the ambush itself. The entire operation was monitored and, though the soldiers in the field did not know this, it was played, real time, during a briefing for the secretary of defense in Washington. Normally the military was careful with letting civilians see live performances because, as per General Lattice, war is chaos and there is never any predicting what exactly might happen.

But over the last several months, the secretary of defense had been growing skeptical about the daily successes the Pentagon described, and the generals could tell that he perceived that they carefully edited the information and the videos they shared with him and with the public both. This ambush was picked to air live because it was expected to be very successful and because General Lattice was there, and Lattice had supporters within the secretary's office who had lobbied hard to resist what appeared to be Jeremy Jackson's inevitable elevation to head of CENTCOM. Jackson was one of only a few senior officers who publicly questioned the elevated status of the SF. But these days, the regular army did not know how to find the Taliban and Lattice had come to be known as the effective commander he was. When Lieutenant Colonel Matheson took that bullet to the chest, the public affairs guys leapt back in their chairs, mortified. The last seventy SF operations in a row had resulted in no friendly casualties at all. None of them had seen an American shot before. In any context.

As they watched, though, through narrowed and frightened eyes, they saw Lattice leaping into action and taking charge of the operation. In that room, he had more detractors than enthusiasts, but at that moment he was only admired.

Emails began circulating after those who were watching the video feed filed out of the room. BlackBerries and iPhones vibrated and chirped. People who moved in these circles were saddened to learn of Matheson's shooting and were very nearly as interested in the abrupt rise in status that General Lattice had just enjoyed.

Now, twelve hours later, everyone in the department of defense knew that an SF colonel, one who had been picked out for accelerated career progression, had been shot in an ambush staged by General Lattice for the secretary of defense. And that the secretary had finally made up his mind about Lattice and had instructed his staff to start getting him ready for the CENTCOM job. Which would probably lead to chairman of the Joint Chiefs. The buzz about this in Washington was like cicadas on a hot summer night.

❀

Lattice led the men to the compound where the Taliban they'd killed had spent their last night. Deirdre watched as the men kicked in the door and pulled every occupant out, man, woman and child. The children shrieked, the women raged and the men were seethingly compliant. They had been eating their midday meal.

The general asked in Pashto, over and over again, "Where are the Taliban? Where are your weapons?"

Nothing was admitted: they did not know any Taliban, they had no weapons. There were twelve young men here. Cousins, the patriarch said, who had come for a family wedding. No gunpowder residue on their hands, no English, no papers, no evidence one way or the other about who they really were. Lattice lined them up, facing the wall of the compound and had their wrists zap strapped.

In Pashto, he said, "I can show you videotape of the Taliban leaving your compound yesterday morning. I can show you videotape of them killing one of my oldest friends. I will take you back to the Special Forces compound in Kandahar and I can show you the tapes."

The old man's eyes grew wide at that. He shook his head. Deirdre's digital recorder was still turned on in her pocket, though she had not announced that.

Lattice's satphone buzzed. He stopped to answer it. "What? Oh, no. When? Has anyone called Lisa? I should, I think. I can do that from here. Who does SF have in the area, who can go see her? Yes, I know a chaplain will visit her. That's not what I'm asking. Well, find out. You have two hours. No, I have Lisa's number. Is her mother still living in Phoenix?"

And then he turned back to the soldiers. They had heard the conversation and knew what news had been relayed. Their faces sagged with fatigue and grief. One of the youngest among them started leaking tears down his face.

Sergeant Foscart, who was standing at the end of the line of men facing the wall, went white. He went down on one knee, and began punching the ground. Deirdre looked at him. This was not the kind of bond she had known in any other unit in Iraq or Afghanistan. She was ashamed that she was taping it without anyone's permission. Sergeant Foscart's grief was agony to watch, but she could not look away.

Which is why it was her eyes he locked on as he stood and lifted his M-4 to his shoulder and aimed at the head of the last man in line. And when that man fell, the man next to him did, too, and then three at a time after that, then four, then two. Twelve men with bullets in their brains in 3.2 seconds and then his magazine was empty and General Lattice was striding across the compound and lifting his own rifle to butt stroke Sergeant Foscart in the head and Foscart fell to the ground, face first. "Right in front of the fucking *embed*—are you insane?"

This struck Deirdre, even at the time, as unfortunate phrasing.

❁

"The helicopter will be here in fifteen minutes," General Lattice said, woodenly, to Deirdre.

"For Foscart?"

"And you, if you want. But you can't talk to him."

"I'd prefer to stay here, if that is possible."

"Because I said you couldn't talk to him?"

"Because this is still where the story is."

The general looked her in the eye. And he nodded. He walked away. She watched Foscart, standing with his wrists strapped behind his back, his weapons stripped from him: holster empty, grenades piled on the ground a hundred yards away, rifle leaning on top of them. Belt knife on it. Folding knife on the belt knife. It was beginning to dawn upon him just how far up the shit he was. None of the soldiers looked him in the eye. They knew him intimately, all had had their asses saved by him a dozen times, and most of them thought that they could equally have done what he did in the moment they learned of the colonel's death.

It was frightening to think about. Like standing on top of the Chrysler building the first time. For an instant, everyone wants to jump. Difference being, in war people do, because that is what war is. It is the dismantling of barriers. Point your weapon at a moving object and fire before you can even think about it. And if you're in harm's way, stopping to think about it means he shoots first.

Passion is the least important aspect of soldiering, once it stops being make-believe. In the imaginary version of it, it is Friday Night Football, under the lights, all determination and resolve and secondary effort. But passion in football is safe because the range of possible outcomes is so contained. You can take the eight yards you got with the catch. Or, with every bit of strength and ferocity available to you, you might be able to stretch it to a first down.

What you want in combat is no passion at all. The forward air controller needs to describe exactly what he sees and no more than that. If the target is not clearly legitimate it will end up being illegitimate and then someone is screaming "Bad kill." The pilot lining up for the 30-mm shot needs to identify the target dispassionately, and do his situation assessment precisely and needs to do this in an unhurried way with a maximum of precision and a minimum of anything else.

Foscart felt passion: grief and love for his comrade and pain and indignation at his murder. He gave way to it and destroyed his own life. And since there was no saying whether those men were even Taliban— for what?

※

Back at the compound, Gul Haqtar and his wife and daughters were washing the bodies of their cousins. He felt remorse like a giant clamp on his chest, for having acceded to the Taliban's request to sleep in his compound, but he told his wife and anyone who would listen that he had no choice. He knew that disaster had come to them. His cousins had brought the Taliban tea and rice and had asked them many questions. Some of his cousins were contemplating a path that could only have ended with an American bullet in their head. As it did, but so fast, so soon. Little Aqbal was just fifteen years old.

He had sent messages to all of their fathers. When the parents arrived it would be grief like an oil burn.

❀

The next day, General Jackson walked into the SF compound for the first time. The specialist at the gate put his heels together and looked back at his sergeant, who just nodded. They didn't know what to do. For years, the compound had been sovereign SF territory. No one came in here except by invitation. But those were four stars on his hat. Jackson walked up to the duty officer and told him to take him to where Sergeant Foscart was being held. The duty officer, an uneasy captain who had only arrived in theatre that month, tried to phone his battalion commander, but General Jackson interjected, "Now, please, captain."

Foscart was in one of the shipping containers that were used as temporary holding cells for all but the very hottest part of the year. He sat in a corner. When General Jackson approached his barred window and addressed him, he did not answer at first. The smell of urine and shit was ferocious. An American soldier had never before been held in one of these cells.

"Sergeant Foscart," the general said again.

The duty officer took out a pad and began recording the conversation.

"I'm not talking to anyone without a lawyer," Foscart said.

"Sergeant, I'm not going to ask you anything about the incident."

No response.

"Sergeant, apart from Colonel Matheson, were there any other Americans hurt in this operation?"

"No."

"Good."

"Sergeant, is the embed you took with you still out on patrol with your team?"

"Yes."

"Was she there during the incident?"

"You said you weren't going to ask me about that, sir. I want a lawyer."

"I don't need to know anything else except whether she was there."

"She was right there, sir. Right beside me."

"Thank you, Sergeant."

❀

It was only now, on the following day, that Lattice spoke to her again.

"You have to cut these guys some slack. They have been here for six years now. They sleep in the field 250 days a year and they are by formal policy denied almost any public recognition at all. You have to understand what they endure."

She nodded.

"I'm not saying this for my sake."

"I know, General."

"Want some more coffee?"

"Sure."

"We're heading in tomorrow."

"I thought we were going to be out for another three days."

"We've fulfilled our mission objectives."

"Or given it up as impossible, now?"

"Well, there were several applicable mission objectives."

"Are the men shaken?"

"The men are fine. They would do anything asked of them."

"Are you?"

"You can write that I am deeply concerned about the mishap of the other day."

"Mishap?"

"That's what you can write."

"That 'Chaos is the core of Mars' talk you gave me is looking pretty prescient to me. Did you have my piece scripted out before we even left KAF?"

"A man's life has been destroyed. I'm not going to joke about it."

"Twelve men's lives have been ended, actually."

"I grieve for them all, collectively and individually."

"Relax, my recorder isn't on."

"I'll confirm anything I say."

"I'm just going to call it like I see it, General."

"I would expect nothing else from you. Write whichever truth you need to."

He stood up and walked toward his men.

CHAPTER SEVENTEEN

When the helicopter landed at KAF early the next morning, Deirdre walked off onto the tarmac with her bag. She did not speak to anyone. The shit was about to come down and everyone knew it. Lattice disappeared with the soldiers and she was left alone. She headed to her room.

She lay face down on her cot for an hour and then she sat up, went to her little desk and opened her laptop. She began writing. A sadness filled her that she could not contain and she stopped writing for a while. She stood up and picked up a towel and some shampoo. She needed a shower more than she had ever needed anything.

In the steaming fibreglass box, she ruminated, her forehead against the wall of the stall: this was the biggest story she would ever break. It would define the rest of her career. And every word she would write would wound her. Like she was betraying her school, family and country all at once. This was not her. It felt wrong on every level. But it would be written about. There was no changing that. And if she didn't do it, everyone would want to know why. She had to write about it. It wasn't her who decided to shoot those boys. The things that ensued—for Lattice, for ISAF—would not be her doing. The depiction is not the act, the act is the act.

Back in her room, she sat on her chair in her towel looking at the few sentences she had managed. "Not in front of the fucking embed." Clearly that would be a call-out at the very least. She lifted her hands to the keyboard. She set them back in her lap. Again.

❀

In the café, Mohammed sat at the counter, blinking away sleepiness as Fazil baked cakes. He'd heard the helicopters coming in, but this was not unusual at that time of the day. The night raids sometimes lasted until the following mid-morning, depending on how eventful they had proven to be. There would likely be soldiers in soon, looking for coffee. In the meantime, stillness. He stared out the window and watched as the lady reporter emerged from the airfield fencing and walked up Screaming Eagle Way. She looked tired. Perhaps she had been up all night. She walked more slowly than he had ever seen her walk. Maybe her pack was quite heavy. The things she would see, doing that work, would be difficult, he imagined. YouTube had opened his eyes about those night raids. He would not watch any more of those videos. He would not go to any more of the movies, either.

Rami Issay stirred himself enough to rise in the back and make it heavily to a table. He waved to Mohammed, indicating that he would like a chai. Mohammed paused for a millisecond and then rose to make it. His boss had barely slept. He had been so excited it had been all he could do even to remain in the bed. Eventually, in the swirl of imaginings about moving to California and owning his own bungalow, about the reassessment his wife would make of him, he drifted away briefly. And then he was awake again, to the sound of Fazil sifting flour. If the possibilities in front of him were half as great as he was told they were, then anything could happen. But he had never known insomnia such as this before. Were good things worth worrying about so much? Surely he would not have preferred just mindlessly running the coffee shop, would he?

Sara Miller and Chayse Simpson came through the doors just then, waving at Rami Issay, and then waving harder to indicate he should stay where he was.

"Jack Benson only gets involved in projects that will be big," Miller said. "I heard he was following our work before I came out here, but something must have caught his attention—probably that footage you sent in of the chess tournament."

"So what do we have to do before he gets here?"

"Well we should have a modified treatment of 'Stolen Information' ready to show him, one that emphasizes Issay's appeal. And we should have notes on our show, too."

"I'd like to talk about that more. I don't know how that non-realistic dramedy/reality idea works." Simpson winced, internally. That was snider than she'd meant it to be.

"Non-realistic dramedy/reality show? That's perfect. Take it from there. Maybe we cast only soldiers and people who have worked at the café. Maybe we make a complete replica of the café. And then write scripts around that recreated reality. With the carrying device of a pop-culture-worshipping Pakistani Muslim exhorting everyone around him to be more civilized, to understand the momentousness of Lady Gaga and *Glee*. All around him, carnage."

"He has no idea who Gaga is. He watches a lot of movies he doesn't always understand that well. To the extent that he knows anything, that's what he knows."

"He can read a script."

"Grow a beard, whittle up a mallard call."

"Exactly."

"That's a lot of work to do in what, two days?"

"That's how it works in the big leagues, my dear. We might not be sleeping very much. Got any cocaine?"

"What?"

"Joking. Anyway, it's ecstasy you kids use these days, isn't it? "

"If we were at an EMF concert in 1996, maybe." *Shit. That was sharp.*

"You're going to go far, Chayse."
Oh. She likes it.

❀

He met Deirdre at the café, without Fred, at her request.

"Look, I know you have had your problems with him, but I need your advice," she said. "This piece could mean the end of his career. It could torpedo a possible path to success in this theatre. It could affect thousands of lives."

"What did he tell you to do?"

"To write whichever truth I needed to."

"So he was telling you to do your job, basically."

"I guess."

"I've known Tom a long time. It's all he wants, for everyone to just do their jobs. As he defines it, admittedly, but that's all he wants."

"Even if doing my job means wrecking the mission here?"

"He really did sell you on his whole thing, didn't he?"

"No, he didn't."

"He is a meticulous man. Everything he does is something he has considered and decided to do."

"You think he arranged the massacre?"

"Don't be an idiot, Deirdre, of course not. But what he said to you, before and after, was thought out. You can count on it."

"You want him taken down, don't you?"

"No. I think the cult of Special Forces is bad for the army and that assassins, generally, don't pacify countries very well, but I don't want him destroyed. It's okay with me if his wings get clipped, but it doesn't really matter what's okay with me and what isn't. That's what I'm trying to tell you. I'm sure he didn't know the shooting would occur. But Tom would certainly have known that it could have occurred and he opted to allow you to see that."

"You think this sort of thing happens often?"

"Who knows? I'm not SF. But I'd say it happens way more for the SF than for the regular army. Which is another reason to be careful about an expanded role for SF."

"You really are trying to sink him, aren't you?"

"Deirdre."

"Fuck you, Jeremy."

And she stood and left. Everyone in the café had stared at their tabletops and pretended not to listen as they'd craned for every word. Why would a journalist speak with such familiarity to a general?

❦

Just Amachai walked in as General Jackson walked out. She had spent the last half-hour on the telephone telling her parents and her son that she was coming home. She was so happy she had to restrain herself from giggling. Her son had not believed her. Then, when he realized she was serious, he had shrieked, he was so happy. Her parents had been more lukewarm, but she was their favourite daughter, ultimately, and they missed her no matter the money she sent them. Anyway, it was time. They all knew it. She had been abroad for years. Dubai, before here. And before that, Kazakstan. That had been dreadful. She almost came home then.

After she got off the phone she had packed her things. It took about fifteen minutes to fill three duffle bags. She left enough clothes out to wear the next few days. She was going home. It had been as simple as deciding to. She should have done this months ago. Years ago.

And as she sat down, beaming unselfconsciously, Mohammed walked up her, grinning to see her so happy. He carried with him a chai latte. "Oh, thank you, Mohammed, that's very kind of you."

"Is madam having an especially good day today?"

"How can you tell?"

"You are smiling, if you will permit me, like a quarter moon on its side."

"That is beautiful. Did your teacher teach you that?"

"I read it on the computer we keep in the back."

"The internet is full of treasure."

"And many other things."

She laughed. "Yes, and many other things. Mohammed. How are you?"

"I am well. And you?"

"I, too, am well. I have been making arrangements to return home, to my family, in Thailand."

"For a vacation?"

"No, for good," she said carelessly and too quickly, and then she saw his face.

"Well, that's . . ." was all he could muster, and then he ran into the back of the café. Rami Issay looked up to see the boy disappear. He glanced around, mystified. Fazil glowered at Just Amachai from behind the counter. After a few moments he wiped off his hands and followed Mohammed into the back. Just Amachai was dismayed. She had been so callous. She could not follow him into the back of the café. She had to speak to him again. Maybe when he came out.

❀

The first three drafts were too obviously exculpatory. "'You have to understand,' the general said, 'these men are in the field three hundred days a year,'" was the lede on the first go-round. It wouldn't fly. The comments section would hear from thousands of people who did not know the rudiments of rank structure but would hold forth with absolute certainty about war and rules of engagement. Editorial boards across the country, which had thundered their approval of all proposed wars for years, would take the opportunity to seize the moral high ground of uninformed hypocritical condemnation. And worse, the only voices to compete with the critical ones would be the worst possible: "Give 'em two, boys."

The only way forward was to just go pure *AP Style Manual*. Facts, events, statements, one upon the other without comment or inflection. Describe what she knew, what had happened, what was said to her. Let the reader make up her mind.

And, with every word, she would sink a knife deeper into the men she respected most in the world.

CHAPTER EIGHTEEN

Green Beans café, KAF

Rami Issay

The lady journalist is distressed by something. She argued with the general yesterday and has not been the same since. Perhaps he is unhappy with her and this depresses her.

But such a glorious day today, and the auguries could not be more favourable. It appears that this television show has widespread support. Sara Miller and Ms Simpson are very optimistic. Already they are talking of spinoffs! Their last effort, *Firefighters' Hoses,* they told me, ran for two seasons. This discussion of me going to Los Angeles is pretty exciting, I must say. I did tell them that obtaining a visa may be challenging, as, for that matter, is merely getting me on an airplane. How long do people stay on no-fly lists? If those on it are all people of as little danger as I am, it must be quite long, indeed. Could it just get longer and longer forever, until every faithful brown man is included? I must ask more questions about this. One hopes they will not be put off involving me when they learn of my difficulties in the UK.

I must also do something nice for Rashid. He has been my muse in these efforts and to him must go at least a little of the credit for the success of the film screenings and of the chess tournament. I will suggest to my superiors that he assume the mantle of command when I move to California. Fazil will object, of course. But that man lacks vision. He does not understand the poetry of running a café. He does not grasp the significance of the chess and the movies, the shelter a café provides from a difficult world. He understands what the place earns, but he does not see what it nurtures.

But my wife will, when she sees the reality television show. Maybe not *Stars Earn Stripes*—my appearance will be too brief to change anyone's mind about anything. Mine will be just a cameo and cameos must not hijack the production, I understand that. But this spin-off show they are planning could become a vehicle to communicate an idea. And it might allow us all to live together again, and permit me to support her and my daughters.

I get so ahead of myself sometimes. The thing to think about now is the movie tomorrow night. Sara Miller's boss will be there and it will be useful to inspire in him the same level of enthusiasm.

Just Amachai

It is like I touched the boy with a live wire. Dismissed by his own mother, alone on this insane base, one child among twelve thousand adults. He and I develop a friendship that seems very warm—and then all of a sudden I announce that I am leaving. I am a fool.

And now he will not even look at me. Fazil had to bring me my tea. With the disdain of a missionary, but still. It would be easy to just leave. But I think I must put things right with Mohammed. I would take him back to Thailand if I could. But that it is not possible and, anyway, this is where he is from. Like my home is where I am from.

This is exactly how you make a boy grow up to hate women. There are enough of those already.

Perhaps I could write him a letter. I did not make his mother abandon him. I was simply friendly to him at the café he works at. But he is a child and he is lonely and unhappy. We all have an obligation to help him if we can. I think a letter would be good. Does he read English as well as he speaks it? I've seen him write out the chalk menu—so probably. But a letter. I'll never even know if he read it. And he'll know that.

Mohammed Hashto

I cannot look at her. She thinks I am upset that she is leaving but I do not care at all. It is the obscenity of that Jessica Alba movie that torments me. I shut my eyes and pray but the picture of her and her rope stays with me. It was like Satan was sitting in my lap and holding my eyes open and pointing my head at her. She was so beautiful she could not possibly be real, and Satan held everyone there that night and came to us all as we sunk into those impure thoughts.

Afterward I looked Jessica Alba up on the computer. There are many photographs of her, all of them hard to not look at for a long time. The day after the movie, I went to the bazaar and bought *Into the Blue* and the *Fantastic Four*. I watched them that night on Rami Issay's DVD player while he slept. I felt like I loved her. That was Satan, sitting in my lap.

I have not understood how powerful his magic is before. But when I watched those movies it seemed to me that she was no nice and kind and tender that it would simply be impossible not to love her. And however immodest she is in these movies, this is just the wickedness of the men who make those movies. She does what is asked of her, and in that world, women wear bathing suits and revealing clothes. Surely she deserves some praise for her obedience, even if it is to requests pure men would not make of a woman? This is how I thought, because I am young and still learning.

I know now that Jessica Alba is the vessel that Satan has chosen to reach me. He wants me to excuse her, to love her, and to want her.

And it was Satan who brought these soldiers here to kill my people. On the internet this morning, they say that, out in Panjwai, they shot down twenty boys my age who were praying in the house of their uncle, just because they were wearing turbans. And Satan also made me weak, made me want the friendship of the Thai woman and made me cry about my mother with my pillow over my head at night.

Rashid Siddiqui

Poor little Mohammed, in love with Jessica Alba and the Thai masseuse both. How did anyone think that this was a good idea? One boy among all these suspect men and a few women. How could that not be a disaster?

Bright and yet not hot today—a rare combination here. It affects the mood of the whole café. Everyone except Mohammed seems cheerful. Rami Issay is so convinced that he will become an American reality television star that he hardly talks about anything else. Which is fine by me.

Chayse Simpson

I have to admit Rashid is cute. I heard him speak English to some customers earlier this week in an unguarded moment and he sounded like Ben Affleck, all Boston drawl. Issay says he studied at Harvard but I'm pretty sure that is hyperbole. BU, maybe. We'll need to find out, for sure, for the writers. That raises a delicate point: if Homeland Security saw fit to deport him, then what will be said about us if we use him on the show?

Deirdre O'Malley

So it's written. Seven thousand words of nothing-but-the-facts. I sent it to Lattice. I imagine he'll show it to his PA people. They'll be aghast. I'll probably be asked to get on a plane pretty soon.

Yes, twelve dead Taliban sympathizers or recruits are bad. But how many girls will have acid poured on their faces for going to school when this all goes to shit and the Taliban take over again? More than twelve, I'll say that. So what have I accomplished here, really? I preserved my fucking *credibility*.

I want him to just deny it all. Deny the quotes that look so damning in light of the shooting. Refuse to confirm anything I've written. His people might tell him to do that. If they do, and he does, then fine. I've done what I needed to do. Whether the piece runs or not, whether it even survives fact checking, is not my problem.

He kept saying he'd confirm everything though. I'm pretty scared he'll do just that. Like he's prepared to let his career just blow up. He thinks he's this country's best chance to emerge from all this tragedy. And he is. Rolling over for this will be betraying that chance, and this country we invaded. I want to tell him that. I tried to. I called him, but he didn't take my call. Then the press release came out a couple of hours ago about Foscart being under investigation for events surrounding the shooting deaths of suspected Taliban in Panjwai. That would be his PA people who drafted that. "Suspected Taliban." You start lying in these things and you lose all chance of recovering. But he didn't stop them and he could have. Inexplicable.

Captain Robert Waller

So after sifting through every record we have of internet traffic on and off the base in the months prior to the publication of those leaks, the best we can do is admit that we just don't know. *After* the leaks were published, that interpreter sent some of the same files to an address in Lahore. But nothing about him suggested he was involved before that. His email accounts were all clean. And his interrogation—which still makes me nauseous to remember—seemed pretty clear-cut. Fuck. I remember those guys back in 2001, and the things they got up to with prisoners then.

I thought it was just an excess-of-the-moment, buildings-still-smoking sort of thing. Who would ever have thought that would become normal? Sick fucking puppies get into that. The twist is that they sent me here in the first place because I was SF and I was here at the start. It's not like this is intelligence work so much as it is police work. Which is why my working group involved FBI, DHS and NSA, as well as CIA. Who all consider me not enough of a cop to be leading the team. But still I'm enough of an SF infantry sergeant not to put up with that for long.

Anyway. The other lead was that large late-night upload from a week before the first publication, from here in KAF. But we weren't copying all files coming in and out yet. So we just can't say for sure. I am told there are also suspicious-looking uploads recorded on a couple dozen other bases over here and stateside. In retrospect, we were pretty lax. Unless the leaker gets loaded and starts confessing his involvement on some chat platform or something, I can't see this case going anywhere.

What I try to remember is that, big picture, this has been a great opportunity. Now I have field experience in combat arms, traditional intelligence assessment and in counter-espionage investigation. So the thing to do is wrap up the assessment and file the report. Whoever sent me here is looking after me.

The guys I run into over at the SF compound that I knew from my days with them think I did the smart thing moving to intelligence. That's a relief. They say they can't see the years coming up having a patch on the ones just passed. Meaning: the wars are going to shit—but also that we are, too. Which they can't say out loud. My stepdad would agree with that. Anyway, he would if he knew what I spent three days watching and listening to. I won't be able to bring myself to tell him about that.

I lift a hand and order another coffee. Nice to have a little downtime.

CHAPTER NINETEEN

Rami Issay hovered as Rashid Siddiqui pried the crate open. When the nails squealed and the top board pulled up, packing foam flowed out and then the grey metal can holding the filmstock emerged. Rashid reached inside and withdrew it. Neither of them could breathe for a moment. Then they saw the title. *Batman Returns*. They both exhaled in one long breath.

"We have no debacles to amuse the television people."

"Don't worry, boss. You're going to be a star."

"We're all going to have our lives changed by this, my boy."

"Well, you mostly. But it's okay. I'm happy for you."

"You will see. All our lives will be different."

"Even Amr's?"

"Amr is implacable, my dear boy. He allows his life to change exactly as much as he wants it to."

"Most of us don't have as much control over things as that."

"Most of us want too much."

"Is that you, saying this?"

"I know, I know, I hear the irony. But with my recent successes, I see the folly of wanting excessively. I have been reading about Buddhism. It's very grounding, they say."

Rashid looked at him like he had just claimed sainthood. "Well, let me know how that goes, boss." He set to further unpacking the crate.

"I think, Rashid, that I may be self-sabotaging."

The younger man looked up at him.

"I mean it. It all feels a bit too much. Major Horner says Mr. Barnett says he is going to fly me and my family—and my friends, too, I'm sure, don't worry—to LA to complete the shooting and promote the series launch. It sounds incredible. My daughters will walk the red carpet. They will admire me. How can any of this be true?"

"Well, think about the Buddhists, boss. Don't get carried away." He took out the other four cans of film, all marked BATMAN RETURNS.

"I may need some sort of therapy."

Rashid turned to look at him.

"Not now. Later, in California. Jungian, maybe."

"You are joking."

"Of course I am joking."

"I was going to tell you to just enjoy the ride, but clearly you are."

"No one has been better prepared to enjoy this than me. After the misadventures of the last several years, I am ready to enjoy some good luck, I promise you."

"Have you told your family about this?"

"Not yet."

"Does Mr. Burnett not ask about them?"

"Sara Miller has asked."

"You do not want to discuss this."

"I don't," Rami Issay agreed, amiably. "And anyway, I have work to do. Major Horner is as excited about this television program as anyone else. He wants a report on the preparations for tonight."

Major Horner called Rami Issay a few minutes later to confirm that the screening was a go.

"Of course it is."

"Which film showed up?"

"*Batman Returns.*"

"Thank God."

"Our Ramstein trickster seems to have developed a conscience."

"It was either that or Leavenworth. I will not be embarrassed in front of these studio people."

"I think they found the story amusing. I think they will be disappointed to learn that the joke is not being continued. They want to use that story in the pilot, they say."

"Who said that? Miller?"

"Ms Miller did, yes."

"What else has she said?"

"A million things."

"I should have had you keeping notes."

"There would have been too many. I could have worn a wire."

"Don't mock me, Mr. Issay. I have a fair amount of influence over this project."

"Oh, I am not mocking you, sir. I don't know why you would think that."

"When will the screening start?"

"At sunset as usual, sir."

"I will see you at sunset."

"Sir, we will save you a seat, sir."

"Stop that."

❀

Fazil looked up as Sara Miller and Chayse Simpson walked into the café. Following them was a new face, a man apparently just off the flight from Kabul, wearing crisp L.L.Bean outerwear and Ray-Bans. The two women appeared very interested in demonstrating to him how fascinating the café was. Rami Issay leapt off his chair and ran to greet the TV people with obsequious good humour.

❁

Anakopoulus had thought that he would not go to see the *Batman* movie, but the day was so warm and bright that his anxiety had lifted a little. He had a feeling that there were no longer quite as many eyes looking for him as there had been. Probably just wishful thinking.

❁

Rob Waller sat on his cot and packed the open barracks box in front of him. His report, concluding that the leak could not be traced to any specific sender in KAF, had been on someone's desk for just six hours when the order to return to Baghdad reached him. Proof of how in the shit Iraq was now, how much they needed more actionable intel, especially from people who understood the battlefield and, consequently, what the "actionable" part of that phrase meant.

He would be perceived to have failed, but he did not view the responsibility for finding the leaker to have been properly his. If it were not for his SF background he would never have been given this assignment. Against his every expectation, he looked forward to getting back to Iraq, to looking at weapons and reading pieces of paper and partially burnt maps. Data-trolling was not for him.

Anyway, for all the discussion about the all-seeing eye of the state, from what Waller had seen, the brain behind that eye was too limited to use that data. What they needed was more humans to read the millions of words of telephone transcripts and emails that accumulated every day in their files. What they needed, ultimately, was a human observer for every five or six humans in KAF, to read their letters and emails and to listen to their telephone calls. Which would be one sort of world to live in. He had rebadged into intelligence because he wanted to concern himself with the big picture. Instead, he had spent his time here immersed in the small picture of normal people's lives, reading transcripts of telephone calls between lonely soldiers and their wives/

husbands/boyfriends/girlfriends. This managed to make him feel even dirtier than he had after watching that CIA sadist interrogate the terp. That was as low as he thought he could go. Back in Baghdad, he would sharpen up his Arabic and think about al-Qaeda in Iraq and work on understanding its organization, methods and aims. He would do the work of an officer in the intelligence branch of the US Army. Rather than in the KGB.

He had wanted to get back to Afghanistan, with its mountains, bright blue skies and clean air. And now he couldn't get out of here fast enough. He put the last of his socks in the barracks box. Next came the undershirts. Fuck. This place had been the model he had used to illustrate how far astray Iraq had gone.

❀

Rami Issay and Chayse Simpson listened as Sara Miller briefed Mr. Burnett on her idea.

"Chayse, tell him your thoughts about the narrative drivers at work here."

"Oh, yes, sure. It has to do with the complicated status of Mr. Issay's character, as being both completely other and the only solace available in horrible circumstance. He conflates the ideas of comfort and threat in a way that could sustain narrative tension almost indefinitely, if done right."

"That's interesting. Sara, who do you see writing this?"

Simpson answered: "Me, I should write this."

Mr. Burnett turned to her and paid attention to what he saw for the first time.

"What have you written?"

"This will be my first show."

"So, nothing?"

"She could do it, Mark."

"That would be a pretty risky bet."

"We're used to those. Remember the first days of *Firefighters' Hoses*? Let's get her to write a pilot."

"What about *Stars Earn Stripes*?"

"We'll feature him in episode four and then create a social media storm about him."

"So who's writing episode four?'"

"I am," Simpson said.

"Of course you are." Burnett turned back to Miller. "Does she ever let up?"

Miller shook her head.

❀

As the afternoon wore on, Rami Issay began fretting about the screening. People had been coming by all day asking about it. He had the sense that the turnout might be much larger than with either of their previous showings. At about five, he excused himself from Sara Miller and Mr. Burnett. He went into the back and asked Rashid and Mohammed to begin setting up the chairs. He'd requested a hundred more than last time and now he worried that he still wouldn't have enough.

At six, Rashid set up the projector and ran the extension cord to it. Rami Issay pulled the popcorn popper into place and then pushed a cooler he had borrowed from the DFAC beside it. He loaded it with bottled water. Amr came outside to help now, too. Rami Issay had decided to close the café between seven and ten, so everyone could concentrate on the film. Fazil had pointed out that the screening was not an income-generating event, and was only justified as a way of increasing traffic to the café, so what was he accomplishing by closing it? Rami Issay rolled his eyes, and told Fazil that they could talk about this later.

By seven the line approaching the café was a hundred metres long. The day was still quite bright and Rashid was still setting up the last of the chairs. *Batman*. It was the perfect choice. Next he would ask for *Fantastic Four*—another Jessica Alba vehicle—and then *Iron Man*, some of the *Spider-Man* films. Come autumn, he would book more thoughtful offerings. Maybe some of those Clint Eastwood directorial projects. He might even be running the café by that point. Rami Issay could be in California.

⚛

Deirdre O'Malley sat down forlornly in the sea of happy soldiers. She had heard back from Lattice. "Thanx. Will confirm all." She'd put her forehead down on her little desk and breathed in and out just as deeply as she could for a long time. Then she filed the piece. Then she thought to herself that it would be better if she were not alone just then. She got up and walked toward the café. She wondered why there was a lineup on Screaming Eagle Way but then saw the rows of chairs. *Batman.* Excellent.

⚛

Simpson walked in front of the crowd and took a photograph of it. Later this picture would be studied in considerable detail. The thing everyone would always point out was how happy everyone looked.

In the second row, behind the long-legged men, was Just Amachai, who had come with the hope of seeing Mohammed. Beside her, Amr Chalabi sat with his arms crossed in front of his chest. He had loved Batman since he was a little boy. He had bought the bootleg DVDs of the Michael Keaton and George Clooney *Batman* movies, but he thought that this Christian Bale might be the best Batman yet.

Next to him was Anakopoulus. He had not been arrested. His bosses were not acting oddly. At last he felt that the eye of the storm had moved on. On Anakopoulus's other side sat several nurses from the hospital across the road. Despite the nice weather recently, the fighting—or at least the number of wounded reaching KAF—had been light. The nurses were rested, and the medics and doctors, sitting in the row behind them, were, too. *Batman Returns.* And popcorn and fountain drinks. What could be better?

Just Amachai scanned the crowd for Mohammed. She wanted badly to talk to him. She could not find him. Then she spotted him beside the popcorn popper, operating the butter dispenser. He felt her staring at him, perhaps, because at that moment he looked out at the crowd. She waved to him. He glanced at her, then went back to his work. He had seen her, she felt certain. It eased her ache a little.

Burnett and Miller sat in their reserved seats behind Just Amachai. The rest of the chairs were taken and the light was failing. Latecomers sat on the ground to the sides or stood at the back behind the chairs. Soon the film would begin. As would *Batman*. Again.

Rob Waller wandered up around then. His flight was not until the following morning and he was tired of contemplating the idea of actually looking forward to getting back to Iraq. That was too discomfiting to bear much contemplation. He looked around for someone he knew. He saw his old friend, the sergeant from Bar Harbor, but he was with some other SF NCOs and he decided not to join them and found a spot to stand at the back.

A platoon of Jordanian infantry occupied the last row of chairs. This was unprecedented, seeing the Jordanians out after dark. They had neatly stooked their rifles—AK-47s—with one of their number standing guard. The rest of the men looked as if it took every bit of will they possessed not to break out into gleeful laughter.

Rashid made his way to the projector in the centre of the crowd. He had not left enough room between the chairs to permit free passage and as he slipped between the rows, he tripped many times, "Excuse me, excuse me . . ." And he thought he was tripped a few times but he wasn't sure.

Finally he reached the projector. He turned on the warming light for the bulb. He looked at his watch. The desert sky was blue-black in the east and in the west, lit up with oranges and reds. He looked over to Rami Issay by the cash register and popcorn popper. Rami Issay looked at the sky and then at his watch. He nodded. Rashid hit play.

The cone of light stabbed into the darkness, and in its stream could be observed innumerable insects, dancing in the light. The hubbub settled down as the film flickered to life. A softball game was being played in a desert compound; innocence and simple pleasure. A bomb goes off. Then another. This was not, actually, Gotham City. And Jamie Foxx was not in *Batman Returns*. Amr knew this immediately. They had gotten the wrong film again. Of course they had. Title sequence. *The Kingdom*. Rashid turned off the projector.

He looked toward to Rami Issay, holding his palms up. They had seen trailers online for this movie but did not remember the specifics. That miscreant in Ramstein put the wrong film in the cases just to mess with them. But four hundred people were growing restless now and this was the only film they had. It could be worse. *The Kingdom*. A Jamie Foxx adventure vehicle. Rami Issay motioned to Rashid to carry on. He was definitely going to file a formal complaint about this.

But it was much worse than simply not *Batman Returns*. Every Muslim in the film was a terrorist or a terrorist sympathizer. Arabs were brutal, stupid cowards. Amr stood up to leave and he was hissed at for blocking the view. He sat down again. Rami Issay collapsed on a crate. He could not watch the screen. When he did look up he surveyed the audience, who had been puzzled when *Batman* had not shown up on the screen, but had settled in comfortably enough. He searched the faces until he found Mr. Burnett and Ms Miller. They were eating popcorn and whispering to one another. They seemed to be enjoying the show. He glanced at Amr, whose expression was so impassive, someone who didn't know him might have thought he was sleepy.

Then a man was tapping him on the shoulder, asking for popcorn. Rami Issay looked around for Mohammed, but the boy was not there. He could not see him anywhere. Perhaps he gone to use the washroom. So Rami Issay stood and filled up a bag and took the man's money. He motioned to Amr to come help but Amr would not acknowledge him. He looked for Fazil, but Fazil's seat was empty.

This irritated Rami Issay, whose instinct was to avoid getting into the nitty-gritty of anything ever. But after he had served a couple more bags of popcorn, he found that he enjoyed it. One hungry young man after another stepped up and said, "Extra-large, please," and held out a five-dollar bill. Rami Issay knew that the popcorn was costing him about twenty cents a bag. The butter, or rather margarine, was a nickel more.

He forgot about Mohammed's absence, and Fazil's, and Amr's failure to notice his summoning. He got the hang of filling the bags with a couple of quick scoops and taking the proffered money with a smile.

Amr also looked around for Mohammed, concerned about the impression the film might be making on him. He was no longer at the popcorn table. He scanned the margins of the crowd but could not see him. He looked over his shoulder for some reason and then he saw him at the back, near the Jordanians. What was he doing there? The man guarding the rifles was staring at the movie screen, transfixed, ignoring the boy.

Rami Issay was filling popcorn bags as fast they appeared in front of him. He was like a popcorn dispensing automaton. Then he couldn't hear a thing because a helicopter was winding up its rotor, thump, thump, thump, from somewhere near the airfield, and where was Mohammed, anyway?

Then he realized that was no helicopter. That sounded like an AK but on the screen Jamie Foxx was only talking to one of his underlings.

No, it was an AK, and it was very loud. He looked around the field. The AK was in little Mohammed's hands, and he was firing in short, aimed bursts at the crowd.

The first person to realize what was happening was Amr. He leapt to his feet and over the row of chairs, running at the boy roaring, "No!" Mohammed saw the figure emerging from the gloom and shot Amr through his forehead, shot his protector and his fellow chess player and his consolation. Amr died in the gravel, with an exit wound in the back of his head the size of a baseball. Just Amachai realized what was happening, too, and she stood as well, and waved her arms noiselessly at Mohammed, who was not thinking anymore, just firing, and Just Amachai fell, too, with a bullet in her chest and another three in her abdomen.

Anakopoulus did not understand what was unfolding around him, but he was on his feet. In standing, he drew fire to him, a bullet striking his left shoulder, and spinning him around. Directly in front of him, Deirdre O'Malley heard a bullet whistle past her ear and then another shattered both forearms. One-fifth of a second later a third was en route toward her forehead, but at the same time Anakopoulus was falling. And in falling, he was hit in the chest by the bullet that had been meant for Deirdre's head. She saw his body shake as he was hit and then she dropped to the ground, bullets whistling just like they had in the ambush she had been in with the Canadians. It took her a moment to understand that the bones in her forearms and hands had been shattered.

These were unprepared, unarmed and unarmoured men and women, in the night, with a bright screen in front of them blinding them to the source of the gunfire. And as they collectively realized they were being fired upon, they rose and began running randomly, tripping over people on the ground, falling on them, and being fallen on in their turn. As men stepped on bodies in the dark, the sound of bones breaking could be heard amid the shots and among the screaming.

Mohammed continued firing. One of his bullets struck the projector and set it spinning and falling, its bulb extinguished in a great burst of sparks.

Sara Miller pulled Burnett with her through the crowd and they ran off into the night. Rami Issay saw them escape, and noted it with relief. He walked around the popcorn table and, no longer able to discern Mohammed, held his arms up as he approached the muzzle flashes that marked the boy's position. With the next burst, he thought, *Oh, that was close.* And then felt his shoulder being spun around and wondered who'd grabbed him, and then he smelled his own blood rushing out down his arm and he fell, too.

Of the people who had slid off their chairs to the ground after Mohammed began shooting, many carried pistols. Most of those remained pressed into the soil just as tightly as they could get themselves, but there were a few, MPs and infanteers, who lifted their heads and scanned for the source of the gunfire. Mohammed had emptied the magazine of his rifle before anyone could react in the bedlam. And then came the moment when he had to change magazines.

He apparently knew how to do this, but in the fear and excitement of the moment he found it difficult to remove the old magazine and when he finally did, it was all he could do get a new one into the weapon and to chamber a round. In that silence, eight pistols were raised but with the projector extinguished nothing could be seen of the shooter. That would have been the moment when Mohammed might have tried to slip away and perhaps he could have and perhaps he would not have been identified as the shooter.

This was not the fate he had chosen. Instead, he held the rifle to his shoulder awkwardly and fired a fresh stream of rounds through the frightened people on the ground. And then the eight pistols fired almost as one at his muzzle flashes. And again and again until they were all empty and then there was no more shooting at all.

And little Mohammed Hashto lay on the ground, punctured in a dozen places, as he had punctured so many others. He took a breath, and it hurt, because his ribs had been broken by the pistol bullets. And then he coughed. Bright, foaming blood poured out of his lips. He wished his mother were there. He missed her embrace, wished she could stroke his forehead and make him feel less frightened. And then he died.

CHAPTER TWENTY

Just Amachai was carried to the hospital on a stretcher by two medAs. She was unconscious when the IVs were inserted into both arms. Then, as the bags of blood that were hung over her stretcher began filling her arms, she roused. She was not certain what had happened to her. She saw light, and heard noise—there was a lot of it. She felt the fear of the nurses and doctors in the hospital, who did not know exactly what had happened either, but understood that there was a shooter, a green-on-blue attack of some sort. It sounded like it was close, was all they knew, but they had to focus on the patients in front of them.

Someone cut off her clothing with a pair of industrial-looking scissors. She was too frightened to be ashamed at her nakedness in front of these strangers. She thought then of little Mohammed. She felt that she bore the responsibility for his rampage, and she felt terrible about that. She had not seen what had happened to him, and that hurt, too.

A woman in a bloody smock who seemed to be in charge turned her attention to Just Amachai's abdomen. She looked at the three holes in her belly and clucked her tongue. She smeared some cold gel onto her skin and put an ultrasound probe on it. She looked over at a screen out of Just Amachai's field of vision. She put the probe down. The other women said something about the patient's blood pressure. For the first time, she met Just Amachai's eyes. "Do you speak English?"

Just Amachai nodded.

"You are very badly hurt. We need to operate on you."

Just Amachai nodded again. And then she felt her stretcher being wheeled backwards. She entered a room with bright lights. A man in a bright blue gown attached a syringe to her IV fluid. He injected something that made her taste metal and then the world darkened. As the light went away, she thought about Thailand, and the way the birds start singing there an hour before dawn, so loudly you would want to throw stones at them, if they weren't so pretty.

After Just Amachai came a flood of wounded soldiers—Americans, Canadians, Jordanians and Brits. Some were already dead, others died in the bedlam of the triage station, and others were staring open-eyed all around them, fully conscious and aware that they were dying, trying to make sense of this moment, trying to understand what this death meant and what their life had meant, but knowing only that it had been much too short. They died or were stabilized and taken to an operating room.

Rami Issay waited in one corner, with his arm in a reddening sling, dozing from the shot of morphine he had been given. Deirdre O'Malley was brought in, conscious and stable. She had extremity trauma only and was left on a stretcher beside Rami Issay. When Anakopoulus was carried in, clutching the side of his chest, Deirdre sat up, certain that he had saved her from being shot in the head. His clothes were cut away by the same person who had stripped Just Amachai, and Deirdre looked over at him, terrified that he might die, having blocked the bullet meant for her, certain that the act had been deliberate.

Anakopoulus's chest sprayed bloody foam in and out with each of the big man's laboured breaths. The nurse took his blood pressure and waved the Dutch surgeon over and told him the blood pressure and showed him the wound. The Dutch surgeon put in a chest tube and she and the nurse moved Anakopoulus to the operating theatre next to the one Just Amachai was in.

Her abdomen was a mess. Two of the three bullets had gone through bowel and had spilled feces throughout the peritoneal cavity. The surgeon washed out the abdomen and performed a colostomy and a small bowel repair. But as she studied her surgical field, she saw venous blood upwelling from behind the liver. The third bullet had gone through the liver and hit the hepatic vein. It's a terrible place to have a major injury. You can move bowel aside, you can take a pregnant uterus right outside the abdomen, and a patient can survive entirely without a bladder or a kidney or a spleen. But the posterior aspect of the liver is shielded from the surgeon by the liver itself, which can't be moved the same way. She tried the Pringle manoeuvre, which involves clamping the hepatic artery and portal vein. The anaesthetists had long since activated the walking blood bank, and fresh whole blood was being run into the operating rooms by the psychiatrists, whose usual work would come later. But it did not stop Just Amachai's bleeding for the simple reason that there was a 7.62-mm hole in one of the largest veins in her body. No clot could cover it.

And Just Amachai, thirty-four years old, slipped away in that operating room. Four thousand miles from her little boy, two years after she last held him.

Deirdre was brought in next, and the orthopaedic surgeon looked at the X-rays of her arms, and told her he thought she'd recover most of her function. In battlefield orthopaedic surgery, the complex business of inserting plates and screwing in medullary rods is generally foregone, because the risk of infection is high. External fixations, consisting of bone pins that attach to a framework of steel rods to immobilize the broken fragments, are preferred. These devices remain in place until the wounded are evacuated to Ramstein, or the Walter Reed, where the plating and rodding are performed. Elaborate wire-and-rod cages were constructed around Deirdre's arms as she slept on the bed Just Amachai had died on. And when the external fixations were complete, she was woken. She was aware of the pain in her arms being gone. And she asked about Anakopoulus. But no one there knew whom she meant.

255

In the operating room next door, Anakopoulus was being roused. His shoulder wounds had been soft tissue only. The bullet tracks were irrigated and cleaned. The bullets themselves, too deep to justify exploration, were left in.

The chest wound was also an uncomplicated repair. The bullet had contused some lung that looked viable—other than that, he was uninjured. Which is not the normal outcome when one is shot three times by an AK-47 at fifty yards. The surgeon told him as much, but he was too confused to understand the point being made. He retched, and then he retched again when he was brought to the recovery room. And then he fell asleep.

When he woke again he was on a stretcher across from Deirdre O'Malley's. As his eyes opened and his vision cleared he saw her, lying on her back, her arms encased in wire cages, and staring at him.

"I know what you did," she said.

"Do you?" he asked.

"Yes. You should not have done that."

He did not reply.

"I'm going to write about it."

"Please don't."

"I have to. The world has to know what you did."

"Can you please wait? Until I get over this surgery, at least?"

"Okay. I'll call you in a month."

"How will you get hold of me?"

"The military will put me in touch. They'll want this story out there."

"I doubt it."

"Oh, they will."

And he turned away from her to face the wall. From his weeping, Deirdre thought his pain was poorly controlled. She motioned to the nurse with her head. The nurse brought some more morphine and soon he was asleep again.

When Rami Issay awoke, a military policeman was talking to the surgeon who had operated on him. The surgeon turned to look at Rami Issay with lip-curling disdain. He said something more to the policeman and nodded. The nurse sat Rami Issay up, and then the military police-man put his hands behind his back and handcuffed him, wrenching his wounded shoulder badly. "What is happening?" Rami Issay asked in alarm. "Can someone call Major Horner?"

No one responded.

The nurse took out his IV. He was helped off his stretcher, and then walked to the door of the hospital. Outside, a Humvee was waiting. He was put in the back seat.

"Where am I being taken?" he asked.

He got no answer.

Rami Issay looked out at the camp from the back of the truck. Whatever time it was, it was not yet dawn, but the place was as active as an anthill under attack. Trucks and jeeps roared around the roads. Floodlamps had been erected around the shooting site, his café, which swarmed with soldiers. There were so many helicopters in the air, with searchlights probing, that it was not possible to speak and nearly impossible to see. In the SF compound, he was removed from the truck. General Lattice—second-place finisher in Issay's chess tournament two weeks earlier—stood talking to an officer. The officer pointed to Issay and Lattice nodded. Issay tried to smile at him. A hood was put over his head.

CHAPTER TWENTY-ONE

Rashid had helped carry wounded people toward the hospital, but within fifteen minutes of Mohammed's death, the medAs took over the process of transport and triage. He circled back from the hospital to the café, giving the stream of wounded a wide berth. Mohammed's body still lay in the dirt where he had fallen. He was not covered. Neither was Amr's. The other dozen dead lay in heaped and inelegant clumps. He didn't know what to do. He didn't know where to begin.

He walked into the café, turning on the lights. He looked for Fazil. He was not there. He walked into the back room, flicking on that light. There was no one there. Everyone else was either dead or at the hospital, except for him and Fazil. He looked at Fazil's bunk. Everything seemed as it usually did. Except for the bundle of letters from his wife that he had kept beside his pillow. It was gone.

Rashid walked back into the café. He had hoped Fazil would tell him what to do. He took a piece of chocolate cake out of the cooler. He made himself a cup of chai. He ate a forkful of the cake. He bent his forehead to the table so that he could weep.

When he lifted his head, a military policeman was standing in front of him.

❀

Major Horner was sitting at his desk. His uniform was blood spattered and bits of bone and gristle were in his hair. He just did not fucking know how to approach this. He was probably supposed to be out there making sure the television people were being looked after. Oh Christ, if any of them had been shot, that would just fucking be it—the end of his career. That asshat colonel at CENTCOM would walk all the way up and down him—and he a fucking rebadged washed-out *logistics* officer, who the fuck does he think knows more about the media? One fucking clue: it would not fucking be *him*. In another hour he could call his wife. No, he couldn't. There would be a base wide PERS COMS shutdown until the NOK were notified. Fuck.

Why did he ever leave New Orleans?

❀

In the morning, the interrogations began.

Rob Waller watched as a sergeant pulled Rashid Siddiqui out of the sea can he had been locked in. Of course he had not got on a plane to Baghdad.

It had been very cold in that steel box all night and Rashid had not slept. He had thought over and over again about his arrest and had theorized that the military was simply casting the widest possible net around Mohammed's acquaintances and would seek to establish whether any of the rest of them were threats, too, whether the café could continue operating safely, whether Rami Issay could have his television show. His best strategy, he thought, would be to remain calm, to not try to declaim his secularism too obviously, and to tell what he knew of his co-workers. Which was that Rami Issay was a fat and lazy man who could no more run a business on his own than make a proper espresso. But that he was not a radical and had not a homicidal bone in him.

And that Amr was a sullen and angry man whose misanthropy extended to the horizons, including imams and teachers and sergeants—

there is a story about the missing eye and his military service—and to any collection of humanity larger than himself and one other, possibly, and on some days not even that. He was a part of no conspiracy because no conspiracy would have been tolerable to him. The moment a collective action would be agreed upon, he would have felt compelled to belittle it.

Fazil was a man for whom only one thing mattered: his family. His need to provide for and eventually reunite with them would surely preclude jihadist nonsense. He loved his wife with the ardour of a schoolboy and worried about his children compulsively. A man like this does not join an insurgency. No doubt he ran away when the shooting began because he was, like any sensible person, frightened.

These were things he expected to be able to say while a tape machine was running and a serious man took notes and asked questions. This is not what happened. He was pulled into the headquarters building and taken into a back room. Not a word was said to him. A hood was put over his head and his clothing was removed. Straps were attached to his ankles, and the straps to a rope. And then he heard a block and tackle squeak and, falling forward, he was hoisted off his feet, his legs pulled up, and like a free-falling naked skydiver he hung there, his head engorging with blood. The rope was tied to a strong point and then the door opened and then it closed again. The pain in his head built. And within a minute the pain in his knees and hips came to almost match it. The worst thing was that no one was in the room with him. There was nothing he could do, nothing he could say, no one he could betray to make this stop. He wondered how long this could go on. And then he made himself stop thinking about that.

❈

When they pulled Rami Issay out of his cell, they had to wake him up. The drugs from the anaesthesia were still in him. He hadn't slept the night before the last screening, and hardly at all for three days before that. And now his entire world had collapsed upon him once again, just as it had in Leeds, just as it had in Lahore. His restaurant was taken from him, his computer sales network was taken from him, and now even this bloody little café in bloody Kandahar would be taken from him, and just, *just,* as he thought he might make good his losses. It had all been a mirage. It was never going to happen, not really. He was not really going to go to California and star in his own reality television show.

As he sputtered to consciousness he managed to ask how he could help. No one answered him. He, too, was propelled into the headquarters building, into a concrete and well-insulated room. Though he did not see him through the window in his door, he passed Rashid's room. Rashid had stopped yelling already, stopped imploring, though the rooms were quite soundproof and Rami Issay would have heard nothing, anyway. Even if he were not already weeping with fear.

⚛

Out on the base, the lockdown had been lifted. The DFACs were still closed and hard rations had been distributed from the backs of trucks in front of every unit headquarters. The journalists from the press tent were given six cartons of boil-in-the-packet ham omelettes, known by the troops as "the lung." When they emerged from the press tent to retrieve them, they were told that they could move around the base once again, but that the SF compound and the hospital should not be approached.

Major Horner's phone had been ringing all night and all morning. CENTCOM and the PA brass in the Pentagon had been on his case about the role the on-base reporters would be allowed to play in the covering the massacre. Though there appeared to be no other shooters, Horner recommended that the base commander declare a lockdown for six hours, in order to keep them in their tent, and get the message ready.

He had the elements of the press release in place:

Thirty-eight people have been shot and eighteen killed at close range by a foreign national of Afghan origin who was employed in a nutrition facility on the base. The shooter was heroically taken down by several bystanders.

The shooter is not known to have had any Taliban affiliations, but this point is being aggressively pursued. He used a weapon seized from an allied military force. The weapon was guarded. How the foreign national of Afghan origin managed to overpower the guard is being investigated. The initial evidence is that the guard resisted bravely. Further details will be released as the situation evolves.

That had gone back and forth by email nineteen times. CENTCOM PA was very reluctant to let Horner organize a press conference on an event of this magnitude, but General Jackson had been terse. "I plan to speak at 1400. Please be prepared." Horner had asked Fred Shaw if he could get a copy of Jackson's speaking notes to review, and Shaw had simply said, "No, you can't."

Horner had alerted his superiors about this and had been told that they had less influence with General Jackson than he did. Which meant this was all somehow on him. For blame was in the air now, seeking out the people to whom it would attach itself. It moved like a black cloud, coiling around first one subject, then the next, tasting them with a view to feasting. Blame would be attached to whoever the joker in Ramstein was who couldn't send the movies that had been ordered. It would attach to the unfortunate Jordanian platoon commander who had brashly taken his men to see that movie. And whose rifle was used to do the killing. It could attach to Major Horner for facilitating the film club. Notwithstanding the email from Jackson's office, telling him to assist in any way he could.

Blame would attach itself to Kellogg Brown and Root for hiring the boy in the first place. What was a minor doing working here, anyway? Who had done the security screening?

The people who fell with holes in them were just the start of it. Everyone involved was going to be injured by this.

But it would especially attach to General Jackson. He was the ranking commander in Afghanistan, and he had been on the base when it happened. Something had gone wrong. Something had become lax. Chaos had been invited into their midst.

Which was the problem with this war, all this laxity, everywhere. Hadn't anyone seen how soft these rear echelon motherfuckers were?

❁

At the hospital, Anakopoulus had been given a ward bed after he had slept off his anaesthesia. By noon the next day his back was already sore from lying in it, and after the surgeon took out his chest tube he asked if he couldn't just go back to his extra-long cot in the warehouse. He was only taking ibuprofen for the pain. On any other day the surgeon would have said, Don't be ridiculous, your chest tube has only been out for an hour. But the doctor looked around at the bedlam in his hospital and said, "Promise me you'll come back if you feel short of breath."

His guys brought him over a clean uniform. As he buttoned the shirt he looked around for Deirdre O'Malley. He couldn't see her. He recalled their conversation and searched his memory of it for evidence—some improbability, some fuzzy edge—that he had imagined or misremembered what she had said. But he hadn't. He knew it.

He stood up and tightened his belt. His guys offered to help him walk but he dismissed the offer. With each step, he felt a sharp pain where his ribs had been opened and he had to force himself not to wince. When he got to the hospital door and saw the truck waiting there, he was relieved.

❁

Eventually, incredibly, Rashid had fallen asleep. That changed when the sergeant threw the bucket of ice water on him and hollered, "*Wake the fuck up!*" The terp beside him leaned in just as viciously, echoing him in Pashto.

When Rashid jolted awake, the pain in his now completely dislocated shoulders reached a searing crescendo. "What is it?" he managed to ask. The sergeant nodded at the terp to leave, as he wasn't needed, and he did. The sergeant leaned close to Rashid's ear, and said, "I'm going to ask you something and you could spare us both a great deal of bother by just telling me the truth. Did you radicalize Mohammed Hashto?"

"What?"

The sergeant put on a pair of bright blue latex surgical gloves. Then he put on black leather gloves over them. He put a yellow water-impermeable hospital gown over his uniform. Then he put on a pair of eye protectors. Universal blood and bodily fluid precautions were required, by regulation, when exposure was probable. They had all had the lectures by infection control experts about risk-mitigation in this work. Hepatitis B is endemic in this part of the world. The sergeant wasn't going to catch hep B for no good reason, that was for sure. First thing you lose is your "fit for deployment" designation. And after that, your career.

❀

Rami Issay had not fallen asleep. When the door opened, he simply said, "I'll tell you anything I know," in perfectly clear English. The terp sighed with disappointment and looked at the sergeant, then turned and left. The sergeant shut the door behind him. He was tired now and notwithstanding the hospital smock and glasses, he was splattered. Behind the mirror he was being watched. He sucked it up and got to it.

❀

Later that afternoon General Jeremy Jackson visited Deirdre O'Malley in the hospital. "I heard about your press conference," she said. "That was dramatic."

"My resignation? It was coming, anyway. Better to get ahead of it."

"You think you were going to take the fall for the shooting?"

"Yes. And the bigger picture here isn't going in the right direction."

"Since when?

"Maybe 2003."

"For the last six months I've heard nothing from your field commanders and public affairs guys except that every day, in every way, things are getting better and better."

"We are a can-do organization."

"What are you going to do now?"

"Go home."

"To your wife?"

He nodded.

"Politics?"

"I don't know."

"Of course you do. I bet Fred has the PAC started up already."

He smiled at her. She knew him so well. "I've had some inquiries from interesting organizations in every sector I can think of. Finance, armaments, diplomacy, academia—I'll take my time."

"Have you talked to Tom?"

"No. He's busy."

"He's seen my piece on the massacre in Panjwai, you know."

"What did he say?"

"That he will corroborate everything I wrote."

"Can I see your piece?"

"I filed it just before I went to the screening. And anyway, you don't want anyone asking if you had access to that piece before it went to press."

"No, probably not."

"So we're all going home."

"We should get together for a game of golf or something."

Deirdre laughed then. "Hey, I'm going to write about a soldier who did something very brave the other night."

"At the shooting?"

"Yes. And when it comes out, I want you to make sure he's recognized. Like, officially. A commendation. Something that will get him attention."

"I'm going to have a lot less influence, you know."

"But you'll know who to call. And they'll still take your calls."

"All right. I should get going now. There are lots of wounded to visit here."

"Okay," she said. She moved her armature-encased arm and pinched his little finger between her thumb and index finger. "Still . . ." she said, and looked at him for a long time.

"I know," he said. And after a moment he opened her fingers gently and released himself. He stood and drew back the curtains around her bed and left.

❀

A week later.

The sergeant sat, exhausted, at a table in the SF OPS centre. Waller and three more SF interrogators and a CIA interrogator sat with him. Lattice stood by the door. Waller said, "I like the manager. He's got the right bio: professional humiliations, rejected by his wife. He's got that crazy brother-in-law. He spent years in Peshawar. He's had more influence over the boy than anyone else. They had a quasi-parental relationship. He had to be instrumental in shaping the boy's world."

"I don't know about that," the sergeant said. "But I'm pretty sure the young guy doesn't know anything."

The CIA interrogator said, "He and the manager's story have some interesting correspondences. Both lived abroad and flamed out. Both superficially secular. Both involved in this chess tournament."

Waller: "Both bilaterally symmetrical. Vertebrates. Both read words. Both Muslims."

Lattice raised his eyebrows at him.

In the room behind this one, Rashid sat, his head drooping, as Slayer's *Hell Awaits* played so loudly the concrete walls faintly vibrated, though the sound transmitted was minimal. His chin slowly approached, and finally touched, his chest, which ran with bile-stained vomit. A soldier with ear protectors poked him in the ribs with a broom handle. This time it took four hard jabs, the fourth one with a foot of wind-up, to get Rashid to lift his chin off his chest.

It was not a prized assignment. The man had been caught napping on sentry duty himself, after a thirty-hour hike, chasing militants into the Hindu Kush. He had some sympathy for what Rashid Siddiqui was enduring. Though not for his role in organizing that shooting.

Motherfucker. How do these people become like this? Look at him: swollen eyes and lips, head hanging, hair matted with blood and snot. Fucking animal. He poked him again.

The other SF interrogator said, "I don't think we just let Siddiqui go. a) He still might know something, and b) we may have just radicalized him ourselves. We might as well say it: everything to do with this disaster is going to be scrutinized by endless commissions of inquiry. If we let him go and he turns out to have been the plant, or even if he wasn't but he takes umbrage at our conversations with him this week and decides to throw his lot in with the bad guys and gets caught on the battlefield—well, that will be talked about endlessly." The CIA guy made a move to respond, but the soldier talked over him. "So let's give him to NDS. They'll take him to Sarpoza and let him contemplate his situation a bit and maybe something interesting will come to light. And if nothing does, at least he's not planting bombs in the roads at night."

All of them nodded.

The sergeant spoke. "Issay is another story. He's just false. I know it."

Lattice said, "Can you be more specific, Sergeant?"

"Every time I catch him looking at me, I can tell he's trying to figure out what I want to hear."

"That could have something to do with the beating you have been laying on him."

"Maybe, sir."

Waller: "Sounds like we're not ready to draw any definite conclusions, yet."

"I'm not ready to say he's clean, that's for sure," the sergeant said.

"So what's the next step? More of this, here?"

"We're not making progress."

The CIA guy said, "You could send him to Salt Pit."

Waller said, "He's not a CIA prisoner. He's military property."

"You can continue the interrogation there, or sit in on them with us helping, whatever you like."

Waller looked at Lattice.

Lattice nodded. "Send him to Salt Pit. Waller, you're going with him." He looked at CIA. "Waller travels with him, on the same flight. Waller is present for, or conducts, all interrogation. I need a memo, agreeing to this." To Waller: "Get packed."

The CIA man nodded. Lattice left the room.

※

Rashid was unchained from the wall and a couple of soldiers helped him to stand. He was made to sit on a wheelchair and strapped in. He was turned around and the door was opened and he was wheeled out.

Though they had not communicated, he had spent the last two weeks never more than thirty feet from Rami Issay. In this time they had been asked about each other so many times that each felt as if the other was in the same room—a sensation that grew more powerful as the interrogations proceeded and the attendant sleep-deprived delirium grew more profound. Each was confronted with contradictory claims from the other so often that it was clear they were both being interrogated. The other had to be nearby.

And now Rashid was being removed. He was suddenly anxious that they might be separated, that this was the last time they would be even in mediated contact. And he thought, *Peace be upon you, Rami Issay.*

After an hour-long truck trip into Kandahar City, he was led into the Dantean stench of Sarpoza prison. Thousands of men were confined here, in dim light, amid a cloud of flying and leaping ectoparasites, and hot tuberculous air as if from the mouth of a fevered animal.

John Wayne looked up as Rashid was dropped on the floor of the cell next to his. They did not recognize one another. Rashid's face was grotesquely bloated in the way his own had been when the Americans first gave him to NDS. Rashid lay on the ground for many long minutes after guards left his cell, locking the door behind them.

"Be at peace, brother. You will not see them again today. The Pakistan–South Africa cricket match is on. It is all they have talked about all week," John Wayne finally said, in Pashto.

Rashid groaned.

"I don't think they will bother you again today," John Wayne tried, this time in Urdu.

❀

The flight went directly from KAF to the Salt Pit and Rami Issay was the only detainee on board. The CIA facility was north of Bagram, built purely for the purpose of interrogating high-value detainees. As a black site, its existence was supposed to be the tightest of all secrets. For the first few years, it had been, but now the knowledge of its existence was seeping through the SF, if not the regular army, like an evil rumour. Things that were too ugly for the detention barracks at KAF were supposed to be done there.

Rami Issay was on a stretcher the whole time. It was easier to restrain him safely with his ankles strapped to the rails of his stretcher, and anyway no one could say for sure whether or not he could walk.

It turned out he could, barely. They established this when they lifted him out of the stretcher and helped him sit down on the floor of his cell. The CIA physician and nurse who had accompanied him left then, and only Rob Waller and the CIA case officer from KAF were there, together with the Salt Pit staff. Who were keen to complete the intake paperwork and then get back to sleep. It was 0200 and they had been pulled from their beds for his arrival.

"A lot of this can wait until morning. We have a process," the senior man said.

Waller said, "He's army property. The only process that matters is mine. Is that understood?"

CHAPTER TWENTY-TWO

When Deirdre was wheeled into the Manhattan offices of the American News Syndicate, the staff lined up at the foyer of their building to greet her. She had gotten back to New York two days earlier, after a stop in Landstuhl, where her external fixation apparatus was replaced with internal plates and screws. She'd spent a week recovering from that and had then got on a plane, desperate with boredom. In the interim, her piece on the SF atrocity had appeared and been picked up around the world, and on top of all that, she had been wounded. In theatre.

In New York, her employers had rented her a suite in a hotel she could never have afforded herself. There was an assistant, Kendra, waiting for her at the airport and she took her into town in a hired car—all this was new. She had leaned against the back corner of the seat as it approached Manhattan and tried to understand what was going on. Kendra explained that she was supposed to stay with Deirdre, make sure she had whatever help she needed, given that both her arms were in casts. When she saw Deirdre's look in response, she added, "Of course, if you'd prefer, I could tell them you declined."

Now, at offices she'd rarely visited, applause broke out. Kenwood stood at the front of the crowd, waiting to greet her. They embraced and Deirdre leaned into his ear, "Kenwood: whiskey tango foxtrot?"

He whispered back, "You're a rock star now, Deirdre."

"Since when?"

"Since the beginning, if you ask me."

"You're not getting all wobbly on me?"

"Is that you, turning into Margaret Thatcher?"

She smirked. "I was always partly her. What am I supposed to do now?"

"Say thanks. Shake a few hands. So to speak."

She nodded and turned around. Her casted arms were in slings tied from Versace scarves that the stylist had brought. The stylist. She made a motion to raise them in acknowledgement. The crowd loved that. There was a CNN film crew here and they caught it. The producer gestured to her do it again. She did. The producer gave her a thumbs-up.

"Not in Front of the Embed" was already considered by the bookies as the probable Pulitzer Prize winner for long-form journalism. Everyone was commenting on what an evolution it represented in her style—sombre and restrained and so much more potent as a result. She was asked a dozen times whether it would become a book.

It was complicated, getting so much attention over a piece she would have paid money not to have written. After she filed it, it just spun away on its own trajectory. The fact checkers called her a few times while she was still in Afghanistan about trivial questions, and then the chief fact checker got in touch to ask if she had made some arrangement with Lattice, since he had confirmed every single quote without objection—unheard of—and had even expanded on several of the most graphic and damning anecdotes she had reported. The chief quoted him: "Ms O'Malley is, if anything, being too restrained. What I recall saying is, 'Not in front of the fucking embed, are you crazy?'"

She twisted for Lattice. First, the news that she had been hurt in the shooting broke and everyone in the media assumed the posture of a worried friend. And then the piece appeared and *that* was all anyone could talk about. The link between the two stories being her incredible courage. Lightning was caught in a bottle and out of thousands of journalists covering those wars, she became the celebrity. This morning, before her car had picked her up to bring her here, Kendra had appeared with that stylist plus a makeup artist at her hotel room. *Jesus Christ.*

❀

John Wayne whispered to him as the lights were turned off, "Brother, do not sleep tonight."

He took it as a warning. The guards had been hard on him that day, but not much harder than they had been on every other day in the two weeks he had been in the prison. He had been beaten and tripped to the floor and thrown into the stone walls of the interrogation room, as on every other day since he had been detained. Nevertheless, this was nothing as bad as what the Americans had done to him, and he was stronger now than he had been when he arrived. The food was foul, but he had resolved to eat every bit he was given, even if he had to hold his nose to get it down.

He thought it was just a matter of time before they really got to work on him. He thought he had a better chance of surviving it, now that he had healed a bit. The question he pushed out of his thoughts every time it intruded was, *For what?* What did getting through any of these sessions mean except that there would be more?

He lay in the straw in his cell and listened to two thousand other men whispering to one another as he considered, or tried not to consider, these questions. This was not like other nights. The intensity of whispering and the sense of electricity in the air was different than it had been for the last two weeks. *What exactly is being planned for me?* he wondered. Then realized this could not be about him. He had suffered, but the remarkable thing about his suffering was just how unremarkable it was in this warehouse of pain. They had all been caught by the Americans, had all been questioned by them and released to NDS.

He could make out individual words in Urdu, Dari, Pashto, Uzbek, Arabic and Farsi. But he could not make out sentences. The meaning in this buzz was not in the sentences but simply in the fact of it.

And instead of fading as the night wore on, as it had every other night, it just kept crackling, thrumming on, not so much indifferent to the audience as being its own audience—Rashid listened to it like it was water music, and felt himself expand with wonder. He stopped worrying about being taken from his cell that night, though if that was not what the warning to stay awake had been about, he could not say what it possibly could be.

When the truck exploded, it caved in eighty feet of the three-foot-thick mud wall of the prison. The entire building nearly collapsed. Forty prisoners were killed outright. The floors on three storeys of the building sagged toward the shattered wall and pulled away from the bars. Within seconds of the first explosion, another rocked the other side of the prison, and another long stretch of mud wall was destroyed. The dust billowing through the abruptly dark prison was suffocating. The steel cages now gapped away from the walls, allowing cell after cell full of men to slip out and into the passageways. Guards could be heard shouting in the distance. And there was something else: the shouts of faithful men, and rifle fire. Someone was suddenly outside his cell, yelling, "Get up, get up! By God, you have your chance now, get up!"

Rashid slipped through the gap in his own bars and followed that voice. Other prisoners fell in behind him and a minute or two later, they were jumping out of a hole in the hall, ten feet down to the courtyard below. Every fifth or sixth man injured his ankle as he landed— the longer they had been in there, the weaker their bones were—and the snapping of bones and groaning could be heard above the whispered exhortations to hurry.

There was another gaping hole in the opposite wall of that courtyard and men streamed through it, dispersing on the other side like an estuary meeting the sea. Rashid stepped over the rubble and ran. After three or four hundred metres, he was exhausted. He slowed to a lope, and then he walked. He had no idea where he was, except in a field. He stood for a moment and looked at the stars, trying to orient himself. He found the familiar constellations. South and east was where he thought he should head. And away from Kandahar City. He looked around. A trio of ragged men were standing only fifty feet away.

"Brother, are you with us?" one of them asked.

"I am," he said, not certain who or what he was with, but pretty sure that he had never needed friends more badly in his life.

"Then let's go now. There are food and shelter and friends waiting for us to the south," one of them said.

They heard the ferenghee soldiers arrive at the prison half an hour later, but by this time they had covered three kilometres. The sound of shooting carried far in that otherwise still night, and it urged them on. Twelve hundred men had been freed with those explosions, and every time they crawled behind a wall or under a tree to rest for a moment, they found the spot occupied by other frightened and eager men. After a whispered consultation, they headed on. Several times, it seemed to Rashid, they accidentally traded members of their groups. In the pitch black, it was not impossible that he, too, had changed groups.

When the sky began to lighten to their left, in the east, they were relieved to see that they had made it well away from Kandahar City. They found a treeline next to a field thick with wheat and far from a nearby road. They lay down silently, deep within shadows. None of them could sleep. They were headed for the mountains, for the border. Toward friends.

❁

Rob Waller spoke from his chair. "Mr. Issay, we have asked you these questions many times, and still you are not being truthful with us. We know this. We have read your emails and we have spoken to witnesses. They contradict every word you have told us. Please stop lying. What we are interested in is your role in radicalizing the boy. Who put you up to this? Who gave you the AK-47 to give to the boy?"

Rami Issay hung naked from his shackled wrists and did not reply. He had answered these questions many times. He could make up answers for them, but that would only anger them more. They had been down that road already. Anyway, he didn't care. He just didn't care. His god had abandoned him. His friends had abandoned him. His family. He had nothing he feared losing. Shit ran down his bare leg and he scarcely noticed. He didn't reply.

His co-interrogator, who called himself Mr. Clark for Rami Issay's benefit, put on a pair of black leather gloves.

Waller got ready to take notes. Most of the time he looked away and just listened. He told himself he did that to concentrate on the information-rich signal—the detainee's words. His Pashto, his Urdu, and his Dari were all pretty good now. He understood even guttural gasps. To do that, you really had to have a feel for the language.

"Now then, about your relationship with the *Stars Earn Stripes* show. Why were you so intent on appearing on it? Were you planning a massacre of the stars? Did you have a special plan for Mr. Palin?"

Rami Issay said nothing.

Mr. Clark lifted a balloon-tipped rectal tube the CIA doctor had given him. He knelt down. Rami Issay shut his eyes tighter. Mr. Clark inserted the tube and inflated the balloon. It hurt, but not as much as being hit. Mr. Clark hung a plastic bag from one of the hooks on the ceiling. He connected the rectal tube to it. He opened a valve.

Rob Waller stepped outside.

Overhead, the Afghan sun flared. The desert all around reflected back brightly and it felt like the light was falling on him from a hose. The air was cleansed by the light and the desert wind that never stopped blowing. He smelled woodsmoke, vaguely. Maybe someone was cooking with garlic somewhere. Inside, he heard a soft thud and a groan. He was supposed to be present for every second of the interrogations. He would file a report on the process for KAF in another couple of days. This was the highest profile green-on-blue yet, and at the hands of a fifteen-year-old. Some evidence of progress toward understanding it had to be made and presented to the public. Fifteen-years-olds don't just do something like that. Apparently he had been learning English and wanted to continue his education. Someone had got to him. Even if it wasn't Issay, Issay knew who it was. And that he wasn't giving him up said everything you had to know about where his sympathies lay. Which made it even more likely that it was him. Who else could it be?

Waller turned and re-entered the room. His eyes had accustomed themselves to the bright, and he could see nothing. He heard another thud, and the sound of breath being forced from lungs.

❀

Once they got south of the Panjwai, they saw fewer soldiers. The farther south they went, the fewer drones and helicopters they saw. They decided to start sleeping at night and travel during the day. They stole some hoes to carry, so they would look more innocent as they walked. They didn't imagine they would fool any of the people whose lands they walked through, but if they looked like farmers to a drone camera, perhaps they would be less likely to hear that sudden shriek. Anyone could see that none of them was carrying a rifle. Apart from the hoes, they carried nothing at all. A pack on any of their backs could mean the end of all them.

The season made their escape possible. In the late summer, the orchards and vineyards were heavy with fruit, which allowed for easy grazing. They stopped in drying huts when they saw them and helped themselves to raisins. Still, they craved rice and meat. They were all so thin, from the diet and the abuse and the dysentery of the prison. Though walking twelve hours a day did not make gaining weight likely, they each felt better every day. One night, over a handful of raisins, one of the men looked up at Rashid and told him, "You know, you don't even look like the same man we started out with. You almost look like a real person now." Rashid shrugged. He didn't care what he looked like. He had noticed, though, that his mind felt like it was uncoiling.

He had begun to think again, and to wonder and to look forward. All those habits had disappeared while he was being interrogated. He had crouched internally as much as he had externally. This represented a change far more important than some bruises healing. And as his thoughts began to uncoil, they let slip anger like he had never known in his life. When he felt it emerge, the unfamiliar insistence of it felt so uncomfortable he wished he were still crouching. This was a demon that could take him over, entirely. He pushed aside the anger and thought about his parents. He reviewed the fundamental theorem of calculus. He remembered being hung by those chains. And that filthy man hitting him. Calculus is the mathematics of change.

To say that any of them was no longer afraid would be entirely wrong. Every moment of the day they glanced skyward, looking for drones and aircraft. They stayed away from any road solid enough to accommodate a LAV or an MRV. They preferred footpaths and would take them even if they added miles to their journey. And they knew at all times that as conscious as they were of these threats, they could not be eliminated. Every one of them had heard stories of relatives and friends, uninterested in any aspect of the insurgency except as a danger to avoid, being killed by missiles. And they were considerably less innocent than that. Since the jailbreak, they imagined, the ferenghee must be scouring the countryside for men just like them.

The sooner they made it to the mountains, the happier they would all be.

❀

On KAF, the UK supply sergeant, David Shipman, sat in his chair in his office. It was the first day things had seemed partway normal since the shooting. His friend Anakopoulus had gone home. His own deployment had another two months to run. Then he would go back home, probably for the rest of his time in. The Brits were almost out of Iraq, and he had done his share here now—unless he wanted to be promoted, which he most certainly did not. The good news is that those InformationIsFree leaks seem to have been pushed to the back burner. All anyone wanted to talk about was terrorist cells on NATO bases.

Shipman looked out his window at the mountains to the south. He thought about the Sarpoza breakout. Where do twelve hundred men go? Into the homes and houses all around them, he thought. Which told you where the sympathies of the people in those homes must lie. Some of the escapees were probably making for their own home villages, and some of them for Pakistan. Look at those mountains. Imagine climbing them in the night, in sandals without a map. Twelve hundred men and they were soaked up in the countryside, just like that. Like summer rain, gone an hour after it fell.

He had met Anakopoulus's replacement. Harold Thorvaldson, from Minneapolis. He was less snarky than Anakopoulus, though Shipman wondered how much of his friend's sourness was the product of the years-at-an-end deployment he had endured. Not all of it, probably. Thorvaldson marvelled at how well run the supply depot was, said Anakopoulus was hard to replace, especially without having been able to get a handover from him. Fortunately, his subordinates were pretty well trained and they had a handle on how things worked. Shipman had told him that if he needed help, all he had to do was call. He was ready to give him some pointers.

Oh my God. He had turned into Anakopoulus. Shipman laughed and reached into his desk for his flask. Well, he could do worse, he thought.

CHAPTER TWENTY-THREE

On the twenty-ninth day after the shooting, Master Sergeant Anakopoulus was in Walter Reed, doing rehab for his shoulder. He didn't want to go home to Texas. He found Washington more pleasant than he could ever have expected. The hospital itself was a miracle of light and high, white walls and glass atria around every other corner. Anything the wounded soldiers wanted was made available to them, in the way of tickets to football or baseball games. There were excursions laid on to all of the local national parks. He had visited the Smithsonian several times.

He was just walking back from the pool when he saw the physiotherapist, a sexy captain from Seattle, coming toward him. "Hello, ma'am," he said.

"Hey, Master Sergeant, good to see you. Listen, there's someone from public affairs who wants to talk to you. Some reporter who met you in KAF, wants to do a story on you or something? I have a number I'm supposed to give you. Sergeant? Are you okay, do you want to sit down?"

❀

Major Horner's agenda was lighter than it had been in months. CENTCOM had flown out some help after General Jackson's surprise resignation. Horner was still held responsible for that, because the general had so clearly communicated his intentions to him. And somehow, the shooting itself was partly his fault, too. Mark Burnett and Sara Miller's witnessing of it could have been prevented, had he only foreseen that it was coming. It wasn't like the Pentagon itself hadn't had the biggest hard-on in the world about *Stars Earn Stripes*, too. That was still going ahead, though they had decided to shoot it entirely in the States now. Probably the safest—and most beside the point—thing to do.

※

Anakopoulus sat beside the Washington Mall Pond and watched it shimmer. The water was the most beautiful thing he could remember ever seeing. Behind him was the Lincoln Monument. The water in the reflecting pool looked like cool molten metal.

He wanted to phone Susie to give her a heads-up about this, but he couldn't bring himself to. He had sent her a three-line email from the Landstuhl hospital, just to let her know that he was okay. The shooting had been all over the news. She had written back, long and tenderly, thankful that he was okay, and thanking him, on behalf of the kid and her new boyfriend Scott, for his service to his country.

He hadn't answered that. "On behalf of Scott and myself." Nice.

※

At one time, walking for twelve hours a day would have struck Rashid as its own kind of torture, but as they walked in file along the narrow footpaths through these fields, he felt a kind of ease return to him that he had not known in many years. He recoiled from even the idea of the city, now, which he had once considered mankind's highest accomplishment.

He had lived his whole life in cities of one hundred thousand or more. With his family, in Peshawar, and then Islamabad for school, and then Boston. KAF was the smallest community he had lived in in his life, and there was nothing non-frenetic about it, either. This, he realized, this around him: the sunshine and the wheat and millet fields and the vineyards and the orchards, this is where he wanted to live now.

He had not been afraid of strangers before the detention. He had not recoiled from settlements. Now, his idea of paradise was just him, sitting on a hill that allowed him to see in every direction for thirty miles and no one at all to be seen.

As they made their way south, the land gradually became more hilly and the houses farther apart. The mountains loomed up in front of him. All they had on their feet were sandals. Would these "friends" meet them before they had to climb the mountains, or were they going to do that in their sandals?

It didn't matter. They would not be going back so they had to move ahead. They would do what was necessary and if that meant climbing mountains barefooted then that is what they would do. And they could all just stop talking about these friends who would meet them. The harder they made it to be found by them or anyone else, the better. There were no friends. There were soldiers with cameras that could see forever, looking for them. They had to keep going, as fast as they could.

※

It was late in the day and Anakopoulus worried that no one would be around. Military police detachments at military hospitals are not generally staffed with prospects for accelerated promotion. A couple dozen cases of petty theft a year, a sexual harassment charge or two, and that was about what constituted the case load at a hospital's MP detachment. When prisoners from Quantico or one of the other big detention barracks got sick and were sent here, sometimes they got involved with the guarding of such patients, but mostly the sending organizations took care of that. They understood the staffing levels of the hospital detachment. And with whom it was staffed.

When he found the office, a pleasant young woman was working behind the desk, processing a stack of parking tickets. She didn't even notice him walk in. After a few minutes he had to clear his throat to draw her attention.

She looked up. "Oh, hello, Master Sergeant."

"Hi."

"I'll be with you in just a moment."

"Take your time."

"Thanks." She grinned at him. He had a lot of ribbons, and sometimes those long-time field guys were permanently pissed off. It was nice to see one with a bit of patience for a change.

When she was finally done, and asked him how she could help him, he set down the magazine he was reading and stood up. "I'm afraid I might be about to ruin your evening, Sergeant," he said.

"Why?"

"Here," he said, holding out his wrists. "You'll want to handcuff me."

She backed away from the counter and fingered her sidearm. "Tom! Can I have some help out here?" she called to someone not visible.

"What?" a sleepy voiced called back from somewhere.

"Tom!"

"Coming."

A portly white-haired man with sergeant's chevrons on his wrinkled shirt appeared from out of the back.

"This man wants to be handcuffed."

"Why?"

She looked at Anakopoulus, who thought that his last minutes of freedom were proving odder than he had expected. "It's not that I want to be handcuffed, it's that I think you'll want to handcuff me."

"Why would we want to handcuff you?" the older man said.

"Because I'm the guy who leaked that helicopter video to InformationIsFree."

"I have no idea what you are talking about. Do you, Susan?"

Susan shook her head.

"I think we'll be giving the psychiatry inpatient unit a call. Who did you say your doctor is? And what's your name?"

Anakopoulus sighed. "I'm not a psychiatry patient. I'm the leaker everyone is looking for. Call your boss. Or his boss."

"What should we tell them?"

"Tell them you have the InformationIsFree leaker."

"How do you spell that?"

"I-n-f-o-r-m . . ."

"Slow down, mister."

CHAPTER TWENTY-FOUR

"**M**aster Sergeant Anakopoulus! You will stand at attention when staff enter your cell, is that understood?"

He nodded. He stood beside his bare cot and put his heels together. His scrotum jiggled with the movement and the sadistic twenty-five-year-old second lieutenant barking at him stood on his toes to lean into Anakopoulus's face, or chin, anyway. "So you wish to have sexual relations with me, Master Sergeant!"

"No sir."

"We both saw what you just did, didn't we?"

"No sir."

"Don't you 'no sir' me!"

He had been in Quantico, naked, standing beside his bed for twenty-two hours a day on suicide watch since the day after he surrendered himself. Even for the two hours he was allowed to lie down, all the lights left blazing, two men sat on the other side of the bars, watching. Mostly, he was not allowed to see his lawyer. Once, when he was allowed, his lawyer told him that this treatment amounted to torture and she would be filing a complaint with the court and with the UN.

Anakopoulus had begged her not to. "That might get you a little more attention and media interviews, but it will not help me in the least. It will only anger them."

"Listen to me," she replied, stung, "the constitution applies here, to everyone. They can't do this."

"They can do anything, absolutely anything they want to me. I am a traitor. I am responsible for thousands of deaths because of that leak."

"No, you're not. You are not."

"You seem to know my circumstances better than I do. How is that possible?"

"Master Sergeant, they've messed with you. They've made you agree with them."

"I did what I did."

His lawyer sat back at that. For the first time in her adult life, she had no words.

❁

Deirdre's new offices were more opulent than she would have wanted anyone she worked with in the Suck to know. She had her own show and staff and personal assistants. Some days it was as if the air currents just picked her up and pushed her through her life. When Anakopoulus's ex-girlfriend had left a message that she wanted to meet, Deirdre had leapt at it. She had been planning to do an entire show on Anakopoulus's actions during the shooting, with Jeremy present and maybe an on-air awarding of a medal, when the press release about him being the InformationIsFree leaker came out. She had been floored. Fortunately, she had not spoken much to anyone at work about her plan to do a show honouring the man. The leak story had just about gone away, buried under the shooting story and the various bombings and acid splashings of the day. And then there was Iraq, which was worse and worse every day, worse even than Afghanistan. Apparently he had been discovered by the MPs at Walter Reed. She wondered how.

After two days of insomnia, she felt compelled to tell the world what she knew of Anakopoulus. The *Times* had published her op-ed. He had been unavailable to speak to their fact checkers, but given the nature of the piece and the prominence of its author, it had been cleared.

That day she got an email from the ex-girlfriend, wanting to talk to her about him. This intrigued her. The woman said she would fly to New York the next day. They agreed to meet at her office.

When Susie walked in Deirdre greeted her from her chair. Getting up was still painful for her. She apologized and Susie waved it off and sat down across from Deirdre.

"Thank you for writing the article."

"It wasn't a very popular thing to do, around here," Deirdre replied.

"Even though you didn't actually come out and say you thought he was innocent? Or even possibly innocent?"

"Ms Alvarez . . ."

"Please, Susie."

"Susie. I don't know whether he leaked something or not. The MPs certainly think he did, for some reason. We'll see what he admitted to at his trial. In the meantime, I just wanted the world to know what he did for me."

"He was high on pain killers, he had had just a session of rehab therapy. Don't they give painkillers for that? He could have admitted to anything."

"I know."

"What can we do for him?"

"We can ask hard questions about his treatment in Quantico. We can make sure the trial is well covered and fair."

"Fair!"

"If you don't mind my asking, he's your ex. Why are you involved?"

"Because he still matters to me. And my son. And he served his country . . ."

"Does he know you're talking to me about his situation?"

"No. I visit him, when they permit him visitors—he still has me listed as his next of kin, but he won't talk to me or let me talk to him. So far, we've just sat there."

"That must be painful, to see him in these circumstances."

"It is important to me that someone helps him. If he hadn't gone so far away for so long, we would still be together."

"Complicated situation for all of you."

"No it isn't, Ms O'Malley. It's very simple. Every one of us should be outraged. Especially those of us who owe their lives to him."

Deirdre handed her a box of tissues.

❀

Their handlers brought them all to makeup an hour before the discussion was to begin. Charlie Rose was already in his chair being primped, and avuncular and cheerful as he waved at the generals and their spouses, and then Deirdre and Stewart Robinson. Mrs. Lattice and Mrs. Jackson embraced, affecting pleasure at the sight of one another. Mrs. Jackson paused for an instant before shaking Deirdre's hand, and Deirdre was not able to say what she knew or didn't know but was anyway uncomfortable enough that she let the woman's hand go the instant she could and retreated to talk to a producer in the corner.

Stewart Robinson approached her then—his hand touching the small of her back. Jeremy Jackson noticed and his wife noticed him noticing and the two of them looked away, in opposite directions.

"Deirdre," Robinson whispered. "Such a pleasure to see you again. When I heard about the attack I was worried sick. When they released your name . . ."

"Stewart," she replied, and turned to embrace him, catching Jeremy's eye over his shoulder for a nanosecond as she did. "How are you?" She stood back to survey him to spare herself the thermal injury of that look from across the room.

287

Deirdre had lost weight after being shot, and still wore a cast on her right arm. Jackson never varied his workout regimen or diet and had always seemed as much a university professor as a soldier. He wore the suit comfortably. But Lattice was the most obviously diminished. He looked absurd wearing anything but combats. He had been gutted by the response to Deirdre's piece. The title said it all, was the conclusion of innumerable internet commenters. With popular opinion against him, his supporters in the Pentagon had backed away, too, and within days, he hadn't a friend in the army. He reached out to men he had served and fought and bled with and for the first time ever no one would take his calls. He had hoped his "Don't apologize, don't explain, don't deny" approach would work in this instance, as it had so often. But this was just too big.

He was, if anything, the most innocent among them, and he had paid, was paying, the steepest price of all.

Mary Lattice hated Deirdre for different reasons than Sherry Jackson did, but she hated her with a deep ferocity that prevented her from looking away from the woman who had destroyed her husband. The essay about the Foscart massacre, and the headline, splashed across every newsstand, "Not in Front of the Embed," had been like a bomb going off. The day after it appeared, Lattice had been summoned to the White House. When he got to Washington, he met with the president's chief of staff. The secretary of defense and the chair of the Joint Chiefs were left entirely out of the conversation. It didn't matter. The president needed to be seen to be doing this, and not through a committee or at a distance.

The president also needed to be seen responding to the green-on-blue massacre at KAF, which spelled the end of Jeremy Jackson's military career. Fred Shaw told him and Sherry Jackson that the timing had been perfect. No reasonable voter would view him as personally responsible for the shooting, and would see this as a political firing, for which they would hold the president and his party responsible. Nevertheless. Jeremy Jackson was out of uniform and living in his own house seven days a week for the first time in decades. His wife was conscious of his diminished stature, and hers. A Super PAC had been started with a large initial contribution from Kellogg Brown and Root, and she met with Fred Shaw nearly daily. Jeremy himself was working on his book, though he had not given her anything to read yet.

"Deirdre O'Malley, I'd like to begin with you if I could. The coverage of the recent wars has been a departure from war reporting in previous conflicts. The practice of embedding is new, and some say, not coincidentally, the coverage of these wars and of the military has been much more sympathetic than was seen, for instance, in Vietnam. Has the military played the media in these wars?"

"Great question, Charlie. The war was necessary and remains necessary and however critical we must be, appropriately, of our own conduct, it is important to remember that the enemy is vastly worse. Our nation is at war with mass murderers. With men who throw acid in the faces of girls for the crime of attending school. So if you ask me, do I have opinions about the merit of our wars, the answer is, You bet I do. And I have opinions about the brave men and women taking the fight to those monsters."

Charlie Rose replied, "But you are among a very small number of journalists that both embedded with the troops and wrote critically about the conduct of the war. Can you give us some insight into the difficulty of the embedded reporter's position?

"Well, I think my own record shows how overblown many of these concerns have become. Reporters are reporters. When we are in the field there is no confusion at all about our role there. We wear different-coloured body armour, our only weapons are our cameras and notepads, and what we are interested in is the story.

"The military itself has no doubt about our role. Soldiers permit us to come with them and tolerate us only because they understand that the press is an important part of the democracy they are trying to defend with their lives. They'd just as soon we weren't there. They'd very much prefer it, actually. But we are. And on the ground, no one questions our loyalties or purpose."

❀

At that moment a short Marine gunnery sergeant pushed the naked Anakopoulus upright. "You will stand at attention, Sergeant!" The second lieutenant on his other side stood ramrod straight, immediately in front of Anakopoulus's chin. He was determined to be evaluated well on this, his first assignment. He imagined he had caught someone's attention somehow, and was seen as having particular promise and so was given the prominent mission of supervising the treatment of the country's worst traitor since the Rosenbergs. In this he was mistaken to the point of delusion. Soldiers with promise are kept far away from radioactive assignments such as the Anakopoulus case.

Anakopoulus only knew that he had mostly not been permitted clothing for a month now, except during his lawyer's and Susie's visits, and that they seemed not to be prepared to beat him. He'd retreated within himself. In the distance, he could hear the second lieutenant screaming at him. In the foreground, he remembered meeting Susie for the first time. He remembered that first day he arrived in Afghanistan. He remembered hearing Mohammed's first shots. It was a little after seven. In two hours he might be permitted some sleep. Or they might keep him awake all night. His preference was that they would let him sleep, but he doubted he had much influence over this.

❀

"General Lattice, you were held up as the last best hope for Afghanistan. What do you make of the violence sweeping the country now?"

Lattice had been remembering being in the field and whispering in Deirdre's ear, breathing rather than speaking the words . . . the worst betrayal he ever committed. He had not told his wife about it and so that memory burned ever deeper into him. He was not used to possessing shameful secrets. But he did now. Telling Mary would only send her white hot rage into a place he thought might break her. And so he had decided to hold onto that coal himself. And pass it from hand to hand, never able to forget about it, never able to put it aside. As he was unable to put it aside now. And so he paused blankly for a moment after he was asked the question and then he turned to the interviewer and nodded.

"Well, there are several ways to look at it, Charlie. In terms of our mission, the position of the United States has always been that we would give the Afghans the option of developing a secure, inclusive government and society. Of course, the final decision as to whether that happens will be in the hands of Afghans themselves. I think that to the extent that we have provided that option, Americans can be proud of the work we have done in that country."

⚛

And at that moment, at four a.m., in Afghanistan, another kick fractured Rami Issay's right fifth rib. He was a thin man now, much thinner than he had been. When he was kicked again, in precisely the same place, a shard of the just-broken rib was driven in like a knife and lacerated one of the blood vessels in his chest. He coughed. Bright red blood ran out of his mouth and onto the floor. He tasted it and opened his eyes in surprise. His mouth filled again with blood and he tried to inhale, but all he did was suck the blood back down for a moment. He coughed again. A quart of bright blood ran out of his mouth and onto the cement he lay upon. In the dim light it glistened, and the smell of fresh blood filled the room. Metallic and sweet. He began to pant, but with each exhalation, another quart of blood ran out of his mouth, and as short of breath as he now was, it bothered him less because he was dizzy and feeling like he might pass out. And then he did. And he took a few more breaths like that, lying on the concrete as his tormentors watched, and he dreamt of his wife and his daughters for a moment, and then he dreamt of nothing at all.

Rami Issay was about to die, but he was kicked again and woke up for a moment and looked around. He saw the concerned and frightened face of the man standing over him, who had never killed anyone before.

He looked him in the eyes and wanted to tell him that he was forgiven. But he could not speak because no air moved across his vocal cords, only blood.

As he felt his life draining from him, another thought leapt, a last final surge of love, for movies, for the soldiers he had entertained, for the men who had worked for him and, he imagined, loved him, too. He forgave the man who resumed kicking him even as the blows broke more ribs. His eyes found Captain Waller, but Captain Waller was looking at the corner of the dark shed and waiting to ask more questions.

❀

"General Jackson: the country is tired of war. The invasion of Iraq did not go well, and in Afghanistan it is increasingly difficult to identify anything we've accomplished that is significant enough to justify what we have lost there. What do you, as the most recent commander in Afghanistan, have to say to people that say you led us on a fool's errand?"

"Charlie, the military is the servant of the people. We do what we're told. The *people* demanded, in the days after 9/11, that we address the source of that atrocity. It was not the military that lobbied to go to war, either in Afghanistan or Iraq. The people demanded that we do these things, and so we did. Ms O'Malley will be sure to tell you that no one over there doing the fighting enjoys themselves. Everyone wants to come home. They are there at the insistence of the people. As, I might add, are the heroic journalists covering these conflicts. Everyone wishes they were home, Charlie. And, God willing, they will be someday soon."

❀

Mr. Clark stopped kicking him. Rami Issay was very tired. Mr. Clark and Captain Waller left the shed and locked the door behind them. Rami Issay closed his eyes. He slept.

When he awoke, a thin finger of light slid through the gap between the door to this shed and the concrete pad he lay upon. Past dawn, then.

He remembered how when his children were young they would wake up at dawn every morning, no matter whether that was at five in the morning, in the summer, or at eight. He remembered those summer mornings, and wishing to God that they would go back to sleep. He remembered silently willing that, and letting his hopes get up in the short intervals of silence. But in the end, there was no pretending they were asleep. Though he pulled pillows over his ears and tried his best to eke out another hour of sleep.

He shouldn't have. He should have gotten up every one of those mornings and said good morning to his daughters. If he could change something, it would be that. It wouldn't be the business at the film. He had not caused that, so he could not apologize, even to himself, for what happened there. But he had decided to stay in bed those mornings when his children awoke. And he shouldn't have.

CHAPTER TWENTY-FIVE

That same early morning, Rashid sat in a café in Peshawar. He was very thin and dirty. He had been introduced by his companions as one of the faithful, and so he was permitted to sit there and was given a glass of hot tea. He had walked for weeks and was only just now getting used to not waking up in the grass at dawn to start walking.

Crossing the mountains had torn his feet open and he had fallen many times. When he got here, he used the toilet in the café and he had looked at himself in the spotted mirror on the wall and been surprised at yet another transformation. He was skeletally thin. Between the depressed healing fractures in his cheeks and the missing teeth, he looked nothing like he had. He seemed misshapen and diseased, when he had been beautiful. He did not care much about that, really, though he was surprised by how much he had changed.

What was more important to him was the way he had recovered his own interior posture in the mountains. The exertion of climbing had acted as a sop for his anger. He learned to direct his rage into his legs, as they burned. He climbed like that: his legs feeling stronger, and his rage departing his head and lodging in his thighs. It made him feel capable of anything. When they had got to the tops of the highest passes, the view of Afghanistan and Pakistan had been more beautiful than any-thing he could have been prepared for. The Afghan plains stretching out to the north, all the way to Kandahar, had looked like a sawn plank. And to the south, the mountains of Waziristan rolled forward like waves in an angry sea.

Rashid thought that he should not linger here—in this café or even in this city. It was expected that he and the other men he had walked across the mountains with would leave at the end of the month for a training camp in North Waziristan. In recovering his own interior posture, he had understood again his revulsion for what would be learned there. He was his own self. Not what he had become while he was in that little room.

In the morning he would leave. Quietly and without discussion. He knew how to travel at night now and not draw suspicion. He would survive. He sipped from his glass of tea. He would need some clothes. He looked up and down the street. There were two laundries in sight. He would need some money. This required more thought. But not so much that he should remain here another day.

Outside, in the street, a truck pulled up. Men who were sitting in the back jumped out and hoisted their bags. They looked around and up and down the street. They knew one another but not this place they had come. Rashid watched them. One of them was the interpreter, John Wayne. The man driving the truck stepped out of the cab. Fazil.

Rashid watched them both as Fazil pointed to the door and the men from the box of the truck trooped slowly inside and sat down at a long table set aside, perhaps just for them. Fazil followed them in. After he closed the door behind him he looked around the café and saw Rashid Siddiqui, but did not recognize him. His eyes moved on to the other strangers, assessing them for threats.

Fazil sat down at the long table, too. The men he had driven here had all been in Sarpoza prison and had walked over the mountains. All month, very thin men had been descending out of the mountains with that story. Two new training camps had been built to accommodate them.

❦

Rami Issay lay on the floor of that little room. It should have been beginning to get warm, under the morning sun, but he had not known such cold. He breathed shallowly and rapidly. His broken ribs hurt less this way. He felt like he was standing just on the edge of consciousness. He thought that he was tired. Tired from the long night following many long nights. Tired of loss. He decided to give way and let himself rest. And he did. He inhaled very deeply, and then slowly let out all that air.

He did not breathe in again.

❀

Stewart Robinson was sleeping but Deirdre O'Malley could not. It was late at night in New York and she sat up in a chair looking out her window on 8th Avenue. She was remembering what she had said and what Jeremy and General Lattice had said on the Charlie Rose show. She did these shows regularly now—she had replaced Jeremy as the Sunday panel go-to guest for Afghanistan—and she knew this was usual, this wincing about awkward phrasings and imprecisions. She needed to let it go. But more and more, now, she couldn't. She rewrote everything she said in her head but still she didn't get anything right. She did not understand why she could not let it rest. She did not understand what was so dissatisfying about what she had said and that revising it satisfactorily was not possible.

Outside, ambulances and police cars let their sirens run almost continuously. The streets were busy, even so late, and watching the restless motion outside eased some of the anxiety within her. She watched Stewart sleep, in her bed. They had met the third day after she arrived in Afghanistan. He had been only halfway through his walk. She liked that they went back so far. Before either of them was famous. In the cab from the studio to the restaurant, Stewart had told her that he had decided to do no more interviews and stop writing any more about the war. He had become too associated with it. And anyway, now it was clear that the war was lost. He thought the reckoning to come could be terrible.

She challenged him on this. "Should we not be talking about that as much as we can?"

He said, "I supported and argued for the mission for a decade. I think it's time to listen to people who had better judgment about the situation in the first place." It was quiet in the cab for a while.

Then she asked, "What's next for you, then?"

"I am at loose ends. Maybe a novel."

"About what?"

"A Brit, living in New York and trying to make sense of popular music."

"You could not be more of a fuddy-duddy if you tried."

"I know."

"New York, huh?"

"It's just an idea. Alternatively, I've been thinking about trying to write a detective series set in Cyprus."

"Cyprus is pretty."

"It is."

"Have you ever spent a winter in New York? It's appalling."

"So I hear. In Cyprus, they hardly have a winter at all."

"Exactly."

Then they were in front of their restaurant.

At that moment, as she sat in her streetlight-lit chair looking out the window and wearing only a shirt, Rami Issay died, and she, and everyone else he had touched, felt that touch leave. For Deirdre it came as a sudden pain. In her darkened apartment in Chelsea she felt a stab under her right breast so sharp it made her gasp. It worsened for a long moment and she wondered what it was that was hurting her. But that was no more clear to her than anything else, that night.

Stewart woke up then, and looked at her, hunched over on her chair. He got out of bed and knelt beside her. She could scarcely breathe. He put his arms around her and that helped a little.

❀

In Peshawar, Rashid knew exactly what had had happened. He doubled forward in the little café, and he breathed slowly and carefully. Because he was young, and had not yet lost many people, it was the most pointed sensation he had experienced. He waited for it to pass. It continued. He looked over at Fazil.

Fazil had stopped speaking, too. And he held his abdomen and breathed lightly. He did not know what had just happened and Rashid would not tell him.

John Wayne looked at Rashid's face at the other table, and he looked at Fazil's at his. He wondered who they could possibly have in common. Because John Wayne had not spent much time in Rami Issay's company, his pain was not as intense. In another moment, it was gone. He watched as first Rashid and then Fazil gripped the table edges in front of them and breathed in slow, deliberate respirations and shut their eyes, waiting for the sensation to pass.

A waiter brought a tray of rice and some flatbread. John Wayne had not eaten in days. He needed to put some weight back on, get his strength back. He waited just a moment or two and then he reached for some bread. That training camp sounded demanding.

❀

"So I've been talking to your lawyer again."

"I'd just as soon you didn't, Susie."

"She has some strong arguments for an appeal."

"But I confessed."

"Nevertheless, she says there are circumstances where confessions may be vacated. Have you not read about the whole false confession issue? It's generating a lot of discussion."

"Susie, we're not talking about some frightened kid, bulldozed into signing something. We're talking about me. I did it. I confessed to it because I did it. And if anyone asks me again, I'll tell them that."

"Okay."

"It's not that I don't appreciate . . ."

"I know. I just don't understand why you don't fight a bit more."

"You are not me."

"I get it."

After several moments of silence, he said, "School starts soon again, huh?"

"Yeah. We've been shopping all week."

"Is he still seeing that girl?"

"I think that might have been more in his imagination in the first place, than a real thing. Nothing seems to have come of it."

"Poor thing."

"It's the age. He'll be okay."

"Yes."

"You should see his room. Covered in books. Floor-to-ceiling stacks of them."

"A little like his mom."

"I read a lot at that age, but nothing like he does."

"It's great."

"Oh, I know. He could be out doing who knows what instead."

"Still, it would be nice if a girl was nice to him."

"Were they nice to you, when you were his age?"

"No, not much."

"And see how you turned out."

Anakopoulus looked around him.

"I mean before this. And after, when you're out."

"Susie."

"I know."

Susie said goodbye to the guard at the gate and walked to the car waiting for her in the parking lot. She would come back next month. It was very hot in the Kansan late summer sun. The corn and the wheat had both been harvested and now there was nothing but stubble in the fields. Nothing to restrain the dust. The sun blazed.

In the car waiting for her was her son, in the back seat, reading a magazine called *Hobby Modelist*. Behind the wheel was Scott. She got in and he started the car. They had a long drive in front of them.

ACKNOWLEDGEMENTS

Though some of the events depicted in this novel may echo things that have actually happened, this is a work of fiction. There really was a network television show called *Stars Earn Stripes*, for instance, but it was broadcast later than the show depicted in *News from the Red Desert*, and the people who participated in it are not those I've imagined here.

The troublesome thing about wars is their actuality—if war bore more relation to its fantasized version, war novels would be both less necessary and easier to write. In order for war novels to deal with their subject meaningfully, the novelist has to hew closer than usual to the things that have happened. To do that, I leapt ahead in time to borrow two snippets from the real coverage of the war on pages 75–6, where Deirdre reads what her competitors are up to at the *New York Times* and the *Washington Post*, quoting from Scott Shanes' piece published in the *Times* on August 11, 2011 and from a story by Karen DeYoung published on October 24, 2012 by the *Post*. Neither of them would have been written when Deirdre is reading them, but both capture the necessary tone and content. Nevertheless, this is a work of imagination.

I wrote most of this book in the Vault Café in Nanaimo, and for hundreds of long afternoons, the better the writing went, the less coffee and the fewer of Lolo's (fabulous) Super BLTs on beer bread I ate, and yet not one word was ever spoken to suggest that I might pay for my seat somehow. So thank-you, Amanda Scott, proprietor and curator, and my friend. And thank you to Hubertus and Gordie and Amanda Pitz and Lolo and all the other eccentrics and kind people who live there.

And thank you to Anne Collins, of Random House Canada, who has been my brave and loyal editor for eighteen years now, and is also one of my best friends. And to my agent, Martha Webb, and to Jane Warren, and Megan Saunders, and Ronald Wright and Deborah Campbell. Mike Kenyon and John Ronald also went to Afghanistan and are much more than colleagues. Thank you, also, to my children, Molly, Selamu, and Sisaye, and to Shauna Klem. My gratitude to my parents, Roger and Margaret, and to my brother, Mike. And to Marta Demuth, Patti Sonntag, Steve Hunt, Brian Daly, Nan Talese and Hilda Lambie.

KEVIN PATTERSON grew up in Manitoba, and put himself through medical school by joining the Canadian army. Now a specialist in internal medicine, he practises in the Arctic and on Vancouver Island. His first book, a memoir called *The Water in Between*, was a *Globe and Mail* Best Book and an international bestseller. *Country of Cold*, his debut short fiction collection, won the Rogers Writers' Trust Fiction Prize as well as the inaugural City of Victoria Butler Book Prize. He is also the author of the critically acclaimed novel *Consumption*, and co-editor of *Outside the Wire: The War in Afghanistan in the Words of Its Participants*. He lives on Salt Spring Island, BC.